The Paintr⌣

Interwoven stories based on the life of a forgotten Scottish artist.

Jane Anderson

HOME STREET PUBLISHING

For Louise, Calum and Helen
Also for my darling godmother, Netta

Chapter One

October 2017, Moscow, Russia

St Petersburg had been my dream destination since I was ten years old. That we'd be there by the end of the day, had me as excited as a child. I added my toiletries and zipped the trolley bag closed. Then, unplugged Nick's phone and coiled the charger beside it to remind him to pack it. My glare at this gadget which so often invaded our home life, willed it to behave. Our St Petersburg booking in September had been postponed by a crisis at Nick's work. He walked in with shower-wet hair, dressed only in a towel. 'Boiled eggs for breakfast?' he suggested.

'Yum,' I replied.

But it was a call on my phone which spliced the atmosphere and sent adrenalin surging through me. The expectation of bad news kept my heart racing.

'Morning, love, sorry to bother you so early, but I thought I'd better ring before you catch the St Petersburg train,' Mum said.

'Granny's gone?' I already knew from her voice.

'She has. An hour ago. I sat with her all day yesterday, but she never regained consciousness.'

1

'I'm so sorry I wasn't there.' Tears choked my words.

Nick put a comforting arm around my shoulders.

'You said your goodbyes before you went to Russia. She got so frail and confused since then. It was her time to go, Anna,' Mum replied.

I took the tissue Nick gave me. Tried to pull myself together. 'Are you okay?'

'Just worn out. It's been a long week. What time is your train?'

'Ten. Well, if we go. I don't know...'

'Anna. Please go. That you were going to visit her precious Christina Robertson paintings was the memory Granny clung to after everything else had gone. When she still talked, she asked me every day.' Mum sighed. 'She never could remember the answer.'

'You sound exhausted, Mum. Go and get some sleep.'

'Yes. I'm going home to York tomorrow. Call me after you've been to the museum.'

Our taxi journey through the busy Moscow traffic was stressful. Grief hit me properly on the St Petersburg train. Mile upon mile of huge, grey, concrete apartment blocks in the Moscow suburbs. Depressing. It suited my mood. Later, we passed through endless green forests punctuated by lakes. Small trackside settlements, houses with roofs of corrugated iron. The low cloud outside flattened the light and threatened snow. I barely noticed. My head was full of childhood summers spent in Edinburgh with Granny.

Eventually, Nick broke the silence. 'How was your mum?'

'Okay, I think. The strain of going up north to visit was exhausting and sometimes Granny didn't know her.'

'It's good you saw your grandma last year. I'm sorry I didn't come with you. Sorry I missed meeting her.'

I managed a smile. I'd not taken Nick to meet Granny because she found new people confusing. I think she remembered me but as a teenager. Mum asked me not to talk about the wedding. Facing Granny with facts that didn't fit in with her memories could make her upset. 'It's been tough on Mum. As she said this morning, it was Granny's time to go.'

Nick squeezed my hand. 'A few days in St Petersburg will cheer you up, and we will look for her artist too.'

I nodded. 'I want to go back for the funeral.'

'Of course. Would you like me to come?'

'No need. I know you're busy. I'll go with Mum and stay on with her for a bit.'

St Petersburg's Hermitage Museum looked like the work of a deranged pastry chef. A glorious confection of green and white that could have been constructed from marzipan, except it was big enough to house a village.

Nick whistled under his breath. 'Jeez, Anna, the Romanovs didn't go for understated elegance, did they?'

Inside, it seemed the man in charge of the icing bag had gone berserk. The Jordan Staircase stopped us in our tracks. Light poured from enormous windows on all sides, illuminating the ornate gilded plasterwork against stark white walls. Above us, the marble balustrade swept around the double staircase. Gilt sconces, classical statues, a painted ceiling. It was gorgeous and over-the-top in every possible way. Was it credible that I had a family connection to this place?

'Let's save the paintings until last,' I said. We walked through an endless succession of marble-walled halls, crossed acres of gleaming parquet floor, stared up at countless glittering chandeliers. The whole thing was overwhelming. The treasure-filled galleries were awe-inspiring, but the excess of opulence made me feel nauseous.

Four long hours later, we found ourselves back at the top of the staircase. The Portrait Gallery of the House of the

Romanovs was our last stop. What if I hated these paintings? Was this just a sentimental childhood story that I'd blown out of all proportion? We entered a corridor lined with portraits. Walked past the fierce-looking faces of the early Romanov tsars towards the women further down. I was drawn to pause in front of an enormous portrait of a young girl in a rose-pink dress. Her dark hair was simply parted and braided around her ears, and her expression was wistful. Peering down at the label, I inhaled sharply.

'I've found her.'

Nick came to stand with me in front of the life-size portrait. 'Grand Princess Alexandra Nikolayevna, by Christina Robertson,' he read aloud. 'So you think this Christina is your great-granny or something?'

I flipped his leg with the back of my hand. 'Cheeky bugger, it was painted in 1840! An earlier ancestor is what my granny thought.'

'When you told me the story before, you said your mum thought your grandma made it up?'

'Mum always thought the Christina Robertson story was wishful thinking, but Granny was convinced we are descendants. When I was a little girl, Granny told me stories about an ancestor painting princesses in faraway Russia. I loved the idea. It sounded so romantic.'

'Too sentimental for my taste,' he said, screwing up his face.

The painting's description said the princess was born in 1825. 'Don't be such a grouch. She was only fifteen. What young girl wouldn't love a silk dress in candy floss pink?'

I turned to look at the painting on the opposite wall. 'Here's the Empress. Alexandra Feodorovna. I think that's the same spaniel as in the painting of the princess in pink.'

The Tsarina wore a cream silk gown in the same off-the-shoulder style as her daughter, but there was no mistaking her superior rank. She was dripping in jewels. Large pearls and precious stones adorned her bodice. Strings of huge pearls hung around her neck, and three more draped down the front of her dress in long ropes. Strands of pearls to measure in feet, not inches. The artist had captured the gleam of each individual pearl, and the precise textures of her ermine-lined, blue velvet cloak. There were three more portraits. Two more daughters, Olga and Maria, and Maria, a daughter-in-law.

Nick put his arm around my shoulder. 'I'm so glad we found your paintings.'

I grinned at him. 'Isn't it fabulous?' I pointed to the moustached man in military uniform. 'They're the family of this guy, Tsar Nicholas the First, Catherine the Great's grandson. Five enormous paintings. How incredible. Christina Robertson must have lived here for months and months to complete so much work. That must have been remarkable in the nineteenth century. And yet no one has heard of her?'

'Well, she is obviously remembered in Russia. Five royal paintings. But, Anna. Please, can we go and get something to eat now? I'm starving.'

I laughed. 'All right. I'm hungry too.'

Retracing our steps felt different. When the building had been the Winter Palace, Christina might have been in this very room and gazed out over tall sailing ships in the wide, grey Neva River. I paused at the top of the staircase, rested my fingers on the cold marble banister, and stared again at the sumptuous decoration. It was without doubt the most extravagant staircase I'd ever seen. Imagine the atmosphere when there were richly clad ambassadors walking up these steps. Imagine the pretty Romanov sisters gliding down them in their silk dresses. Was it possible Christina Robertson was really a relative? Now I needed it to be true.

. . .

Outside, the vast plaza had been cleared of tourists by the vicious wind. Two costumed photo touts were bent over a shared cigarette, an incongruous friendship between a be-wigged gentleman and a six-foot-tall zebra. They looked towards us hopefully and I shook my head, saving them the trouble of the walk over.

'Is it too early for wine?' Nick asked.

'Nope. I want to toast Christina. I'm so glad we came.'

The trendy wine bar was off Nevsky Prospekt, just a couple of blocks up. We followed the hipster waiter's recommendations and soon had a charcuterie board and a bottle of Georgian white wine in front of us. A large group of cyclists gathered in the pedestrianised street outside. Central St Petersburg was full of young people and reminded me of Paris. The tall buildings were similar in style, with narrow alleys leading to shady courtyards, and the bohemian atmosphere was enhanced by pavement art. Picturesque bridges over the canals topped it all. Paris with a hint of Venice. I absolutely loved it. The city centre must have looked much like this when Christina was here.

Nick's phone rang. 'Work. I'll be back in a minute.'

He took the call outside, smiling as he talked. I wondered who he was speaking to.

Nick returned and sat back in his seat, glass in hand.

'A toast to your artist,' Nick said, raising his glass.

I raised mine. 'To Christina Robertson and to Edith Robertson Gallagher, my wonderful granny.'

'The Robertson middle name, just like you. I'm surprised your mum did that if she didn't believe the story.'

'She said it was important to Granny,' I answered with a shrug. 'It's Mum's middle name, too. Apparently it used to be common to give girls a family maiden name in Scotland. Only in ours we kept one particular name going.'

So all the girls back to the middle of the last century?'

'I'm not sure. I'm thinking I might look into it. See if I can trace my family tree back.'

'It could be a good project for you, keep you busy,' Nick said.

My grip tightened on my glass. He didn't mean to be patronising, and he was right. I was bored, and I did need something to do. My experience of the last few months, giving up work and moving to Moscow for Nick's job, was very unfamiliar territory.

Browsing through the Hermitage website on my phone, I typed Christina's name into the works of art section. 'The Hermitage actually owns twenty-two paintings by Christina Robertson. Do you think I could get access to those they have in store?'

'It might be worth asking,' he said, signalling to the waiter for the bill.

When the waiter left, Nick leaned over the table to kiss me. 'We can come again next year, when the weather's warmer. Let's have an early night. Put some work in on that other project.' He raised his eyebrows suggestively. I laughed, but my insides clenched. Failure to conceive was making me more anxious every month.

We walked beside the canal, back towards our hotel. Nick put his arm around me, and I rested my head on his shoulder. The floodlit image of a large colonnaded building reflected on the canal surface. Ahead was an ornate cathedral with multicoloured domes. St Petersburg was as pretty as a dream.

'Imagine how perfect it would be if I conceive here. We could give the baby a Russian name,' I whispered, allowing myself to hope.

'More Russian than Anna and Nicholas?'

'Good point. Maybe it's an omen. Meant to be.'

Nick stopped walking and drew me into a hug. 'I'm sure

it's meant to be. And it'll be a girl so we can give her the Robertson middle name.'

'God, I never thought of that. What if I don't have a girl? All those generations passing down the name and I break the chain.'

He smiled and took my hand. 'Trust you to think of something new to worry about. Anyway, why does it have to be a girl? Robertson is a perfect middle name for a boy. Just so long as you don't insist on Ivan. You'd be condemning us to a dead cert for terrible twos.'

We both laughed and Nick tugged my hand. 'More speed now, Anna. If I freeze my nuts off, it will royally spoil our dynasty plans.'

We paused beside the church. Up close, its bright paint was garish and perhaps too reminiscent of Disney.

'Church of the Saviour on the Spilled Blood,' Nick said, reading the sign in a mock horror film voice.

We'd visited this church the day before. It was built on the spot where a tsar was assassinated. 'Can you remember which tsar it was?' I asked.

'No, but weren't they all either Alexander or Nicholas?'

'Apart from Peter. And of course, baby Ivan,' I answered.

'Ivan Robertson Jenkins. I guess I could get used to it,' he said with a smile.

I lay in the dark, willing a miracle to happen inside me. The timing was good. That thought banished sleep. I didn't want to wake Nick with the bright phone screen, so rolled on my side and dangled my arm over the edge of the bed to do another internet search on Christina Robertson. Now I'd seen the paintings I wanted to be related to her.

There were a couple of leads on the Wikipedia page. It said she was trained by her uncle, a successful painter called

George Sanders. If I was related to Christina, then I must be related to him, too. The second paragraph read:

During the 1830s she was travelling away from her artist husband and her own children. She worked in Paris in the mid-1830s and she was tempted to St Petersburg.

I read it again, struck by the odd tone. An accusation of child abandonment, and the use of 'tempted' seemed censorial too. Who writes these things? A man, I guessed. Another link revealed that the National Portrait Gallery had black and white engravings in their archives. Maybe I could request to see them the next time I was in London? My arm developed pins and needles. I put down my phone and rolled onto my back. Nick's hand crept over my naked stomach.

'Let's just make sure,' he whispered.

I lay awake afterwards, willing the stars to be aligned. The risk of miscarriage weighed heavy on my mind. Some websites quoted rates as high as one in four. Terrible odds. Nick had joked about our 'project', but I'd long lost my sense of humour about the whole thing. Half an hour later, Nick got up to go to the bathroom. I was desperate to pee, but instead I thrust my pelvis up into the bridge position and pulled a pillow below my back. Of course, it probably made no difference; even teenage Anna knew you could get pregnant standing up. The irony of years spent trying to avoid pregnancy hadn't escaped me.

Nick laughed when he came back into the room. 'What a vision!'

'I know. You're supposed to hold it for ten minutes. Do you think I'm crazy?'

'Crazy and gorgeous.' He smiled and kissed me. 'We have two hours before the train. What do you want to do?'

'I'd like an authentic Russian breakfast, and to soak up the St Petersburg atmosphere.'

.   .   .

We stepped out of our modern hotel and into the nineteenth century. The cobbled street ran beside a densely forested park. Old trees created deep shadows behind ornate floral railings. The temperature had dropped overnight, and I pulled my jacket tight around me. I imagined myself swathed in furs like Anna Karenina, the chill of the pavement seeping up through the soles of her high-laced leather boots. When the road ahead was momentarily free of cars, it was easy to picture Vronsky striding round the corner in his handsome uniform. I still felt alien in our Moscow life, drifting without purpose in a high octane modern city, where I could neither read nor understand the language. However, St Petersburg was strangely familiar. A grand and gorgeous incarnation of my Russian reading imagination.

Just before we reached Nevsky Prospekt, we spotted a restaurant and went in.

It was busy inside, but we found a table near the back. The young waitress wore her hair in a high ponytail, accentuating heavily made-up eyes. She had the slim frame of a ballet dancer, not impossible in ballet-mad St Petersburg. 'Do you speak English?' I asked, and she nodded. 'We'd like a typical Russian breakfast.'

'Kasha,' she replied. 'Russian porridge. The chef here does good.'

She returned with two bowls of porridge topped with berries and a sprig of mint, floating in a puddle of butter.

'Granny always made us porridge in the winter,' I said, dipping in my spoon. The taste was a surprise, both familiar and completely different, a delicious mix of sweet and salty.

'Quick walk now?' Nick said when we'd finished. 'We should probably get back to the hotel to pick up the bags an hour before the train.'

. . .

Nick and I walked arm-in-arm up Nevsky Prospekt. Both sides of the wide street were flanked by elegant old stone buildings, five or six storeys high. Why did I find this city so beguiling? Born in York, I was used to being surrounded by the past, but while York's ancient town was all narrow lanes and squat buildings, the scale of central St Petersburg was grand and expansive. It ought to have had more in common with the Georgian streets of Granny's Edinburgh, but most of central Edinburgh is serious grey sandstone, and this main street was multicoloured. Ordinary ground floor shops were housed in architectural marvels painted in wild colours, ripe apricot, custard and turquoise.

I took photos on my phone, amazed that one of my ancestors lived in this exotic city. My granny would have loved to see them. I'd missed the chance to show her photos, but I'd do the next best thing and find our link to Christina Robertson.

Chapter Two

May 1823, Marylebone, London

Christina Robertson let the fine sable brush fall from her fingers and put her head in her hands. Her paint palette sat beside her elbow on the desk. The viscous puddle of paint she'd mixed was the perfect shade and this miniature painting was nearly finished. But the final touches were delicate and she'd had so little sleep this week, her hand shook.

The silence was split by a costermonger's shout from directly outside. The bellowing call offered sprats, and the smell he brought with him from the docks drifted in through the open window. She glanced over at the cradle and saw a small fist fly up into the air. Baby Agnes began the grizzling noises that preceded a full-blown scream. Could she be hungry again? Her daughter's appetite seemed insatiable. Christina sighed and stood up.

God had granted all her prayers. Her debut exhibition at the Royal Academy was in a few days and they'd admitted five paintings. Baby Agnes was born two weeks ago, a year after she and James were married. This child was strong and healthy, full of life. But she cried a lot and hardly slept at night, so Christina didn't either.

As Agnes suckled, she gazed up with serious, knowing eyes. Christina felt herself in the presence of an old soul, someone reliably weighted to this earth. Pale blue now, she wondered if Agnes's irises would deepen to sapphire like James's, or fade to grey like her own eyes. The warmth of the infant's tiny body and the quiet sound of her breathing flooded Christina with grateful, calming love. Meanwhile, the glossy paint on her palette dulled and hardened.

The first day of the 1823 Royal Academy Exhibition arrived. Christina prodded Agnes's puckered mouth with her little finger. The baby had fallen asleep on the breast and she needed her to drink her fill. Ten minutes later, she handed the baby to Eliza to wind. Christina was already dressed to go to the Academy Exhibition and didn't want baby sick all down her gown.

'I'll be back within two hours. I'm hopeful she'll sleep.'

Eliza propped Agnes expertly against her shoulder. The housekeeper was in her forties with four grown-up children. Christina was so grateful for her help and reassuring expertise. The child burped almost immediately. Christina shook her head in disbelief. When she did the same, it took forever.

She pinned on her new bonnet. It was made of simple straw, but the wide three-quarters brim made a pleasingly symmetrical arc around her face. A green silk ribbon around the crown was repeated in two more ribbons, hanging down from the brim's edges. She secured the ribbons in a large bow just below her collarbone. The green was a good match for the piping on last year's pelisse robe. Christina rushed downstairs to their small sitting room. James stood with his back to her.

'Is the carriage here?'

'It's been waiting for you this past half hour, my dear,' James replied. He turned, revealing a new tailed coat in midnight blue and pale, tight-fitting trousers with stirrup straps. The outfit accentuated his wide shoulders and small waist. The coat brought out the colour of his eyes. Her husband would be the most handsome man in the entire gallery.

'Where did you find the money for such an outfit?' she blurted out.

He raised his eyebrows. 'All the eyes will be on us, Christina. Would you have me turn up looking like a country carpenter?'

'I doubt anyone will give me a second glance,' she said. But every lady in the room would notice him. She would be like a dull peahen beside a glamorous peacock.

James scrutinised her face. 'You're pale. Are you sure you're well enough to go?'

'I'm not ill, just tired. Uncle George isn't here?'

'I told him to meet us there. You would think it was his exhibition, the fuss he's making.'

'He's proud of me and I wouldn't miss the first day for anything.' Christina picked up her paisley shawl and handed James his top hat from the chair. He passed his hand over the glossy new crown to smooth away imaginary dust. She still hadn't got used to going out with James in public. She knew people's opinion. How did such a handsome man come to marry such a dowdy girl?

James offered his hand as she climbed into the coach. 'Take us to Somerset House on the Strand, driver,' he said.

Top-hatted drivers queued to set down their passengers from shiny black carriages. Christina and James walked through the arched entrance into the busy courtyard of

Somerset House. Christina had been in that crowd often and the buzz of excitement never failed to make her heart race. Today, for the very first time, people had come to see her work. A dream come true.

Uncle George appeared at her side and she hugged him. 'I was afraid you wouldn't come. James said...'

James glared at him and he broke off.

Christina took James's hand and squeezed it. 'James knows I'm exhausted, Uncle. But I couldn't miss this.'

'It seems like only yesterday that I brought you here first,' George said.

'I was just thinking about that and it's fully ten years ago. You had to work so hard to persuade Aunt Agnes to allow me to come south for that first time. As soon as I stepped in the first gallery and looked up at the hundreds of portraits, I was seized by the wild idea that my work might one day be on those walls.'

And, she thought, the day I vowed to support myself one day. She'd had to lean on George through her first months in London, but she was determined to forge her own path now.

'It's your dedication and hard work that got you here, Christina,' Uncle George replied.

'I couldn't have done it without your help, Uncle.'

'And then I met you just after you came home to King-horn from the exhibition. Your seventeenth summer,' James added. 'I knew you were destined for fame as soon as I saw your sketches.'

'Plenty of people have talent,' George added, 'but Christina also has the gift with words to sell her work.'

She glanced anxiously at James. He painted alongside his carpentry work, but hadn't yet sold a single portrait.

'You taught me that too, Uncle. Come. Let's go inside.'

Christina swallowed hard as they ascended the staircase

and entered the Great Room. Would the public like her work? She lifted her heels off the floor, resisting the urge to go on full tiptoe like a child. The fashion for ostrich feathers and large flowers on bonnets was a great nuisance for viewing the lower paintings, and her own shortness was a handicap.

Then she spotted her painting of the child. She'd spent so much time studying this boy's face, she knew it as well as her own. The two men followed her over to stand below the gilt frame. Christina let go of the breath she'd been holding. Even set high on the wall, the boy's angelic charm shone through. You could make out the nap on his blue velvet suit and he was full of such youthful energy, as if he might run off after the terrier at his feet.

'I don't know how you manage to paint children so well, Christina. I find them unable to sit still,' Uncle George said.

Christina laughed. 'I devised a game for Edward that required him to make the puppy sit at his command. He was so intent on the dog, he never guessed I was capturing those brief moments of stillness.'

'It's a shame your first large Academy portrait is not of a society person,' James remarked, turning to look at David Wilkie's portrait of the Duke of York.

'Not at all,' Uncle George said in an offended tone, 'Christina's portrait was chosen on the merit of the painting, not the sitter. I couldn't be more proud, my dear.'

'Thank you, Uncle,' she replied, 'but James is right. Most people are more interested in faces they recognise. The profusion of paintings blurs all but the famous.'

She took Uncle George's arm to dissuade him from saying more. He had reservations about their marriage. James and he were always disagreeing about something. It was the only blot on the landscape of her new life. 'Shall we look at the other rooms?'

They entered the next room. A painting of a Scottish gentleman, dressed from head to foot in garish red and green tartan, including his hose, hung on the wall directly in front of them.

James burst out laughing. 'What in the name of God was he thinking?' he said through his laughter.

'Shush, James,' Christina said. 'George Watson is extremely influential in Scotland. If he hears of your reaction, I can forget ever exhibiting in my native land.'

However, James's laughter was proving infectious. Several people around them were smiling. 'But the bonnet feathers, Christina,' he added, then could hardly talk for laughing. 'Where on all earth did he find such a huge pheasant, and he appears to have skinned his mother's white cat?' He pointed to enormous ermine sporran extending below the man's shiny belt buckle almost to the kilt's edge.

The young lady next to them had a fit of the giggles and was admonished by her parents. Christina pinched James hard. 'Enough now,' she said under her breath.

Uncle George cut in, his tone reprimanding. 'The object of your mirth is Sir Evan Murray Macgregor, the clan chief, and apparently eagle feathers are traditional.'

James chuckled. 'Come on, George. Admit it, you've never seen the like before.'

'I have not. But apparently, King George wore a similar outfit at a reception in Holyrood Palace and in the red Stuart tartan. It seems Sir Walter Scott has him enamoured with all things Scottish since his Edinburgh visit.'

'You should consider plaid for your next new dress, Christina,' James suggested. 'We might profit from our Scottish connections if it's to be in fashion.'

'Perhaps,' she replied, wondering when she might afford a new dress.

James and George strode ahead. The enduring pain from the birth slowed her pace, and she found herself behind the giggling girl's party.

'Who is that uncouth fellow?' the girl's father asked his companion.

'A noisy presence in London's salons. His wife, Mrs James Robertson, is an exhibitionist this year.'

'Is the paintress any good?'

'Competent portraits of women and children,' his companion answered with a dismissive shrug.

Stung by his words, Christina gritted her teeth and walked behind them with her head held high. Even if they turned, she'd be invisible to them. Known only by her husband's name and dedicated to an art form they deemed uninteresting.

She caught up with the others in the Antique Academy room. 'What hour is it, James?'

'Ten after two.'

'Then I need to get back soon. Agnes will be hungry.'

'Do you really want to leave without seeing all your exhibits? It surely won't do her any harm to wait a few minutes.'

'Then let's use the catalogue to go to them directly. The Drummond-Burrell girls are in this room too.' Christina felt a surge of pride, contemplating the portrait of the young sisters.

'Now then, James. You wanted a society portrait and there you have it. Ancient families with earls on both sides,' Uncle George said.

James nodded. 'How old are the girls?' he asked.

'It's years since I painted this. I suppose Clementina must now be fourteen and Elisabeth thirteen.'

'Let's hope they'll want full paintings when they're older,' he replied.

'We got on very well. I think it's possible.'

They found two more of her paintings hung nearby. Their positions could have been better, but on the whole Christina was more than satisfied with her first exhibition.

'Congratulations, Christina,' George said. 'All your portraits are praiseworthy. I'm very proud.'

'Thank you,' she replied. 'Now please, James. We really must go home.' Christina squirmed inside her bodice. She had never been away from her baby for so long and her engorged breasts made it too tight.

'Not without viewing your self-portrait, my love.'

She sighed and followed him to where the small gilt-framed picture was hung. The miniature was barely six inches long, designed to sit on a desk, so it was lucky it was positioned on the lower section of the wall.

'It's a marvellous likeness, Christina,' Uncle George said.

'I agree that the technique is first class, but I wish you'd painted yourself looking a bit more like a newlywed. Your expression is so solemn and the linen cap is frumpy,' James complained. 'And what letter have you in your hand?'

'Perhaps it's an apology to your tailor for the unpaid bill,' she replied, causing James to frown.

'Surely that's your normal preoccupied painting expression?' Uncle George said.

'Of course. How else would I present myself? I'm holding a sketch. My paint palette is on the table.'

'Darling Christina, you are just too modest. Since you refuse to paint yourself in a flattering light, I might do it myself,' James said.

'I would love that, James,' she agreed, regretting her harsh words. 'But I really must go now, James. You may stay if you wish.'

'I'm coming, don't fuss.'

They struggled to push through the gallery crowds. As

they emerged, she realised that Uncle George was by her side but where was James?

She looked around and George nodded to where James was talking to two young men. They walked over and she caught the end of the conversation.

'So you'll be living off your talented wife from now on then, you lazy dog.'

Christina froze. She'd feared this kind of teasing.

'I wish,' James replied with a laugh. 'I've worked my fingers to the bone completing that desk.'

James had crafted a desk for a customer, but it was the only piece of income he'd brought in this year. He hadn't noticed Christina and George approaching and continued his conversation.

'You know how it is. A lady's artistic muse must be cosseted. Meanwhile, we men must attend to business.'

George gasped beside her. She silenced him with a look and a shake of her head. Of course, James would conceal that she was the main earner.

George coughed. James turned around. If he noticed her uncle's glare, he chose to ignore it. 'You'll have to excuse us now, gentlemen. We're expected at home.'

She'd no time to spare for dwelling on the lack of introduction, but it did infuriate her to hear him belittle her.

By the time they found a carriage, they'd been gone for over three hours. As soon as it pulled up at their front door in Marylebone, Christina could hear Agnes's screams.

'Good lord, is that racket coming from our tiny daughter?' James said with a laugh.

'She's hungry,' Christina replied through clenched teeth. She was already racing up the staircase, her skirts scrunched up in her fingers, when he called behind her.

'You must ask Eliza to look for a wet nurse, or we'll never be able to go out again.'

He was laughing, but she had to blink back tears. Agnes's cries made her breasts ache and the front of her gown was damp with milk.

Chapter Three

October 2017, Moscow

I arrived back in our Moscow apartment with my thoughts full of Christina Robertson. I reactivated my subscription of an ancestor tracing website. It would be a quest, something to do for Granny. I'd attack it from both ends: my grandmother and her family; then hopefully I'd find some connection to Christina, too.

Details on the internet about the painter were sparse. Although I had her date of birth and birthplace, there was no trace of Christina's birth record. However, George Sanders, her uncle and mentor, had been born in the same village of Kinghorn on Scotland's Fife coast. He was born George Saunders. Apparently, he'd changed his professional name in London because there was already another portrait painter with the same name. Since Christina's maiden name was Saunders, she must presumably have been his brother's daughter? It turned out George had many siblings.

Nick padded into the kitchen, his eyes screwed up against the light. 'What are you doing? It's after three in the morning, Anna. Come to bed.'

'Okay. Sorry. I'll just finish this.'

He stood behind me and looked down at the screen. 'Since this artist's been dead over a hundred years, I think it could wait until tomorrow.'

I put my hand on his where it rested on my shoulder. 'I've discovered the family used Saunders and Sanders interchangeably. It might explain why I didn't find Christina's birth records when I looked before.'

'Wouldn't it be easier to look for your grandmother's family first?'

I rubbed my eyes wearily and stood up. 'I know, and I will.' But if I couldn't find Christina and her children and tie us to them, it would be so disappointing.

I went to bed but slept fitfully. When I woke, the grief hit me before I remembered why. This deep sadness was more complicated than my grandmother's death.

Nick brought me tea in bed. 'What are your plans for today?'

'I'm supposed to meet Kerry Ross to talk about helping with the Christmas charity ball.' I held the hot mug in both hands, taking comfort in the warmth.

'Christmas? It's not even November yet,' he replied with a laugh.

'I know. Apparently the fundraising is complicated. I might ring and call off.'

Nick kissed me on my forehead. 'I think you should go, Anna. You'll mope if you stay inside all day.'

As soon as the front door closed behind him, I jumped out of bed, determined to continue my research. The morning was spent with tea and toast and uncovering birth-dates for George Saunders' twelve elder brothers and sisters. At the last minute, I realised that it was too late to cancel my lunch appointment. I ran down the stairs of the apartment block and out into the street, having only had time to drag a brush through my hair and mascara my lashes. I'd regret that when I met Kerry. She always looked immaculate.

I hurried down the escalator into the underground station. The Moscow metro system had been a revelation. Clean, efficient and many of the stations had beautiful architecture. This gorgeous Pushkinskaya Station commemorated the famous poet and featured granite floors, white marble columns and massive brass chandeliers. It was by no means the most beautiful of the stations. Others featured stained glass, bronze statues and halls as elegant as palace ballrooms. Today, I strode towards the train without a sideways glance.

Emerging into the street, I made myself walk. A grown woman running looked crazy, and I didn't want to arrive out of breath. I found central Moscow intimidating. The streets were ultra-clean compared to the UK, and everyone adhered to the strict rules about using pedestrian crossings. Maybe it was that extreme sense of controlled order, but I always imagined I was being watched. Nick had laughed when I admitted my fears, saying he doubted anyone would be interested in my social life. I grimaced again at the thought. Even I didn't find my social life interesting. I hadn't met many other English-speaking women of my age. Those with young children lived near the school, which was well outside of town. The couples who took small gardenless apartments in the city were mostly older, like Kerry, with grown-up children. In my thirties, with no career and childless, I stood out as an oddity.

As I got nearer to the restaurant district, the pedestrians changed. This area was like Bond Street on steroids. Loads of expensive shops and smart cafés. The Muscovites were very well-groomed, sharp suits, lots of high heels. Tourists too, the majority from the Far East. Wealthy individuals with designer handbags, and large groups being herded by guides.

My spirits sank when I entered the restaurant and saw the

woman sitting at the table with Kerry. I hadn't realised anyone else would be there. Kerry stood up. There was no escape.

'Anna, you're here! I worried you might be ill.'

'No. I'm fine. Sorry I'm late. Um...'

Her eyes flicked over my outfit. Did I really look that terrible? Glancing down, I saw my un-ironed blouse was missing a button. I put my hand over the gap.

'Are you sure you're all right?' Kerry asked. Her gaze was penetrating.

'Yes. No. Perhaps I shouldn't have come... I've just heard that my grandmother died.' I blurted it out. I hadn't intended to tell her.

'Oh, you poor dear. Let me get you a drink. Come and meet Lisa. I think you'll like her. Take your mind off it.'

I guessed this was Lisa Chalmers. I'd heard about her. English and married to a Russian. One of the few British women my age living in town, and a bit of a legend. Fluent in Russian, senior executive in a pharmaceutical company, mother of three small children and on the charity committee as well. Too bloody perfect by half. To top all that, it turned out she was very pretty, with long, shiny red hair.

'Lisa, this is Anna. I'm trying to persuade her to get involved.'

Lisa smiled. To be fair, she looked genuine. I shook the hand she extended across the table. Perfectly manicured and painted nails, of course.

'Let me get you a glass of wine, Anna. Would you like red or white?' Kerry asked.

'Maybe just a soft drink?' I wasn't drinking when there was any chance I might be pregnant, but I was hardly going to admit to that. Now they'd think me boring.

'Have some of my sparkling water,' Lisa said, pouring from her bottle into a tumbler. 'I've got to go back to the office this afternoon and I can't breathe fumes on the chairman.'

'Poor Anna has had some bad news,' Kerry said. 'Her grandmother passed away.'

'Oh god, I'm so sorry,' Lisa said.

'Thanks. She'd been ill for ages. Dementia. But still...'

Lisa's sympathetic expression nearly set me off crying again. 'It's one of the toughest things about living overseas,' she said. 'I've lost both my remaining grandparents since I moved here. You feel so far away and you just want a hug from your mum.'

I nodded. She seemed understanding. I took a deep breath and tried to focus. 'Tell me about the fundraising. Kerry said you've been involved for years.'

Lisa laughed. 'Once you start raising money for disadvantaged kids, you'd seem like a real shit to say you're quitting.'

'She's too modest, Anna,' Kerry said. 'Lisa is the best fundraiser by a country mile.'

'I'm just making use of both my worlds. I source paintings from up and coming Russian artists,' she explained, passing me the bread basket and pushing over the oil and balsamic bottles. I took some bread and nodded to show I was listening. 'They give me a good price to support the kids' charity. Also, the ball is high profile and the exhibition we stage exposes the artists to new clients. Maybe you could help? If you have time, that is. There's a brochure to put together, then making sure the lots get to the right bidder after the auction.'

'I'd like that. I was a journalist until recently, and I have experience of setting up a page.'

'Marvellous,' Lisa replied. She turned to Kerry. 'Can I steal Anna for my auction project, Kerry? Her skills are perfect and I'm behind with the brochure.'

'Of course. I was going to suggest it.'

We ate lunch. Lisa and Kerry talking about how best to get corporate support from various local businesses.

'What kind of journalism do you do?' Lisa asked, when their conversation was over.

That she used the present tense pleased me. Most conversations here opened by being asked what my husband did in Moscow. Something that drove me wild. 'Bit of a generalist, really. Everything except sport. Before moving to Moscow, I worked for a big media group who own several titles in north-west London.'

'And did you enjoy it?' she asked.

'I used to. I loved the buzz of deadlines and the variety of the stories. Now though, there's no money in it. People get their news free online. I took voluntary redundancy.'

'Don't they need journalists for online stories?' Lisa asked.

'Sometimes, but they use freelancers. Nick, my husband, was offered a great job here and we live on his salary.'

'Except?' Lisa asked, perhaps hearing the 'but' in my tone.

'Except I'm bored.'

'And now you're bored and sad, too. That's rubbish and I'm really sorry.'

She sounded so sympathetic, I found myself opening up to her in a way I hadn't expected. I described how my research into Christina Robertson had become an all-consuming project. Lisa listened attentively. Then, she looked at her watch. 'Shit, I'm late.' She pulled a business card from her wallet. 'Look, I've got to run, but let's go for a drink next week? Or supper if you have time? We can talk about this brochure. I really do need some help.'

'I'm waiting to hear the date for my grandmother's funeral, but if I'm here, I'd love that. I don't have a card but I'll text you my phone number.'

'Hopefully see you next week then,' she said.

I stood to leave too. 'You were right about Lisa,' I said to

Kerry. 'I do like her, and I feel better for getting out of the house.'

When I left the restaurant, Lisa still stood on the other side of the road. She waved at me as a shiny black Mercedes pulled up beside her. I waved back, and she got in the car. The sound of a familiar laugh took my gaze further up the street. A couple were about to enter a restaurant on the opposite side of the road. Nick? What was he doing here? And who was with him? He held the door open for his female companion, his hand resting on her lower back. Jealousy and doubt hit me like a sledgehammer.

Chapter Four

March 1824, London, England

C hristina watched James get out of bed and cross to the washstand. The tendons in his calves flexed at each step, and muscles in his naked buttocks clenched and relaxed beneath his skin. He was the most beautiful creature she had ever seen.

When he was in the company of others, James was constantly aware of his audience, the way he held himself, his manner of speech. But here in this bed and its immediate vicinity, he was different and completely hers. Their relationship was like the mixing of two paint colours. His would be bold and striking on its own, a vermillion red maybe, and hers would be unassuming, the pale yellow of a primrose, perhaps? But together they created something glorious, like a spectacular sunset, or fire itself. He transformed her. It had been that way from the beginning.

James turned from his ablutions, rubbing his face dry on a linen towel. He smiled. 'I adore the changes in your body when you're with child,' he said, and ran his hand over her rounding stomach. 'You ripen like a sweet plum.'

Christina sighed. She would have liked to stay there in the

harmony of that moment, but James's brothers were expected today and there was lots to do. Adam and Tom worked together in their furniture business in Alnwick, as James had done before moving to London. They were travelling south to deliver an order to the Duke of Northumberland, and the commission was too important to entrust to anyone else. The eldest brother, John, wasn't coming. From what Christina could gather, John and James had quarrelled before he moved to London.

'Will you supervise the men who are coming to put Uncle George's spare bed in our living room?' Christina asked.

'I wish George had volunteered to host them at his house,' James complained. 'Shifting beds and sofas up and down stairs is a great deal of unnecessary trouble.'

'Uncle George doesn't know your brothers. It was kind of him to offer the bed,' Christina answered. 'You know how much George likes his privacy, and it will be lovely to have everyone under the same roof.' Christina ignored James grumbling under his breath.

Eliza's voice floated up from downstairs. 'Come down from there.' Agnes had recently learned to walk and was delighted to discover she might go where she pleased. James opened the bedroom door.

'What's this creature creeping up my stairs?' he said in a playful voice. 'Is it a little mouse?' He ran down the steps with a mock roar, and Christina heard her daughter scream with laughter.

Eliza followed father and daughter into the bedroom. 'Sorry, mistress, every time my back is turned, she goes to the stairs. I'm terrified she's going to fall.'

'Must we build a cage for you, little monster?' James said, burying his face in her chubby stomach and making noises as if he were eating her, sending Agnes into paroxysms of delight again.

'Leave her here, Eliza,' Christina said. 'I shan't go to the studio this morning. There's too much to do.'

Eliza put Agnes into her wooden cradle. The child immediately stood up and grabbed the rails. 'Papa,' she said, causing James to laugh and pick her up again. She'd begun demanding his attention at five o'clock this morning. By seven he was tired of playing with her and told Christina to take her downstairs to Eliza, to give them some time to themselves. Such privacy would become even rarer when this new baby was born.

'I'm going to meet Adam and Tom at Northumberland House. Help them take in the furniture,' James said, after breakfast.

Christina smiled to herself. James was no fan of manual labour, but she knew he'd be curious to enter one of London's grandest buildings. The Duke's enormous London home sat at the edge of Trafalgar Square, and the marble statue of the Percy lion proclaimed the family's importance across London's rooftops.

'That's fine,' she said. 'I've some accounts to attend to and I brought home a miniature to work on.'

'Surely all your Academy submissions are ready?' James asked.

'They are, but I've other client commissions to complete, and I'll have no time when the baby arrives.'

Their need for income was urgent. She'd not be paid for her Academy exhibits until after they were delivered. A completed portrait commission this month and next would tide them over. This baby was expected in June. At last year's Exhibition she'd struggled with the needs of a newborn. This May she would be waddling like a farmyard duck.

. . .

James helped George's footman bring the bed up their narrow staircase. Once it was in place she and Eliza put on clean bedlinen. When all the guest preparations were complete, Christina sat down to her ledgers. However, Agnes found the couch's transformation into a bed, the most tremendous joke. She insisted on climbing on to it, so Christina daren't take her eyes off her. When it came time for her to eat, she wasn't happy to be scooped up. Eventually the tantrum ran its course, and Agnes fell asleep. Christina got out her paints.

An hour later, a boy brought a note to the door.

Meet me outside Northumberland House. There's someone I want you to meet.
James x

Christina disliked socialising during the day because her painting hours were too brief. There was no hope now that she would finish the portrait this afternoon. She asked Eliza to sit with Agnes, who was still napping in the middle of the guest bed, and set off, deciding to walk to Trafalgar Square. She often walked to her studio and it was only ten minutes further. The sharp click of her boot heels echoed against the tall buildings in Portland Place. Crossing in front of the elegant rotunda of John Nash's new All Souls Church, she passed the end of Foley Place. Christina shared the studio there with Uncle George. This was where she first thought of herself as a professional artist. She was proud to be able to cover her share of the cost now.

Her marching woke her baby, and a kick reminded her of their changing circumstances. She and James needed a larger home, but couldn't afford more rent this year. Christina dreamed of a property with its own studio space. She had originally thought they'd also need a workshop for James's business, but the stark truth was that he showed less and less interest in cabinet making. He'd only sold a couple of items this year and constantly found excuses to paint instead. But then, how could she deny him the right to improve his skills? He was a more than competent painter and his charm would help him get clients. He'd started her portrait, but put it aside. Capturing a likeness was hampered by his intention to flatter. Now he was practising the human form, filling his sketchbook with a series of hands.

Tom, Adam and James were standing outside Northumberland House on the far side of Trafalgar Square. Tom's hand rested on the back of an ornate dining room chair. An incongruous vision in this setting.

'Did the Duke reject your work and throw you out?' she joked, when she reached them.

The three men turned smiling to face her. James looked particularly pleased with himself. Adam grinned and stuck out his hand. Christina grasped it, then hugged first him, then Tom.

'We're right glad to see you, Christina,' Adam said.

She liked Adam and Tom. They were barely more than boys, Adam being twenty-one and Tom nineteen, but having been apprenticed from childhood they were both skilled craftsmen. James had told her the Duke of Northumberland was so impressed with Tom's fine woodwork skills that he'd promised more commissions.

'Why the chair?' Christina asked.

'The gilding got scratched on the journey,' Tom replied. 'Shall we take it to your workshop, James?'

James gave her a sideways glance. 'I'm not using that place anymore. The journey to Shoreditch was tedious, and the rogue wanted to increase the rent again.'

Christina frowned. He hadn't told her that. 'How will you

work without equipment, James? You must seek out another cabinet maker who can give you space to work.'

James took her hand in his, turning to answer Tom. 'A little bit of gilding will take you no time at all. We can use George and Christina's studio.'

'So long as it's somewhere dust free and dry. I can be done in an hour,' Tom replied.

James smiled at her. 'We'll go in early and be out of the way before George arrives. And as for my work, I can manage to make small items with my hand tools, and I've done a piece of work this day that will see our fortunes rise.'

Adam and Tom's expressions reflected his excitement. James tilted his chin, before announcing grandly: 'Charlotte Florentia, the Duchess of Northumberland, wishes to meet you.'

'What? Why?' she replied.

James tapped his temple. 'I guessed the Duchess might come to greet us in person. She always used to in Alnwick. She was most pleased to see me again and asked after my new life in London. I told her about my marriage to you and described my pride in your Royal Academy success.' At that, James retrieved her self-portrait from his coat pocket. 'Then I showed her your painting.'

Adam and Tom laughed and clapped.

'You took my miniature on a furniture delivery?'

'I planned this,' he replied. 'The Duchess is a gifted draughtswoman and most interested in the art world. She was delighted to hear I'd joined that world myself.'

Christina let that last remark slide. He'd sold not one single piece of art, but she knew full well James chose to call himself an artist. Nevertheless, arranging an introduction to a Duchess was no small feat. 'You are a genius,' she said, and hugged him.

'So let's go in,' James said.

'What, now? James, if I knew we were to meet a Duchess I would have changed.'

James gave her an up and down look. She knew her dark blue dress was respectable, but dull, her boots well-worn.

'It will do,' he replied. 'It's more important to grasp the moment.' He turned towards the main entrance.

'We should use the tradesman's door, James,' Christina protested.

'Not for calling on a Duchess, she's expecting you.'

'We'll wait for you here,' Adam said.

'I'll take you up to the Foley Street studio afterwards,' James called back.

A footman answered the door.

'Mr and Mrs James Robertson, the Duchess is expecting us,' James said.

The footman nodded and ushered them into the hallway. 'One moment, please.'

They stood at the foot of an enormous marble staircase with an ornate iron balustrade. The scale of the grandeur increased Christina's apprehension. When the footman returned, he made a small bow towards her. 'The Duchess will receive you in her private sitting room, madam.' The man put extra emphasis on the word *you*.

'The Duchess specifically asked me to bring my wife to meet her,' James answered, his smile frozen on his face.

'And she will receive her now,' the footman replied in a curt tone. He turned his back on James and extended his arm, showing Christina the way.

Christina placed her hand on James's sleeve. 'I'm honoured to be offered some moments of her time,' she said, hoping James would understand her pleading look. A member of a carpenter's team was clearly not considered suitable company for the Duchess.

James shrugged. 'I'll take my brothers up to the studio

and meet you at home.' He kissed her cheek and whispered, 'Good luck,' giving the footman a final glare before turning to leave.

Two enormous candelabras, large as lampposts, flanked the foot of the staircase. Christina's feet sank into the rich carpet over the marble steps and her heart quickened with nerves. She'd had no time to prepare for this interview. What would she say? The footman halted in front of a door and rapped lightly. A female voice said: 'Enter.'

He opened the door, allowing Christina to step inside before closing it again behind her. A woman, sitting on a red velvet chair near the huge window, smiled up at her. 'I'm pleased to meet you, Mrs Robertson,' she said.

Charlotte Percy, the Duchess of Northumberland, was a small neat woman in her late thirties, with auburn hair and large, dark eyes. This red painted drawing room was overwhelming. There was a huge arched mirror over the white marble fireplace, and many more enormous mirrors on every wall. Gilt metal scrollwork embossed the pilasters framing the mirrors, and these seemed to be made of coloured glass too.

Christina bobbed a curtsey, then followed the Duchess's gesture for her to sit on the matching velvet couch.

'I thought your miniature charming. Your talent for capturing a likeness is formidable. Mr Robertson perhaps told you that I like to paint?' The Duchess gestured to an easel near the window. 'I mostly attempt landscapes, but I'm afraid I have more enthusiasm than talent. My current project is not going well.'

'On the contrary, James mentioned that you are an excellent painter,' Christina replied.

The easel looked out of place in such a grand room. However, Christina supposed that if she owned a room full of reflected light, she might choose it to paint there.

'Perhaps your husband is prone to flattery?' Charlotte Percy's smile was mischievous.

'I've heard that said before,' she admitted. 'Is your problem something specific?'

'There is a myriad of problems, today's is the impossibility of clouds.'

'A notoriously tricky subject,' Christina said.

'Would you take a look?' the Duchess asked in a tentative voice.

Christina rose and the two women went over to the easel. 'Colour and depth make clouds a particular challenge,' Christina said.

The Duchess's painting showed some skill with line and perspective, but the clouds were flat and monotone. 'We imagine that clouds are white or grey, when if we look more carefully they're composed of many colours. Also, I might suggest a different brush. A rounded brush allows you to apply the paint in a circular motion,' she added, miming the action in the air.

The Duchess gave her a searching look. 'I have a proposal. I love the idea of a portable likeness that might sit on a desk. Would you paint me as a small gift for my husband?'

'I would be honoured, Your Ladyship,' Christina replied, trying to keep the excitement from her voice.

'In addition I'd like to hire you to give me some painting lessons.'

The Duchess's eyes strayed down to the bulge in her skirts. 'Oh, but perhaps you won't have time?'

Christina laid her hand on the bump. 'I have a couple of commissions to complete and this baby is due in June. I should be free to start a new project towards the end of July. Is that too late?'

'Not at all. That would be perfect. And the cost?'

Christina quoted a price ten per cent higher than normal.

'Most reasonable,' the Duchess said, 'and you must charge extra for the lessons.'

'If you find my input useful, we will come to an arrangement,' Christina replied.

Christina caught a carriage home, excited to give James the good news. Agnes's laughter and the rumble of male voices came from the sitting room.

All three men turned to face her as she walked in. Adam had Agnes in his arms. 'Your daughter is delightful, Christina.'

James set his head to one side, his eyebrows raised. 'And?'

'A commission for a miniature and also some art lessons.'

James hugged her. 'Your first duchess. Congratulations, and it seems I wasn't needed at all.' He pulled a face.

'You got me the critical introduction,' she replied.

'Tom is to draw up a design for some side tables, so an excellent day all round. I thought I'd take the boys to the chop house?' James said. 'We should celebrate and there's hardly room for us all to eat in here.'

Christina thought of the chicken stew she'd planned to serve, but James loved the noisy camaraderie of the chop house. It would cheer him after the humiliating episode with that confounded footman. 'That's fine. I'm tired anyway. I'll see you when you get back.'

'I'll go ahead to secure us a table,' James said.

Agnes started to cry as her father was leaving. Her wails showed every sign of intensifying, so Christina made her excuses and bid them enjoy their evening. She detoured to the kitchen to fetch warm milk for Agnes. Then, carrying an oil lamp against the darkening afternoon, she bundled the now sobbing Agnes up to their bedroom, where she hugged her angry daughter in the fireside chair until her cries subsided into hiccups. Once Agnes had drunk her cup of milk, Christina murmured a Scottish lullaby into her small and perfect pink ear. It wasn't long before the child's head fell against Christina's chest.

Staring into the flickering fire, she could hear Adam and Tom talking in the room below, the chimney arrangements made their words audible. Christina smiled to hear them praise Agnes. She'd got to know them well in her visits to Northumberland. Christina had liked Alnwick. The extended Robertson family living and working together there, reminded her of her mother's family in Kinghorn.

'What do you think of James's artistic ambitions?' Tom asked his elder brother.

'Undoubtedly he has talent,' Adam replied. 'Don't forget, he was solely responsible for that masterful fresco in Alnwick Castle. Trouble is, he's never had the patience for the tedious parts of any job. When it came to decorating a plain wall or gilding a cornice, he was easily distracted. John was always complaining he was lazy. It was his failing as a cabinet maker too.'

Christina's shoulders drooped at Adam's words. He'd voiced what she feared.

'Maybe he'll persist better with fine painting if that's his real love?' Tom replied.

'Maybe.' Adam sounded unconvinced. 'We'd all thought he might marry a monied lady. The Duchess isn't the first woman to find him charming.'

'Christina is better than any monied lady,' Tom replied crossly.

'She is,' Adam agreed. 'Their marriage caused me to revise my opinion of James. They make a fine family.'

The kind words unleashed the emotion Christina had been trying to hold back. A tear fell into Agnes's curls, followed by another.

The men went back to talking about Northumberland

House, and soon Christina heard them go out. She sat for a long time, staring into the yellow-edged red of the smouldering embers. The lamplighter's footsteps outside preceded the glow of the street lantern, flinging long shadows into the dark room. Christina hugged her sleeping infant closer, and rubbed her cheeks dry with her sleeve. Self-pity was an emotion she daren't indulge. Her hope that James would become more money-focused was unrealistic. She knew her peacock's limitations.

Christina could do nothing about her nursed secret, creating a constant undercurrent of sadness and fear in her life. However, confirmation of James's idle tendencies was not an insurmountable situation. She had the skills to provide for her family. Hopefully, the Duchess's commission was just the beginning. Christina filled her lungs with a determined breath. So be it then.

Chapter Five

October 2017, Moscow

I strode towards the river, only stopping for breath when I reached the horse fountain in Alexandrovskiy Garden. The spray misted my face with water. Was Nick having an affair? The thought made me feel sick. But it made no sense. We were happy, and he was fully behind our plans to start a family.

I started to walk, keeping the Kremlin walls to my right. Tourists wandered, wide-eyed at the famous surroundings. I marched fast like a demented woman. I tried to slow down, taking deep breaths as I crossed Red Square. My emotional state was fragile. Getting married, giving up work, moving countries, I was literally out of my comfort zone. All necessary changes to have a baby, but I hadn't anticipated how it would feel if the last critical step in the plan failed. My body wasn't cooperating, and now this. Could I trust my own judgement? I needed to get a grip. Focus on my Christina quest.

I stared up at St Basil's Cathedral with its coloured and gilded onion-shaped domes, an ancient church that had been here for centuries. Had Christina Robertson ever come to Moscow?

I'd visit the Armoury Museum again to look for items linked to Nicholas I's reign and get a sense of what her world would have been like. The museum had been our last stop when Nick and I had visited the Kremlin complex. I'd assumed from the name that it would be a military museum, but in fact it contained lots of other items: clothes, jewellery, carriages and incredibly beautiful sledges. The guide had explained that passengers in horse-drawn sleighs could speed from St Petersburg much faster and more comfortably in the winter than in summer, when carriages had to bump along on muddy or rutted roads. Imagine that, a sledge piled high with furs, the jingle of bells on the horses' harnesses. Very Anna Karenina. Christina must surely have travelled in a sleigh?

My phone buzzed. A text from Nick.

Don't make supper for me. It was someone's birthday and I went out for lunch with the team.

My shoulders relaxed. I'd been fretting about how to raise the fact that I'd seen him. How to explain why I hadn't shouted and run across to talk to him. I was being an idiot. Making something out of nothing. I turned towards home. I'd no need for supper either, so I could get back to my research.

I looked up and smiled when Nick walked in.

'Please tell me you didn't sit here all day,' he said, bending over to encircle me in a hug, briefly resting his head on top of mine.

'No, I went to the lunch and I'm glad I did. I'm going to help with a brochure for the charity ball art auction. It's run by an English woman called Lisa. I liked her.'

'That's brilliant,' he said, heading for the fridge. 'I'm going to have a beer. Do you want one?'

'No, thanks. How was your lunch?'

'Good,' he said, rummaging about in the drawer for the bottle opener.

'It's on the draining board,' I told him, then waited, willing him to say more.

He smiled, an open, guiltless kind of smile.

'Who had a birthday?' I asked. My bright voice sounded false. So much for getting a grip.

'Oksana, my translator.'

'So you took her for lunch?'

'Along with all the guys. I took the whole team,' he replied. 'Her birthday was the occasion.'

'What's Oksana like? You never talk about her.'

'She's great, very efficient. I'm lucky.'

'No. What's she like, as a person?'

He shrugged, scowled. 'I don't know. We don't really chat much. Work is full on, and she has kids, so she's always in a hurry to get home.'

'How old is she? What does she look like?'

Nick smiled and shook his head. 'I get it. Have the expat witches been winding you up about Russian seductresses? Oksana's just a colleague. She's at least five years older than me and looks ordinary. Whereas you, my love, are extraordinary.' He kissed me.

That was the point I should have told him I'd seen her. That she had long, glossy, dark hair and shapely legs in high heels. Not ordinary at all. But I didn't. I said I'd have a small glass of wine after all and allowed my jealousy to fester.

The next few days were absorbed in painstaking and time-consuming internet searches. I was excited to find both the banns and the marriage in the Marylebone district records, confirming that Christina married a James Robertson in London in 1822. I started to look for their children. Then, I saw a critical detail. Christina's maiden name wasn't Saunders at all, it was Robertson. I'd been looking for the wrong name on a birth record.

On Saturday morning, Nick made us breakfast. 'It's stopped raining and I need some fresh air. Let's go for a walk.'

We got the metro to catch the cable car across to Gorky Park. Associated with spy thrillers and murder scenes in my imagination, but in reality a beautiful and deeply wooded riverside park. The cable car bubble soared up over the river and the treetops. Moscow's incredible panorama opened up behind us. I knew I was privileged to get this chance to live in Moscow. If I was serious about having children, there had to be compromises. I simply had to work harder at settling in here.

We walked to the viewpoint, hand-in-hand. There were lots of families doing the same, and there seemed to be toddlers and babies everywhere. Nick took a selfie of us in front of the gothic facade of Moscow State University, then another with the Moscow backdrop. This view captured several more of the city's 'seven sisters'. Stalin commissioned these monolithic structures to be modelled on the Manhattan Municipal Buildings, so now all I could think of was *Ghostbusters*, an odd and disorientating vision. We wandered through the trees down the hill, then walked along the river to catch a ferry back to the city centre. A woman with three small children was walking ahead. She had long, dark hair.

'Is that not...?' I started. Then remembered I wasn't meant to know what Oksana looked like.

'Not what?' Nick replied.

The woman turned to call to a straggling boy on a bicycle. She was in her twenties, too young.

'Nothing.' I must stop this. The old London Anna wasn't given to jealousy.

While we were sailing down the river, Nick showed me the photos. 'These are good. You should send them to your mum.'

I wouldn't send Mum the one with the Moscow view. My hand was protectively placed on my stomach, and my eyes looked anxious in the photo. A moment of truth captured. Hope and fear pulling me apart.

Lisa texted me the next day.

You up for supper this week? Wednesday or Thursday maybe?

I replied: *I'm heading back to the UK on Friday for the funeral. Wednesday would be better.*

Great. If you text me your address, I'll swing past for you at seven.

On Wednesday, Lisa texted me again.

Change of plan. Can we grab a takeaway at my house? My house-keeper has something on and Dmitry is going out. I'll pick you up after work at seven as planned.

Lisa turned up as arranged in the same Mercedes I'd seen outside the restaurant.

'Sorry to change the plans but I have lots of photos I want to show you, so this probably works better.'

Lisa spoke in Russian to the driver, and I was pleased to recognise the word for home. We stopped in front of an imposing looking old apartment building.

'We'll just out jump out here,' she said opening the car door. 'The turning circle inside is a nightmare.'

Black security gates swung open when Lisa pressed a remote on her keyring. A uniformed security guard raised his hand as we walked past his kiosk in the courtyard. Lisa led us to a door in the left-hand block. Inside, the hallway had stone floors, and a banister of twisted, painted metal with a gleaming wooden handrail. Very much a cut above our own relatively modern and modest apartment block.

'Are you okay to walk up?' Lisa asked. 'The lift is tiny and I need the exercise after sitting at my desk all day. Just two floors.'

We had to do the usual awkward shuffle on the landing of the second floor, to allow the heavy metal door to swing towards us. Moscow fire regulations demand that all apartment doors open outwards, but most landings weren't designed that way. Inside, was a long corridor covered in woodblock flooring. Light poured through big windows in the room beyond. I heard a chair scrape back, then a small boy came hurtling into the hall. He wound himself around Lisa's legs and she laughed.

'Anna, this is Misha my son.' She stroked the boy's blonde hair and gestured to the two girls who stood in the kitchen doorway. 'And these are his sisters Eva and Nina.'

All three children were in their pyjamas.

'How was school, girls? Have you had supper?' she asked.

'Yes, Mama.'

'You'll never guess what a boy in my class did...'

Both girls spoke at once as a middle-aged woman appeared behind them.

'You can tell me all your stories in a minute. Let's allow Mila to get on home first.'

Lisa swapped to rapid Russian to talk to her housekeeper, who soon had her coat on. 'Goodbye, madam,' she said with a nod in my direction.

'Right, Misha, go get your book. You can let Anna hear your excellent reading, then it's off to bed.'

In the large high-ceilinged sitting room, a big TV screen

hung on one wall. All the other walls were covered in abstract oil paintings of animals, birds and trees. Lisa sat on one couch and the girls perched either side of her. When her son came running in carrying a book, Lisa pulled him up onto her knee.

'What a beautiful room,' I said. 'I love the art.'

'Dmitry, my husband, is a professional artist. I'll tell him you admired them. He'll be so pleased.'

The boy read in Russian, his small face screwed up in concentration and his finger tracing along the page.

After a few minutes, the boy closed his book. Lisa stood, pulling her son onto her hip.

'Right then, Mikhail Dmitriyevich, teeth and bed. Say goodnight now.'

'Do you like Chinese food?' she asked me.

'Love it.'

'I'll order our usual selection.'

'Us too?' Eva asked.

Lisa laughed. 'I know you've had supper and it's much too late. If you are already in bed once I've settled Misha, you can have some dim sum at breakfast.'

The girls followed their mother.

Our food arrived a few minutes later and Lisa brought in a tray bearing the Chinese boxes, cutlery, plates, glasses, and a bottle of white wine.

'Join me?' she asked, opening the bottle.

'Just a small glass,' I replied.

Once we'd eaten, Lisa put a bulging folder on the table. 'I thought it might be helpful to go through some photos for this year and show you last year's catalogue.'

I leafed through the brochure, trying to absorb the layout. 'Okay, so you have the larger, more expensive paintings at the front, then it's grouped by paintings of similar subject,' I said.

'Exactly, you've got it.'

I knelt on the floor beside the low table and pushed the photos into groups. Many featured Moscow landscapes, some were sentimental and touristy, others more modern in style.

'Great! You have an eye for it. There's some politics in the art world, and some artists are better not on the same page, but I can sort that.'

'How should I go about writing the artists' descriptions?'

'I'll mark those that are in last year's brochure and send you website links where they exist. Most websites have English translations.'

'But you'll want Russian text too?'

'I'll handle that,' Lisa replied.

I held up a photo of an abstract bird, a dark shape in a violet-tinged shade of blue. 'Is this your husband's work?'

'Yes, well spotted. He's putting in two this year.' She pulled out another photo of a stylised boat.

'I might not get much done before Friday, but I'll take them to the UK with me.'

'The folder's for you to take home, but don't weigh down your suitcase. I'll send you electronic copies.'

'I'm really looking forward to this, something to get my brain working,' I said, sitting back in my chair.

I looked around the room. 'This place is really stunning.'

'Thank you. It belongs to Dmitry's family. We couldn't afford it on our income, but I do love it here. Shall I top up your glass?' She held up the wine bottle.

'No thanks.' I don't know why I hesitated. I liked Lisa and felt I could trust her. 'The truth is, I'm trying to get pregnant.'

'How exciting,' she said. She filled her glass and raised it. 'Good luck.'

'Thanks, I might need it,' I replied with a grimace. 'We hoped it might happen quickly once we married and started living together full-time. But apparently the universe is not aligned to fit in with my plans.'

Lisa smiled in sympathy. 'Don't worry too much, it often takes time. I was married for five years before I had the twins.'

'Yes, but we started trying years before we got married.'

Lisa nodded, her expression thoughtful. 'I understand how stressful it is. And I can't believe I just told you not to worry. It's exactly the kind of platitude that used to drive me crazy when I was struggling to conceive. The twins were IVF, then Misha was our lucky bonus.'

'Well, you have a lovely family now. Having twins must have felt like hitting the jackpot.'

'We were delighted, if a little deluded about how much work it would be.'

I opened my mouth to ask about IVF, then hesitated. It might sound too needy. She pre-empted my question, perhaps reading it on my face.

'If you start considering intervention, just give me a shout. I'm familiar with the system and some of the fertility professionals here.'

'Thank you. I appreciate the offer. I think we might be getting to that stage.'

'Fingers crossed you won't need it.' Lisa glanced up at the clock. 'Would you excuse me for a minute? I'll just check on the girls.'

I stood to study some smaller paintings on a far wall. On the shelf, next to some art books, was a framed photograph of a teenage boy. I leaned in to look at it more closely.

'That's Vadim, Dmitry's son from his first marriage,' Lisa said as she came back into the room. He usually comes here at the weekends.'

We sat down again. Lisa tucked her bare feet to her side on the couch. 'I know our life looks perfect, but it wasn't at all easy in the beginning. Dmitry's family was afraid I'd entice him to live abroad and Vadim was convinced he'd be shut out.'

'How did you bring them round?'

'Tact and time, then eventually giving his parents more grandchildren helped. So, how is your painter research going?' she added.

'It's been frustrating, but I finally had a breakthrough. When I looked more closely at her marriage documents, I realised she was recorded as Christina Robertson, spinster.'

Lisa looked puzzled. 'What? A Miss Robertson became a Mrs Robertson?'

'Exactly. I've gone back to the birth record search again.' I gathered my things to leave. 'This ancestry stuff is so time-consuming, but I promise I'll prioritise the art brochure now,' I said, as I gathered my things to leave.

'Just do what you can,' Lisa answered and gave me a hug. 'I'm really relieved to have some help.'

My period came early the next day.

I sat alone on the bathroom floor and sobbed, filled with rawness, self-blame, loneliness. This mounting sense of loss every month had grown monstrous, and difficult to hide. Nick and I had started out as a hopeful and excited team. Now, he didn't want to deal with a full-scale drama every four weeks. We'd stopped talking about it.

I dragged myself back to my laptop, wrung out and exhausted, but needing distraction. I found Christina's mother's birth and marriage record. George had one younger sister called Margaret. Not born in Kinghorn like all the others but in nearby Kirkcaldy. Her husband was a John Robertson. A new trail to follow.

Chapter Six

August 1824, London

Christina set off for Northumberland House. In this third sitting with the Duchess she must capture the final elements of her sketch. Tomorrow, the Duke and Duchess would escape London to go up the Thames to their Syon House country residence. Christina would be stuck here in the intolerable heat with the rest of Londoners. As her open carriage travelled down Haymarket, the Duchess's other reason for quitting London was horribly evident. Christina clamped a handkerchief soaked with lavender oil over her mouth and nose. A choking miasma of foul air drifted up from the Thames and the fear of disease made Christina's heart beat faster. Their second daughter had been born at the beginning of June. Smaller and frailer than Agnes, Christina feared for her health. James had greeted her arrival with the same enthusiasm as for Agnes.

'She is adorable, Christina. We do create the most beautiful babies,' he'd said.

'I'm sorry you didn't get your boy,' she replied.

'There's plenty of time for boys, but I insist on Christiana this time. That is what we agreed, Christiana for a girl and

51

James William for a boy. James will arrive when we've fulfilled our pledge. Agnes is a lovely child, but I fear she'll chastise you for her dull name.'

They'd long ago discussed naming their first daughter Christiana as an acknowledgement of both her names. Her parents had christened her Christian, but Aunt Agnes changed it to Christina, declaring her too wilful for such a pious name. Christina couldn't dissuade James and wouldn't divulge her secret, so she shortened it to Tiana.

Christina was jerked out of her thoughts by the driver reining the horse to a sudden halt. A barefoot beggar child scooted out from in front of the horse's hooves and fled down an alley. The angry stallholder who'd been pursuing him was left shaking his fist. Her driver shouted a rebuke after the boy, and Christina hoped whatever he'd stolen would appease his hunger enough to save him from taking another near fatal risk. As the carriage wheels started to turn, she became aware of a droning noise. A swarm of bluebottles that had settled on the huge pile of horse manure in the road flew up in an angry buzzing cloud around her face. She flailed at them with her handkerchief, exposing her to the putrid smell again. At last they reached their destination, and she escaped into the cool, clean corridors of Northumberland House.

Christina entered through the tradesman's door. The Duchess had said she should come through the front, since her easel was set up near there, but Christina had learned over the years the importance of keeping in with the servants. She paused in the kitchen to ask after cook's health and sent a message to the Duchess's lady's maid, requesting an audience with her mistress. Christina had become close to the Duchess through the portrait sessions and their weekly painting lessons, but the politics of a big house were much more complicated than the whims of its mistress.

Christina propped her sketch on the easel at the foot of

the staircase. She'd established the broad outline already, the curve of the Duchess's arm, the set of her chin. Today she'd concentrate on getting the details of her hair, her tiara and other jewellery. She'd return here after the Duchess had left London to perfect the ornate, marble-topped table on the side of the painting.

The Duchess's voice came from the top of the stairs. 'Christina. Sorry to keep you waiting.' She started to descend. 'I got dressed at the last minute today. It's altogether too hot for this gown.'

The Duchess's velvet dress was gorgeous, but much too heavy for today's weather.

'Would you prefer not to pose today, Your Grace? I could come out to Syon House next week.'

'No, it's cooler down here. The sunlight has turned the drawing room into an oven.'

Christina worked quickly to complete her sketch, then she got out her paints.

'Would you grant me ten more minutes, Your Grace? I'd like to capture the green hues in your dress. I may have to do a couple of mixes to get it right.'

'How exciting. May I come and watch how you do it?'

They spent a companionable half hour chatting about painting technique and the challenges of creating the different shades to depict the folds. Christina recorded the proportions of the colour mixes she'd chosen, then cleared away her paints. 'I expect to have the portrait done within a month,' she promised.

'It's my birthday on the twelfth of September. It would be marvellous to have it by then,' the Duchess replied.

'Then if it's convenient, I'll visit you on the first day of September for one final sitting,' Christina suggested.

'Excellent plan, and the Duke should be at home. I aim to introduce you and persuade him to sit for a portrait. I fear the King's plans for him will often take him away.'

Christina kept her eyes down, hoping not to betray her wild joy at the prospect. A portrait of the Duke could take her art to another place entirely. She made a steady trade in miniatures of women and children, but she'd never had a commission from an important man. The Duke of Northumberland was the King's confidant and one of England's most influential figures.

'I would be extremely honoured, Your Grace.'

'I wish you'd call me Charlotte when we're alone, Christina. I feel over these weeks that we've become friends. I so appreciate what you've taught me.'

'I believe I've enjoyed painting you more than anyone before. James told me you were a gracious lady, and he didn't exaggerate.'

'Another example of your husband's silver tongue,' the Duchess said with a laugh.

On the carriage journey home, Christina's thoughts went back to the sweltering day she met James. She'd been sitting with her back against the warm harbour wall, tucked down out of sight from the road, in case her aunt might spy her. She was pretending to sketch the harbour, lifting her gaze in its direction often enough not to raise the suspicions of the fishermen. These men working on their nets were the actual subject of her sketches. Their gnarled hands and weatherbeaten, lined faces were challenging to draw. Since her May visit to London, she'd been possessed with a fervour to improve her skills. Art was all she cared about. She looked up when a tall shadow fell over her page. The boy who stood there was as fine featured as a Greek statue. A total contrast to the fishermen she'd been drawing.

'I was told of a legend,' he said, with laughter in his voice, 'that deep in sleepy Kinghorn I'd find an artist, a Robertson girl masquerading as a Saunders, like a beautiful cuckoo amongst a nest of speugs.'

She laughed. 'And how does an English boy know how to name a Scottish sparrow, and why do you know so much about me?'

He didn't answer, but sat himself down on the ground beside her and took her sketchbook without asking. 'These are good,' he said. 'Robertson talent and no mistake. My name is James Robertson. Are we related?'

'I've no idea,' she replied.

That summer, they conspired to meet almost every day. Her aunt would not approve of the meetings, but Christina had years of practice in discovering Kinghorn's secret places. They walked the woods above the village, sticking to the hedgerows and avoiding public paths. He brought his sketchbook, and they worked together. She was content for the first time in her whole life. When he said he must return to work in Alnwick, she thought her heart would break. Pressed against the rough trunk of a Scots pine, he kissed her for the first time. She knew she shouldn't allow it, but it felt like joyous freedom. Her heart took flight like a skybound hawk and when she gave in to the urge to kiss him back, it was a swooping, perilous dive. Complete commitment.

He broke away with a mischievous smile. 'I'll see you here next year, Miss not Saunders Robertson. Don't go forgetting me.'

He kept his promise and came back the next year, and although their love had faced many challenges, she'd been his from that day onwards.

. . .

Christina expected to find James in the living room when she got home. Eliza had the afternoon off and he'd promised to entertain Agnes. Instead, she found Tiana's wet nurse sound asleep in the chair. No toddler, no baby, no husband. She frowned. Becky usually nursed Christiana in the bedroom, or sat darning near her cradle whilst the baby slept. The sound of crashing, followed by Agnes's laughter came up from the kitchen. She went out to the stairs and found James coming down them.

'Who's watching the girls?' she asked.

He smiled at her. 'Don't worry, they're quite safe. Becky is feeling a bit off colour, so she brought in her eldest daughter to help out. She's come a couple of times recently and the girl is a natural with children. Agnes loves her.'

Christina hurried down the stairs. The kitchen was in uproar. Agnes was on the ground beside a girl of around ten, who had Tiana in her arms. They'd requisitioned a wooden spoon and two pots from the cook. Agnes was banging them with all her might and laughing. Christina opened her mouth to say something when Becky's voice came behind her.

'Get up at once, Grace. Look at the state of Agnes's dress.'

Christina heard the fear in the woman's voice. Becky had seven more children younger than Grace and could ill afford to lose her place. Christina took a deep breath to subdue her anger. She would direct it at James later. He was meant to be in charge.

Agnes shouted, 'Mama!' then tottered over to wrap her arms around Christina's legs. Her upturned face was smiling and bright red.

'Sorry, Ma, 'twas just a game,' the girl said.

Christina reached out to take the baby from the girl,

whose face was as scarlet as Agnes's.

'I'm sorry, Mistress,' Becky said. 'Little Fred has kept me awake at night this last week. Our house is hot as hell and he's teething. Grace has a knack with the young ones. She has plenty of practice at home.'

Her tone was pleading. The truth was, Christina had no intention of dismissing Becky. A wet nurse was not easily replaced and anyway, she was sympathetic to the woman, juggling so many children and trying to earn extra income.

'The kitchen's not a good place for Agnes now she's walking. She might get under the cook's feet when she's dealing with hot pans.'

Christina laid her hand on Agnes's head. The child was very warm.

'It won't happen again, Mistress. You get on home now, Grace.'

Becky's daughter was absently scratching her chest. Did she have fleas? 'Yes, Ma,' she replied, now moving her worrying fingers to the crook of her elbow.

Christina reached for the girl's wrist. Her extended forearm was covered in unmistakable red spots.

'Measles,' Christina whispered, meeting Becky's terrified gaze.

'I'm right sorry, Mistress,' she muttered. She grabbed her daughter's hand and fled.

Christina sat up all night with Agnes in the nursery, then kept the same vigil for three further days. She banished James to their bedroom with Tiana. Christina had measles as a child, but James wasn't sure if he had. She was still feeding the baby at night, but her nipples were soon sore and bleeding. The child sucked her dry and cried for more. Christina tried to tempt Tiana with softened bread, but she wouldn't swallow.

On the third night, after a fraught hour of sucking the baby fell asleep. Christina rose to go back to Agnes. James touched her arm. His face was grey with worry.

'Will she starve without Becky's milk?'

Christina winced as she eased her aching breast back inside her petticoat.

'No,' she replied. 'My milk will come back stronger soon. It's Agnes you should worry about. I can't keep her temperature down.'

He nodded, grim-faced. 'I'll send to the dock for more ice.'

Christina hadn't the heart to be angry with him. She knew he blamed himself.

Eliza brought bowls of rags soaked in ice chips, which Christina used to try to salve her daughter's torment, but Agnes writhed and bucked in her fever. On the fourth day, the first tell-tale spots appeared on her chest.

'Is there any word from Becky?' she asked Eliza.

'Her son died yesterday and her twins are sick too,' Eliza whispered.

'Poor woman,' Christina replied.

When Eliza left, hopelessness came over Christina in a nauseating wave. She sat beside her sleeping daughter and wept. Was this her punishment for putting her artistic ambitions ahead of her children?

A couple of hours later, she stood stiffly and went to the cot. After days of thrashing about, Agnes was sleeping quietly. Christina touched her daughter's forehead. It felt normal. She ran up the stairs. Inside their bedroom, she found James standing over the crib.

'Agnes is over the worst, James. I think she's going to live.'

He raised his head, but instead of joy, she saw anguish. 'Christiana is very hot. I'm so sorry,' he said.

. . .

Tiana's fight wasn't like her sister's. She hadn't the same strength. For two days the baby refused to feed, twisting her head away. On the third day, Tiana jerked like a marionette, her tiny body wracked with fits. Christina sensed her baby was leaving. They sat beside her all night. Tiana slipped away just as the first spots bloomed on her neck.

Dawn light glistened on the slate tiles of the rainy London rooftops. Christina's throat was raw with crying. James was still weeping beside the cradle, unable to tear himself away. Christina stood up. Her limbs ached and grief hung on her shoulders like a sodden cloak. But Agnes was alive, so she must cling to that and live too.

She swallowed painfully and gasped. That familiar metallic taste in her mouth. The change in her saliva was unmistakable. She was pregnant again. How was she going to face the terror of trying to protect another baby?

Chapter Seven

October 2017, Edinburgh, Scotland

When I cleared customs in Edinburgh airport, I found Mum waiting for me. I dropped my bag at her feet and burst into tears. She hugged me and the smell of Estée Lauder's Private Collection was like a hardwire to my childhood.

'Oh, Anna love, you're going to set me off,' she said, holding my shoulders and scrutinising my face. 'Are you all right? You look a bit peely-wally.'

'I'm fine, just tired from the journey.' I pulled a wry face. 'And my period is terrible this month.'

'Oh, right,' she said, nodding, understanding the implications. 'Let's get you home. You look like you need a cup of Edinburgh tea.'

We exchanged a smile. Granny always maintained that tea in England didn't taste as nice, because it wasn't made with Scottish water. We got into Mum's old Volvo estate in the airport car park and were soon on the road into Edinburgh.

'Are you sure you're okay about us staying at Granny's house tonight? There isn't even a proper bed. All Granny's furniture has been in storage. The rental helped cover her care fees. Uncle Jimmy is bringing all of her stuff tomorrow. I'm sure I could find a B&B.'

'I'm looking forward to seeing the place again, and those camping mattresses worked fine in plenty of lumpy Lake District campsites.'

'God knows what's going to turn up tomorrow,' Mum said. 'I wish I'd gone through everything when we cleared the house.'

'I remember the stress of settling Granny into the care home. There was no energy left for anything else.'

Mum grimaced. Granny had managed with carer support in her own home for years, but began to forget she didn't cook anymore. She burned through the bottom of a saucepan. The fire brigade came, and the council threatened to turn off her gas.

'Poor Mum,' she said quietly. 'If I start to go that way, you have permission to shoot me.'

I squeezed her hand on the gearstick. 'I don't think I need to get my firearms licence just yet.'

Granny's house was in an area universally known as The Colonies, in Edinburgh's Stockbridge. Quirky rows of small terraced houses built as affordable homes for Victorian workers. It was a particular style of housing I'd seen nowhere else. Each terraced cottage was actually two flats, the lower one accessed by a front door in one street and the upper one accessed via an external stair in the next street. That meant each had the luxury of a small garden and its own front door with no shared staircase. That must have seemed unbelievably luxurious to city dwellers who'd perhaps come from crowded tenements. Granny's house was one of the 'double-uppers' at the end of the cul-de-sac with sight of the Water of Leith running alongside. I'd loved visiting as a child. I used to play with the local children in the low-walled gardens and quiet road, cobbled with granite setts. When I was older, I joined the gang of children who ranged further to the wooded riverbank and nearby Inverleith Park.

It was a tiny house, mayhem when Mum, my brother, and I descended on Granny for a holiday. There were only two bedrooms, so the three of us shared, with Euan in a sleeping bag on the floor. I smiled at the thought as I put my holdall beside the mat and sleeping bag on the bare floorboards. Euan had always complained about the injustice of me being in the bed with Mum, so this would make him laugh. I walked over to open the dormer window, taking care not to bang my head on the eaves. All I could hear was the gurgle of the river and a blackbird singing. We were within walking distance from the centre of Edinburgh, but it was like being in the country. My shoulders relaxed. This had always been a home-from-home.

'Tea's ready,' Mum called from downstairs.

As I reached the bottom of the narrow staircase, there was a gentle tap on the outside door. A woman in her fifties, with lots of curly auburn hair, stood in the doorway.

'I'm Mandy, a neighbour. I heard about Mrs Gallagher. She was a lovely lady. I just wanted to say, I'm sorry. Oh, and I brought some cake, save me from eating it all.'

Mum thanked her and took the offered the tin.

'That's so kind of you, Mandy. I'm Emma, Mrs Gallagher's daughter, and this is my daughter, Anna.'

'I just made tea, if you'd like a cup.' Mum gestured for her to come inside. 'Although I admit we don't actually have any chairs. The furniture is coming tomorrow.'

Mandy laughed. 'I'm sure you've got lots to do, but I can lend you a couple of kitchen chairs overnight if you would like?'

'That's really kind, thank you,' Mum replied.

'Jack, my teenage son, will be home from school any

minute. I'll send him over with them.' Mandy shot Mum a glance. 'So, are you moving in?'

'No, I live in York, although I expect I'll be here for a few weeks. I need to sort out all Mum's things from storage, then I suppose we'll put the house on the market.'

Mandy's face fell. 'Oh, right. Of course. Well, anything I can do to help, just let me know.'

Mandy left and Jack appeared with the two chairs twenty minutes later. After he had gone Mum made more tea and we sat down with slices of Victoria sponge.

'Mandy seems nice,' I said.

'Yes, I remember your granny saying she liked her. So tell me all about your St Petersburg trip. What with all the drama, I never got to ask you.'

I told Mum how much I'd loved the city and the excitement of discovering the Christina Robertson paintings.

'Do you have any photos?' she asked.

'There are great images on the Hermitage website. Although it might be better to look when I can get wireless access. I switched to a cheap UK contract, it doesn't have very good data.'

'There's Wi-Fi. The tenants left recently and I told the letting company to keep it on. The password is on the router in the living room.'

'Really? That's great news. I've some work for a charity thing to do when I'm here.' I told Mum all about working with Lisa, then about the ancestry research I'd started on Christina Robertson.

'Fancy the story about the artist being true all along. It just sounded so far-fetched.'

'I haven't confirmed the link to us yet. You might be able to help me with Granny's family. I haven't got very far with our branch of the family tree.'

'Maybe,' she answered. 'There's a tin full of old birth and

marriage certificates and I think a family Bible. It'll arrive tomorrow in one of the boxes.'

We spent the rest of the afternoon cleaning. By five o'clock, we were exhausted and decided to head to the local fish and chip shop for sit-in fish suppers. Although it was already getting dark, there was just enough light to take the riverside path. We crossed the bridge which led out of the last street in the Colonies. Mum said 'evening' to a man who stood smoking at the water's edge.

'Five more minutes, boys,' he shouted to three children, who were playing chase on the bank.

'Euan and I used to play here when we visited,' I said.

'And unlike that responsible father, we just let you run wild. It's a wonder you didn't drown.'

I laughed. 'It's not very deep.'

Strolling arm-in-arm, we listened to the sounds of the Water of Leith bubbling past and the muttering of ducks settling on the bank for the night.

'It's odd being here in the autumn. It never seemed to get dark when we came here in the summer.'

'Light all summer and dark all winter, that's Scotland,' Mum replied.

We crossed another bridge, its shape and the overhanging willow evoking Monet's art, then climbed the steps up to the main road. A delicious smell signalled we were approaching the chip shop.

'Is Don looking after the shop while you're gone?' I asked once we'd sat down.

Mum had run Dad's antiques business since he died ten years ago. Don had worked for Dad from the beginning.

'Yes, but he's retiring at Christmas.'

'I suppose he must be well past retirement age. Will you look for someone else?'

'He's seventy, and I'm not sure. I might sell the business.

I've had an offer from Henderson's, the shop in Micklegate. They're looking for bigger premises.'

'Wow. That's big news. Are you going to retire too?'

'I haven't decided, but I think I'll accept their offer. It's too good an opportunity to miss. Granny left this house to me, so either I can live off the rental income, or use the capital for a new business.'

The server came over. 'Two fish suppers wi' salt and sauce. Do youse want anything tae drink?'

'Just water for me, please,' Mum said.

'Me too,' I added. 'Salt and sauce, yum. There's nothing beats a Scottish fish supper.' I put a piece of fish into my mouth, savouring the hot, crisp batter with the vinegar tanged brown sauce. The taste took me straight back to Friday nights at Granny's house. Euan and I would eat ours on the outside steps, not to miss a moment of hanging out with our friends. 'This is perfect.'

Mum nodded.

'Will you stay in York?' I asked.

'I'm not sure about that either,' Mum replied. 'Would you be very upset if I didn't?'

'No, and anyway, you should do what you want.'

'Once I'm not tied to the shop, I'll be able to come and visit you in Moscow.'

'I'd love that. We should go to St Petersburg together. I'm itching to go back and see the paintings I missed.'

The next day, Uncle Jimmy arrived with a small truck of furniture and boxes. We all stood and stared into the full van.

'If I didn't know that it all definitely came out of this house, I'd say it wouldn't fit,' Mum said.

'I should've suggested you come and have a look when it was in the shed,' Jimmy answered.

'I want to get it all unpacked before Euan arrives, then he can see if he wants to take anything back,' Mum replied.

I laughed. 'I kind of doubt that Granny's things are going to sit well in Euan and Alan's fancy apartment in San Francisco.'

'I expect you're right,' Mum replied.

Uncle Jimmy shifted from one foot to the other. Granny's cousin was an ageing Fife farmer. Living a life as far from that of a gay couple in a San Francisco condo as was possible to imagine.

'I've brought Harry and Mac tae help carry stuff in,' he said. 'We'd better get a shift on since this van is blocking the road.'

Once the house was filled with furniture and boxes, Jimmy said he'd be off.

'Won't you stay for tea? A neighbour gave us cake,' Mum said.

Jimmy shook his head. 'The pay and display here is gey expensive.'

'Tell me about it,' Mum answered. 'You have to be a resident to get access to parking in this road. I should have left the car at home, but I'm sure I'm going to want to take some things back with me.'

'Why don't you bring the car tae the farm?' Jimmy said. 'Now that barn is empty, you could park it in there.'

'I might take you up on that, Jimmy. I don't know how to thank you for everything you've done.'

'It's the least I can do for oor Edith. It's a sad time, so it is.'

Once Jimmy had gone, we started to unpack the kitchen boxes.

'Why in all earth did one woman need so many saucepans?' I said.

66

'And that's after binning the one she nearly set fire to the house with,' Mum replied.

After we'd done as much as we could for the day, we sat on the couch and I showed Mum all the Christina Robertson paintings on the Hermitage site.

'They're beautiful, so romantic. We must definitely go together. It'll be like a family pilgrimage,' she said.

'Exactly. I suspect Nick will be pleased that I've got someone else to go with.'

'Did she do any work here?'

'Yes, much more than I thought when I first started looking. The Royal Academy has a link to the original catalogues. It seems she exhibited year after year.'

'You would think she'd be more famous,' Mum said.

'That's the weird thing. I suppose portraits mainly end up in houses rather than museums, and it seems she went out of fashion. Anyway, I'm hopeful I might track some down.'

'We could visit Kinghorn when we drop the car at Uncle Jimmy's. It's only about five miles from his farm.

'I'd love that. I'd like to have a look in the graveyard.'

Mum stretched out her neck and yawned. 'Thank goodness for Jimmy's boys today. I thought it would take hours to unload that van when I first saw it.'

'I heard him refusing to take any money. That's really good of him. Removal firms are so expensive.'

'He point blank refused, although I tipped the lads when he wasn't looking. It's not just today, either. Jimmy would never take anything for the storage, said he knew how expensive the care home must be.'

'Nothing? That would have saved Granny a fortune. She must have been a favourite cousin.'

'They lived together most of Granny's life. Her mother

already had Granny when she married Jimmy's dad, when his first wife died giving birth to him,' Mum answered.

'Really? What happened to Granny's biological dad?'

Mum gave me a peculiar sideways glance. 'I'm not sure that Granny knew who he was. I once overheard Jimmy's sister Margaret describing her illegitimacy. Perhaps that's why Granny didn't talk about it. Being born out of wedlock was a shameful thing in her day.'

That night, I couldn't sleep. I'd expected to uncover secrets in my search for ancestors, but never imagined it would involve Granny. Why had Mum said nothing before? If Granny's illegitimacy was generally known, that must have been hard for her. I put on the bedside light and reached for the blue tin we'd found in a box today. Stacks of yellowing certificates were piled inside. My mother's family back through the ages. I reached the bottom of the tin somewhere around four in the morning, having ploughed through generations of birth, marriage, and death certificates. Absolutely everything except Granny's birth certificate. Why was it missing?

Chapter Eight

January 1825, London

Christina had thought she might go insane with grief. The pain from her engorged breasts was a terrible punishment to add to the loss. When her milk dried up, that was agony of a different kind. James was tortured with guilt for allowing Tiana to be exposed to disease. He spent a great deal of time out with his friends and he was drinking too much. Christina sensed that witnessing her own pain made him feel worse, or at least that was what she told herself to excuse him staying away. She survived because of two people, little Agnes and the Duke of Northumberland, a very incongruous pairing.

The Duchess advised her to quote a substantially larger fee to the Duke. 'His friends will ask about you and what you charged. I'm certain it will lead to more commissions. I've no doubt his portrait will be first class and you should be properly rewarded.'

Painting the Duke's portrait was much more time-consuming than his wife's. The outfit the Duke had chosen to wear presented an enormous challenge. He was to represent the King at the coming coronation of Charles X in France and the Duke was posing in full regalia, holding his coronet. Christina understood his wish to mark such an auspicious occasion, but this level of formality didn't lend itself to her style. It was also an extremely heavy costume, so the Duke couldn't tolerate standing still for long. Her Uncle George was a master at such formal paintings of England's aristocrats. Powerful men looking very serious and some would say pompous. Christina would never tell her uncle, but she thought the style outdated. Christina feared she would be unable to capture the character of the man, when the viewer's eye was overwhelmed by the over-elaborate outfit. She arranged to get access to the clothes and jewels in separate sessions. Spending long hours drawing every ruffle on his collar and sleeves and exact detail of his jewels, required concentration through the darkening days of November and December. By early January, when the painting was almost complete, she realised that occupying her thoughts had taken the worst edge off her terrible pain. Her pregnancy was now very evident and she must ready her heart to welcome another baby. The risk terrified her.

Christina asked the Duchess to be present when she met the Duke for the last time, to capture the fine nuances of his face. She got the Duchess to sit where the Duke's gaze settled. Her ruse had the desired effect. It brought a warmth, a certain softening of the eyes and mouth. When she gave the Duchess the finished work, she cried with joy.

'You can see the love in his eyes, Your Grace. To others it will look like an official and serious portrait, but you will always remember he was looking at you.'

Her task complete, she turned her attention to James. 'You promised to paint my portrait as a gift. Do you mean to keep your pledge?'

His wounded look was the first time he'd met her eyes in months. 'I find I don't have the heart for it.'

'You could present it to the Royal Academy committee for consideration for this year's exhibition.'

He shook his head as if irritated by an insect. 'They wouldn't admit my poor efforts.'

'The painting is not poor, it just needs more work to perfect it. You've two other portraits sitting there almost finished and what about the miniature you promised Mrs Hamilton?'

She took his hands and looked deep into his eyes. 'I know how hard this is. I miss her every day, too. Do it to honour Christiana, like a memorial, and for Agnes. She should grow up knowing that the world recognises the talent of both her parents.'

His expression changed. Her arrow had reached its mark.

'I'm very short of time. Do you think it possible?'

'My commissions are done. I have seven miniatures complete to submit to the Academy, including the Duke and Duchess. I can attend to everything else so you can work.'

He kissed her. 'Damn it, I'm going to try. For the sake of all my girls.'

And work he did, in a way that Christina had never seen before. He gave up his late night drinking and went to the studio every day. Of course, she continued to draft new commission sketches at home and pursued leads for more work. Christina was delighted that James was working diligently, but so far only Mrs Hamilton had commissioned a portrait, which meant his paintings were unlikely to bring them much income.

This didn't diminish her pride when James finished all four portraits on time. She wrote the submission letters to

Henry Howard, the Academy Secretary, for her own miniatures and the four paintings by James. The wait was excruciating. Pushing James had been a gamble. If the Academy
turned all his work down, she might have done more harm
than good.

The weeks after they heard that the Academy had accepted
all eleven paintings were some of the happiest in their
marriage. James joined them on their daily excursion to Hyde
Park. Agnes had grown into an active two-year-old who
needed to be outside when the weather was dry. James could
chase after Agnes when she wandered off, something
Christina found increasingly difficult in these last weeks of
her pregnancy. The sight of Agnes's stout little legs making
determined progress under her petticoats made them both
laugh.

James's sociable nature was evident in the number of
acquaintances who stopped to talk to him. She loved to see
his pride when he introduced his daughter and told people
that his work was to be honoured. Many of his friends were
artists, and they knew the importance of this Royal Academy
milestone. Even strangers were drawn to chat to this handsome man walking hand-in-hand with a small girl. Most men
had no patience with children, but James had a gift for it.

The Academy Exhibition opened on the second of May.
Christina had a real problem fastening her dress over her now
enormous stomach. The baby moved, and she snatched her
hand away. She'd been resisting the inclination to stroke this
baby. The bond with her girls had begun before they were
born. Love of a child was like walking around with your soul
stripped raw, the strength of the bond matched only by its

frailty. That Agnes had survived measles was a good sign for her longer term health, but Christina watched her constantly. She'd touched the child's brow so often that Agnes put up her podgy hand to push her fingers away.

'No, Mama,' she'd said, her little face screwed up in annoyance.

Now here was this new baby, already asserting itself. 'All right, little one, just please don't come today,' she whispered.

She and James walked into the Royal Academy arm-in-arm. They met the Duchess of Northumberland leaving the gallery with a group of her friends. The Duchess introduced her as the talented artist responsible for their two portraits, and her friends were loud in their praise. When Charlotte also introduced James as a fellow artist and Royal Academy exhibitor, Christina could have kissed her. James gave a restrained nod of his head, but she knew he was beaming inside. They came to the miniature of the Duke of Northumberland first. It had an excellent position and there was a crowd of gentlemen looking at it. Christina recognised Lord Barrington in the group. Her portrait of his wife hung only a few feet away. She and James exchanged a covert look and edged forward to eavesdrop.

'Damn fine portrait,' one man said.

'I predict you'll hear more of this paintress. She has captured my wife's likeness exactly,' Barrington replied.

'Do you think Hugh Percy intends to wear his coronet at the coronation?' the first man asked. 'The French monarch might take offence.'

'The two are well acquainted from Charles's time in South Audley Street,' Barrington replied.

'Still, I question the wisdom of sending a representative to such a papist spectacle,' the man muttered.

Lord Barrington glared in response to his friend's indiscretion. Christina led James away, anxious not to be caught listening.

Next they went to look at the Duchess's portrait. James had been given a nearby position for one of his paintings. She had hoped the association would bring him an audience. Many ladies stopped to comment favourably on the Duchess's painting. Not a single person paused to look at James's portrait. Christina had worried he might get discouraging criticism. The truth was that his work was competent, but didn't stand out. James was used to people looking at him. Being ignored would hit him hard. She needed to get him away.

'James, would you mind if we went home now? I feel some pain. It wouldn't do if this baby came here.'

A few days later, Uncle George told her James had stopped going to the studio, but her anxiety about her husband was swept away by swift and intense labour pains. They hardly had time to summon the midwife before she safely delivered a baby boy. Christina was astonished at how different it felt to hold a male child in her arms. The complete otherness of the sensation. Then the tender look on James's face when he cradled his son made her cry. She was sure of his love for Agnes, but she could also see how much it meant to him to have a boy. James took the child to be baptised and named him James William.

Over the next weeks, James spent a lot of time with her and the children, seemingly recovered from the exhibition opening. Not for the first time, she thought that he liked to be known as an artist, but that he wasn't driven by it as a vocation. He simply didn't care about it the way she did. Three weeks after the birth, Christina started going back to her studio. It was expected she would remain at home for at least a month, but she had so much to do.

August came with a heatwave. Christina daren't take the children out into London's stinking streets and Agnes was getting more fractious by the day.

'Phillip is hosting a family party in his garden tomorrow. Why don't we go together?' James asked.

Christina had little interest in James's social circle. His friends were a group of artistic and musical young men who rarely met in the presence of their families. When she'd gone to one such gathering, she had found herself sat with the wives, while the men had a noisy wine-fuelled debate about the merits of landscape painting over portraiture. She was one of the few commercially successful artists at the gathering, but her opinion wasn't sought. Their notion that art should have some serious subject led to more than enough paintings of famous battles and biblical scenes. Her patrons wanted a painting of a loved one; there would always be clients for this universal need.

'Please come, Christina. Agnes will love it, and I want them to meet Will,' her husband urged. Will had emerged as baby James's nickname.

Meanwhile, Agnes tugged at her father's sleeve, saying, 'Park, park.' Despite her limited vocabulary, Agnes had no difficulty making her wishes understood.

Philip lived on the edge of the city, where the air would be cleaner. 'All right, we'll come. Agnes will enjoy being outside.'

The house was on the edge of Hampstead village. When they emerged into the beautiful garden, she was glad that they'd come. Phillip seated her on a wicker chair under the shade of a tree. Baby Will was sleeping in her arms and this arrangement excused her from standing with the others. James loved a crowd. Whilst she was happier in the one-on-one intimacy of painting a portrait.

A little girl, a few years older than Agnes, was sitting on the grass nearby. She'd been supplied with a large basin filled with water and an assortment of cups and spoons. Agnes walked over and sat beside the girl, who was creating an imaginary tea party for her wooden doll. Christina smiled. Every day Agnes showed more and more that she had inherited James's confident nature. The other child played on, not acknowledging Agnes.

'Now then, Christine, you must share your cups with this little girl,' a man said.

Christina glanced up in surprise, hearing what was surely an Edinburgh accent.

'Hello, Christine,' Christina said. 'This is Agnes. Can you she play with you?

The little girl, who had given no sign of hearing her father, turned to look at Christina and then Agnes. She gave Agnes two cups and showed her how to pour from one to the other.

'Perfect,' the man said. 'Now she has a playmate to keep her entertained.' He held out his hand. 'David Roberts, pleased to meet you.'

David Roberts had dark hair and brown eyes. Christina warmed to his soft Scottish accent. She could tell that like her, Roberts came from a non-aristocratic background.

'Christina Robertson,' she replied and shook his hand. 'It seems I almost share a name with little Christine.'

'My mother is called Christina. Both versions are bonny,' he replied. He gestured to the rush-seated chair beside her. 'Would you mind if I joined you? I promised my wife I'd watch Christine this afternoon. Margaret loves this kind of occasion.'

He gestured over to where a pretty woman with blonde ringlets was standing in the middle of a group of men, including James. She was telling some animated story that caused her to wave her hands about, apparently oblivious to the wine spilling from her glass.

Mr Roberts give a small sigh. 'Margaret was an actress, and she finds the life of a wife and mother rather constricting,' he said.

'It can be very exhausting,' Christina agreed.

Laughter from the two little girls drew their attention.

'Oh dear, they're soaked,' he said.

'They're happy and it's so warm they'll soon dry,' she reassured him. 'What brings you down to London, Mr Roberts?'

'I'm a painter,' he replied. 'I paint theatre scenes at Drury Lane, although I hope one day to have success as an artist. The British Institution took a painting of Dryburgh Abbey last year.'

'Congratulations, I'll look out for your work. Is that your usual type of subject?' Christina asked.

'It is so far. I enjoy architectural challenges, Scottish churches and the like. However, I travelled to France last year, and I found the light there inspirational.'

'How exciting. I've never been to France, but I should like to go,' Christina replied.

'Is your husband a painter? I would certainly say it's a destination for artists.'

'Yes, James paints, that's him, the dark-haired man talking to your wife. The Academy took four of his miniatures this year.'

David Roberts turned to look directly at her. 'Are you Mrs James Robertson?'

'I am,' she replied.

He looked surprised and full of remorse. 'My dear lady, please accept my sincere apologies. It's the sort of thing my wife complains of all the time. I'm in the presence of a renowned artist and all I've done is talk about my own small efforts. Your miniature of the Duke is first class.'

'Thank you. He represented quite a challenge, but his wife was pleased. That was always my chief aim.'

He shook his head in disbelief. 'I'm most impressed, to execute such fine work when you obviously have your hands full. However do you manage it?' He gestured to Agnes and the baby in her arms.

Christina didn't burden him with the story of losing Tiana, although the loss was always at the front of her mind. It would only spoil the atmosphere of this pleasant afternoon.

'Will was born after the exhibition,' she replied, 'and James is very supportive.'

There was a peal of loud laughter from Roberts' wife. She stepped back and almost lost her footing on the soft grass. James had to put out his hand to steady her.

'Excuse me, Mrs Robertson. I've so enjoyed meeting you, but I must remind Margaret that wee Christine has been in the sun long enough.'

'Let me introduce you to James before you go.'

David Roberts picked up his daughter. James arrived beside them, and Agnes immediately raised her arms.

'Hello, mouse, you're very wet. Have you been having fun? Come over and join us, Christina. I'd like to introduce little Will to my friends, and you too, mouse.' He tickled Agnes, making her giggle.

'James, this is David Roberts, a fellow artist from Scotland,' she said.

James shifted Agnes from one arm to the other to hold out his hand. 'Pleased to meet you, David. I believe I've just met your wife.'

'Delighted to make your acquaintance, sir. Two Academy

exhibitors in one family, what talent,' David Roberts said. 'I do hope we'll meet again.'

Later that night, they lay on top of their bed. The bed curtains were open to try to catch any breeze from the window.

'That wasn't so bad, was it? Are you glad you came?' James asked.

'Yes. We were lucky to find a playmate for Agnes and I did like Mr Roberts.'

'I've heard said he has talent,' James added. 'His wife is certainly very amusing. Do you know she used to be an actress?'

'Her husband mentioned it.'

James pulled her towards him and kissed her neck. 'It's been too long a time,' he whispered, undoing her nightgown buttons.

She turned and kissed him, then sat up to pull her shift over her head.

'But James, please. We're so lucky to have Will, but I'm not ready for another baby yet.'

'Don't worry, I'll be careful,' he said, pulling off his nightshirt and moving to straddle her.

Chapter Nine

October 2017, Edinburgh

I'd fallen asleep exhausted and frustrated, then overslept in the morning.

When I went into the kitchen, Mum had her coat on ready to leave. 'I made you toast. I wouldn't rely on Jimmy's catering being up to much. Are you all right? You look tired.'

I put the piece of toast in my mouth and pulled on my jacket. 'Didn't sleep much. I got thinking about Granny, and couldn't resist opening the tin. I found lots of certificates to help me create this tree, but not her birth certificate.'

'Surely you'll find it online?'

'I expect so, but I'd left my laptop downstairs. I didn't want that creaky stair to wake you.'

There was something else behind my hesitation. Why had Granny never talked about her father? Had he done something terrible? Or very likely I might find he was married already. There could be a whole other family of relatives we know nothing about. If Mum had never tried to find out before, was it my secret to uncover?

. . .

We drove in silence until we crossed over the elegant new Queensferry Crossing.

'If I'm right,' I said. 'Christina was born in Edinburgh, and her mother's family were in Kinghorn. The two communities would have had close links because the Fife ferry came from Kinghorn.'

'So you're not sure about her birth?'

'I think that her mother was a Margrate Sanders, or Saunders, her father used both versions. Her family came from Kinghorn and a George Saunders was the witness at Christina's baptism in Edinburgh. It's not the exact birthdate quoted in other places, but the combination seems too close to be coincidence.'

'Margrate?' Mum asked.

'Or maybe Margaret, or Margret? Perhaps it depended on the man writing the register. I've found lots of spelling inconsistencies in my research.'

'Jimmy's sister was called Margaret,' Mum said.

'So were two of George Saunders' elder sisters,' I replied. 'It's so sad that they reused a name if a child died.'

We reached Jimmy's farm at the top of a hill above the town of Kirkcaldy. Mum drove up a rutted lane, then over a cattle grid, before turning into a muddy farmyard. The farmhouse had an incredible view across the Forth to Edinburgh beyond.

'Is this where Granny was brought up?' I asked.

'From the age of eight when Jimmy was born.'

Jimmy appeared in the farmhouse doorway. 'Just put the car directly in there,' he shouted, pointing to the open doors of a large shed. 'Sorry aboot the state ae the yard.'

We parked up and picked our way around the puddles and into Jimmy's kitchen.

'Go ben the living room, I'll bring in some tea,' he said.

'Can I give you a hand?' Mum asked.

'No, I'll manage. You probably don't want to be looking too closely at my kitchen arrangements. I've kinda let things slide since Carol died.'

He came through with a teapot in a stripy knitted cosy, a pint of milk and three mugs hanging from his large fingers.

'My washing-up skills aren't up tae much, but you'll be glad tae know the dishwasher's working fine,' he said, with a sheepish smile.

'It must be hard managing on your own, Jimmy,' Mum said.

'It's fine. I'm no farming anymore. The byre and the fields are leased tae the farmer next door. I should really move out ae the farmhouse, but I've been here my whole life. I cannae imagine where I'd go.'

'I can picture you and Granny running around here as children.'

'I told Anna about you being brought up together,' Mum said.

Jimmy sighed, gazing at his hands clasped on his knees. 'Dorothy, your granny Edith's mum, was good tae me and I loved her. But my sister Bessie was twelve when our ain mother passed, and she took against Dorothy. She did her best tae make Dorothy's life a misery, and wee Edith's life too. She used tae pinch Edith's airms black and blue. I learned tae pretend tae side wi Bessie or get the same treatment.'

The thought of my granny being bullied brought tears to my eyes. She used to tell me not to pay attention to play-ground teasing; I'd no idea she'd endured much worse.

'That must've been really hard for you as a wee boy, Jimmy,' Mum said quietly.

He shrugged. 'Dorothy did her best tae protect me and Edith, and I never heard her complain. Bessie married and left home when she was sixteen. I never hardly saw her aifter that, but things at home settled down.'

After tea and Tunnock's wafers, Mum and I climbed up into Jimmy's Land Rover and he drove us to Kinghorn. On the way, I told him all about Christina Robertson's life and how I was trying to trace our family link back to her. 'I now believe Christina was born in Edinburgh's Canongate. The old ferry route meant there were strong links with Kinghorn.'

'If it's the ferry you're interested in, you might want tae walk over tae Pettycur, that's where the auld ferry used tae leave fae,' Jimmy replied.

We got out and said our goodbyes.

'See you at the funeral on Friday, Emma,' he said.

'Thanks again, Jimmy. I hope you'll stay on after. I've taken the restaurant behind the Raeburn Hotel, in Stockbridge. Just high tea. Sausage rolls and the like.'

'Widnae be a Scottish funeral wi nae sausage rolls,' he replied.

Mum and I walked down to the village harbour.

'So if you think Christina Robertson was born in Edinburgh, are you sure she actually lived here?' Mum asked.

'She was always described as coming from Kinghorn. Maybe her family moved back?'

The old churchyard was right beside the harbour. The ancient gravestones were hard to read, and we found no Saunders or Robertsons.

The tide was a long way out, and the few boats were high and dry. 'You can see why this was no use for a ferry.'

'We could over walk to Pettycur Bay if you like,' Mum replied. 'It's very pretty and we can catch the later train.'

'Prettier than this?' I asked, spreading my arms to take in the sandy beach and the small quayside cottages. 'Although the railway bridge does spoil the village view.'

'I suppose so, but the railway makes Edinburgh accessible for work,' Mum replied.

We walked to the next bay, along the base of the cliff. 'Christina must have played here as a child.'

'I certainly did,' Mum replied. 'We'd sometimes come with our buckets and spades on the train. It was less crowded than Portobello and the water is shallow.'

Once we rounded the point, it was obvious why people would visit. Pettycur Bay was a massive expanse of rippling sand, stretching out for hundreds of yards to the sparkling water of the Forth estuary. Edinburgh's skyline and Arthur's Seat were visible in the distance.

'This would be a great place to bring children.' A vision of a smiling toddler came into my head and I swallowed, gazing at my feet.

Mum reached out and squeezed my hand. 'Let's head back. We could look in the bigger graveyard up on the hill.'

The second graveyard had a few nineteenth century graves, but again no Saunders or Robertsons.

'Are you sure the family lived here?' Mum asked.

'Yes. The birth records for George Saunders' family are all in Kinghorn. The death records are a bit patchy, but I suppose some will have died elsewhere.'

We set off towards the railway station.

'Did you know about Granny's childhood?' I asked Mum. 'Imagine being an only child, then dropped into a family who hated her.'

'She never talked about it, but I expect being a child without a father would have been difficult too,' Mum answered.

'I'm so glad things turned out better in the end.'

'She did talk about her and Jimmy having a happy life on the farm. I suppose that was after Bessie left. Maybe she was too young to remember the earlier years?'

I thought of Granny's eyes when she comforted me about being teased. 'I think she remembered.'

The next day I worked on the auction brochure, and sent my suggested pages to Lisa for comment. Something in Jimmy's responses made me hesitate about searching for Granny's birth certificate. I needed to talk to Mum about it again first. She'd gone out to visit the lawyer about Granny's will. She was annoyed that she couldn't go to the airport to meet Euan off his plane, but he'd just laughed at her when we Skyped him together the day before.

'Don't be daft, Mum. You just told me you've left your car at Jimmy's. I'll jump in a taxi or I might even try out this infamous tram. I'll see you at Granny's house tomorrow afternoon, then I want to take you both out to dinner.'

I opened the front door when I heard the taxi arrive. Mandy was dead-heading roses in her garden and I waved to her. Euan unfolded his six-foot-three frame from the taxi. Even after twenty-four hours of travelling, my younger brother managed to look handsome. I noticed Mandy's interest, although she was of course wasting her time. He was blissfully happy with Alan and I had never known him have any interest in girls. When he came out at university, nobody was in the least surprised.

He bounded up the stairs to hug me. 'How's my favourite sister doing?'

'Your only sister is just fine.'

He held my shoulders at arm's length to look me over. Was that a slight hesitation as his eyes slid over my flat stomach? It's a look I've come to expect from friends, so I might have imagined it.

'What about Mum? Is she coping? I think I'll revert to being a sobbing cry-baby when we lose her.'

'Thanks, Euan, that's a cheery thought. But to answer your question, she's doing okay. A bit tired. We've been really busy sorting through Granny's stuff.'

Once inside Euan sprawled across the two-seater couch. The house walls seemed to come closer together in response to his presence.

'This is like a doll's house. I can't believe the three of us used to live here with her for weeks.'

'That's exactly what I thought, but I've got used to it now. You'll be glad to know you've got your usual spot on the floor.'

'The floor?'

His expression was laughable. 'I'm just joking. I'm in with Mum and you've got the spare bedroom for your stay. Mum and I slept on the floor on our first night. Now with all the furniture and boxes, it's difficult to find any floor.'

Euan used his toes to push off his shoes, which were smart and shiny. I'd have travelled in trainers. Euan was always the one with style.

On the morning of the funeral we sat silently in the living room waiting for the car to arrive. Mum was pulling the skin off the side of her finger nail. I put my hand over hers. 'Stop fretting. It will be fine.'

'What if no one comes?' she said. 'I've lost track of how many of her friends are still alive. We might be one row at the crematorium and there's six tons of food at the Raeburn Hotel.'

Euan put his arm around her. 'Don't worry, Mum, people will come. And anyway, Anna says there's to be sausage rolls. Jimmy and I will polish off enough for ten men.'

She smiled, but looked unconvinced.

'Don't you have any funny stories or good news, Euan? You've hardly said anything about what you've been up to,' I said.

'Ah,' he replied. 'I do have something to tell you, but it can wait until after the funeral.'

'That's not fair,' I whined. 'Good news or bad news?'

'Good news, but don't even try to guess, you'll never get it,' he replied.

He and Mum exchanged an excited look. Some secret they were keeping from me? Was he moving back to the UK? He had always said he'd like to at some stage.

The black car arrived. When we got in, the sight of the hearse parked in front set me off crying. Mum took my hand, I saw her cheeks were wet, too. Euan's jaw was clenched tight and he looked resolutely ahead. I sat next to him in the crematorium, and I could see his struggle in the strained muscles in his neck.

'Let it go,' I whispered. 'It's okay to cry.'

He took a white hankie from his pocket and gave me a distraught glance. 'She was such a lovely lady, it wasn't fair what she had to endure at the end.'

I'd been dreading the crematorium. I hated the one at Dad's funeral. Too modern, too brash, too brightly lit. This was better. A stained glass window behind an altar with candles. Wooden chairs. Gentle light. I'm not religious, but the church-like atmosphere was an easier place to bear the sorrow. It was near Granny's house. On her patch. She'd probably been here many times to say goodbye to friends.

Despite our fears, dozens of people turned up to pay their respects. The Raeburn Hotel was mobbed and Jimmy was well-attended by a group of elderly ladies. Perhaps they thought him a catch? He looked genuinely alarmed, so I went over to rescue him. 'I need you for a few minutes, Jimmy,' I said, and led him over to a quiet corner. 'Can I get you something else from the buffet?'

'Maybe just another cup ae tea?'

When I brought him back his tea, he nodded at me. 'Did you find the birth certificate?'

'No. And actually, I want your advice. Is it something better left alone?'

Jimmy shook his head. 'It was a painful business at the time. Edith was my half-sister. Faither had an affair wi Dorothy and my mother knew about it. I guess she forgave him or I'd no be here.'

'Jimmy! Is that why Bessie hated Dorothy?'

'Aye. She'd grown up hearing my mother call Dorothy a whooring bitch.' He gave me an apologetic look. 'Later, when I met and married my Carol, I thought back tae how Dorothy and my faither looked at each other. It made me wonder if they were aywis in love?'

When we finally got home, we were all exhausted.

'Are you sure all those people actually knew her?' Euan asked. 'Half of Edinburgh was there.'

'She would have been pleased,' Mum replied.

Euan opened a bottle of red wine and I told them what Jimmy had told me. I watched Mum's face for her reaction, but she didn't look shocked.

'I already suspected that.'

'What was his name?' I asked.

'Archibald Kirk. Archie,' she replied. 'I don't remember him. He died just after I was born. When I asked Mum about him, she described him as being a good father to her. There seemed no point in raking up painful memories by pushing her.'

'I can't believe you never told us,' Euan said.

'It was her story to tell. I think she preferred not to think about it,' Mum replied.

'Maybe we've had enough drama today. My news will keep,' Euan said.

'No way,' I replied. 'You've stalled us long enough.'

Euan topped up our glasses and lifted his. 'On this saddest of days, let's raise a toast across the generations. To my lovely granny, and to Archie, her father. Also to us, and those who will follow. My fingers and toes are in agony from being crossed so long, but Carla sailed through the week twenty scan last month and everything is looking fine. Edie Grieve is due to make her appearance at the end of January. You're to be promoted to Granny, Mum.'

'What?' I said stupidly, as Mum jumped up to hug Euan. 'Who's Carla? What about Alan?'

Euan frowned at me. 'Don't tell me you think I've gone straight,' he said with a mirthless laugh. 'Carla's Alan's sister. You met her at the wedding.'

'So a surrogate?'

Mum's frown confirmed that I wasn't reacting as I should. My tongue was stuck to the roof of my suddenly dry mouth. I was consumed by the urge to cry huge, hot and selfish tears.

'It wasn't very high tech,' Euan said. 'Being a vet gives you access to all sorts of fancy syringes, but yes a surrogacy. Carla volunteered, and Alan put together all the proper legal papers. Turns out a vet and a lawyer is a dream team for this kind of thing.' His smile was a bit lop-sided, his eyes sad. 'I thought you'd be thrilled for me, Anna. I'm gonna be a dad.'

'Oh god, congratulations, Euan,' I hurtled towards him, burying my head in his shoulder, desperately fighting the urge to cry. 'I'm so happy for you, it's the best news.' I took a deep breath. 'Right then. Half a bottle of red wine will not do for this occasion. I'm going to the Co-op to see if they've got champagne.'

I returned Mum's strained smile and nodded reassurance to her. Once outside, I allowed myself the five minutes' walk to the shop to bawl my eyes out and curse. Luckily, it was a quiet road. The walk back would be enough time to sort myself out and give my lovely brother the reaction he deserved.

Chapter Ten

January 1826, London

Christina tried to ignore the signs, but by January, it was clear there would be another baby this year. The prospect didn't fill her with joy, and acknowledging that made her feel guilty. She also feared for Will's safety. Somehow in her head, she'd connected the loss of Tiana to her pregnancy with Will. As if some fierce deity only gave protection to two of her children.

She'd worked extremely hard and had eight miniatures to submit to the Academy, the maximum allowed by any one artist. The portraits included the Marchioness of Wellesley. Her list of high society sitters had grown, and price increases seemed to put nobody off.

Christina hoped the baby would arrive in early June so they could escape London in the summer. The plan was to visit James's family in Alnwick.

One morning after they had made love, she turned and leaned on her elbow to face her husband. 'We need to have a different arrangement after this baby is born.'

He blinked, but said nothing.

'I know that lots of women have a baby every year, but I

can't carry on that way. Apart from anything else, our success as a family is limited by the working time I lose.'

James's brow furrowed. 'I did try. If there was a slipup, then it was only once or twice.'

Like a child, he only thought to avoid the blame. She sighed. 'However it happened, this baby is coming. I adore Agnes and Will, but I never stop worrying about them. A new baby will bring extra love and risk, too. It's exhausting.'

James flung himself onto his back.

'We have to think about our future, James.'

He turned to face her. 'I know, and I want to contribute more. I've been thinking that if we had a home we could entertain in, I'm sure I could find you more clients.'

'I've been thinking about our need for a bigger house too. We could have a sitting room suitable for entertaining, perhaps a small studio.' She took a deep breath. 'And more bedrooms.'

'Of course. Agnes needs her own room now. Will can have her bed when the baby has his cradle,' he said.

She rolled onto her back and spoke towards the ceiling. 'We need separate bedrooms, James.'

James laughed. He took his weight on his hand, his smiling face hovering above hers. He'd barely changed from the handsome boy she'd first loved ten years before, whilst she felt aged and weary.

'I know you, Christina. You enjoy our coupling as much as I do. We cannot be like strangers to each other.'

Christina didn't respond to his teasing smile. 'We can't keep having a baby every year.' She moved away from him and sat up. 'Maybe we should spend some time apart? I thought I might go onto Edinburgh from Alnwick.'

James frowned.

She resented that she was having to drive this. That he didn't realise the necessity. 'I could use the time to get more

Scottish clients. A couple of ladies have expressed an interest.'

James pulled a face. 'I hate the idea of being parted. I'd worry about you travelling alone and what about the children? Would you take them to Scotland?'

Christina clenched her fists. Sometimes she felt like she was dealing with another child. He wanted everything; he lived in the moment, but one of them had to look to the future. 'I don't know. Let's pray that we're blessed with another healthy child. But if we don't spend the autumn apart, there's sure to be another baby this time next year.'

They didn't revisit the conversation, and Christina put Scotland out of her mind. Even if James had supported the idea, it wasn't practical. She'd have no free time, accompanied by three small children. They arranged to let their house go when the lease came up in July. They could rent cheaply in Alnwick over the summer and save for a bigger house in London.

Christina and James had supper with David and Margaret Roberts in April. Their first meeting since the garden party. That evening they were celebrating David's painting of Rouen Cathedral being accepted by the Academy. They'd also taken all eight of Christina's miniatures. Roberts shared that he would soon move to Covent Garden Theatre.

'Congratulations, such a prestigious appointment,' Christina said.

'Thank you, Mrs Robertson. The better salary will allow me to provide for the family and save a little, but I fear I'll have less painting time.'

'Balancing creativity and income is a constant battle,' she agreed. 'Please call us Christina and James,' she added.

'If you will return the courtesy,' he replied.

'Will you travel to France again this year, David?' Christina asked.

'Sadly no, there's too much to do here. I don't think I'll get up to Scotland this year either. Do you ever go back?'

'Not since I left, no,' Christina replied. 'My mother died young. Her older sister brought me up, but she's dead now too.'

'I'm sorry,' David Roberts replied.

Christina shrugged. 'I have Uncle George here. To be honest, I don't feel any interest in going back to Kinghorn. I'm not fond of village life.'

David Roberts smiled. 'I was brought up in the village of Stockbridge, so I do understand. Still, I love Edinburgh and you should think about visiting. I could introduce you to my artistic contacts. There is a market for a portraitist of your calibre.'

'Thank you. It is something I've been considering.'

James met her eyes, then turned back to Margaret who was lively and beautiful, but now Christina observed she was talking loudly and leaning in too close. Soon, James said they should be going.

They walked back through the streets to Marylebone, arm-in-arm.

'David Roberts is a good sort, but I'm beginning to find his wife rather overbearing.'

'I wonder if she's nervous. Some people drink too much when they're anxious,' Christina said.

'She's an actress, Christina. I doubt she suffers from nerves.'

The 1826 Royal Academy Exhibition went well and, as with the year before, Christina attended very pregnant. James had made no mention of submitting again, and she was glad.

Another baby boy was born at the end of June and they christened him John. A month later, the family travelled to Alnwick, where James's brother Tom had found a very reasonable house that could accommodate them all, as well as Eliza. Christina planned to nurse John herself in Northumberland. She'd engage a wet nurse when they got back to London after the summer. Uncle George would hopefully have found a larger property for them by then.

Everyone in Alnwick was in high spirits. Adam had recently married and Tom was courting, too. Christina thought both girls charming, and they made a tremendous fuss of Agnes, Will and John. It was lovely seeing both her brothers-in-law in happy relationships, and their business was thriving. Christina was resigned to not working for the entire month. The house they'd rented near the cousins in the Narrowgate hadn't enough light and John seemed to never be done feeding.

Adam organised a trip to the beach in the first week. Agnes and Will had never seen the sea, which seemed very strange when she and James had both had seaside childhoods. Tom organised to borrow two carts from a farmer friend to transport the extended family. Adam's wife Jane brought along her mother Anne and older sister Sarah. Although only twenty-five, Sarah was a widow. Her son Andrew was slightly younger than Will, but her husband Danny had been killed in a farm accident just before the boy was born. Her delight at being included in the seaside trip made Christina's sympathy for the girl even more acute. Their cart crested the dune track and revealed the view of endless empty sky and miles of sandy beach. James had to be quick to grab Agnes when she leapt up in excitement. They'd not finished unloading the carts before Agnes had her shoes and stockings off and was dragging her father to the water's edge. Both Will and Andrew had just started learning to walk. She and Sarah held their hands and stood them where the incoming tide washed over their toes. At first, both boys cried in fright at the cold shock, but were soon splashing with their fat little feet and laughing. The beautiful stretch of sand was almost deserted and the cool sea breeze made the sunny day comfortable. Gulls screeched and wheeled overhead. Such a contrast to the fetid air of London in August.

James looked so relaxed, walking in happy companionship with his brothers. Tom had hoisted Agnes onto his shoulders and her hair streamed loose behind her. Later, James set up a blanket hidden in the dunes for Christina and Sarah to breastfeed the babies.

Sarah pulled an apologetic face. 'You'll think me indulgent, but I may never have another baby. I don't want Andrew to be grown up just yet.'

'Not at all. I'm sure Will would like it too, but I've always had a new baby to take my one-year-old's place.'

Sarah nodded. 'I've had that, too. I had a little girl called Janie, a year older than Andrew. She died soon after I got pregnant with him.'

Christina put her free hand on the girl's shoulder. 'You've had a terrible year. I'm so sorry. I also lost a daughter between Agnes and Will.'

They exchanged a look of understanding. Their experience was commonplace, but their shared grief was a bond. The plaintive cries of distant curlews sent a shiver down her spine. Would there ever be another happy day that wasn't shadowed by sadness?

Two days later, both Agnes and Will developed runny noses. Christina told herself not to be so over anxious. The summer cold barely bothered Agnes, but hour after long hour, Will got worse. He cried and refused to eat or drink. Christina looked in his mouth and found the back of his throat was red. That night, he started to cough and Christina didn't sleep. She flitted between the dark rooms, alternating between feeding John and trying to soothe Will. In the darkest hour of night, she sat beside Will, holding his hand and listening to his ragged breathing. It was getting worse.

Please, please not again.

Eliza had taken Agnes in with her so they could keep the three children apart. When she judged Will was quiet, she went to lift John from his cradle in their bedroom, desperate to get John to feed quickly so she could rush back to Will. It felt so much like the previous year. A streak of dawn light fell on James's face, and she saw he was lying awake, terrified, too. Christina went down to the kitchen to make Will a tincture with lemon and honey. She tried to feed it to him with a spoon. He twisted his head away and wouldn't swallow. When Eliza came in, Christina saw the terror in her eyes that rose in her own chest. Will's neck was swollen. It took every effort not to sob.

In the course of the day, Will's cough changed to a deep and desperate noise. Croup. His back arched as he tried to get a breath. Christina placed her hand gently on his ribs and made soothing noises to try to calm him. Beneath her palm, she could feel his little heart fluttering like a netted bird.

They sent for a doctor, but he had no useful advice. The next day, Christina opened his mouth again. The pale grey mass at the back of Will's throat was stark above his red tongue. His mouth looked so vulnerable with just four baby teeth. She'd heard this disease called 'the strangling angel of children'. Surely not a phrase coined by a mother. There was nothing angelic about this.

Will didn't go quickly like Tiana. He fought for three

more days. Christina refused all help or sustenance except water. She held her son in her arms and sung him lullabies. He was dying, but she needed him to feel he was never alone.

When he became still on the fourth day, she kept singing, kept rocking him in her arms. Hours later, they had to prise him away from her. Christina curled up on his small bed and faced the wall. She felt so light now, barely attached to this world herself. James came in. She heard the tears in his voice, but his words couldn't reach her. Later, Sarah came and knelt at her feet.

'Christina, Johnny is crying, he's hungry. They're asking if I'll feed him. Please, is it all right if I feed him?'

Christina nodded. When Sarah had gone, she opened her eyes and stared at the wall. If she left them now, they would be all right. She needn't bear this pain anymore. Needn't face this agony again.

But they wouldn't leave her in peace. James picked her up and took her to their own bed. Eliza tried to feed her broth.

They brought in Agnes to kiss her cheek. 'Love you, Mama,' she said.

James lay beside her with his hand on her back at night. In the day, Sarah sat in the armchair and crooned to baby John while she fed him. The cool cabbage leaves Sarah laid on her breasts eased their ache, the tincture Sarah persuaded her to drink rid her of fevered nightmares. As much as she wanted to die, her body persisted.

'Mistress, I made you eggs. Please eat.' Eliza's pleading tone and anxious expression forced her to swallow a couple of mouthfuls.

Sarah was the only one whose presence was tolerable. She chatted about what Agnes and Andrew were getting up to. Sarah had lost both her daughter and her husband, yet somehow found a way to endure living without them.

Days stretched to weeks. Instead of dying, Christina sank

into a silent lethargy. Time drifted. She'd settled in a place between life and death.

One morning, Eliza stripped and washed her, then helped her into a clean nightgown. James wrapped a shawl around her shoulders and carried her out into the garden.

'You're too thin, too pale. You need some sunshine,' he whispered in her ear.

He sat her in a garden chair. Eliza put a cup of warm, fragrant chocolate in her hands. Adam lowered Agnes into a swing hanging from the bough of an apple tree. The seat was fashioned of wood, like a little square basket with holes for Agnes's legs. Adam pushed her, and she giggled. Her daughter's laughter, the squeak of the swing, a blackbird's song. These were the first sounds that pierced the bubble of her grief.

James held her hand. 'Today you should eat. You must be fit to travel soon.'

Christina shook her head. 'I'm not going anywhere.'

'I think you should. It's all arranged. I had a letter from George today. He's already left London. His boat will reach Leith by the end of this week. He's rented some rooms for you both in the centre of Edinburgh. A flat with a painting studio. George took your painting materials with him and there's an appointment made with a Mrs Anstruther-Thomson. I know you'll not leave George with the task of telling her you've changed your mind.'

Christina stared at her husband. He was talking about a life she'd left behind.

Tom walked into the garden carrying a wooden box. The polished mahogany shone in the sunlight, the swirling inlaid mother-of-pearl and brass gleamed.

'It's a writing slope,' Tom explained, laying it on the table in front of her. 'I made one for the Duchess of Northumberland, and this one especially for you.' Tom opened the lid to turn the box into a sloped writing desk lined with cherry red leather.

'I'll write to you every week and I hope you'll reply,' James said quietly. 'You could use it for working on miniature sketches, too. If you want to take Agnes and John, Eliza and Sarah will come with you. If you prefer to leave them here, they will be fine.'

James pushed the writing box until it was within touching distance. Without meaning to, she reached out and stroked the pretty cut glass ink pot. She trailed her fingers over the pens and paintbrushes. James placed a small artist's palette on the slope beside her hand.

'It's a beautiful thing, Tom. Thank you,' she said.

James took her hand in both of his. 'I'm sorry,' he whispered. 'Please, Christina, don't give up on us.'

Chapter Eleven

November 2017, Edinburgh

M um declared herself worn out and went to bed. I moved to sit next to Euan on the couch, and we spent the next two hours talking. He showed me the blurry scan image of his baby. His joy was infectious, and the tension between us dissipated. I'd never seen him so happy.

'Do you think Mum is okay about me naming her after Granny?' he asked.

'Of course,' I replied. 'Edith would be an old-fashioned name for a baby, but Edie is perfect. You could give her the Robertson middle name, keep the family tradition going.'

'Isn't it a female line thing? Your prerogative then. Just like Mum, Granny and Dorothy, and who knows who before.'

'I'm not making much of a job of extending the female line so far.' I grimaced.

'It will happen, Anna. Anyway, we've agreed she'll have Lyle as a middle name, after her other father and her mother. I'd have been happy for Grieve Lyle, but Alan and Carla both think Edie Lyle Grieve sounds better.'

'So she'll have three Scottish names. It's such a coincidence that Carla and Alan have a Scottish sounding surname. Do they maybe have Scottish ancestors?'

Euan looked at me as if I was an imbecile. 'They're Afro-Caribbean heritage, Anna. Honestly, for a journalist, your knowledge of history is appalling.'

The penny dropped. 'God, Euan, are we talking about descent from a slave owner?'

He shrugged. 'It's possible. There was a lot of rape going on but slaves were given their plantation owners' name anyway.'

I sat silently for a minute, letting the implications sink in. 'I've started work on our maternal family tree. What if I find a slave owner in our past?'

'It's not impossible. Lots of plantations were owned by Scots. If you think about it, almost every Scottish town has a Jamaica Street. Anyway, let's hope not. Tell me all about what you've been up to. St Petersburg must have been fascinating.'

I brought him up to date, and banged on too long about my Christina Robertson obsession. I could sense his relief when I started to tell him about Lisa's painting auction.

'Do you want to see the artwork?'

I reached for my laptop and opened the folder. 'Help me choose one to bid on for Nick's Christmas present.'

Euan flicked through the photos. 'If it were my choice, I'd go for this one.'

He passed the laptop back, and I smiled. 'Great minds think alike, Sherlock. That's my favourite too. It's by Lisa's husband. I love the atmospheric blue. Almost like the soul of a bird.'

We drained our glasses, and I yawned. 'I realise you're on US time, but I need to get to bed. I'll see you in the morning.'

'Anna, are you alright about this baby? I was really nervous to tell you. Mum told me you've been trying.'

'Of course. I'm really sorry I messed up my reaction. My

emotions are all over the place right now. Really, I'm so happy for you.'

'I asked Mum not to tell you until we were sure. Didn't want to jinx it. Alan and I had been discussing adoption. We couldn't believe our luck when Carla suggested surrogacy. To have a child with both our genes seemed too much to hope for.'

'It's brilliant news, and I can't wait to be an auntie.'

He nodded, hesitating before speaking. 'What about your plans? Will you consider other options if you don't conceive?'

'I've started to think about it.' I shrugged.

'Are Alan's parents pleased about the baby?'

'Over the moon, especially because she's a girl. Martha is haunting all the baby stores already. I do feel a bit sorry about Mum, though.'

'Mum? Why? You can see how happy she is.'

'Because it means I won't ever move back to the UK. It's something Alan and I had discussed, but I couldn't prevent Edie having Carla, Martha, and Paul in her life. That wouldn't be fair.'

'Of course. Anyway, I'm sure Mum will be out to visit lots. Did she tell you she's thinking about retiring?'

Euan nodded. 'It's great timing. I'm hoping she might come out for the birth. You too, if you want to come.'

'Maybe not for the birth, but I'll be out next year some-time. You try keeping me away.' I kissed him. 'Night, Daddy-to-be.'

'Night, Auntie Anna.'

I crept in beside Mum and lay thinking about all the complicated conceptions in my family. Surely one more was not too much to hope for?

. . .

I slept through Mum getting up the next morning but was woken by a call from Nick.

'Were you still asleep?'

'It is only eight in the morning here, and yesterday was exhausting.'

'How did the funeral go? You didn't call.'

'It went well. I decided you'd have more time to talk today.'

'That's why I'm calling early. I'm going out of town. The signal might not be good.'

'Where are you going?'

'Oksana's family dacha, her parents live there.'

Bloody Oksana, of course.

'Is it just you going?' Jealousy twisted like a clenched fist in my guts.

'She invited all the foreign singletons. Pierre and Gerard are going too.'

'You're not a singleton, Nick.'

'Well no, the French guys are married too, but their wives stayed in France. They've been out to the dacha before. They insisted I should come this time since you're away. Apparently, it involves lots of vodka.'

'Definitely not my kind of thing then.'

'Exactly. That's why I've always refused before. The car will be here soon. I'll call you tomorrow.'

'Have a nice time,' I said, flicking a v sign at the phone.

I looked up to see Mum standing in the doorway. She gave me a quizzical look.

'Nick,' I said.

She raised her eyebrows further. 'Is he well?'

'He's fine.'

'I came to say I made French toast for breakfast.'

'Brilliant, you're spoiling us like kids.'

'You are my kids,' she replied.

. . .

After breakfast, we took a nostalgic walk to the Botanic Gardens, a childhood haunt.

'Granny and I came here together when I was last in Edinburgh,' Mum said. 'She often asked me to take her home. This was the nearest I could manage.'

I squeezed Mum's hand. We paused at the crest of the hill. Edinburgh's Georgian New Town lay in the foreground, and there was a view of the castle through the bare branches. The ground was strewn with leaves, their golds and reds fading as the nutrients returned to the earth.

'Her favourite bench is free,' Mum said. 'Let's stop for a bit.'

The sky was icy blue. The castle barracks' stern outline spoke of its military back story.

'Who'd like an ice cream?' Euan asked.

'Does the café sell ice cream in winter?' I asked.

'They do, Luca's best. Granny never forgot to ask for ice cream.'

When Euan left, I slid along the bench and put my arm through Mum's. 'I'm sorry I screwed up yesterday. Euan and I are fine now.'

'I should have insisted on warning you. I didn't think it would happen so quickly.'

'He made me question why I'm just waiting and hoping, instead of doing something more active.'

'Maybe it's time to consider that?' Mum answered.

'I was stupid to go abroad without getting everything checked out by the NHS first.'

'Would you go private?'

'I'd need to talk to Nick. I expect it would cost a fortune.'

'You could maybe have an initial consultation here. There must be some simple tests they could do first.'

'That's a thought, but I doubt there's time.'

'No harm in ringing them to ask, Anna.'

'You're right.' I kissed her cheek.

Euan came back with three tubs of vanilla ice cream. Despite the chill in the air, it tasted like heaven. Licking the last of the ice cream off the tiny wooden spoon, I imagined bringing a toddler. A flicker of hope. If my brother could become a father against staggering odds, then I had to try harder.

In the evening, we made Mum put her feet up, whilst Euan and I made spaghetti carbonara. When we took the bowls through, there was a large wooden box I'd never seen before on the coffee table.

'What's that?' I asked.

'A surprise and you're not allowed to touch it. I'll tell you after supper,' Mum replied.

After we'd cleared up, Mum pulled a leather box out of her cardigan pocket and placed it on the coffee table. 'So, talking to the solicitor yesterday, she says that once we've sorted all the funeral costs, Granny's will should get through probate without any problems. We three and Jimmy are her only living relatives and more or less everything is coming to me. We're so lucky compared to most people whose relatives end their days in care. The rental from this place paid towards the care home costs.'

'That's down to Jimmy too,' I told Euan. 'Paying to store Granny's stuff would have cost a fortune.'

'Anyway,' Mum continued, 'looks like there will be enough to pass on the financial gifts she wanted to give you both. Five thousand pounds each.'

My brain raced ahead. I could go and see a fertility consultant.

'She also left this for you.' She handed the small box to Euan. He opened it to reveal a handsome silver fob watch with a white face.

'It belonged to Grandad Gallacher. She wanted you to have it,' Mum said.

Euan picked it up, spooling the fob chain into his hand. 'What a beautiful thing. Does it work?'

'Yes,' Mum replied, 'but it's losing time. You'll need to take it to a specialist to have it serviced.'

'I absolutely love it. I can't wait to show Alan. I'll buy a Scottish gentleman's tweed waistcoat. I've always wanted an excuse.'

'That's for you,' Mum said to me, nodding to the wooden box on the table.

The box was in a dark wood. Mahogany, I guessed. The corners were bound in brass and delicate mother-of-pearl decorated the lid. It was stunning.

'Let me show you how it works.' Mum turned the key and opened the box, revealing the transformative trick. It folded out into a small, sloped desk faced with very pale pink leather. At the back of the desk, there was a glass ink pot and a compartment for pens. Mum lifted the front section, revealing another box containing writing paper.

'Oh, Mum. It's just beautiful. I don't remember ever seeing it in Granny's house.'

'It arrived back from Jimmy's inside an old suitcase. I think it was under the spare room bed for thirty years before it went into storage.'

'So was it meant for travelling?' I asked.

'Yes. I've seen similar military versions in the antiques shop. Don calls them campaign writing slopes, but this one is obviously styled for a lady.'

'Was it Granny's?'

Mum shook her head and smiled. 'Look at the maker's label.'

I squinted at the engraved brass plaque. 'Thomas Robertson, Alnwick.'

I rocked back on my heels and looked up at Mum in astonishment.

'It can't be.'

Mum held out a piece of paper. 'Granny wrote that page of her will herself.'

Joseph's silver watch for Euan and Christina Robertson's lap desk for Anna.

Chapter Twelve

September 1826, Alnwick, North England

Christina didn't remember actually agreeing to go to Edinburgh, but somehow the plans came together. Once she realised the momentum was unstoppable, she told James she must take the children.

'I'll go back to London,' James said. 'George has said I can stay in his house to delay leasing a family home. You'll find it easier to return to London by sea, but don't even think about risking it until the better weather comes next spring.'

Christina nodded. The pain of Will's death had settled into a numbness. She was taking full charge of the children, and would soon have to meet some very influential people in Edinburgh. She had only the length of the coach journey to assemble her wits around her.

She hugged James beside the coach. 'I'll miss you.'

'As will I,' he replied, 'but you've work to do. I can see already that you'll manage.'

James raised his hat as the coach wheels started to turn. 'Give George my regards and thanks,' he shouted.

. . .

The familiar outline of Arthur's Seat grew steadily larger on the horizon. Christina clasped her hands so tightly that her knuckles ached. Although it was her birthplace, she didn't associate Edinburgh with happy memories.

At the edge of the city, they moved into a local coach, and she gave the address Uncle George had sent to her. Sarah's delight in the spectacular view of the castle was a light moment that cut through her nerves. Christina had found her company a welcome diversion on the journey. Sarah had left her precious son in the care of her mother. She must surely be wretched inside, but she managed to hide it. This virtual stranger had weaned her own son to feed John. How could Christina repay such selfless kindness? She'd never had a loving sister, nor a close female friend. Every day, her fondness for Sarah grew.

When they entered the area now being called the New Town, she was as impressed as Sarah and Eliza. This was not an Edinburgh she recognised at all.

'Why, it's as grand as Mayfair,' Eliza exclaimed.

And so it was. Their coach took them along Heriot Row, a particularly elegant street of pale sandstone townhouses overlooking newly laid gardens. Christina was astonished when the coachman stopped just beyond this exclusive address. Surely Uncle George hadn't rented in such an area?

He must have seen them from the window, because he appeared at the front door. 'I hope you're ready for a climb. We're on the second floor and the stair is steep.'

Once inside, George gave her a warm hug, but didn't mention Will. He showed them the bedrooms, the kitchen, the large airy sitting room. Finally, he opened the door to a small room which contained only two chairs, two easels, a desk and their painting materials. Despite the central location, this apartment was much more modest than the expensive houses in Heriot Row. There were only three bedrooms, but they could all squeeze in if Eliza and Sarah shared and she took the children in with her. Christina loved the light from the enormous sash windows and the whole place had a calm atmosphere. It felt like somewhere she might begin to heal.

The next day Sarah and Eliza took the children for a walk in the nearby gated gardens. Christina carried her writing box into the art room.

'That's a beautiful thing,' George said.

'Tom made it for me.' She opened the box to expose the writing slope, then lifted the lid to retrieve some paper.

'Ingenious,' Uncle George said.

'I must write to James and tell him we're here safely.'

George picked up her sketchbook from inside the box and leafed through. He hesitated over a sketch of Will's face. She'd been trying to commit it to paper. She could no longer retrieve a sharp vision of Tiana from her memory.

'I am so very sorry, Christina, you've had to bear too much,' he whispered.

She nodded, unable to speak.

'I remember that painting helped you after Tiana. I pray it may have the same healing effect.'

Christina stood to hug her uncle. 'Thank you. You know me so well.' She took a determined breath. 'I'm ready to do my best.' She nodded towards the large blank canvas on the easel. 'And who are you going to paint?' she asked.

'I bought that canvas for you. You haven't found time to do a large painting for years. I believe the challenge of scale will be the kind of consuming project you need.'

'My miniatures are too in demand for me to have time for anything bigger.'

'You can find time here. I'm sure you'd get larger commissions if people knew what you're capable of.'

'I'd need a sitter.'

George held up a sketch she'd done of Sarah. 'I would say you've already found one. She's a pretty girl.'

'Sarah is lovely in every way, but painting only for my pleasure would seem like an indulgence.'

'You're too hard on yourself. Most of the male artists exhibiting at the Academy aren't commissioned, James included. Give your talent room to grow.'

'I'll think about it,' she replied. She dipped her pen in ink, but found her eyes drawn to the window. The hills of her native Fife were on the horizon. The Forth estuary and the coastal villages were hidden by the fields and trees in the foreground. She reflected on how Uncle George had rescued her from so many crises in her life. James thought him a bit of an old lady and made snide remarks about his lack of female companionship, but she would never judge this man. His loving support was a constant she could always rely on.

'Mrs Anstruther-Thomson called past and left her card yesterday,' he said.

'I saw it on the sideboard. I'll call on her tomorrow. Thanks to your introduction, I've to meet her elderly father, and sister-in-law too.'

'Painting Lord Adam will attract commissions from other influential men,' Uncle George remarked. 'I doubt the old man's been painted since Raeburn.'

'They only want miniatures,' she replied.

'Intimate pieces and therefore most important.'

Christina returned from her first sitting with Clementina Anstruther-Thomson to find a letter waiting from David Roberts.

5th September 1826
My dear Christina

I heard only this week about your terrible loss. Please accept my sincere condolences.

I hope that your stay in 'Auld Reekie' will give you space and time to grieve. I've taken the liberty of writing to David Ramsay Hay. David and I have been best friends since boyhood and he is very well connected in Edinburgh's artist community. I have asked him to call on you and offer any assistance you might require. I am sure you will have the Scottish art world completely charmed in no time.

I trust that little Agnes and the baby are well, and I look forward to seeing you again.

Yours, David Roberts

She smiled at Roberts' thoughtfulness. Strange that he made no mention of his wife.

The following week, Uncle George came in looking very sombre.

'I'm to travel to Kinghorn for a funeral tomorrow, Christina. Your cousin's been killed in an accident.'

'Which cousin?' she asked, not daring to meet George's eyes. The air seemed sucked from the room. She laid down her paintbrush, conscious of the tremor from her fingers. She'd wished a man dead and it wasn't the first time.

'Rob,' he answered. 'Will you come over for the burial?'

A shiver washed down her back. Finally, after all these years, her wish had been granted. It was a wicked thing to have longed for, but it was the truth. 'Robbie and I weren't friends, but I don't think I need to dance on his grave.'

Uncle George looked shocked. 'I didn't know you felt that strongly.'

Christina took up her brush again and simply replied: 'Give my best regards to the others. Tell them I'll bring the children over to visit before we leave Edinburgh.'

A week later, Christina and Agnes travelled to Leith with Uncle George, to catch the Fife ferry. John hadn't slept well, so she left him with Sarah. Jean, George's elder sister, had urged him to bring them over on the next nice day, since the crossing would get more difficult as the year edged towards winter. Christina was reluctant to face that ferry, but she wanted to see Aunt Jean and it was safer to make the journey now.

The harbour was packed with dozens of tall ships and the quays thronged with sailors and porters. Agnes was making a fuss to be allowed to walk, but Christina refused to let her down.

'There are too many people, and we're too near the water,' she told her squirming daughter.

'Come to me, Agnes. If you let me carry you, I'll give you a peppermint when we get on the little boat,' Uncle George said.

He held out his arms to receive Agnes, but his sudden expression of horror caused Christina to whirl around. And there he was. An old man, a sour expression, but unmistakably her father, John. The man who gave her away.

Christina was aware of George's hand on her wrist and his voice in her ear. 'Come away, Christina,' he pleaded.

What did she feel? Was the old anger and that terrible pain still there? Her father was arguing with a man selling fish. The woman beside him was carrying a grubby, barefoot child. The resemblance was undeniable. Surely her half-sister.

She allowed Uncle George to lead her towards the harbour wall, and they climbed down into the small boat that served as the ferry to Fife. The same ferry that had taken her from Kinghorn six years previously. Yet again, Christina climbed aboard with her heart aching. She was glad not to recognise the captain who gave command to cast off. A sailor coiled the rope on the deck as they headed out to sea. Christina took Agnes onto her knee, and kissed the top of her head. The smell of lavender drifted up from her freshly laundered white dress. The child on the dock had looked dirty and scrawny, her mother harassed, the kind of family that lived in harsh conditions and knew hunger.

'What's her name?' she asked.

'Isobel, same as her mother, who died some time ago. I don't know the name of the child.'

Christina nodded.

'I didn't know you knew he was alive,' Uncle George said quietly.

'Aunt Agnes told me he was dead, but Rob delighted in disproving that lie when I was about twelve. He tricked me by saying Aunt Agnes wanted us both to go and fetch something from Leith. He took me to where my father's new wife worked on a stall in the market. I recognised my father and saw his children. A girl my age and the boy older than my brother.'

'No wonder you didn't like Rob,' Uncle George said.

'Being cruel to me was his chief enjoyment. He told me my father sent me away because he'd never loved me.'

'Oh, Christina.' Uncle George laid his hand on her arm.

She kept her face towards the sea, to hide her tears from Agnes. 'Everything fell into place that day. I understood what my mother meant when she made you promise to save me.'

They sat in silence for several minutes. The wind dried

her cheeks. She'd long ago resolved to never shed another tear for her father. She never would again.

'I was only thirteen when my father died, your mother Margaret only ten,' George said. 'When our mother passed a year later, I'd already gone to Edinburgh as an apprentice. Jean had recently married, so she took in Margaret. When father's big house beside the harbour was sold, we all came into some money. Those savings funded my move to London, and your mother had a sizeable dowry. It seems that your father John had debts which he repaid after their marriage. We only found out later that he'd never given up Isobel. That she had his children. Someone told Margaret.'

'How awful for my mother,' Christina whispered. 'The woman with my father looked poor,' she added.

'I heard that Isobel, your half-sister, made an unfortunate marriage. Her husband is a drunkard.'

'How terrible,' Christina replied.

The piping sound of oystercatchers heralded her arrival in Kinghorn harbour. She'd left under a cloud of scandal. This time she kept her head held high.

Aunt Jean must have guessed they might come today. The smell of baking met them at the door. A stack of freshly gridled drop scones sat next to the range. She served them with homemade raspberry jam and newly churned butter. Agnes's dress was soon no longer pristine and white.

'I'm right glad tae see you, Christina. My sister was wrang tae turn you away, I think she aywis regretted it.'

'I had Uncle George to go to,' Christina replied.

'I blame Robbie. He was jealous fae the beginning, and he turned her against you.'

'He'd been the youngest. I can imagine why a younger cousin in his home wouldn't be welcome,' Christina said.

'That's maybe true, but he was a born a bad lot, much like his late faither. He looked like Rob senior and Agnes never accepted what the rest of us kent fae the beginning. Red-haired vicious little shites baith ae them.'

George looked up sharply. 'Jean!' he exclaimed, gesturing towards Agnes who was stroking a cat lying in the hearth.

'She's too wee tae understand, and it's time tae put the record straight. This story about an accident's no true either. Everyone kens Rob laid his filthy hands on farmer Scott's youngest daughter. It wasn't the first time that some faither threatened tae kill him. Robbie finally got what he deserved.'

'Jean, you mustn't say such things. His death was an accident,' George said.

'A story for the authorities but it was no accident. Naebdae in the whole village blames Jock Scott. And although he was my ain kin, Robbie got what was coming tae him.'

Christina let go of a deep sigh and turned the information around in her mind. She experienced a distinct shift, like the disappearance of a cloud shadow. All those years of pain. Could she put it to rest now? Just then Agnes tottered over and climbed on her knee.

'You look well, Christina, and this wee lassie's a credit tae you. You said she's the eldest?' Aunt Jean asked.

Christina held the old lady's questioning gaze for a few seconds, blinked, then answered. 'Yes, we've had to endure sadness along the way, but her little brother is doing well.'

Jean nodded. 'That's good tae hear and I wish you and your family all the luck in the world. I'm sorry we didnae make a better job ae looking out for you when you were wee.'

Christina thought again about her half-sister. 'I have many happy memories of Kinghorn, Aunt Jean. Aunt Agnes did her best. Now, I have high hopes for the future.'

. . .

That afternoon she stood at her easel and reflected on her day. In the space of a few hours she'd rid herself of two malevolent ghosts. One was dead and one was not, but she'd never think of her father again. She looked down at her sketch of Sarah, then she dipped her brush in the paint and made one bold brushstroke across the canvas.

Chapter Thirteen

November 2017, Edinburgh

I rested my laptop on the open slope of Christina's desk. Mum raised no objection to me looking for Granny's birth certificate. Armed with the date of birth, it was easy to find, and sure enough, there was no father's name. I tracked down Jimmy's birth certificate, naming his mother as Elisabeth Kirk, and found her death certificate for the same day. Jimmy had two elder sisters. What unimaginable awfulness for Archie Kirk, to find himself a grieving widower with three children, including a new-born baby. I searched for his marriage registration, and Archibald Kirk married my great-grandmother, Dorothy Robertson Linton, later that same year. No wonder Jimmy's sister was resentful. Then my eyes strayed to the next record on the marriage register search. An Archibald Kirk had married an Elisabeth Linton twelve years earlier in 1936. I opened up the record with a sinking feeling; it confirmed that my great-grandfather's first wife had the same maiden name as Dorothy. Linton was not a very common surname. Stunned by a thought, I let my hands fall into my lap.

Mum came in. 'What's wrong?'

'Was Granny's mother related to Archie's first wife?'

'I don't know,' she replied. The two marriage register entries were positioned side-by-side on my screen. Mum took a sharp breath.

'Jimmy's eldest sister was called Bessie, right?'

Mum nodded. After a few minutes of frantic typing, I had the whole story in front of us. Archibald and Elisabeth had a daughter at the end of 1936, Bessie's proper name was also Elisabeth. I got Dorothy's birth certificate out of Granny's tin. Her mother was Mary Robertson Linton. She lived in Kirkcaldy and an ancestor search threw up two daughters: Dorothy Robertson Linton, the eldest, my great-grandmother, and Elisabeth her much younger sister. Did this answer the question about Granny's father? Had Archie had fathered a child with his wife's sister?

'What an utter mess,' I muttered.

Mum just shook her head.

A little more research uncovered more details. I opened my notepad to start drawing a family tree. Mary Linton died before her youngest daughter married at seventeen and Elisabeth's baby was born four months later.

Granny Gallagher Family Tree

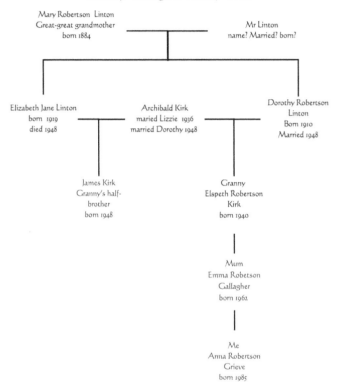

'A hasty marriage and a very young bride,' Mum whispered.

'Since her mother was dead, you'd expect her elder sister to have been very involved, perhaps a frequent visitor to the farm. Could Archie have been Granny's father? Poor Elisabeth Kirk, what a disaster. Then Dorothy brings up her baby boy.'

'And Jimmy said nothing about them being sisters?' Mum asked.

'No, but he must have known. If I'm right, the events didn't reflect well on Archie Kirk. The way he described him, Jimmy obviously adored his father.'

'I'm sure your granny loved him too.'

Mum went back downstairs, and I stared at the screen. Granny was born in 1940, in the early years of the war. Farmers would have been one of the few young men not away fighting. If my hunch was right, could that have been a factor? Also, Dorothy was a thirty-year-old spinster. She might never have had children if she hadn't had Granny. Perhaps she longed for a child of her own? But badly enough to ruin her sister's world? I knew what it felt like to ache for a baby and worry about running out of time. How far would I go? I loved my brother to bits. I would have said I'd never do anything to hurt Euan, but my initial reaction to his baby news revealed how I was capable of selfishness. Certainly, having sex with your sister's husband was hard to defend. Was it a full-blown affair, or something that only happened once?

That set me wondering if Mum had conceived immediately. I was afraid to ask. Might I be the first 'Robertson' girl in generations not to get pregnant at the drop of a hat? I closed my laptop and cradled my face in my hands. Pressing my eyeballs, breathing through my fingers. That familiar, dreaded feeling swept through me. It seemed to get stronger every day. It felt like shame. Why was my body letting me down?

Pull yourself together, Anna. I didn't want Mum to catch me crying. I had an appointment to meet a gynaecologist on Monday. If there was a problem, it was time I got to the bottom of it.

I opened my laptop again. The Christina Robertson research was keeping me sane. Dorothy Linton was born in 1910, so her mother Mary must have been born in the nineteenth century. Only a few generations after Christina. Could I find the links to Mary Linton?

The doorbell rang an hour later. Neighbour Mandy stood on the doorstep with an elegant Border Collie. 'Hi, Anna. I've promised to walk my friend's dog today and my delivery is late. Is it okay if I ask the delivery company to bring it here?'

'Of course, no problem. Mum and I are both in.'

Mum appeared beside me. 'What a beautiful dog, Mandy. Is she yours?'

'No. Meg belongs to a friend, but I usually walk her on a Friday when I work from home. My afternoon always goes better after an hour in the open air.'

'It's a lovely day for a walk,' I said, looking at the blue sky beyond the Colonies' rooftops.

'Why don't you come with me?' Mandy suggested.

'Great idea, go on, Anna. I can wait for the parcel,' Mum added.

Five minutes later, Mandy and I were following exuberant Meg up the riverside path in the direction of Inverleith Park.

'I'm glad I decided to stay on a few days longer. The weather has been so lovely. We should have snow any day now in Moscow. It's late this year.'

'You live in Moscow? How fascinating,' Mandy said. 'I'd

love to visit. I went to St Petersburg five years ago, and I adored it. The Hermitage Museum is amazing.'

'Isn't it? I visited recently and Mum has promised to come with me again next year. I'm researching a family connection.'

'Now, that is intriguing.'

I launched into my Christina Robertson story. It was lovely to relate it to someone who was obviously interested. 'I've hit a stumbling block searching for information on Christina's daughters. I found their birth certificates, but nothing after that. Now I've fallen down another rabbit hole to keep me busy for weeks. The Royal Academy of Art has a searchable catalogue, and Christina exhibited year after year. I'm trying to track down photos of her work by using the sitters' names.'

'I've got a book you might find interesting,' Mandy said. 'I work for a publishing company and we brought out a book about the Edinburgh artist David Roberts a couple of years ago. He must have been active around the same time. I'll drop a copy round.'

'I'd love to see it. Why don't you come for supper? I've made a massive lasagne. Bring your family, there's enough to feed the street.'

'That's really kind. Jack is at his dad's for a few days, but I'd love to come.'

Nick called just as I was setting the table. I could hear his footsteps echoing on the pavement and the sound of cars in the background. 'Hi there. I was going to call you tomorrow. I can hear cars. Where are you?' I asked.

'Just crossed over the Kamenny Bridge. The traffic is extra busy tonight, so I decided to walk. I forgot my gloves, though. My fingers are freezing.'

'Would you like me to pick up some wireless earbuds at

the airport? Save you having to hold your phone in the winter. Call it an early Christmas present.'

'Nice idea. Thank you. What are your plans for the weekend?'

'Nothing much. Euan went back to the States. Mum and I are still busy sorting through the last of Granny's boxes. Although a nice neighbour called Mandy is coming for supper tonight. She's due any minute, so I'll have to go if she arrives.'

'Is it worthwhile getting friendly with your grandmother's neighbours? I thought your mum was planning to sell?'

'She hasn't decided about the house yet. Anyway, I like Mandy. I've been telling her about my Christina Robertson project.'

'How is that going?'

'Fine, making progress.' I didn't tell him about Granny's birth circumstances, especially the latest twist. Granny had loved Archie Kirk, and I didn't want to have to defend him.

Just then, the doorbell rang. 'I'll get it,' Mum shouted from upstairs.

'You'd better go,' Nick said

'Shall I call you back later? I doubt we'll finish late.'

'I'm tired. I think I'll have an early night. Then I'm going to the country with the boys again tomorrow. I'll call you on Sunday.'

'You mean you're going to Oksana's dacha?'

'Yes,' he replied, then paused. 'It's great to get out of the city and it will be more difficult once the snow arrives.'

'Of course.'

'Talk to you on Sunday. Love you,' he said.

'Bye,' I replied. But the line had already gone dead.

Mandy came into the tiny kitchen. 'I've brought some

chrysanthemums. Your mum said the vases are in here.' She looked at me quizzically. 'Is there something wrong?'

'No,' I replied, shaking the anxiety from my head. I smiled and took the flowers. 'And thank you for these, although you didn't need to bring anything. Go through and sit down. Can I get you some wine? White or red?'

'Red would be perfect. I brought you this, too.' Mandy handed me the David Roberts book.

In the living room, I gave Mum and Mandy their wine and then sat and examined the book's glossy cover. A desert painting on the front and a portrait of Roberts in Middle Eastern clothing on the back. Lots of illustrations inside. British looking church ruins early on, then increasingly exotic overseas scenes later. 'This is beautiful,' I murmured.

'Can I see?' Mum asked.

'It's been one of our most successful titles. We commissioned it in partnership with the Scottish National Gallery who were staging an exhibition of his work. They sold lots of copies through their gift shop, then the exhibition went to the V&A and they sold even more. That was several years ago, but sales still tick over.'

'He must have led a fascinating life, visiting all those places. When was he born?' I asked.

'I can't remember, beginning of the nineteenth century, I think.'

'It says here 1796 to 1864,' Mum said, and passed me back the book.

'Born the same year as Christina. I wonder if they knew each other.'

'Your artist lived in London?' Mandy asked.

'As an adult, yes. Her mother Margaret was the youngest in a large Kinghorn based family. She had Christina in Edinburgh but it seems the family moved back to Kinghorn, both Christina and her uncle, George Saunders, were described as coming from there. The next record I can find is Christina's marriage in Marylebone when she was twenty-six.'

'David Roberts was born here in Stockbridge, then moved to London as a young man too. Are these Christina's portraits?' Mandy asked, reaching for the stack of images on the coffee table.

'Yes, I've printed out some of my favourites. Look, these are the Tsar's family.'

'What stunning paintings. The dress style reminds me of a young Queen Victoria.'

'It's the same era. Christina painted these around 1840.'

'Are there any paintings here in the National Portrait Gallery?' Mandy asked.

'One miniature. I'm going up to see it tomorrow.'

'They might hold more information on this artist if she was Scottish. The curator is Esme Stevenson, I know her from the David Roberts project. I'll introduce you if you like.'

'I'd love to meet her next time I'm back. I'm returning to Moscow next week.'

Mandy set her head to one side and looked towards Mum. 'So you're not selling this place just yet?' she asked.

'Not yet,' Mum confirmed. 'I've got to go back to York next week. I have an antiques business there. But I am thinking I might leave York soon. I've got a buyer for the shop.'

Mandy smiled. 'Well, I do hope you decide to move back. I'd love to have you as a permanent neighbour.'

Supper was successful and Mandy entertained us with publishing stories. Later, lying in the dark, I found myself wondering if Nick really went to bed early. Moscow was two hours ahead, so I certainly couldn't call him now. I must stop torturing myself with irrational jealousy.

. . .

The next day I got a text from Mandy.

Can I come with you to visit this painting? I'm in town and I'm curious.

Sure. Mum and I are planning to be up there around 2.

The information desk attendant told us Christina's painting was in the library. This turned out to be a sombre room, lined with dark bookshelves and also containing an unsettling collection of death masks. We found the painting hidden inside a glass-topped drawer. Not tiny, to be worn around the neck or held in one hand, but nearly the full depth of the drawer. It depicted three unknown blonde-haired children with impish expressions.

'Quite a contrast to the enormous paintings I saw in St Petersburg. But it would be more effective on a wall, the drawer glass reflection makes it difficult to see,' I said.

'To create such detail on a small portrait takes skill, though,' Mandy added.

We went into the café and ordered coffee.

'Are you making much progress with your Christina research?' Mandy asked.

'I'm not sure if I'll ever uncover the truth about her life. There's too little in the public records. But Christina Robertson deserves to be remembered. She exhibited at the Royal Academy every year from 1823 until she left to live in Russia in the 1840s. One hundred and thirty portraits in total at the RA and she exhibited here in Scotland too. She mostly did miniatures in her early career, the large portraits came later.'

I showed her some more of the images I'd saved to my phone.

Mandy flicked through the photographs of the paintings. 'Have you thought about writing a book?'

'Of course, I'm a journalist. I'm sure we've all dreamed of that. But I've never had the time nor a good idea for a book.'

'Well, you have both now,' Mandy replied. 'I'm sure my company would consider a book about Christina, if you make a good pitch. It doesn't have to be a detailed biography. Think of it more as an illustrated guide. If you can track down some really eye-catching portraits that link back to her life, I could see that working.' Mandy held up the image of two little girls in velvet dresses. 'This is charming.'

'That miniature of Clementina and Elizabeth Drummond-Burrell was in Christina's first Royal Academy Exhibition in 1823, but it seems to have been painted when she was only twenty-three. It's the earliest example I've found so far. There's a nod to her Uncle George in this too. The painting on the wall behind the girls is George Saunders' painting of their mother.'

'So, like an appreciation of his mentorship?' Mandy added. 'That's exactly the kind of personal detail that could bring a book to life.'

I felt an exhilarating buzz of excitement. 'Do you really think your company would be interested?'

'I can't promise, but I'm sure they'd consider it. You don't have to write the whole book up front. We just need a proposal. Give me your email address and I'll send you the submission guidelines.'

My gynaecologist appointment was at lunchtime on Monday. The receptionist had me fill in a form. Then I sat down to wait in the otherwise empty waiting room. I was nervous but also grateful to the doctor I was about to meet. He'd squeezed me into his schedule when I'd explained I was only in Edinburgh for a few more days. The man who stood to greet me when I walked into his room was tall. In his late forties, I guessed, with a mop of hair and the build of a rugby player. His disarming smile immediately put me at ease. He gestured me to sit opposite him.

'So, tell me what I can do to help?'

Unexpected tears pricked my eyes. An offer of help. This was what I needed to hear. He didn't appear impatient as I blinked and struggled to compose myself. Just folded his huge hands in his lap, smiling patiently.

'My husband and I have been trying to have a baby, and I'm worried that it's taking so long.'

'Let me take some history,' he answered, and ran through some questions with me. 'I'll get you to pop up on the couch, if you don't mind. I want to do an examination of your abdomen.'

He made a phone call and nurse entered, carrying a syringe pack. 'I'll examine you first, then we'll do a blood test while you're up here,' he said. 'Sorry, my fingers are a wee bit cold.'

His hands on my abdomen were firm. His calm, practised probing inspired confidence that he knew what he was looking for. 'Everything feels fine,' he said. 'Dawn will take your blood while she's here. Nurses are famously better at it than us doctors.'

Once that was done, the nurse left. I got off the bed and sat back down to retie my trainers. 'When will I get the blood results?' I asked. 'I live in Moscow and go back on Thursday.'

'I'll ask the lab to rush them through, so hopefully you'll get them before then. Give me a call when they arrive and we can talk about it.'

'And what would you advise if there is a problem?'

'Let's see what the results say. I've pulled together some general information on fertility issues. They detail possible next steps.' He handed me some leaflets.

I left in a more positive mood. Euan had been right. It felt better to be taking charge of this.

The test results arrived on Wednesday. My hands shook as I opened the envelope. What if this was the moment I found I was infertile? I squinted at the results. They seemed to say that I was ovulating, but that my fertility was low. Not infertile, but heading in that direction. Shit. I called Dr Matthews' secretary and asked for him to call me back.

'So the results aren't great?' I said when he returned my call.

'I wouldn't say that at all.' His deep, reassuring voice had a calming effect. 'We would expect reduced fertility by your mid-thirties and you are ovulating so spontaneous pregnancy is possible. You're a good weight, you don't smoke and you don't report any symptoms of fibroids or endometriosis. There is every reason to be hopeful.'

'But my chances reduce over time?'

'That's just the way it works. If you were living here, we could do a blood test at the beginning of your cycle and perhaps an ultrasound.'

'Would you recommend starting fertility treatment?'

'Of course, it's up to you, and I understand your concerns about the cost of private treatment. Hormone injections to increase you egg production could be a next step. I'm sure you could have that done in Moscow.'

'I'll discuss it with my husband.'

I finished the call and stared at the phone in my hand. Surely it made sense to try to improve my chances and Nick was bound to be in favour of that. We were managing to amass some savings in Moscow, and now I had Granny's money, too. I'd ask Lisa about her consultant when I got back.

. . .

Sitting in the departure lounge of Edinburgh airport the next day, I got Mandy's guidelines out of my bag. The very idea that I might have a book published made me remember what it felt like to fizz with ambition. An idea of how I'd approach the Christina Robertson proposal was forming in my mind. I was on the scent of a story.

I detoured to the airport pharmacy on the way to the gate to grab another couple of packs of ovulation tests. There was a whole industry in this. You could get fancier ovulation predictors that linked to an app on your phone, but these would do for now. I felt like I'd signed up for a cross-Channel swim and was currently paddling in the shallows. The cashier smiled at me. She was around my age, and I felt a frisson of empathy pass between us. I wondered if she was swimming in this new world too.

When I exited security in Sheremetyevo airport, Nick was there, smiling broadly and holding a large bunch of flowers.

'Welcome home, Anna.'

I was glad to see him and I walked into his arms.

Chapter Fourteen

August 1827, London

Christina's portraits of Sarah were hung either side of the marble fireplace in the drawing room of their new home. She and James had moved to London's Argyll Street the month before. Christina had just reached up to straighten one of the frames when she heard James's step on the parquet floor behind her. His arms encircled her waist, he nuzzled his face into her shoulder and kissed her neck.

'You look lovely in your new gown. The bright plaid will draw all the eyes in the room this evening.'

'I certainly hope not.'

James released her from the hug and let his hand skim over her stomach. He hesitated. 'Are you?' he asked.

She sighed. 'It's hardly a surprise. God willing, this baby will come at the beginning of March.'

She saw a flicker of concern in his eyes. No comparison to the chasm of fear she felt in her own chest. She'd hoped for a longer gap.

'Do we wish for a boy or a girl?' he asked.

'I only wish for a strong, healthy baby, just like Agnes and John.'

The evidence of the strength of Agnes's lungs and character came from a voice on the stairs. 'I want Mama.'

Seconds later, their four-year-old burst into the room, followed by Eliza with little John in her arms.

'Agnes wanted to say goodnight,' Eliza said.

James took John from Eliza's arms, then bent to scoop Agnes up onto his hip. He lowered his face near his son's and said: 'Papa.'

John dutifully repeated the word, causing James to laugh and cheer. It was his only word so far, and James must have said it to him a thousand times since they returned from Edinburgh in April. Christina had found the strength to dampen her grief in Scotland with Sarah's help. Parting in Edinburgh allowed Sarah to return to her son, but Christina had found it horribly painful. But their absence had come at a cost for James. He'd hated being away from her and the children. When they'd returned to London, fourteen-month-old John hadn't known his father, and had cried when he came near. James's expression at the boy's rejection cut Christina to the core.

The sound of shouting drifted from outside. Two carriages were stuck facing each other in New Argyll Street, both drivers refusing to back up. A queue of carriages had formed in both directions behind them.

'Is there an event in the Argyll Rooms tonight?' she asked.

'A concert, I believe.'

Christina sighed. 'A flat with such magnificent windows was a find, James, but this must be the busiest corner in London. Surely an inconvenience for our guests.'

'I disagree. This is the happiest corner in London. Almost all our visitors will have fond memories of visiting the original Argyll Rooms.'

'There's Uncle George,' she said, recognising the gait of a top-hatted gentleman. 'How good of him to be punctual.'

'He needs the extra ten minutes to manage the stairs,' James muttered. 'But that's Lord Glenlyon's carriage. I'd better go down.'

Eliza took baby John from his arms. 'Kiss your mama now, Agnes. It's time for bed.'

Agnes folded her chubby arms across her chest. 'No,' she said, her face screwed up in determination.

'You may come downstairs with me to greet the first guests,' James replied, giving into her whims as usual.

Christina raised her eyes to look at Sarah's portrait. 'Here we go again,' she said.

The room filled up quickly, and the temperature started to climb. The breeze from the open sash windows couldn't compete with the crush of bodies. Many ladies required extra space to accommodate the new fashion for wide sleeves. Christina had resisted her dressmaker's suggestions on this, considering the busyness of her tartan gown, quite distracting enough. She took James's arm and began a dutiful circuit of the guests. An unusually tall and broad elderly man came through the door. He was accompanied by a lady about Christina's age.

'Who is the tall man with his daughter?'

James turned his head away and coughed, to hide his snort of laughter. 'The gentleman is Lord John Rolle. He owns half of Devon, and the lady is his wife.'

James bent in closer to whisper. 'The age gap has inspired a verse.

How comes it, Rolle, at seventy-two
Hale Rolle, Louisa to the altar led?
The thing is neither strange nor new
Louisa took the Rolle for want of bread.'

Christina glared at her husband. 'People can be so cruel

and it demeans you to repeat such nonsense. Can you introduce me? I want to meet this lady.'

Lady Rolle paused in front of the fireplace, gazing up at Christina's portraits of Sarah. 'Look, John, these are magnificent! Do you think they were executed by this paintress?'

'Good evening, Lady Rolle, Lord Rolle,' James interjected with a small bow. 'May I introduce my talented wife, Christina, and I can confirm Mrs Robertson did indeed paint these portraits.'

Christina bobbed a curtsey, her cheeks burning. The whole point of these evenings was to promote her work, but she found it excruciating.

'Mrs Robertson, I believe these are the loveliest paintings I have ever seen. May I ask the identity of the sitter?' Louisa Rolle asked.

'A relative. Her name is Sarah,' Christina replied.

Lady Rolle's face fell. 'Ah, family pictures. I should have guessed from the candid expressions. So they're not for sale?'

'I'm afraid not.'

'The portraits are intended to demonstrate the breadth of my wife's talent. Most people know her chiefly for her miniatures,' James interrupted. 'She could create such a portrait of you, Lady Rolle.'

Louisa Rolle shook her head. 'Oh no, I shouldn't like that at all. I'm not nearly pretty enough to grace a wall, not even ours.'

'My wife is too modest,' Lord Rolle added.

'Not everyone enjoys being painted,' Christina answered, 'but I disagree about your suitability. Sarah's eyes are the features that draw you to these portraits. They let us see her kind and honest soul. I would say the same is true of your eyes.'

Lady Rolle smiled at Christina, her head slightly to one

side. 'I'm not accustomed to compliments, Mrs Robertson, but I will accept that one. Thank you.'

Lord Rolle took his wife's hand. 'You have seen what I know to be true, madam. I am the luckiest man alive. We must certainly persuade my wife to sit for a miniature. If I ask it as a gift to me, she will not refuse.'

'If it pleases you, John, but I doubt Mrs Robertson wants to traipse all the way to Bicton to make a small painting.' Louisa Rolle turned towards Christina. 'I'm very busy with a project for our garden in Devon. I don't often come up to London.'

'You should have pushed her for the full length,' James whispered after the couple had moved away.

'If she wasn't willing, the portrait would have no life,' Christina replied.

Unable to face any more obsequious chatter. Christina sat on the couch and allowed her hand to settle on her already bulging stomach, giving her an excuse for sitting.

Uncle George came and sat beside her. 'Sarah's paintings look very fine in here, Christina. Surely they will lead to commissions for larger paintings. You might even sell them. Sarah is a very handsome subject.'

'Lady Rolle already expressed an interest, but I wouldn't dream of selling them.'

'I can see why you're loathe to part with them. These are your best paintings yet. You've captured such subtle emotions, I can actually see the maturing of your friendship in Sarah's eyes. In the first she looks shy, but the second betrays the sadness of your imminent parting.'

Christina gazed again at Sarah, looking back over her shoulder. 'I'm glad you can see what I intended. When I saw her off on the coach to Alnwick I thought my heart would break, and Agnes was inconsolable.'

'Have you heard from her?'

'Of course. We correspond every week. In any case, my wish to keep Sarah near me was selfish. She missed little Andrew, and he needs his mother. I've wracked my brains to find a way to bring them both here, but we can't afford it.'

David Roberts was heading towards her. Finally, a friendly face in the crowd.

'Good evening to you both. I'll join your cosy corner if you'll permit it.' Roberts drew in a chair.

'I'm delighted to see you. Is Margaret here?'

'Sadly, she's feeling under the weather this evening. She sends her sincere apologies.'

Was the flicker of emotion that crossed his face at odds with his reply?

'I'm so sorry to hear that, but I'm glad that you were able to come this week. We'd begun to worry that we'd offended you.'

'Not at all. I'm afraid I've been so busy at Covent Garden that I've barely found the time to sleep.'

'I do hope you found some time for your own art.'

'Of course,' Roberts replied with a wry smile. 'I just sleep less.' He looked up at the portraits of Sarah. 'Although I'm afraid I didn't achieve anything of this standard, they're extraordinary. Why did you not show them at the Royal Academy?'

'They weren't finished, and also we wanted to keep them to show in the house. The room needs large paintings and James wants people to know they can trust me with more than miniatures.'

'Lady Rolle admired them,' Uncle George interrupted.

Roberts nodded. 'These show your versatility and talent for portraits of any size. Is the subject a society lady?'

Christina laughed. 'Not at all. Sarah is a relation of James's brother and now my dearest friend. She accompanied me to Edinburgh.'

David Roberts closed his eyes briefly. 'I'm so very sorry about your wee boy.'

She sighed. So many people avoided the subject but David Roberts' thoughtfulness endeared him further to her.

'Thank you.' Christina reached over to touch Uncle George's arm. 'It was Uncle George who arranged for me to go to Edinburgh, and he was right as usual.'

'What do you think of this new Scottish Academy, Mr Roberts?' George asked.

'I'm in favour,' he replied. 'My friend Hay has made me promise to send up a painting for next year's exhibition. Would you consider sending something, Christina?'

'Perhaps,' she replied. 'If they thought my work would be of interest.'

Loud shouting from downstairs caused them all to look towards the door.

'What on all earth?' she said. But in the same moment Christina recognised the Scots voice, even although the obscenities were far from ladylike. David Roberts went red and jumped to his feet.

Margaret Roberts appeared in the doorway. She put her hand on the doorjamb to steady herself and glared around the room. The footman they had hired for the evening arrived just behind her, looking out of breath and thoroughly terrified. He put his hand on her arm. 'Madam, please...' he pleaded.

'Get your hands off me, I have an invitation!' Margaret said loudly, brandishing Christina's handwritten card above her head.

David Roberts made a move towards her.

'There ye are, ye miserable, cowardly wee worm,' Margaret said. People stepped back as she barrelled across the room. She stopped right in front of David Roberts and yelled up in his face. 'How dare ye hide my invitation? Ye ken fine I'm fed up stuck at hame. My friend Christina invited me and here I am.'

Margaret shouted the last sentence even louder and turned towards Christina. She had to think fast. 'Margaret, how delightful.' Christina passed her arm around the lady's waist and whispered in her ear. 'Don't tell anyone else, but I want to give you a personal tour of the house.'

Margaret smiled and gave a very theatrical wink. Christina guided her towards the door. It was a struggle to keep her advancing in a straight line, and she prayed they wouldn't fall. 'Take the banister, Margaret. I want you to see my private sitting room and the staircase is steep.' They met Eliza running up the steps, no doubt alerted by the noise. 'Eliza, I feel a little faint. Would you bring tisane for myself and Mrs Roberts to my sitting room?'

'Are ye poorly?' Margaret asked, her eyes full of concern.

'You know how it is in the early months of pregnancy. I feel constantly nauseous and tired. Would you stay and keep me company while I rest?'

'Of course. Fancy making you receive guests in your condition. Men are brutes.' Margaret Roberts burst into tears.

Christina guided her into a chair. The smell of alcohol was almost overwhelming. 'Please don't cry. You're here with me now and it's much cosier than upstairs.'

Eliza came in with the hot drinks. She hovered anxiously near the door.

'Thank you, Eliza, that will be all. Mrs Roberts and I already feel better away from the crowd.'

'There was a time when the crowds used tae come to see me perform, not laugh at me,' Margaret muttered.

Christina poured the tisane and wrapped Margaret's hands around the hot cup. 'My friend Sarah collects and dries the herbs and flowers for this herself. The recipe is secret, but I believe it's chiefly chamomile.'

Margaret sniffed the drink and took a sip. Tears ran channels through her face powder. 'I'm sorry I disrupted your party,' she whispered. After a few quiet moments, she added: 'I saw them all staring at me, but I was so angry wi' Davy, I couldnae contain myself.' Her face crumpled. 'He never takes me out. He's ashamed of me, ye see.'

'I'm sure it's not that. David told me he has to work long hours in his new job.'

Margaret shook her head. 'But he doesnae come home when he's finished. He blames me for drinking, but I'm so lonely. I cannae face life sober anymore.'

Margaret's plight twisted Christina's heart. Her words were slurred, but her misery was clearly genuine. 'Let me top up your tisane,' she said. When she turned back with a fresh cup, she found Margaret had fallen asleep.

Christina sipped her drink while her companion dozed. Margaret was still beautiful but had aged visibly in their short acquaintance. An hour later, James and David Roberts appeared in the doorway. Christina put her finger to her lips.

David Roberts shook his head. 'She'll not wake now. This is how it always goes. She rages, she weeps, then passes out. I'm at my wit's end and little Christine is more frightened of her every day. I'm talking to my sister in Edinburgh about sending Christine up there for a while. We can't go on like this.'

'She tells me she is lonely.'

'I know, but I'm working day and night to provide for them, and you can see she isn't fit for polite company. There are many young women at home with their children and they don't resort to gin. I'm convinced now that she had the daily habit before we married, but I mistook her high spirits for gaiety. There's nothing gay about our situation now.' Roberts then put his arms under his wife and lifted her off the chair. She groaned and her head fell on his shoulder.

'Sorry, Davy,' she muttered, without opening her eyes.

Christina heard James hail a carriage for the Roberts, then a muffled conversation with some other gentleman. She couldn't make out what was said, but the man sounded angry. Christina looked out the window and saw a cloaked man in a flat cap walking away. He turned around and flung a few more words in James's direction. His whole demeanour seemed threatening. She shivered. The front door banged shut and James hurried up.

'Whatever's the matter now?' she asked.

'Just a ruffian. I sent him packing.' James poured himself a brandy. 'What a night,' he said, collapsing into the chair recently vacated by Margaret Roberts.

'Were you not pleased with the salon tonight?'

James loosened his cravat and took a large swig of brandy. 'On the contrary, it was our best yet. I was worried that confounded woman had ruined it, but the incident rather energised the conversation. People do like a bit of drama. I feel most sorry for poor David Roberts, though.'

'My heart breaks for them both,' Christina replied. 'It's a desperate situation.'

James took a card out of his breast pocket and handed it to Christina. 'Lord Rolle spoke to me again before he left. If you change your mind about those portraits, he will give you four hundred guineas for the pair.'

'That's too much, but they're still not for sale.'

'I told him, but I think you should make the journey to

Devon to do that miniature. If you get on with Lady Rolle, she might be persuaded to sit for something larger.'

'Perhaps she'd prefer a family piece. Have they any children?'

'No. I'm sure that was his hope for their union, as he has no heir from his first marriage, but they've been married for several years now.'

'Nevertheless, they seem a happy couple despite their different ages. I fear David Roberts is not a good match for his wife. He is quiet, and she wants to be in company. Spending all her time with no companion but her child clearly doesn't suit her at all.'

'You are quiet, whilst I love company, and we manage just fine.'

'Hmm,' Christina replied with a wry smile.

Chapter Fifteen

November 2017, Moscow

Nick ordered in Chinese food. We sat side-by-side, using chopsticks to eat spicy noodles straight from the cardboard cartons.

'It's lovely to have you home,' Nick said after supper.

'It's great to be back, and I've lots to tell you.' I rifled through my handbag for the earbuds I'd picked up in the airport, pulling out the publisher's submission guidelines and the gynaecologist's report as well.

'Thank you. These are perfect,' he said, turning the box over in his fingers. 'What's all this then?' he asked, gesturing at the pile of papers.

'The top page is a brief on how to pitch a book to Mandy's publishing company.'

'Mandy?'

'The editor I told you about. She lives in Granny's street. Hang on though, there's other stuff in my case I want to show you.'

I returned with the plastic bag full of ovulation predictor kits, and the stack of leaflets the gynaecologist gave me. Nick already had the doctor's report in his hands. He didn't look up.

'The earbuds sit inside their own charging unit.' I could hear the anxiety in my voice. For god's sake say something!

He raised his head. 'This is terrible news.' His expression was anguished.

I felt like he'd punched me in the stomach. 'That was my first reaction too, but the doctor talked me through it. I'm not infertile. We still have a chance.'

He shook his head, looking stricken.

I took a deep breath. 'It's disappointing, but surely not that unexpected?'

'Why didn't you tell me?'

'I only got the results yesterday.'

'Did you go back to see your GP?'

'No, I'm not registered there anymore. I went to a private clinic in Edinburgh.'

'Private?'

'Granny left me five thousand pounds in her will. She would approve of me spending it on this.'

He nodded, staring at the letter. 'Could this doctor say what's caused the problem?'

'My age mostly, I guess.' I struggled to keep my tone even. I was feeling blamed. 'I'm thirty-five next year, Nick. We've always known time was an issue.'

'I know, but I thought...'

I put the stack of leaflets on the table and pulled one of the ovulation kits out of the bag. 'These will tell us exactly when I'm ovulating.'

'Looks like a pregnancy test.'

'It is a urine test, same idea, but testing for a different hormone.'

'Then when it says go, we have to have sex to a schedule?'

'I suppose, but is that such a hardship?'

'I guess not.' His smile looked strained.

I'd had enough of this. 'I feel a bit overwhelmed too, Nick. Why don't you read the leaflets? They explain everything better than I can describe. I'm going to bed. I was up really early this morning.'

I stood up. 'Let's talk about it tomorrow.'

Next morning, Nick left early, as usual. The stack of leaflets looked untouched.

Lisa's text was a welcome diversion:

The brochure outline looks great. Well done. I'm going to visit the charity ball venue this afternoon. Would you like to come along?

I tapped out a reply: *I'd love to. Where is it?*

Meet me in Bosco Café in Red Square at 2?

I gazed up at the incredible façade of the massive GUM building as I walked across Red Square with the Kremlin to my back. The green-tiled roofs and fairy-tale styled towers made it look more like a castle than a retail emporium. Bosco Café was towards the St Basil's end and Lisa's red hair made her easy to spot.

She stood to hug me. 'Welcome back. It's great to see you,' she said. 'How's your mum doing?'

'She's okay. Granny had been ill for a long time.'

'And what about you? I can't believe you found time to put the brochure together.'

I opened my mouth to say I was fine, but the words got stuck. My eyes filled with tears.

Lisa put her arm around my shoulders. 'I'm so sorry. Were you very close?'

'Yes, but the Granny who knew me had been gone a long time. It's just I stayed on to see a gynaecologist in Edinburgh and...' I scrambled to find a tissue in my bag.

146

'Do you want to talk about it?'

I took a deep breath and nodded. 'I only got as far as doing blood tests. My fertility is low, but that's hardly a surprise. But it's Nick's reaction,' I paused, struggling to be truthful but not judgemental. 'He seemed so shocked. I don't think he had really understood how likely this was.'

Lisa nodded, but left the silence for me to fill.

'I'm ready to discuss fertility treatment, but I sense Nick's not.'

Lisa made a wry face. 'Dmitry was the same. He'd had a baby easily with his first wife, he assumed it would be straightforward. Would you like me to make an appointment with the fertility clinic I used? A consultation doesn't commit you to anything. I'll come with you if you like.'

'Would you? I'd really appreciate it. I'm still rubbish at getting around Moscow and just in case there are any language problems.'

'Dr Smirnova's English is fluent, but I'm happy to come as moral support. Nick will get his head around it soon, then you'll have all the information to discuss the next steps.'

Lisa got out her phone and made a call. After a friendly exchange in Russian, she looked up at me. 'Is Friday afternoon any good? I can work from home that day and take a few hours off.' I nodded. 'It's fixed for two-thirty,' she told me after she'd ended the call. She looked at her watch. 'The GUM event manager is expecting us in ten minutes.'

'The venue is in here?'

'Yes. Upstairs. They have a lovely ballroom and a gallery we can use for hanging the paintings.'

We walked through the café, past the grand piano, and into the shopping centre. I stopped to stare up at the galleried floors above, topped by the curved glass ceiling. The shopfronts were housed in repeating arches of pale stone.

'I hadn't appreciated quite how grand this is. I visited once before but the crowds and the designer shops put me off.'

'There are designer shops, but they sell all sorts of other things. When I first came to Moscow, this building was practically empty and becoming derelict. It's just luck that Stalin didn't tear it down. GUM has huge history, built at the end of the nineteenth century and on the site of the old market used by the original Tsars. Wait till you see this function room. It's brilliant.' Lisa got a large metal tape measure out of her handbag. 'I want to work out how many exhibition boards I need to hire. We can't drive nails into the walls, of course. The boards need to be the optimum size to take all the paintings without spoiling the beautiful ambience of the gallery.'

I found myself striding along in Lisa's glamorous wake, grateful for her kindness, and for sweeping me up in her busy project.

The following Friday afternoon, I jumped into the back of the waiting Mercedes. Lisa smiled, but looked strained. Her phone beeped, and she frowned at the screen.

'Is everything alright?' I asked. 'I can easily go to this appointment on my own if you're busy.'

Lisa dropped her phone in her bag. 'Sorry, just problems at home and to be honest, I'm glad to be out of the house.' She screwed up her face. 'Vadim has come to us a day early this weekend. He's upset about an argument with his mum.'

'Are you sure you don't need to be at home with him?'

'Dmitry is there, and I try not to get involved. Honestly, I have some sympathy with his mother. She dumped her useless partner and is dating again, while Vadim is full of fifteen-year-old hormones. He doesn't want a new man in the house, which is kind of understandable.'

We travelled into a part of Moscow I'd never been to before. I was glad I hadn't tried to find it on my own.

'Did you talk to Nick about coming?'

'No,' I admitted with a grimace. 'He's been working such long hours this week. I thought it better to do this first. I want to get a clear idea about the costs.'

'Dr Smirnova's first appointment is deliberately priced very fairly and she'll give you a full price list. And if you don't warm to her, I'll help you find someone else.'

We stopped outside a multi-storey building. 'The clinic is in here.'

Lisa's phone rang again. 'I need to take this.'

'There's no need for you to come up. Which floor?'

Lisa held up four fingers.

I spent half an hour with Dr Smirnova. When I came back to the car, Lisa was still on the phone. She grimaced and rolled her eyes. I couldn't follow the Russian. It sounded like she was being very firm. Lisa had been nothing but kind and patient with me, but I didn't doubt she could be tough too.

She ended the call. 'Sorry, Anna. Office politics. Thank goodness it's Friday. How did your consultation with Katya go?'

'Really well. I liked her. Lots to think about,' I answered. 'I need to talk to Nick, and I'm not looking forward to that. She wants him to go in and have tests.'

Lisa nodded thoughtfully. 'The hormone injections are a huge faff, then if you do full IVF, it's pretty brutal. You both need to be committed.'

. . .

I delayed starting the conversation until we finished eating. I topped up Nick's wine and poured a small glass of my own to find the courage. 'I went to see Lisa's gynaecologist today.'

Nick's head snapped up. 'You didn't say you were going.'

'You've been so busy, and anyway if I hadn't gelled with her there would have been nothing new to say.' I took a deep breath. 'But I did like her and there's some stuff we need to discuss. Also, she'd like you to go in.'

'I would have thought my input is minimal. She doesn't want to supervise, does she?' He laughed.

I frowned. 'You have to provide a sample, of course. Did you not read the leaflets?' I glanced over at the stack of leaflets on the coffee table. The one about male infertility had definitely been moved to the top of the pile.

'I've been too busy this week,' he replied. 'Can't you take in a sample? I really don't think I could do the thing with dodgy magazines in a cubicle.'

I'd been dreading this conversation and Nick's flippant tone was making it worse. I swallowed my irritation. 'I don't know, I'll ask. But I think she will still want to meet you. If we decide to go ahead I'd have a scan first, then she'd take a cell sample. If everything looks good to go, she'd start monitoring my cycle and I'd have to do hormone injections at home. She said she'd teach us both how to do it.'

Nick screwed up his face. 'You know me and needles, Anna.'

I ached for him to put his arms around me. He didn't move. I searched his face for clues, for some empathy. Instead his hopeless expression filled me with dread. This was what I'd been afraid of.

Chapter Sixteen

November 1827, London

In anticipation of her confinement, Christina had worked every available daylight hour over the last three months. She'd finished all the eight miniatures intended for the Academy Exhibition next spring. Now the whole of one wall of their Argyll Street home was covered in small paintings laid out in a grid pattern.

'They look splendid hung together,' James said. 'I wish we could persuade the Royal Academy to always display them this way. Miniature portraits are so easily lost amongst the larger paintings.'

'I shall be more than happy if the Academy accepts all eight wherever they hang them.'

'Isn't it too long to wait until next summer? Ask the sitters if we may deliver, then borrow them back for the Academy Exhibition. That way you can invoice them this year.'

Christina looked questioningly at him. 'I already asked them if I might display them in our salons in the run up to the exhibition. In any case, most of them are destined for

Scotland. There is enough risk in the transportation, without attempting it twice.'

James shrugged. 'Never mind. The income would have been useful, but this work for Tom will bring money in.'

Christina had been astonished when James told her he would join Tom and Adam to help make and install wood panelling in Syon House. It was the kind of time-consuming and most likely dull project he'd previously abhorred.

'Is there some extra problem in our finances that makes you so suddenly keen on joinery, James?'

'The usual bills, nothing to worry about,' he replied.

In the afternoon, they took the children to watch the Thames section of the Lord Mayor's procession. They managed to find a spot on the Embankment between the old and new London Bridges. The incomplete new London Bridge was adorned with huge flags, and there were men and boys swarming all over the arches, which would soon carry a new road spanning the Thames. James hoisted Agnes on his shoulders. She let out a shout of 'hooray' and waved the tiny flag they'd bought her. The people around them echoed her cry. When the Mayor's barge passed under the bridge, everyone cheered.

It took them more than an hour to find a carriage home. By the time they reached their front door, both children were asleep. As Christina passed Agnes out to James, a man came up behind him, wearing that familiar cap. He suddenly seized James's shoulder, causing him to stagger, and Agnes cried out.

'What in God's name?' James swung around. 'Get away from me,' he growled under his breath.

'So sorry to disturb this lovely family scene, but you missed our appointment, sir. It's lucky I saw you,' the man said.

James glowered at him and lowered his voice to a whisper. 'Not here, for God's sake.' Then in loud tones, 'Unhand me, sir. Whomever you seek, I am not your man.' Agnes whimpered again.

The man smirked, then had the audacity to place his fingers on Agnes's arm. 'Fear not, young lady, your father will keep you safe.' With a glare at James, he walked away.

Christina exchanged a look with James. Guilt was all over his face. He hurried inside with Agnes but she stayed to watch the man disappear around the corner.

When Christina went inside, James was standing in the hallway, reading a letter. She knew from his expression that it was bad news. 'What's wrong?'

'The Duke has delayed the work for a week. Tom and Adam won't come tomorrow.'

A week's delay should not have been a huge issue, but his jaw was clenched. Whatever the problem, she must get to the bottom of it today.

Christina stayed with the children until they were fed and in bed. Eliza went to her own room, and Christina carried their dinner tray up. She set their plates down and placed her accounts book on the table between them. 'Let's eat, then you are going to tell me the truth.' Her tone was deliberately even. Necessary if she was to get the truth out of him.

James refilled his claret glass. He spoke without looking at her. 'That man is a debt collector. I missed a payment and without money from Tom tomorrow I will have to miss another.'

'Why are we in debt? My ledger indicates a small surplus in our accounts.'

James stared at the ceiling. 'I exceeded the amount allocated for my living costs when you were in Scotland. I spent the money we had set aside for the deposit on this place, and lacking the funds, I went to a moneylender.'

The thought of such a debt made Christina feel cold. She'd lived in poverty throughout her childhood, but her aunt had never resorted to borrowing money. She'd seen the consequences of a debt with interest. Witnessed the families flung from their houses and their goods loaded on carts bound for auction. 'You should never have signed for a rent we couldn't afford,' she said. 'And why in God's name have we been running salons when we are in debt?'

James clenched his fists on the table. 'Our best hope of better income is high society commissions from the salons. Your commissions this year exceed the amount I borrowed. I could have paid the interest with the money from Tom, then when we deliver the miniatures, I can settle the whole amount.'

'Paying off interest is a fool's game, James. I'll contact all my sitters tomorrow, and tell them I'll send their portraits now, then you must settle with that vile man.'

James's expression was miserable. 'But you will have nothing to exhibit next May.'

'I still have four months. I'll just have to find more commissions,' she replied.

Later, Christina got into bed.

James lay on his side facing away from her. 'I'm sorry,' he said.

She put her hand on his shoulder. 'Why didn't you tell me?'

James rolled over to look at her. 'After Will died, and you went to Edinburgh, my state of mind was not much better than yours. I was overwhelmed with hopelessness and couldn't sleep. I took refuge in drink and the company of friends.'

'You should have said,' Christina whispered.

'The last thing you needed was to worry about me. I couldn't bear to be alone and living in George's house underlined how little I'd achieved compared to him.'

'That's nonsense. George is over fifty and has no children. He has had time to build his fortune.'

'That's the point. I'm over thirty with a family. I couldn't protect Christiana and Will. I felt a failure.'

'I know how it felt, James. I felt it too. I still do.'

He turned his anguished face towards her. 'I'm sorry,' he said again.

'The children are robust and we have the means to pay off the debt. But please, James, promise me there will be no more secrets.'

James nodded.

Christina woke early. James was already up and dressed. She watched him use his candle to melt some sealing wax over a letter. When he turned and saw she was awake, he walked over to kiss her. 'I've been up for ages and I've been thinking. We must do a salon this week before we distribute the miniatures. The collection looks so wonderful, it's a waste of an opportunity if we don't.'

'I don't know,' she replied. 'What about the expense?'

'It's an investment. It's my fault we can't keep them up all winter for people to see at their leisure. Let me assemble the crowd you deserve.' He held up an envelope. 'I'm going to catch the mail stage. I've written to Tom to ask if he and Adam can be here for Saturday. They will want to see what you've achieved.'

'It would be nice to see them,' she replied, warming to the idea, though not fully convinced.

'I've asked Tom to bring my share of the Duke's deposit, so I can pay for the catering.' At that, he crammed his hat on his head and clattered down the stairs.

Christina wrote to all her sitters at the beginning of the week. She'd known, even as she made her pronouncement that she'd deliver all her Academy miniatures early, to clear James's debt, that it wouldn't be that simple. These conversations were delicate. The two ladies who lived in London were delighted to take early delivery and promised to make immediate payment. Even in the best marriages, most women understood the awkwardness of being reliant on their husbands for money. As for the others, she had turned to Uncle George for help.

She was at her easel on the day of the salon when George came in. He kissed her cheek and placed a pouch of money on a side-table. 'Your sitters all paid up, to a man.'

'Thank you. I hope it wasn't awkward.'

'No, although since James caused the problem, you could have made him sort it out.'

'You are right, but he's embarrassed, and I knew you would handle it better. It's not about sparing his feelings, but that he simply hasn't your tact.'

George shrugged. 'I've known most of them since they were boys. My age has damaged my knees but earned me a level of respect.' He patted the couch. 'Sit down, Christina. You look tired.'

She laid down her brush and picked up a rag to wipe her hands. Sinking onto the couch beside her uncle, she tucked her feet under her skirts to hide her swollen ankles. 'I'm fine, but I need to go and get changed soon.' She picked up the bag of coins. The weight was a pleasant surprise. 'You really managed to collect from them all?'

'Yes. It's lucky that the Lords have been in Session this week, so all your Scottish gentlemen were in town. I got payment and a promise from three of them to attend the unveiling at the salon tonight. Even the plainest of men likes the idea of his face being admired by his friends.'

'Good news. James has worked tirelessly and we expect at least fifty people. Lord and Lady Rolle are amongst them. I plan to ask her if I can come down to Devon to do her miniature next month.'

George nodded. 'I came across him on the steps of Whites, and he mentioned it.'

'Is Lord Rolle a gambler?'

'I don't think so, but Whites keep an excellent cellar. If James's interest in Watier's was for the quality of their claret, the debt would have been less.'

'Watier's?' Christina asked.

George reddened. 'I thought... Well, my footman told me... I expect he was mistaken...' he blustered.

Christina knew of Watier's. It was a notorious gaming club. James had not been truthful with her. 'Don't give it another thought, Uncle, and I fear your footman was correct.'

James had gone to meet Tom and Adam off the coach. An hour before the salon was due to start, Christina heard the outside door bang.

'Sorry I'm late. The coach was delayed. I left a note telling them to make their own way here. I'll just go and change.'

Christina grabbed his sleeve to prevent him rushing past her. 'It's good they are delayed because I must talk to you before the guests arrive.'

He looked perplexed, a flicker of anxiety in his eyes.

'You have a debt at Watier's in addition to what you owe to that money lender.'

The deflating of his posture gave Christina the answer.

'I daren't tell you. I don't know what got into me.'

'Did you imagine the debt would go away?'

'I haven't been there since January and I left no forwarding address.'

His childlike posture and eyes directed at the floor enraged her. 'Gambling is for fools, James. When did I become married to a fool?'

He raised his head. 'Cribbage is a game of skill, not just chance. I'm good at it.'

'So good that you accrued a debt that wiped out our savings?'

'I was set against a man I'd beaten before. I was certain I could win. When he beat me by the narrowest of margins, he offered me double or quits.'

Christina clenched her fists in rage. 'How much, James?'

His audible swallow gave her a second's warning of the magnitude. 'Five hundred guineas.'

So much larger than she'd feared. She gasped.

James gave her a guilt-ridden glance. 'I must get ready.'

She followed him to their bedroom. There was only one answer. 'You'd better hope that Lord Rolle is still enamoured with his young wife. When he comes, you will offer the portraits of Sarah that she covets but tell him only on the condition that he pays before the end of this fortnight and the price is five hundred guineas. I will paint her miniature portrait as part of the deal. Don't fail me in this, James.'

The salon was obviously going well, but Christina couldn't bring herself to mingle. Sarah's portraits were on the edge of her vision, but she didn't turn to look at them. She couldn't trust herself not to cry. Christina was sad to lose their owner-ship, but more than anything, she was terrified for her family's future. Gamblers' wives ended up on the streets, their children in the workhouse.

In the course of the evening, James brought over two different MPs' wives who'd been persuaded to commission a portrait. The guests had begun to drift away when Lord Rolle came over and bowed.

'Thank you,' he said, sitting beside her and lowering his voice to a whisper. 'Louisa's birthday is at the beginning of next month. If you can bring the portraits to Devon without her knowledge, I will tell her the miniature sitting is my gift, then surprise her with your beautiful paintings. She truly will appreciate them, I promise.'

'I'm sad to part with them, but very glad they will go to your home,' she replied.

The sound of James greeting Tom and Adam downstairs caused a tiny lift in Christina's spirits. Adam and Tom came in. Their smiles turned mischievous as they deliberately stood apart. There in the doorway, like a joyous apparition, stood Sarah.

'Oh, thank God,' Christina whispered.

Chapter Seventeen

December 2017, Moscow

Lisa was scowling at her laptop screen. It turned out that organising the paintings in the brochure was the simple job. Now she was trying to make the groupings work in the mock-up for the display board layout. In theory, the seventy paintings would fit onto the twelve display panels Lisa had booked, but in practice the varying sizes made it nigh on impossible.

'How many paintings do we have that are over a metre in height or width?' she asked.

I picked up the draft brochure to do a tally. 'Six.'

Lisa broke into a smile. 'Then I have a solution. I'll borrow some easels and display the largest paintings in the entrance area.'

'That's a brilliant idea. Will giving some paintings more prominence cause problems with the artists? Two of the big ones are by the same guy.'

'Probably,' she said. 'But you can't please everyone. My primary concern is to raise as much money as possible and that's in the artists' interests too.'

'Then leave the rest of the planning for me to finish. With

six fewer paintings, I'm sure I can manage it. I'll send it to you to approve tomorrow.'

'Thanks,' Lisa said. She stood up and stretched. 'I'm going to make some tea before Dmitry brings the kids back from swimming lessons. Will you join me or do you have to get home?'

'Nick is working late, so I'm not in a hurry. I'd love tea.' I followed her through to the kitchen.

'Did you discuss your appointment with Dr Smirnova?'

'Yes. We agreed we'd try one more cycle on our own, using the ovulation predictors. If it doesn't work this time, then we're supposed to start with hormone injections through the clinic.'

'Do I sense a but?' she asked and gestured for me to sit down at the kitchen table.

I pulled a face.

'The whole thing is a mess. After years of being mad keen on starting a family, I sense Nick is stalling. He's being awkward about giving the clinic a sperm sample, and I can't get him to commit to an appointment to talk to Dr Smirnova about the hormone injections.'

'Perhaps it's just that he's realised his fertility is under the spotlight too?'

'Maybe. I hope he'll get his head around it soon.' I looked at my watch. It was gone six. 'I'm going to head home now. Is there anything more I can do for the auction?'

'Thanks, but we're on track this week. Our next task is assembling the artwork. One of our distributors is lending me a secure warehouse from the beginning of next week. You might help me by picking up some of the paintings from the artists?'

'No problem. I'll send you the exhibition plan tomorrow.'

. . .

Next day, I submitted the painting layout to Lisa, then turned my attention back to Christina Robertson. The research was totally absorbing and blocked out my unease about Nick. Christina had exhibited at the Royal Academy every year and very often they accepted eight portraits, the maximum allowed. She showed one large painting in her first exhibition in 1823, but then only miniatures for years. I spent ages searching digital archives for images of the portraits, trying to get a sense of her evolving style. Most of the listed paintings had disappeared without trace, but I managed to find at least one from every year. Many of these came from a publication called *La Belle Assemblée*, which had commissioned portrait engravings of high society ladies. It seemed like it was a sort of nineteenth century version of *Hello*. Clearly, celebrity culture wasn't a new phenomenon. I began to recognise Christina's style. The women were posed in a similar way, depicting head and shoulders, and their expressions were thoughtful and characterful.

Then, I found an extraordinary image from the 1834 exhibition that was completely different. This full-length portrait of a young woman wearing a red, ermine-edged cloak and looking back over her shoulder had at one time been attributed to Sir Thomas Lawrence, but the British Museum said it was by Christina. The Museum described Lady Louisa Barbara Rolle as being posed on the steps of Westminster Abbey. I felt sure that I'd seen a similar painting amongst Christina's Russian portraits. Inside my now bulging file of images, I found the image I'd remembered. Empress Alexandra was facing a parade of mounted soldiers, but looking back at the viewer over her shoulder. Both the pose and the style of the painting were similar to the 1834 painting, and surely the work of the same person. Did Lady Rolle's painting mark a significant moment for Christina's art?

My phone alerted me to a text message from Mandy and my heart skipped. Was this the answer I'd been waiting for?

Great news – you've got your book deal! AND I've been talking to Esme Stevenson from the Scottish National Portrait Gallery. They are already planning an exhibition focusing on nineteenth century Scottish artists and they are VERY excited to extend it to include Christina Robertson. I've sent you an email with all the details.

I squealed with joy and rang Nick. My call went straight into voicemail, so I left a message. Next I tried Lisa's phone. She picked up.

'I'm so sorry to disturb you at work, but I'm desperate to tell someone. I just heard that I have a publisher for my Christina book!'

'That's fantastic news. Congratulations.'

'Even better, there's going to be a tie-in with an exhibition. Mandy, my friend at the publisher, has been talking to the Portrait Gallery in Edinburgh. She showed them my pitch about Christina's life and they're going to include her work in an exhibition of Scottish artists.'

'That's marvellous. The exhibition will bring you readers. I'm so pleased for you. Do you have a deadline?'

'About a year to finalise the book, although the exhibition isn't until the year after. Mandy is going to set up a phone conversation with the museum curator, but they've asked me to meet with someone based here in Russia. A guy called Pavel Sidorov is cooperating with them over lending art from the Hermitage, and the Scottish curator wants me to discuss the possibility of including some of Christina's work.'

'So are you going back to St Petersburg for the meeting?'

'No. I do need to go back at some stage, but Sidorov happens to be coming to Moscow next week, so I'll meet him here.'

'I'll ask Dmitry if he knows him.'

'That would be useful. Thank you.'

'Brill. Congratulations again, I'm so pleased for you.'

I allowed the elation to sink in. This changed everything. My work on Christina wasn't just some personal project to keep me busy. I had a new profession. I was an author. Joy flooded through my chest. I reached out to touch the brass corners of Christina's writing slope. I'd bought a remote keyboard so I could sit my laptop up on the old desk. The direct link back to Christina was inspiring. I ran my fingertips over the faded pink leather and imagined her writing letters home. The many years of separation from her family must have been difficult. I found it hard being apart from Mum, and Christina had apparently travelled without her husband and children.

'I'll make sure people remember your extraordinary life and I believe you might have saved mine,' I whispered.

My sense of self-worth had been dented, but the next time I met someone new, I wouldn't have to resort to describing myself as Nick's wife. I was a writer working on a book about Christina Robertson, a Scottish painter who lived and worked in St Petersburg. Granny would have been so proud.

When Nick came in, he had a bottle of champagne in his hand. 'I got your message. It's great news, Anna,' he said and hugged me.

'Thank you, I can hardly believe it.'

'Will you allow yourself a glass?' he asked.

'My period came this morning, so I can have several,' I answered.

He grimaced. 'Are you okay?'

'It's fine. I knew I was in Scotland at the critical time.'

He popped the champagne cork and poured two glasses. 'To Anna Robertson Jenkins, famous author.'

I took a deep breath and raised my glass. 'Mandy and I talked about my author name. Would you be very offended if I used Grieve instead of Jenkins?' It's been my name for over thirty years and Mandy thought it sounded better.'

'Whatever you prefer,' he replied, although I could tell he was a bit hurt.

We sat together on the couch, and I leaned into him.

'It's a sign that our luck is turning,' I whispered. 'Dr Smirnova will help us realise our other dream and baby Ivan will be a Jenkins.'

Nick kissed me. 'I'm sure you'll have a little girl. What will we name her? I don't fancy Ivana. What were Tsarina Alexandra's daughters called?'

'Maria, Olga and Alexandra.'

'Maria then.'

'To Maria Robertson Jenkins,' I raised my glass again.

Chapter Eighteen

January 1828, London

Christina gave birth to a little girl on the last day of January, a whole month before her due date. When her waters broke and she went into early labour, she expected the child wouldn't live. The tiny, doll-like creature breathing in her arms was like a visit from an angel. She told James they would name her Christina.

He answered her, wild-eyed. 'I thought you considered it unlucky.'

She held up her index finger encircled by a tiny hand. 'She's here as a messenger from Tiana. She will take back both my name and my love.'

Little Christina hung on. She breathed like a bird and suckled like a mouse. Having accepted this baby's fate, Christina was calm. She kissed the sleeping infant. 'I'm so glad to see your face again,' she whispered.

Christina refused to be parted from her and slept only in snatches. James paced and fretted until she had to banish him from the bedroom. 'I want her never to experience anxiety, to know only joy, warmth and love. We can give her at least that.'

Sarah came into the bedroom quietly, without a fuss. She brought a basin of warm water and broth in a cup. 'James says you are preparing to lose her. Do me the honour of letting me hold her for a few minutes. I'll clean her up while you eat.' Sarah took the baby from her arms and crooned to her, while she wiped her clean with warm water and changed her tiny gown. When Christina took the child back, the scent of lavender drifted up from her blanket. She buried her head in the baby's sweet warmth and inhaled.

'A few dried flower buds near her skin. Lavender is the hardest working herb. It signifies love and wards off evil. This child is so calm, you can tell she knows she is blessed,' Sarah whispered.

The next day they braved the short journey to the church to have the infant baptised. Assured of her route back to her siblings, the baby took her leave of them that evening. Sarah and Christina wept silently, while James's sobs seemed to rock the house.

Two weeks later, she embraced James on the quayside. Sarah and Eliza carried John and Andrew aboard. Agnes insisted on walking down the gangplank. Uncle George only agreed on the promise that she'd take the captain's hand whilst he followed behind. George had brought forward their booking in Edinburgh. This time away from James had been planned. Christina was still weak from the birth, so the rest was necessary, but she'd expected to head north nursing a baby. That thought gave her a sharp pang of grief.

'Look after yourself. Write often,' James said.

'I will and I won't pressurise you to do the same. Only

stick to your promise of no gambling. Now you've managed a year, you've proved you can do it.'

'I promise.'

'If I hear to the contrary, I won't return, James.'

He nodded.

They stayed up in Scotland for six months, after the baby's death. It took until May in the following year for Christina's interest in life to return. Now her consciousness had emerged from under the blanket of grief, something new was stirring.

Christina walked through the main galleries of the Royal Academy Exhibition alone. She and James had already attended during the opening week to witness the exhibition of her eight miniatures. It was a proud moment after the previous year's disaster, when she'd not even stayed in London to visit the exhibition. Those portraits painted after clearing James's debt, lacked spirit. Today she'd come to examine the large works of art in the first few rooms of the exhibition. She loved Turner's use of light in his depiction of the Loire, but she was here to concentrate on those paintings featuring people. Christina was studying the expressions of the many characters in David Wilkie's war council painting when she heard her name called.

'Christina, is that you?' David Roberts walked quickly towards her and took her hand in both of his. 'I'm so pleased to see you. I had heard you were back in London. Welcome home.'

'I've been home since last autumn, but James and I have been living a quieter life this year.'

'I'm so sorry for your loss,' Roberts said. 'Such a terrible thing, to carry a child for all those months then have no resulting joy.'

'She arrived too early to survive this world, but little

Christina tarried long enough to bring me immense joy. I'm very glad to have had time with her.'

Roberts turned his top hat brim in his hands. 'I don't know how you ladies cope with what you have to go through.'

Having no good answer to give him, Christina held her peace and looked up at the paintings again.

'What do you think of Lawrence's Duke of Clarence?' David asked, gesturing to the huge painting beside Wilkie's.

'I find it very sombre,' Christina admitted. The King's brother was dressed from head to toe, completely in black. Only his own high colour and the ribbon holding the Star of the Garter gave red highlights.

'Did you hear that the Duke paid six hundred guineas for it?'

'I did,' Christina replied. Her thoughts were mirrored in Roberts' raised eyebrows. 'We portraitists may name the price but sometimes have little influence on our sitters' choice of clothes,' she added. 'I am rather more taken with Wilkie's Spanish scene. I do admire his work.'

'I feel the same. David is a good friend and a mentor. His European paintings give me the urge to travel again.'

'I would love to visit the Continent. That's what occurred to me when I was admiring Turner's French scene,' Christina said.

'I thoroughly recommend European travel for inspiration and I'm sure you'd find lots of clients in Paris. I'm going again next month.'

'Might you keep your ears open for any openings for a society portraitist?'

'Of course. I'm going directly to Scotland from France, so I'll write to you if I have any news.'

'How long since you were in Edinburgh?'

'Several years. Much too long. Also, I've been able to help

my parents move to a better house, so I'm anxious to see them settled.'

'I'm sure Margaret will be pleased to go home too,' Christina commented.

'Margaret is not well enough to travel,' he replied, keeping his gaze on the paintings. 'My sister has taken young Christine to Edinburgh and I'll join her there. She is quite the young lady now and my parents were eager to see her.'

'Did your friend, William Shiels, tell you he visited me in Edinburgh?' Christina asked, skirting around the delicate subject of Roberts' wife. The thought of Margaret caused a pang of guilt, for Christina had intended to visit her. Work, bereavement, and then being away were good excuses, but she knew she was also reluctant to get involved.

David gave her a small smile. 'He did, and I hope you will excuse him for sharing your good news. The first woman to be given an honorary fellowship of the Scottish Academy, you should be delighted. I certainly was when I received mine.'

'Will you forgive my vanity if I admit it means a great deal?' Christina replied. 'I left Scotland without a penny, or much hope for my future, and now I am named amongst the great and good.'

'I never find you vain, quite the opposite,' David replied. 'Have you sent Shiels some paintings to hang?'

'Yes. I persuaded four of my clients to lend their portraits.'

'That's what I admire about you, Christina. We men follow some muse on a flight of fancy, then have to hope someone will buy the resulting painting. Whilst you work to commission. It's a much safer practice.'

'It's nothing to do with being a woman. It's simply that I cannot afford to work for free. Every penny of my income is accounted for to fund the family. We couldn't even spare the expense of James's precious salons this year.'

'I do sometimes wonder if marriage and family are a luxury that we artists would be better to forego,' David said quietly. 'I adore little Christine, but I'm afraid that I'm poor company for Margaret. Painting is an obsession, and when I'm gripped by my work, all thoughts of others disappear.'

'I rarely enjoy that luxury,' Christina replied.

'I'm sorry to hear that. Do you ever feel the urge to paint something on a bigger scale? Those large paintings of your relative were a revelation.'

'All the time,' Christina replied. Then, before Roberts could reply, she added: 'You will have to excuse me now, David. I left the children in the garden and I promised I would meet them on the far terrace at four.'

'Of course. I'll walk with you if I may,' he said, putting his hat on. 'I can catch a boat at the steps. It's the easiest way to get home to Lambeth.'

They walked together down the path that separated the two expanses of grass in the grounds of Somerset House. Dozens of boats plied the Thames beyond the boundary wall. Walking by the river, Sarah turned when one of the children by her side started to run up the path towards them.

'Mama!' Agnes shouted.

'Not too fast, Agnes. Be careful!' Sarah called after her.

'It's the lady from the paintings,' David said.

'Yes,' Christina replied. 'We spent so many months in Uncle George's company again last year, and he became fond of Sarah. When his housekeeper left him, he offered the post to Sarah, and she moved down here with her son.'

'I thought you would say that George asked her to marry him.'

Christina laughed out loud at the thought. 'Uncle George is not the marrying kind,' she said.

'Perhaps that confirms my point about artists,' David added. Christina just smiled.

Agnes arrived beside them, and Christina took her hand. 'Agnes, do you remember Mr Roberts? You met his daughter on that day when you both got wet at a garden party.' Agnes looked up, clearly not remembering. However, when Christina squeezed her fingers, she took the hint to bob a curtsey, causing David Roberts to laugh.

'Delighted to meet you again, Miss Agnes.'

Sarah continued up the path towards them. As usual, Christina's son John was hand-in-hand with Sarah's Andrew. The two had become inseparable.

'It's a shame you never exhibited those paintings of your friend,' David said.

'That's exactly what I've been thinking. I'm meeting Lady Rolle next month in London. We got on very well when I did her miniature last year. I believe I can persuade her to lend Sarah's portraits to the Academy. Since I've already admitted to my vanity, I must confess to ambition too. I mean the world to know I can paint on the same scale as Sir Thomas Lawrence.'

'Bravo, Christina. You can, and I applaud your ambition.'

Christina introduced Sarah when she and the boys reached them.

Shortly afterwards, David excused himself. 'It was very nice to see you again. I shall be sure to view your paintings at the Scottish Academy Exhibition.'

They accompanied Roberts down to the Thames to watch him clamber in a small boat. Roberts raised his hat in farewell and shouted, 'Goodbye, Miss Agnes!' The oarsman pulled the boat out into the fast-running current and soon they sped downstream, while the man pulled hard on his oars to direct them towards the far bank.

'I'd certainly prefer a bumpy carriage ride over Waterloo Bridge, rather than risk my life in such a boat,' Sarah said.

'Are you afraid of the water?' Christina asked her, as they

linked arms and made their way back through the Academy gardens towards the Strand.

'I cannot swim,' Sarah replied.

'I learnt to swim as a child, although I'm sure it would be no help if I ended up fully clothed in the Thames.'

Sarah gazed across the water. 'I'd like to see the seaside village where you grew up.'

'You should have said when we were in Edinburgh, but you'd have to tolerate a boat from Leith to reach Kinghorn. We might take Agnes and John to teach them to swim. Kinghorn's sandy, shallow bay makes it an ideal place to learn. Although, I believe people also swim at Portobello. We could try there if we get nice weather on our next visit.'

'I coped with the ship from here last year, but let's try Portobello. It certainly sounds grand and I know passing through Leith makes you nervous.'

'Is it that obvious?' Christina replied.

'Why don't you like the place?' Sarah asked.

The children had run ahead. It was the time to tell Sarah her story. 'My estranged father lives there,' she explained.

Sarah stopped dead. 'What? I thought your aunt brought you up because you were orphaned?'

'I believed that when I was younger. My mother died in childbirth with my baby brother when I was four. She had asked George to take me to my Kinghorn relatives because she'd discovered that my father had another family with a woman called Isobel. She didn't trust him to care for me.' Christina stopped and turned back towards the river, so the children wouldn't see her tears.

'How appalling! And is he still alive?'

Christina sniffed and nodded. 'So far as I know. I saw him first when my cousin showed him to me when I was twelve. Robbie told me I was rejected by my father in favour of his other family. The second time was with my half-sister when George and I travelled through Leith to visit Aunt Jean.'

'Did you speak to him?'

'No. I resolved then to never think of him again.'

Sarah squeezed her hand. 'I am so very sorry. You must keep to your resolve.'

'It's a shame the boat from London lands us in Leith. I'd prefer to avoid a chance encounter. Although of course he wouldn't know me.'

Will you go to Edinburgh again next year?' Sarah asked.

'I haven't decided. This business of sleeping in Agnes's room cannot go on forever. James has kept to his resolve of staying debt free. It's time I became a proper wife to him again. I just hope I don't fall pregnant immediately. Our finances are recovering and I have a plan to entice some sitters for large paintings. It takes more time but I can ask for a much bigger fee. It's a shame you have no potion to keep pregnancies at bay.' Christina hailed a carriage and instructed the man to take them to Argyll Street.

'If I had a reliable recipe for such a thing, we could buy our own carriage and a grand house on Trafalgar Square,' Sarah replied with a laugh.

'I need your permission for part of my plan,' Christina said. 'I mean to ask Lady Rolle if I may borrow your paintings to show next year. How would you feel about being on the walls of the Royal Academy?'

'If you think they would win you more business, then I would be honoured.'

The coach pulled up outside their door. 'Shall I ask the driver to take you home?' Christina asked.

'No. I'll come in with you. I want to say goodbye to Eliza.'

'What time is your stage tomorrow?'

'First thing. George expects Angus, his friend from his apprenticeship days, to arrive from Edinburgh in the afternoon. It's outrageous that he couldn't have his friend sleep under his own roof when Mrs Anderton was his housekeeper. I thought he might cry when I told him that the gentleman's visit coincided with my promised trip to my mother.'

'Don't mention Angus's visit in James's presence. I'm afraid he fails to acknowledge the importance of their friendship.'

'I'm sorry to say that James is a fool, but then, so are most men. George has rescued me as he rescued you. He should be lauded as a hero, rather than sniggered at because of his choice of companions.'

'I think in James's case, it's misplaced jealousy. He knows I will always adore George, which causes James to want to disagree with him. Several of the young men in James's group of artistic friends are recklessly indiscreet about their preferences and he pretends not to notice.'

They found Eliza darning in the sitting room. 'Don't get up, Eliza,' Sarah said. 'I just came to say that I'll see you next week. I'm off to Alnwick tomorrow.'

'Give my regards to your mother and sister,' Eliza answered.

Sarah adjusted her bonnet in the mirror and pulled on her gloves before giving Christina a hug.

'Tell Uncle George to let me know if he needs anything in your absence.'

'I'll tell him and I'll see you next week,' Sarah replied.

'Could I ask you to take some flowers to Will's grave when you are in Alnwick? I hate that he isn't here with his sisters.'

'Of course, but you know I made sure he would never want for flowers. I planted both snowdrops and primroses, then lavender to see him through the rest of the year.'

'Thank you, that was such a kind thought. I think we

might come up this summer, since we aren't going to Edinburgh.'

'Then I'll make some enquiries about houses with enough light for painting. The place Tom reserved for you last time was hopeless.'

Christina walked to the door with them, bending down to give Andrew a goodbye kiss.

'Good luck with Lady Rolle. I'm sure she will agree to the exhibition and if not, you'll just have to paint two more,' Sarah said.

Chapter Nineteen

December 2017, Moscow

Walking from the metro station to the café, I felt both ten feet tall and absolutely terrified. I'd interviewed all sorts of people as a journalist; it was a part of the job I'd always loved. However, Pavel Sidorov was a curator from one of the world's most famous museums, an art historian and an expert. I had no relevant qualifications and no background in this. On the other hand, my editor had asked me to meet him and this gave me the right. I'd frequently interviewed experts for the paper. I'd just have to keep my nerve.

Entering the café, I channelled my inner Christina. She'd been a trailblazer, crossing continents to earn her living. I could surely handle a museum curator. Sidorov wasn't difficult to spot. I had done my internet stalking, so had an idea what he looked like. What I hadn't anticipated was his height. He stood up as I walked towards him, and I guessed he must be six-foot-five. His wavy chestnut-coloured hair curled down to his collar. When he held out his hand in greeting and smiled, his dark brown eyes exuded warmth. He had a firm hand-shake and his huge hand engulfed mine completely.

'Pleased to meet you, Mr Sidorov. I'm Anna Grieve.'

'Please, call me Pavel. Can I get you a coffee?'

He had a lovely deep voice and only a hint of an accent. I watched him walk over to the counter. His shirttail had become untucked from the waist of his chinos. Presumably a common annoyance for someone of his height. I'd chosen to wear a charcoal grey suit and white blouse, clothes I'd used to interview businessmen in London and I felt overdressed. He smiled when he spoke to the girl serving the coffee, and his words caused her to smile back. I decided this was a nice man.

He returned with two coffees. He took a sip. 'So how can I help you?'

'I'm not sure you've been told. I'm writing a book about the life of portraitist Christina Robertson. She lived and painted in St Petersburg from the 1840s until her death in 1854.' I moved my coffee cup to make room and opened my folder of images.

He laughed. 'I hope you're not going to test me on my knowledge of your artist. I'm afraid I'm no expert.'

'I don't think there are many experts, that's what's so fascinating, but your museum has the biggest collection of her work by a long way.'

'I heard from the Scottish Portrait Gallery that they've decided to include her in their exhibition.'

'That's the plan, but they have only one small painting. We've tracked down several portraits in English collections, but they're all from her early years.'

'So will you decide which portraits will be in the exhibition?'

'That's definitely not down to me. At this stage, I'm focusing on uncovering suitable images for my book. I'm hoping to find portraits to illustrate different stages of her life, including her later years. If my publishers approve my wish list, they will apply for reproduction permissions. Of course I'll want to include those that feature in the actual exhibition.'

'Do you have any idea what they want from the Hermitage? They've already made a request for a pair of William Allans. However, I'm afraid some of Christina Robertson's royal portraits are very large and too important to export.'

'Of course. I've seen Empress Alexandra and her daughters with the other Romanov portraits in the Hermitage. And no, those huge paintings aren't suitable for the exhibition. The event will feature the work of several artists, so there will be a strict limit on number and dimensions. However, I imagine they will want at least one of her later pieces. So far, I've found nothing in the UK from the last fifteen years of her life. It's all here in Russia.'

I flipped pages until I came to the Hermitage images, which I'd put together as a list of thumbnails. 'I'm planning to go back to St Petersburg next year to continue my research. Can you tell me which of these are on display?'

'Can I borrow your pen?' he asked. He marked two of the images with an asterisk. A portrait of Princesses Olga and Alexandra, and a painting of two children with a parrot. 'I'm afraid these two are the only ones currently on display, other than the royal portraits. However, I can arrange access for you to view anything from our archive, if you give me advance notice.'

'Thank you, I really appreciate it. Can I ask which of Sir William Allan's they've expressed an interest in? His name came up in my Christina research just yesterday.'

'They are a pair. *The Frontier Guards* and *The Bashkirs Escorting Prisoners*. Allan must have been an extraordinary man. He lived and travelled in Russia for years at the beginning of the nineteenth century. Nicholas I admired him and visited his studio in Edinburgh before he became Tsar.'

I stared at Pavel. 'He and Christina must surely have known each other.' I grabbed the file and flicked back to my notes around the painting of Lady Rolle. 'I believe 1834 was an important year for Christina. After years of exhibiting only miniatures at the Royal Academy she showed this larger portrait. You can guess the prestige from the other artists exhibited in the same room.' I ran my finger down the list. 'Turner, Landseer, and look here: *Polish Exiles conducted by Bashkirs on their way to Siberia*, by William Allan. This must be the same painting.'

'Maybe there were two paintings? My understanding was that Tsar Nicholas bought Allan's Hermitage paintings in Edinburgh.' He tilted the file to look more closely at Lady Rolle's portrait. 'William Allan might have introduced Christina to the royal family. He returned to St Petersburg for a final time in the 1840s.'

'Perhaps he did. Can I show you something else?' I reached over to flick through the file again. Realising that in my enthusiasm I'd snatched the folder back, I glanced up. He smiled. Was he laughing at me? I hoped not and ploughed on. 'I'm no art expert, but in my opinion, Lady Rolle's portrait is a departure in style as well as size. This particular pose of looking backwards is in many of her later paintings. Look at this.'

'Empress Alexandra. And yes, I do see what you mean. Have you viewed the painting?'

I screwed up my face in frustration. 'It seems it's actually here in the Pushkin Museum collection. I went yesterday, but didn't find it, and couldn't find anyone who spoke English to ask. In fact, their other two paintings are important too. This one of Princess Ivanovna was painted in Paris in 1837, then exhibited in the St Petersburg Academy in 1838. It was so admired, I think it was most likely this portrait that got her royal commissions.'

'We have a copy of the Tsarina in the red dress in St Petersburg. Perhaps the original is in storage? I know the curator at the Pushkin very well. Would you like me to call her and try to arrange a viewing?'

'Would you? I'd be so grateful.'

He sat back in his chair and gave me another amused look. 'I can see why your publisher commissioned you. Your enthusiasm is infectious.'

I groaned. 'Do you mean amateurish? I feel such a fraud, writing this book with zero knowledge of art history.'

'I disagree. I read academic art history works all the time. They generally have little appeal to the general public. Your publisher is very astute. I'm sure that a book weaving a story around this lady and her art will appeal to a wider audience.'

'God, I do hope so. I feel they are taking a massive gamble with me, and I don't want to let them down.'

'I can't see why you would. You seem to have found out a great deal already, and I'd be delighted to help you when you come to St Petersburg. Can I ask you what sparked your interest in this particular artist? I suppose you know she has fallen out of fashion.'

'Promise you won't laugh.'

He put his hand to his heart.

'I went to view the Hermitage portraits because I was christened Anna Robertson Grieve. My grandmother told me I was named Robertson after Christina, and that I'm a descendent.'

'Really? No wonder you're intrigued!'

'I'm still trying to prove the genetic link. I need to find out what happened to her children after she died.' I studied his face, trying to gauge his thoughts. He looked interested. His expression was warm. 'My grandmother died last month.

In part, this is a personal quest to honour her.' The last words caught in my throat. I coughed to try to disguise it, feeling an idiot for betraying my emotions when this was meant to be a business meeting.

Pavel's chin sunk towards his chest. When he looked at me, I was sure I could see emotion in his eyes. 'Then I am even more determined to help you. Grandmothers are very underrated. I lost my own last year. She lived well into her eighties, but I miss her terribly. It can be our secret, a very uncool but committed babushka appreciation society.'

We parted with an agreement that Pavel would try to arrange a viewing of Christina's Pushkin Collection portraits before he left Moscow. I was buzzing with enthusiasm, and Mandy sounded just as excited when I called her to update my progress.

December arrived and Moscow turned into a sparkly wonderland. Acres of blue and gold lights hung above the pedestrians, and now in the darkening late afternoon, the effect was beyond romantic. I was only disappointed there was still no snow. At least this made my task of gathering the paintings easier. Sergey, Lisa's driver, dropped me at the end of Old Arbat Street for my last pickup of the day. He already had four paintings in the back of the car, ready to be taken to the storage unit. Sergey was very apologetic that he couldn't take me to the door of this particular address because the road was pedestrianised, but I assured him I could easily carry the painting. Lisa had explained that this St Petersburg artist sometimes sold his art through a stall on Arbat Street, and he had an arrangement with an antiques shop owner to store his art over the winter.

I found the shop and asked for the painting in my stilted Russian. Thankfully, the owner's face beamed in recognition and he brought me the framed pen and ink sketch. I'd positioned it amongst our tourist orientated works of art in the catalogue, but seeing it face to face, this piece was obviously of very superior quality. It featured a bridge over one of the St Petersburg canals. I immediately wanted it for myself. If my advance from Mandy's company came through in time, perhaps I could afford to put in a bid?

I left the shop in high spirits. I'd picked up all the paintings as promised, and my conversation today with Esme Stevenson, the Scottish Portrait Gallery Curator, had been brilliant. She was pleased with my recounting of the meeting with Pavel, and I could tell from her voice that she shared my outrage that Christina was so overlooked. Dr Stevenson had discovered that the painting of Lady Rolle had been donated to a charity in Devon. She was very hopeful she'd be able to secure it for the exhibition. I smiled at the thought and breathed in a lungful of the chilly Moscow air. The drawing was an was an awkward size, slightly too large to fit comfortably under my arm. I shifted it from one side to the other.

Ahead of me a man and woman came out of a shop. A small brightly coloured bag swung from the man's fingers. Wait though. Was that... Oh my god, Nick? The blood drained towards my feet. As I took in his familiar coat and the swing of the woman's dark, shiny hair, her laughter drifted back towards me and hit me like a blow in my solar plexus, as he put his arm around her shoulder. The intimate gesture was so familiar, I could feel the indentation of his fingers on my own arm. I stood motionless, allowing the crowds to flow around and past me. No amount of wishing could help me deny what had just happened. Eventually I realised my gloveless fingers grasping the picture frame were numb with cold. I was in danger of dropping the precious brown paper parcel and Sergey would be getting worried. I forced myself to move.

Back at the car, I placed the drawing safely in the well behind the driver's seat.

'That's the last one for today, Sergey. I'll get the metro home. There's a shop here I want to visit.' In fact, going into the shop was the last thing I wanted to do, but I needed to know what they'd bought. Did that bag contain jewellery?

It turned out that the shop sold Russian lacquerware. On a different day, I might have found it charming, but today it was like entering a nightmare. I found myself surrounded by a sea of smiling, lurid faces. Matryoshka nesting dolls with huge blue eyes and tiny rosebud mouths. Dozens of Father Frosts, the Russian Santa Claus, stared at me with mocking eyes peering over long white beards. I took a step back and my arm brushed against a rotating stand of Christmas baubles, sending it into a whirl of giddy colours. Subduing panic, I walked deeper into the shop. Had Nick brought Oksana here to choose her Christmas gift? Surely, these items were aimed at the tourist market and would be unsuitable for a Moscow resident. Glass cases lined the walls, containing lacquered boxes in different shapes and sizes. The first case was filled with garish renditions of ballet dancers and cats, not Nick's taste at all.

A sales assistant appeared at my elbow. She addressed me in Russian, but my shocked brain was incapable of summoning a single word. She immediately switched to English. 'Can I help you? Are you looking for something in particular?'

'I want to buy a gift. A small box, perhaps?'

'Of course. We keep stock of all the best artists and they paint in different styles. Perhaps you might like the more traditional versions? Is it for someone special?'

'Yes,' I murmured, voicing my fears.

The woman led me up a few steps. 'Boxes in this section are from Fedoskino. It's one of the best schools and artists have been producing lacquerware there for two hundred years.' She unlocked the cabinet and handed me a box featuring an exquisitely painted winter sunset. I was surprised at the light weight. 'Is it made of wood?'

'Papier mâché,' she replied. 'These Palekh boxes are top quality, too. You might like the Pushkin fairy tales?' She led me to another cabinet, which held many boxes depicting old fashioned scenes. One box illustrated a man fighting a dragon, and another featured a girl with a swan. All were made of shiny black lacquerware with their edges decorated in intricate gold patterns.

'That one is beautiful.' I pointed to a small box. She passed it to me and I cradled it in my palm. More than just a box, this was a miniature work of art. A night-time scene of a girl in a sleigh, pulled by six horses. Surely painted employing the same skills as Christina had used.

'I have another similar at the till point. The previous customers took two boxes nearer the window to decide on their choice.'

I swallowed and hastily placed the box back on the shelf. The ticket revealed a price in roubles equivalent to more than three hundred pounds. My heart was still racing when the assistant came back from the till with another box, also a fairy-tale style scene, featuring a fur clad young woman. I reached to take it, then realised Oksana might have held this object. I clenched my fist and let my arm fall to my side. The assistant looked startled. 'Thank you. I'll come back when I have more time.' I turned on my heel and fled.

Chapter Twenty

January 1833, London

On the thirty-first of January, Christina put on her warmest clothes before braving the cold. She left the children in Eliza's care. Christina would have liked to take three-day-old Mary along to visit her sisters' graves as she had done with baby William two years previously, but she was forced to concede that it was too cold. Eliza didn't want her to go at all, but she knew Christina would never be dissuaded from visiting her children's graves on their birthdays. She had promised to lean on Sarah's arm. When they climbed into the carriage, Christina gritted her teeth to stop herself wincing. She hadn't told Eliza that she was still in pain from the birth.

Sarah had been at the delivery and was less easily fooled. As the carriage set off, she gave Christina a concerned look. When they got out in Paddington Street, she said: 'When we get home, I will make you a poultice and you must rest.' Sarah's words created a cloud of vapour in the cold air.

They crossed the narrow road and entered the seclusion of the Marylebone churchyard.

'If my babies were all as big and strong as William, I

would not have so many names on this gravestone,' Christina said.

'Damaged flesh doesn't stretch. That's why even little Mary caused you to tear again.'

'The truth is that since William's birth, the scarring has caused me pain every time I lie with James,' Christina confessed. 'Loving him used to give me so much joy, but I've come to dread it now.'

Sarah grimaced. 'It might be many weeks before you heal this time. You must explain to James that he cannot be admitted to your bed.'

'I haven't told him yet, but I am resolved that Mary will be our last child. Our livelihood depends on me being able to stand and paint for long hours. I daren't risk another birth.'

'If he needs any persuading, I would be happy to recount my stories of those poor women I visited in Alnwick who are completely confined to the house.'

Christina gave Sarah a questioning look.

'Multiple births render them unable to prevent passing water. It's a common enough condition amongst those few poor old ladies who do not die in the course of a lifetime of annual births.'

Christina shuddered. 'He would be offended if you raised it, but I will tell him if there is any argument.'

They walked to the graveside. The earth was frozen rock hard and sprinkled with fresh snow. Blades of grass crunched beneath their feet. Christina stopped in front of the stone she and James had raised for baby Tiana eleven years ago. They'd returned again five years ago to bury three-day-old Christina beside her sister. When the stonemason added Christina's name to the gravestone, they'd instructed him to put a memorial to little Will in the line above.

James William Robertson, born 5th May 1825, died in Alnwick August 1826.

It gave her comfort to see the three names here together. Christina had brought a posy of snowdrops to lay there. Unable to bend, she handed it to Sarah to place against the stone.

'I needn't have worried about bringing flowers. The bulbs you planted have spread so well.'

'I split the bulbs last year to give better ground cover,' Sarah replied. 'I've done the same thing on Will's Alnwick grave. It's one of the prettiest in the churchyard now.'

'I like to imagine these snowdrops as a gift from Will to his sisters. He was the sweetest little boy.'

'Your little William looks so like him. You will have the pleasure of seeing the first Will in his features as he grows to be a man.'

As they turned to go, Christina looked over at the spot by the wall, which she visited alone every April. There was a glimmer of white at the base of the bricks. She looked quizzically at Sarah.

'I hope you're not angry. I couldn't help but notice you looking in that direction every time we visited. It looked so forlorn with no flowers, so I planted some of the snowdrop bulbs I split out.'

'Oh, Sarah,' was all she could manage through her tears. The weight of the secret made her bones feel heavy. It was time to let it go. She leaned on her friend's arm to walk the few steps to the tiny headstone. It bore a simple inscription: *Christiana Robertson born 24th and died 25th of April 1820.* She closed her eyes and tried to picture her first daughter's face, but it was somehow blurred by the memories of those babies she had lost since.

'I'm so grateful that she lived long enough for me to hold her. When tiny baby Christina was born, it felt so familiar,' she whispered. Christina managed a tearful smile. 'I should have told you before.'

Sarah's eyes were wet with tears too. She clasped her arm tight to her and spoke quietly. 'So when you said Christina was sent as an angelic messenger from her sister, you were thinking of this first baby?'

'Both of them, I have a trio of innocent angels looking after Will, although James only knows of the two.'

Sarah dropped her arm and swung round to stare at her. 'James doesn't know?'

'She was born three years before our marriage.'

Sarah's expression was both pained and perplexed. 'Was she James's child?'

'I believe so. It's complicated.' Christina gave an involuntary shiver as the cold crept up through the soles of her boots.

Sarah put her own shawl around Christina's shoulders. 'Let's take shelter in the church. You shouldn't linger in the cold.'

As they walked through the churchyard, Christina smiled to Mr Dawson, the churchwarden. 'Good day to you, Mistress Robertson,' he said, touching his hat.

'I owe that man huge gratitude,' Christina said when he was out of earshot. 'When I came to bury the first Christiana, I think he knew I had no husband, but he treated me with great kindness. She had no stone at first, but he counselled me to raise one, to keep her place safe. Uncle George helped me buy a headstone, and I have been so glad to have it to visit on her birthday every April.'

'George knew?'

They walked through the studded doors and into the empty church. 'Let us sit here and I'll tell you the whole story. I feel sure our Lord understands, and I will not be the first such woman to cross this threshold.'

They settled in the back pew and Christina stared up at the stained glass window as she told her story. 'James and I met at seventeen. He was my first and only love. He visited me every summer and in the summer of 1819, he asked me to marry him. I had no father to ask, so it was a private agreement between us. We planned to marry the following year and seek our fortunes as painters in London. I wrote to George. Asked for his blessing and advice on how to start out. On the last evening of his time in Kinghorn, James took me to a hay barn, and we lay together. I considered it like my wedding night and I was so happy. James promised to return for me the next spring, then he went out first, to avoid being seen leaving together. That was when my cousin came in and trapped me.'

Sarah's eyes widened. She put her hand over Christina's.

'I'd lived in Robbie's house since I was four years old and he made my life hell from the beginning. I don't believe I gave him any cause to hate me, but I was clever and hardworking, and I think he felt I overshadowed him. Also, Uncle George always made a great fuss of me when he visited. He was an artist from far away London and over the years gained fame. That made Robbie hate me even more.' Christina had to stop talking.

Sarah squeezed her hand. 'Don't tell me if it distresses you. I hate to think of you being bullied.'

'This secret has been kept for too long. I shan't sully this place with the details, but what he did was quick and violent and forever spoiled that precious moment with James. When he left me bleeding, he laughed. He said he had been watching us through the barn doors and he knew I was a whore. If I accused him, he'd tell his mother what he'd seen, and she'd throw me out.'

'And did she?'

'Eventually, yes.'

'How could she be so cruel?'

'When she discovered my pregnancy I wouldn't tell her

who the father was, and I never told James. I was ashamed, and it's not the kind of thing you can write in a letter.'

'Why were you ashamed? That brute is the person who ought to have been ashamed.'

'I knew I was pregnant by the end of September. I hoped I might keep it secret until James came back for me. The thought of telling him filled me with dread, because I'd no way of knowing if the baby was James's or Robbie's. Then in November James's letters stopped. I thought at the time that maybe Robbie had found some way to taunt him.'

'Did he?'

'I don't know. Anyway, it was hard to hide the absence of bleeding in such a small house. One night in December, Aunt Agnes came into my bedroom to confront me and seeing me in my nightgown, she had no need to ask. Robbie had given her an account of catching me in a barn with a strange man. She was furious. She told me to leave, and I used my small savings to come to London.'

'And George took you in?'

'He supported me but we agreed it was better if I took lodgings nearby. I went to live with him after Christiana died. When I started to mix in George's art circles, the decision to call myself Miss Saunders bound me to him and cut the tie to Christiana's records. It was a quirk of fate that she already had her father's name.'

'What? Your maiden name wasn't Saunders?'

'No. My mother was George's younger sister and that man I avoid in Leith was her husband and my father. His name is John Robertson.'

'So George saved you twice. He fulfilled your mother's dying wish to find you a better place to grow up, then gave you his name as well as shelter and means to support yourself when you were in London alone.'

191

'He did. Taking his name was a way to honour him,' Christina answered. 'George has been like a father to me.'

'I wouldn't have believed I could admire this excellent man more.' Sarah hugged her.

'We should be getting back to Argyll Street. Mary will be hungry.'

'Of course,' Sarah replied, helping Christina to her feet. 'Does it pain you too much to describe what happened to your first baby?'

'She was born early, like her sister after her. The midwife I'd paid to attend me in secret wasn't much help, but I think Christiana would have died anyway. It was just too soon. I felt she was James's but wasn't completely sure until we welcomed the babies who came after. Robbie was very fair. Not a beautiful blonde like you, but a reddish-blonde, ratty-faced boy with sparse eyelashes. All my babies arrive with the same dark hair that fades to auburn as they get older. The first Christiana looked like all her siblings.'

'But you never told James?'

'I cannot without telling him about Robbie. I don't think he would be able to cope with the knowledge.'

Sarah tutted under her breath. 'Whereas you cope with everything for him.'

In May, the Royal Academy selected Christina's large portrait of Mrs Pelham to be the first painting in their catalogue, with a prominent place in the Great Room. The commission had been won as a direct result of showing Sarah's large portraits, and Christina invited both Sarah and Lady Rolle to come to the opening. Maude Pelham was a very beautiful, dark-haired young woman. Christina had painted her in an off the shoulder dress that would remind people of young Princess Victoria. Listening to the noisy crowd of ladies standing in front of the portrait, she was pleased to hear that their praise was unanimous. James and Uncle George stood shoulder to shoulder, gazing up at the painting. Their proximity and huge smiles showed how united they were in pleasure and pride. Christina experienced a sensation of deep joy in this family moment. Her ambition and her commitment to her family often pulled her in different directions. Today, everything was in perfect harmony.

Sarah and Lady Louisa Rolle stood arm-in-arm at the edge of the room, unobtrusively observing the scene. Lady Rolle first met Sarah when she had accompanied Christina on her visit to Devon to paint Louisa's miniature. They'd stayed in Bicton for two weeks, and the three of them had got on well. Louisa and Sarah had bonded over their common interest in herbs and plants. They were both very knowledgeable and the mutual respect was clear. However, it was evidence of Lady Rolle's sweet personality that she was so openly affectionate with Sarah in public. A friendship between a miller's daughter and a member of the aristocracy was uncommon. Christina walked over to join them. 'Thank you,' she said. 'I owe this achievement to you both, and I already have two large commissions for the coming year. These ladies came to me because they admired the portraits inspired by one of you and loaned by the other.'

'You owe me no thanks,' Louisa Rolle replied. 'I'm grateful to you every day when I see Sarah smiling back at me from my drawing-room wall. The beauty of the paintings enchanted me first, and now through you I have Sarah's friendship, too.'

Sarah squeezed Louisa's arm against her side as she beamed back at her. 'How can we persuade Lady Rolle to let you do her own large painting? There is room for another portrait on the walls of Bicton House. The lady of the manor should have pride of place.'

Lady Rolle shuddered. 'My plain looks do not lend themselves to such an idea. I accepted John's request for a miniature, but a full length painting would require a type of outfit I never wear.'

Christina smiled. 'I'm quite certain I could paint a large portrait that you would like. In fact, I've already seen you in a suitable outfit.'

'When? I certainly don't own an off-the-shoulder gown.'

'There is no dress that could equal the one you wore under your robes for King William's coronation.'

'Were you there? I didn't see you.'

'Sarah and I were both in the crowd, and you looked absolutely beautiful.'

'Oh, Louisa, you did,' Sarah added. 'What an excellent idea, Christina.'

Lady Rolle smiled. 'I have to agree that was the one day in my life when I felt stylish.'

'It wasn't just the dress, it was your expression. You looked so proud and so serene,' Christina said. 'Would you permit me to recreate that emotional moment?'

'I believe Sir John would be delighted by the idea.'

'Do you still own the dress?'

'Of course, it's at home in Devon. I have robes as well, but not the ermine cape. That's a garment only used for coronations.'

'Then I'm sure I could recreate the look. I'll do you a sketch and a price, then you can think about it. I would need a few hours of your time.'

'We are only in London for another two days. Lord Rolle and I are expecting new specimens for the Palm House and we want to get back.'

'Could you come to my home for an hour tomorrow, then we could travel together to Westminster Abbey? I want to stand you there and I need to check the proportions.'

'Yes. Does it matter what I wear?'

'No. If you accept the proposal, I will sketch a general impression and come to Devon to pose you in the robes.'

The next morning, Christina spent time drawing Lady Rolle in her Argyll Street home. 'Adopt the same pose as Sarah's portrait, facing away from me, looking back over your shoulder. If you choose to hang the portrait in your drawing room, your posture will mirror Sarah's painting.'

'I love that idea,' Louisa Rolle replied.

Christina captured her facial features and general stance. She summoned a memory of the coronation day in her head. The red velvet cloak with a long train falling in soft folds over Louisa's gold embroidered silk dress. A ruff rising from the back of her collar and her diamond tiara sparkling in the sunlight.

Christina asked Sarah to come with them in the carriage to Westminster Abbey, knowing her presence would calm Louisa's nerves. They chatted about the possibility of being reunited in Devon later in the year. Louisa Rolle was obviously warming to the idea. Christina felt a shiver of excitement at the notion of painting the picture she'd envisioned.

The carriage stopped beside the Abbey.

'Let's take a moment,' Christina said. 'I'm going to ask you to throw your thoughts back to how you felt that day.'

'That's easy. I remember exactly what I was thinking.' Lady Rolle closed her eyes and spoke quietly. 'People laughed at me when it was announced I would marry Lord Rolle. I was that plain, awkward, poverty-stricken girl who was forced to marry an old man. But, Christina, they were completely wrong. My childhood wasn't easy. I was only three when my father and mother died within six months of each other. They left behind no money and six young children. Consequently, we were split up and moved about. So, to find myself one of those privileged few to witness the King's coronation... To be dressed in robes, surrounded by a cheering crowd... Then, most of all, to know I was loved and cherished by a man I'd come to love too. I knew I was blessed.' When Louisa raised her head, there were tears in her eyes.

Christina asked Louisa to stand on the Abbey entrance steps, with her back to them. 'Call her name,' she whispered to Sarah.

'Louisa,' Sarah said.

Lady Rolle turned around and Christina captured her gentle expression for posterity. This portrait would be her best yet.

Chapter Twenty-One

December 2017, Moscow

I couldn't shake the shock of seeing Nick and Oksana together. The way he held her shoulder, when I'd thought that gesture was only for me. I was so dazed, I missed my stop on the metro. Once home, I chopped dinner ingredients while my thoughts flailed about, unable to come up with the words to confront him.

The front door banged. 'I've had a voicemail message from the letting agency. Someone has viewed the flat and made an offer,' Nick shouted from the hall.

I could hear him talking French on the phone. I rubbed my palms down the front of my apron and went to the front door. His laptop satchel was in the usual spot, leaned against the wall. Keeping my eyes flicking towards the living room and my ears tuned into his voice, I flipped open the various sections. They held nothing unusual. I opened the coat cupboard. and I slid my hands into the pockets of his overcoat. Nothing.

I seethed with frustration. My *Love Actually*, Emma Thompson manoeuvre was never likely to throw up a package. If they chose her gift together, why would he bring it home? I'd have no peace unless I tackled him on this.

He came into the kitchen and gave me a guiltless smile. My stomach clenched but I waited until we sat to eat before asking what he'd done today.

'Nothing special,' he replied. 'The budget estimates went in yesterday, so the pressure is off. Oh, by the way, I've got to go away for a few days. The power plant in Kalinin is having issues with the control system upgrade. I need to lead the investigation.'

'This week?' I said incredulously. My peak time for ovulation was imminent, and we'd talked about it only yesterday. 'When? How many days?'

'Tomorrow. Three or maybe four days. I'll probably come back on Saturday.'

'Then there's little point in doing the ovulation predictor.'

Realisation dawned on Nick's face. 'Of course. I'd forgotten.'

He did look genuinely contrite, but I could remember a time when Nick was as tuned into my cycle as I was. Was Oksana the reason his interest had waned? 'Is Oksana going to Kalinin with you?'

His expression changed from empathetic to annoyed. 'For god's sake, Anna. You know I can't manage meetings without her. I thought you'd accepted that?'

'I saw you today in the street,' I retorted.

'Where?'

'Old Arbat Street, coming out of a shop with a woman with long dark hair.'

Nick picked up his water glass. He looked over the rim with his eyebrows raised. 'The busiest street in Moscow, a great place for an assignation.'

'What were you doing?'

He put down his glass and gave a loud sigh. The kind an

exasperated parent would direct at a moody teenager. 'Well, you've completely spoilt the surprise.' He screwed up his napkin and dropped it beside his plate. 'We were choosing your Christmas present. Oksana knows the owner and was able to get me a better price. It's a gorgeous thing. Do I really need to bring it home as proof?' He glared at me.

'Of course not,' I replied quietly.

'My relationship with Oksana is strictly professional. She is very good, and she makes my life easier.' The inference that I did not, hung in the air between us. Nick stood up. 'Excuse me. I've got some emails to finish.' He left the room.

Why had I never considered that the gift might be for me? My cheeks burned. I felt humiliated. But also, still jealous and threatened. I couldn't forget the sight of his hand squeezing her shoulder. It might be the most beautiful box in Russia, but I was never going to be able to forget Oksana's involvement.

I dumped the dishes in the sink and headed for bed. In the bathroom, I put the ovulation kit back in the cabinet beside the others. Right now, the gulf between us made sex unthinkable.

Nick got up early and I pretended to be asleep. Once he'd gone, I made coffee and went to my laptop. Unravelling the secrets of Christina's world was my place to hide from real life.

Progress was slow, and the search for portrait images was frustrating. However, I started to see some patterns in the names of the sitters. I had thought Christina had cut contact with Scotland when she joined her uncle in London, but I found many Scots were amongst her portraits. I widened my search, and discovered she'd frequently exhibited at the Royal Scottish Academy and been made an honourable member in

1829. No other woman had been given such an honour. Christina gained commissions from many Scottish aristocrats, including the Duke and Duchess of Buccleuch. I uncovered many family connections between the people in her portraits, particularly when I looked into maiden names. I loved the notion that her patronage was so influenced by women. Christina painted sisters, sisters-in-law, as well as mothers and daughters. Surely it said something about her personality. These ladies must have enjoyed the painting experience as well as the quality of the portraits. It was particularly satisfying when a family connection from the Duke of Buccleuch wove its way through the Clinton family to the enigmatic looking Lady Rolle. My lady in ermine was the daughter of Baron Clinton. The whole thing took hours, but I added another six images to my folder and a sense that I'd found another chink of illumination into Christina's life.

The sense of achievement improved my mood. I even managed to regain some perspective about Oksana. The role of a translator was an odd one. To be paid to hang on someone's every word, to be able to understand and translate both meaning and tone, was bound to create a certain intimacy. They worked long hours and Nick most certainly spent more time with Oksana than with me. I could do nothing about their closeness at work, but I had no evidence of an affair. I'd make myself ill if I didn't trust him.

I texted Nick to suggest we meet at our favourite restaurant for supper. In the evening, I grabbed the new painting images from the printer before I headed out the door.

Nick was there when I arrived. He looked nervous. I kissed him and squeezed his shoulder in reassurance. The waiter brought our plates of steaming pelmeni. This was the restaurant speciality, and we rarely chose anything else. These little meat dumplings came served with sour cream and dill, and on a cold day like today, the explosion of warmth and flavour felt like soul food. I showed Nick the pictures and gabbled my way through supper, describing everything else I'd discovered. Nick was probably less interested than he pretended, but I could sense from his body language that he was more relaxed. Although I wasn't completely convinced, I'd decided to give him the benefit of the doubt. I stretched across the table to touch his hand.

'I'm sorry about mistrusting you.'

'And I'm sorry that I have to go away tomorrow. The timing is terrible.'

'I've decided to track my ovulation, anyway. The dates will be useful for Dr Smirnova.'

Nick nodded. 'Good idea.'

'I'll make my next appointment before New Year. The clinic closes down for the week over New Year and Russian Christmas and I want to have everything ready to start the hormone injections.'

'I'll come with you. We'll be quiet that week too,' Nick replied. He gave me a wry smile. 'And I promise to do the dreaded sample.'

We paid the bill. 'By the way,' he said, 'one of Oksana's children is ill, so I'm taking Pierre's translator to Kalinin.'

I smiled and nodded. No point in pretending I wasn't pleased.

Nick put his head to one side. 'His name is Yevgeniy,' he added.

I'd arranged to meet Pavel in a café in Volkhonka Street, after my visit to the Pushkin. He waved from a table in the corner. As I walked over, I took off my hat and unwound my scarf. The warm café was a stark contrast to the freezing temperature outside. The Moscow winter was building, but still no sign of snow.

'How did it go?' he asked.

'Great. The assistant curator spoke perfect English and was very patient. The paintings are way more impressive face-to-face. It was such a buzz to be able to see her actual brush-strokes. She is going to email me the digital link for applying to use the images. I want to use the Empress dressed in her feathered bonnet, looking over her shoulder to pair with Lady Rolle. Then I need to do more research into Princesses Zinaida Yusupova and Maria Ivanovna Baryatinskaya. I'm finding lots of family links in Christina's earlier portraits. I expect there will be similar connections amongst the Russian sitters. There is so little written about Christina's own life, but I think readers will find her sitters' stories an interesting context for understanding the times.'

'I recognise both names. I believe we have other family portraits in the Hermitage collection.'

'That's what I noticed.'

'Do you know when you'll come to St Petersburg?'

'I'm nearly finished researching the English portraits and most of the paintings she did in Paris were of Russians, so I'm definitely reaching that phase of her life. I'll need to talk to Nick, but I might come in January.'

'Might you be able to come early in January?' Pavel asked. 'I teach an art history class at the university and the students don't go back until the thirteenth. I'd have more free time to help you.'

'Maybe. I'll try.' In my head, I calculated my cycle. The first week in January would be okay to be away. 'When are you going back to St Petersburg?'

'I've booked a train for the twenty-ninth.'

'Of course, you'll want to be back for New Year and Christmas.'

Russian Orthodox Christmas falls on the seventh of January, and I knew from last year that Muscovites revel in celebrating Christmas all the way through our Western Christmas and New Year, right onto their own day.

Pavel shrugged. 'I haven't made any celebration plans.'

'Do you have family in St Petersburg?'

'None since my grandmother died.'

'I'm sorry.'

'I'm making myself sound pathetic when it's really not that bad. I have lots of friends in St Petersburg.'

'When did you lose your parents?' I asked.

'My father was a diplomat. I was fourteen, and we were living in Brussels when Mama was diagnosed with ovarian cancer. It was picked up late, and she died within months. Papa came back to St Petersburg, and we moved in with my grandmother.'

'No wonder you were close to your grandmother.'

'It was a terrible year. Mama's death was so sudden and I found adjusting to my Russian school difficult. Until then, I'd been in international secondary schools, first in London, then in Brussels. And, of course, Papa was heartbroken. I can't imagine how we'd have got through it without my grandmother.'

'Then your father died too?'

'A few years ago. I moved back into the family home when Papa became too sick to look after himself or my grandmother.'

I looked at Pavel with new eyes. He was such a big, powerful looking man, but he clearly had a sensitive side. 'I doubt many men would have done that.'

'My fiancée moved in with us too for the year of Papa's illness. After he died, she wanted to move out again. I refused, and we split up.'

'She wanted you to leave an old lady on her own?'

He shrugged. 'I could see her point of view. My grandmother was a very strong woman and also very forthright. She and Liling didn't always get along. Liling believed she disapproved of me marrying a Chinese girl.'

'Poor woman, that would make living together impossible.'

'I was her only grandchild. My grandmother was always going to be difficult to impress. Forced to choose, I didn't find it hard to decide. I guess that says my relationship with Liling wasn't strong enough.'

'My Scottish grandmother developed dementia and eventually had to go into care. My dad died when I was in my twenties and Mum took over his antiques business in England. I know she felt guilty that she was too far away to care for my granny.'

'That must have been tough. Dementia can become impossible to deal with at home. My grandmother was sharp as a pin. Liling thought she might live for decades. That's not the way it worked out in the end.'

'The Babushka Appreciation Society is my only club here so far. It's a great thing to be a member of.'

Pavel laughed. My phone pinged with a message from Lisa.

Just confirming our meeting on Friday. I should be done with work by 4.30. Also are you and Nick free to have supper with us on Friday night? Why not invite your curator too? Pavel is a mutual friend of the owner of a St Petersburg gallery and Dmitry has an exhibition there in January. He'd like to meet him.

'Excuse me while I answer this. I'm helping my friend Lisa organise a charity art auction this month and things are manic.'

My thumbs flew over the phone keyboard.

Nick is away on business but I'd love to stay for supper. I'm actually with Pavel now. Shall I ask him?

Please! Tell him my husband Dmitry Verenich is an artist and knows the gallery owner Ilya Maslov.

I passed on Lisa's message.

'I'd love to come. Ilya is a good friend and I think I've heard of Dmitry.'

I packed my folder away in my rucksack and pulled on my woolly hat. Pavel took my jacket from the chair and held it for me to put on. 'I'll send you Lisa's address for Friday. We have a meeting in the afternoon but I'll ask what time she wants you to turn up for supper.'

'I'll look forward to it,' Pavel said.

'Me too,' I replied, realising that I really would. Pavel was going to be a great help for my research and I had the distinct feeling that he might become a friend.

Chapter Twenty-Two

October 1835, London

After two consecutive high profile Academy Exhibitions, Christina's portrait order book was full. Painting large portraits as well as miniatures she earned enough to cover their family needs. The next priority was education. Unfortunately James and she disagreed.

'No,' James said. 'Absolutely not. The sound of you and Agnes talking French to each other is insufferable. I will not tolerate it in my son.'

'Surely war is something to put behind us. Our children are growing up at peace with our neighbours. There is a huge market for painting commissions across Europe, and French is the common language of the aristocracy.'

'That was your argument for taking Agnes to Tours, but it led to no French commissions.'

'You are twisting the facts. You know quite well that Agnes's education was my primary reason for going to Tours. The Geraud family are very nice people, but they are not active in society.'

'John is gaining a gentleman's education from Mr Ambleton and gentlemen learn Latin.'

'Latin has its place, especially if John pursues a scientific career. But Agnes learnt more French in two months than I learnt in the whole previous year. She and John are the ideal age for acquiring a language. I wish him to have her chances, just as she should have his.'

'Are we going to go over this argument again? Mr Ambleton maintains that female minds are different. Agnes does not need the same skills as John.'

'Then we should find a more enlightened tutor. It's a waste of an opportunity to pay for private tutoring for only one child. Agnes and John should be in the same classroom.'

'Agnes's interest is painting, and she has the best possible teacher in her mama.'

Christina took a deep breath and suppressed the urge to pursue the subject. James had seized on the idea that his son needed a gentleman's education and nothing would dissuade him. Her income in recent years had brought in enough money to rent this home in Harley Street, which was fit for a gentleman and his family. But it gave her nightmares that they were bringing up the children to expect that kind of life. Unlike the men James liked to socialise with, they had no land or family money to pass on. If for any reason Christina was prevented from working, their way of life would evaporate. She closed her eyes and willed her heart to slow down. Her new fame had allowed her to double her fees. They were secure for a few years, but it was imperative that she looked for avenues to increase her income.

Christina sent a note to David Roberts, asking him to meet her in Hyde Park. She was conscious that such a meeting with a man who was not her husband would be assumed by some to be a romantic assignation. In fact, she wanted to ask him about possible clients in Paris and couldn't raise the subject in front of James. Christina's spirits lifted at she neared the park. She harboured no feelings for David, but she enjoyed his company. It was a perfect day for a walk. She brought the children here often, but it was such a treat to enjoy the park without having to be constantly vigilant. Four-year-old William's fascination with horses, meant she struggled to keep him away from the track.

Today, the trees had gained their autumn colours, and the sky was just the right shade of blue to set them off. Might she find a way to incorporate the vivid combination in a portrait? In her mind, she selected red and yellow ochre and cerulean blue. She'd buy a bolt of fabric in autumnal shades and have it made up for twelve-year-old Agnes, then set it off with a blue sash. They were her God-given colours, with her auburn hair and blue eyes. Christina was still smiling at the thought as she entered the Cumberland Gate. Roberts was waiting for her underneath a horse chestnut tree.

'Thank you for finding time to meet me. I want to ask you more about Paris. I'm still hoping to persuade James that I should go.'

'I must apologise for my lack of tact. I had no thought of introducing discord.'

'I'm the one who should say sorry. There was no excuse for James's rudeness. You couldn't have known that France is a sore subject in our household.'

'Och, Christina, I'd be the last person to make any judgements about the complications of married co-existence.'

David Roberts expressed his frustration by swiping his walking stick through a large pile of sycamore leaves. He had spent a great deal of time apart from his wife in recent years. However, they were now reunited in London.

'Does Margaret keep well?'

He smiled at her. 'For the time being. Margaret is much happier in the Mornington Place house. I'm usually at home now that I've finished with theatre work and have my own studio.'

'So you're not travelling abroad this year?'

'No. I have a book full of sketches to paint up from my tour. My head is full of the Moorish architecture I saw in Spain and the north of Africa.'

'That makes my fuss about Paris sound quite pathetic, but James is not keen for me to go and we cannot agree on the plans for the children.'

'I could not have gone away if my sister had not agreed to have Christine in her home for the duration. I can't imagine how you can make arrangements for four children.'

'I have the support of both Eliza and Sarah. It would be possible to travel without the children, but I'd hoped to take both Agnes and John with me to Paris. I'd like John to learn French, and the sights of Paris would be an education in itself. However, James lost an uncle fighting the French, and he is inclined to dislike them on principle.'

'They were the enemy for so long. James is not the only one who cannot let go of the past. However, learning French as a child is an excellent idea. Like you, I've had to overcome many gaps in my education.'

'I am persevering with my lessons, but I wish I picked it up as easily as Agnes.'

'You must be proud of your gifted daughter and I hear she shares your artistic talent.'

'She shows both promise and interest. I'm hopeful that it might give her the means to earn her own money.'

'Astute thinking. I'm most happy with Christine's little school in Barnes. We'll have to see where her talents might take her.'

They reached the edge of the Serpentine. Roberts

gestured that they might sit on a bench. The lake was busy with rowing boats. Lots of visitors were making best use of the last of the pleasant weather

'So, tell me again about the French lady you mentioned?'

'Countess de Noailles, I'm sure she is an excellent prospect for you. However, now there is another family more immediately on my mind. A Russian gentleman I met in Scotland is in London this week. Vladimir Davydov is charming and would be an excellent portrait subject. What is more, he has recently married into an important Russian family. I met his wife in Paris. Princess Olga Baryatinskaya is one of three beautiful sisters, and I just know you are the perfect artist to capture their good looks. I thought I might ask Vladimir to come to your salon? I imagine James might be more comfortable with a Paris-based family who are not French. Vladimir lived in London before Paris, and was educated at Edinburgh University. In fact, I met him first at Abbotsford. He was a friend of Sir Walter's and a frequent visitor.'

'A Scottish educated Russian. How very unusual.'

'Exactly. Shall I see if he is free to come to your next salon?'

'Would you? We've only just begun to run the salons again after the move to Harley Street.' Christina's cheeks burned with embarrassment. They had hosted two salons at their new address but not sent the Roberts an invitation. James had refused to invite Margaret Roberts, and Christina would not agree to invite David without his wife. Christina took a deep breath and turned to face David, ready to apologise.

David smiled and laid his hand on her arm. His rueful expression told her he understood her discomfort. 'Tell James that I wish to introduce you both to a Russian nobleman who is married to a princess, and that Mrs Roberts is sufficiently embarrassed by her last visit to your home that I can promise she will cause no trouble.'

She let her breath go and smiled back. 'I will tell him and you should expect an invitation for three people to the salon next week. Tell me again the gentleman's name?'

'Vladimir Davydov. I'll talk to him about it and send you a note if he's free.'

Christina gazed up at the newly finished portrait. She had painted Lady Elizabeth Clinton three times. Lady Elizabeth was related to Louisa Rolle. All Lady Rolle's female relatives had admired her painting and clamoured to have a portrait of their own. Louisa Rolle was to attend the portrait unveiling tonight, but she would be disappointed to learn that Sarah was out of London.

Thinking of Sarah's hasty departure made Christina feel panicked. Sarah had rushed back to Alnwick. Tom's wife Ann had contracted consumption and her health had taken a turn for the worse and confined her to bed. Tom needed help nursing her and looking after their three small children. Sarah's letter of this morning described a desperate situation. Young Charles and baby Agnes were both showing the same consumptive symptoms as their mother. Sarah feared for the lives of Ann and all her children. And what of the danger to Andrew and Sarah herself? Sarah had admitted that she believed the disease cut through families because of close contact. Christina knew it was a selfish thought, but if she lost Sarah, she wasn't sure she could carry on. She simply couldn't imagine day-to-day life without her friend. For all of those reasons, she'd wanted to cancel this evening's salon, but James had invited half of London and David Roberts had persuaded Vladimir Davydov to extend his visit by a week to attend. She had to carry on.

. . .

As the hour drew closer, her low spirits were raised by Agnes's excitement. Tonight, her daughter would wear her first proper evening gown and join the adult guests. Agnes's dress was white, as was appropriate for her age, but with her hair worn up and the flush in her cheeks, Christina could see adulthood was just around the corner.

'Papa, tell me again the names of all the important people. I'm afraid I will mix them up and not behave properly,' Agnes said.

'My advice is to be polite and charming to everyone,' Christina said.

'Your mother was never interested in society politics. As a young lady who will be seeking a suitor in a few years, you should pay great attention to their names and titles. Tonight we shall entertain our very first Russian nobleman, and I hear the Russian aristocracy makes our home-grown version seem like paupers.'

James said it in a joking tone and Agnes laughed, but Christina shot him a glare.

'David Roberts tells me Vladimir Davydov is married, and since he was a friend of Sir Walter Scott, I imagine he must be in his later years.'

'Ah, but he may have an eligible son,' James added, ignoring her stern look.

She turned to Agnes. 'If I find you behaving like one of those young women who habitually views every new acquittance in the light of future marriage prospects, you can be sure that there will be no more salons in my house.'

Agnes put her arm around Christina's waist. 'Papa is just teasing you. I'm not sure if I want to marry at all. My dearest wish is to be a painter and follow in your footsteps.'

A wise idea and Christina kissed her daughter on her forehead. How James stuck to his traditional views on marriage, given their unusual financial circumstances, was a mystery.

'Come on, Agnes,' James said, taking Agnes's hand. 'Come to the door with me to greet our guests. I shall pinch you once for a possible beau and twice for a definite.'

'Don't be silly, Papa,' Agnes replied with a laugh. James adored all his children, and they loved him in return. It was good they were so far blind to his faults.

The evening got off to a good start. Christina had got to know both Louisa Rolle and Elizabeth Clinton well during the painting of their large portraits, and enjoyed their company.

David Roberts came in with a handsome, dark-haired young man, whom he introduced as Vladimir Davydov.

'Mr Roberts tells us you were well acquainted with Sir Walter Scott,' James said.

'I had that very great privilege,' the young man replied. 'My years in Scotland were happy and my welcome in Sir Walter's home was a significant factor.' Davydov spoke excellent English and the soft Scottish lilt in his accent endeared him to Christina.

'You were lucky indeed. I assure you that few Edinburgh University undergraduates were afforded that opportunity,' David Roberts added.

'He invited me to his home the first time because he was interested in my uncle, Denis Davydov. He actually had a portrait of Uncle Denis hung in Abbotsford. Sir Walter was researching his story as part of his work on the life of Napoleon, and I was able to put him in touch with Denis to provide first-hand testimony.'

'How very fascinating. Did your uncle fight Napoleon?' Christina asked. She knew this was a line of conversation that would impress James.

'He did. Uncle Denis is quite the war hero and also a renowned poet in Russia. I'm very proud to be his relation.'

'I do wish I'd had a chance to meet Sir Walter Scott,' Christina added. 'I'm a huge admirer of his novels.'

'Sir Walter's fame lives on all over the world. Tsar Nicholas and his wife share your admiration. They read the novels to each other in the evening. It is their favourite pastime.'

'So romantic,' Christina replied.

She saw a tiny twitch in James's eyebrows. She knew he wouldn't consider reading novels to one's wife as a suitable pastime for a gentleman, never mind a Tsar.

'I hope to take my wife to Scotland,' Davydov continued. 'Olga knows London well, but she has never been to Edinburgh.'

'We have a Scottish lady here this evening,' Christina said. 'Let me introduce you.'

When she introduced Davydov to Lady Clinton, he looked up at the portrait. 'I can see I am in the presence of the portrait subject. You must be delighted. What a stunning painting.'

'Mrs Robertson has done such a good job,' Elizabeth Clinton answered.

'A Scottish accent. How marvellous. You make me homesick.'

'You are surrounded by Scots,' Lady Clinton said. 'I, Mr Roberts, and Mr and Mrs Robertson all hail from Scotland.'

Davydov looked at David Roberts in surprise. 'David, you told me that this lady was an incredible painter, but you didn't say she was Scottish. How perfect would it be to have a portrait to combine two loves, Scotland and my lovely wife. Mrs Robertson, would you consider coming to Paris to paint Princess Olga?'

Christina daren't look at James or David Roberts. 'It

would be an honour, that is, if James and my children can spare me.'

James smiled and made a gesture of acceptance towards Davydov. She could imagine him boasting to his friends that she'd been commissioned to paint a princess.

'Splendid. We are leaving Paris soon to spend a few months at our Russian estate. Come sometime in the spring, perhaps?'

'That sounds reasonable. Let us keep in touch.' Christina sidled away from the group, got out the sketchbook she kept in the bureau drawer and retired to the sofa. She spent the next half hour sketching Vladimir Davydov, as he chatted to the other guests. She would give the likeness to Davydov to take with him, in case his wife might need any convincing.

David Roberts came and sat beside her. 'Thank you,' she said. 'I am in your debt.'

'You owe me nothing,' he replied. You are one of the very few ladies in London who has shown Margaret kindness. She is grateful and so am I.'

Christina looked up from her drawing. 'Yet she didn't accompany you? Did you tell her she was invited?' She cast her eyes back to the page, suddenly realising she'd accused him of deception.

'I told her,' he replied in a low voice, 'but insisted she must be sober. Sadly, it appears she cannot face any social outing without the assistance of a drink.'

Roberts' mouth was set in a line, his jaw clenched. She thought he might be close to tears.

'Your invitation brought her some happiness this week. Her inability to do the one thing required to get her here convinces me again that she is beyond redemption.'

'I'm so very sorry,' she replied.

. . .

Christina gave Vladimir Davydov her sketch, which he made a great fuss about. Soon, he and the other guests left. James brought her a celebratory glass of port.

'To a future painting princesses.' He raised his port glass high, as if viewing the room through its rosy hue. 'If Sarah returns, you may take Agnes. John will remain with me, where he belongs.'

Christina's fingernails bit into her palm and she had to force her other hand to unclench, lest she should break the stem of the delicate glass. She had loved James so much. What happened to their marriage, that in such moments she actively disliked him?

Chapter Twenty-Three

December 2017, Moscow

Lisa and I spent the Friday before Christmas at her home, double-checking the exhibition boards against the catalogue before it went to the printers. The ball was scheduled for the day after Boxing Day.

'We're still waiting for nine paintings. There will be huge gaps in the display if they don't arrive in time.'

'Don't worry, this is normal,' she replied. 'I always have to chase, and it's actually much better this year. Some of them think it's fine to cancel Sergey at the last moment. Knowing you are foreign, they see you as a potential client and are less likely to mess you around.'

She underlined four names on the list. 'These four artists speak English. Just call and press them for a time to meet. Sergey can manage these three on his own.' She ticked three more. 'And I'll ask Dmitry to deal with those two.' She circled the last two names. 'They are repeat offenders for being very late. Dmitry can play the bad guy when required.'

Just then, the door opened. A stocky man with his blonde hair pulled back into a ponytail came in.

'Here is my lovely bad guy, right on cue,' Lisa said, with a laugh in her voice.

'What have I done now, Lisichka?' he replied, and came over to kiss her.

I wondered if this was a diminutive of *lisa*, the Russian for fox, as well as a version of her name. I'd learned the word in my last Russian lesson. It was very fitting for my friend, whose hair was the colour of a beech tree in autumn.

'Dmitry, meet Anna, the person who's prevented me going demented this year.'

He shook my hand. 'You have no idea how grateful I am, Anna.' Dmitry flung his jacket on the chair, revealing muscular arms beneath his rolled-up sleeves. The twins came running through and flung themselves into their father's arms. Their long strawberry blonde hair swung as he lifted them onto his hips and my stomach knotted in jealousy. Their children were a perfect blend of parental genes.

'You're home early,' Lisa said.

'It occurred to me that Pavel might ask to see more of my work tonight, and my studio is a mess.'

'I've been telling you that for weeks. I like this man already.'

'I'll just go and say hi to Misha,' Dmitry added.

Lisa looked at her watch. 'I'd better get on with supper.'

'Tell me what I can do to help.' I followed her into the kitchen. 'What are you making?'

'Shepherd's pie,' she answered.

I laughed. 'I was expecting you to cook something Russian.'

'Dmitry loves it and I thought Pavel might like to try some typical British food.'

'I love it, too. My mum made it for me when I was in Edinburgh.'

'How is your mum coping?' Lisa pushed the chopping

board and an onion towards me and got a knife out of the block.

I peeled the onion. 'I spoke to her today, and she's okay. I told her all about the art gallery and my latest Christina discoveries. I think she's enjoying this project almost as much as I am.'

I described my viewing of the Pushkin paintings, and how my ideas for structuring the book were evolving.

'Pavel seems extra helpful. You're lucky. Dmitry tells me he's highly regarded in the art world.'

'Very lucky. I can't imagine how I'd begin approaching the Hermitage without him.'

Pavel arrived, and we sat down to dinner. He and Dimitry got into a very animated Russian conversation. It was obvious they were getting on. Once we'd eaten, Dmitry took Pavel to see his studio.

'Thank you,' Lisa said. 'Dmitry was worried about this exhibition. He knows fewer people in St Petersburg and was concerned about getting enough visitors into the gallery. Now Pavel has agreed to come and publicise it on social media, it could make a huge difference.'

'There's nothing to thank me for. When is the exhibition?'

'It starts on Saturday eighteenth January and will be on for a week.'

'That's a shame. I'll miss it. Pavel has more free time at the beginning of January, so I'm planning to go to St Petersburg for a week, but I'll be leaving around the twelfth.'

'Then we'll overlap. I've taken some leave to help Dmitry set up. We'll probably arrive the weekend before.'

'Maybe I'll see if Nick wants to come out for that weekend?'

I stood to help Lisa clear the plates.

'One of our sponsors can't come to the ball, and has offered up his ticket. What do you think about me inviting Pavel?'

'Good idea.'

Nick and I exchanged presents on Christmas Eve, a practice Nick had picked up in Paris. We toasted with champagne beside the flickering lights of our small Christmas tree. I'd made a homemade garland with greenery and pine cones. The natural woodland scent mingled with that of the Christmas candles on the dining table. I handed Nick the envelope with my handmade card.

'Your Christmas present is more of a promise. I've earmarked two paintings from the charity sale. I think I like them both equally, but if you have a preference, I'll concentrate my bidding on that one.'

'I've already had my earbuds, so you're spoiling me.' He opened the envelope and took out the two photographs I'd printed and mounted on card.

'The pen and ink drawing of the canal bridge is by a St Petersburg artist. The abstract painting is by Lisa's husband, Dmitry.'

'I love them both,' he replied.

'I'll decide on the night, depending on how the bidding goes. They have similar catalogue estimates, but it only takes one other person to love them and the price could rocket.'

Nick gave me the brightly coloured bag I'd seen him carrying that day on the street. The painting on the box was a scene of a couple in a forest glade. It was beautifully executed and very romantic. Unfortunately, the woman had very long, dark hair. She looked nothing like me. I forced a smile.

There was silence for a few seconds. 'What are you thinking?' Nick asked.

I couldn't tell him what I was thinking, so I described what I'd thought earlier, when we were eating our Christmas Eve supper.

'I'm thinking that I hope next year we'll have a completely different Christmas, one like my own childhood. A baby will wake us up early on Christmas Day, and the year after we'll be out of bed at dawn with a toddler begging to open their Christmas presents.'

'My Christmas wish too,' Nick leaned over to kiss me. 'When is your appointment next week?'

'Ten o'clock on Monday. Are you sure you can be there? Dr Smirnova will do the first hormone injection, but after that, it's up to us.'

'I promise, and I checked with your clinic that they're happy to accept the results from the place I found near the office. I've got an appointment tomorrow. This is a better arrangement. It means the first time I meet your doctor it will be with a smile, and not a dodgy container in my hand.'

I laughed. 'Lucky you, retaining your dignity. I'm quite sure I won't be able to keep mine for long in this whole process.'

On 27th December, Lisa, Pavel and I pushed through the crowds, heading towards GUM. Nick sent me a text, to say he was leaving the office and going home to change. Dmitry had gone to deal with some drama at Vadim's mum's house. We'd been about to leave when he got the call and hadn't been pleased to have to rush across town in his tuxedo. Pavel was carrying a large painting that the artist had delivered to Lisa's house only the hour before. Luckily, it was one of the easel paintings, so it didn't need hanging. Lisa, Dmitry and I had worked like demons all day to complete the display of beautiful artwork in time, and the sense of achievement gave me a huge buzz. I'd enjoyed every moment of today. Working late into the afternoon, then rushing to Lisa's to shower and change into my long dress. We'd shared a celebratory bottle of champagne before we set off. Nick hadn't been able to get away in time for the pre-drinks, but I'd sensed his reluctance when I told him the plan. I assumed he'd invented the need to work late rather than feel the outsider. It was weird that Lisa was such an important part of my life now, and Nick had never even met her. Should I have done more to bring them together? Was I ashamed of our modest apartment compared to Lisa and Dmitry's place? Whatever the reason, I needed to put that right. Lisa and Dmitry had agreed to come round for supper before I went to St Petersburg, and Nick had promised to join me for my final weekend there.

We passed an enormous Christmas tree surrounded by a canopy of lights strung like a tent above a small ice rink. Girls were pushed round the rink in sledges, and skaters swayed with their hands behind their back, the sound of their scything blades cutting over the noise of the crowd. We crossed Red Square with the Kremlin on our right; the fairy lights edging the architectural features of the GUM building stood out against the dark sky. St Basil's reminded me of a Christmas decoration at the best of times, and tonight it took my breath away. The whole of Red Square had been trans-formed into a celebration of Christmas. There was an old-fashioned carousel with painted horses and another that sent squealing kids flying around it. The air was scented with glüh-wein and warm sugar, and the high buildings echoed the sounds of fairground music and children's laughter. The festive atmosphere and excitement for the coming ball made me shiver.

Lisa took my arm. 'The Russians really know how to do Christmas.'

Lisa's friendship and my book research had brought me happiness I hadn't expected. I needed to recalibrate my life with Nick, banish my fears, then tie all my special people together. This would be the year I found happiness in Russia. Maybe these were the conditions my body was waiting for to bring a baby into the world.

The ballroom looked stunning. Christmas lights bouncing sparkles off the enormous chandelier hanging above us; an arrangement of crystal circles, each topped by a copper-coloured onion dome, in a nod to nearby St Basil's. Lisa and I stood on either side of the entrance, handing out catalogues. Wave after wave of glamorously dressed guests entered. I caught snatches of English, Russian, French and Italian, united in the language of laughter. The room buzzed with excitement.

'I predict record takings,' Lisa whispered into my ear.

I returned her triumphant smile. Lisa looked amazing in a sheath dress of scarlet silk. She'd laughed when I changed into my red and black Devoré velvet dress. 'We even look like the perfect team,' she said.

When dinner was announced, we joined Kerry and her other guests at our round table near the dance floor. The stage was set for the live band. They'd been doing their sound test when we arrived. Snatches of Robbie Williams mixed with Frank Sinatra, sung by an amazing vocalist. Just the kind of thing to get people on their feet.

The silent auction was in full swing. Lisa rushed out to check progress after the starter course and returned beaming. She leaned towards Pavel and me to whisper: 'Every single painting has at least one bid and a few of the large paintings are creeping towards a thousand dollars.'

The waiters served the main course, and Pavel topped up our glasses. The whole evening was perfect, except for one thing. There was still no sign of Dmitry or Nick.

We ate, and the time crept past nine o'clock. I began to get really worried about Nick's absence. I rang his phone, but it went straight into voicemail.

Lisa gave me a reassuring smile. 'I've had a text from Dmitry. He's on his way, but the traffic is gridlocked. Nick is probably caught up in it too.'

I smiled, but my stomach churned with anxiety. The conviction that something terrible had happened strengthened with every passing minute. Pavel was trying to entertain us with stories of the St Petersburg art world. Just then, Dmitry came in, smiling widely. He sat down and whispered something in Russian in Lisa's ear. Her eyebrows raised in alarm. Apparently, she didn't find the story as funny as Dmitry.

'Sorry to abandon you all,' he said. 'My son came home and disturbed my ex-wife in bed with her new man, then her day got even worse when a drunk driver pranged her car when she was driving the guy home.'

Lisa didn't join in the laughter. 'What was Vadim even doing there? He's supposed to come to our house straight from school on a Friday.'

'That's obviously what his mother thought,' Dmitry answered with a laugh. 'He forgot his Nintendo Switch and went home for it.'

'But why were you so long?' Lisa asked.

'I had to go and pick her up from the hospital.'

'Is she okay?'

'She's fine, but her boyfriend broke his collarbone in the accident and her car's a write-off.'

I registered Lisa's nervous glance in my direction.

'He'd already scarpered before I got there. Oksana said he's going to be in deep shit for being late.'

Oksana? Behind Dmitry's head, I saw Nick enter the ballroom. His dinner jacket hung on his shoulders and his arm was in a sling.

Lisa turned to follow my horrified gaze. 'Anna...' she said.

I leapt to my feet, the chair crashing to the ground behind me. Nick's guilty eyes met mine.

Everyone was now looking at me, so I forced myself not to run. I scooped up my dress and headed for the toilets. There was nothing I could do about the tears streaming down my face.

Chapter Twenty-Four

July 1836, Northumberland, England

Christina and Sarah walked in companionable silence along the beach at Druridge Bay. It was eleven years since they'd come here on a family picnic and it felt like a pilgrimage. Ahead of them, Agnes, John and Andrew were walking barefoot along the water's edge and Christina imagined she could see the ghostly footprints of little Will paddling in the shallows. At least one of her lost babies got to experience sand beneath his feet. The three baby girls were like angels, only hers on loan, but Will stayed in her memory as a laughing, lively boy.

Mary, squirming in her arms, brought her thoughts back to the present. 'Down, Mama,' she said. Now this strong little girl had turned three, she allowed herself to feel hopeful about her future.

When Mary found herself trailing behind her siblings, she began to cry. Agnes walked back. 'Come on, Mary, let's play horses.' She hoisted her sister onto her back and gathered her skirts up to her knees. 'Hold on tight!' she yelled. Agnes charged off. Mary shrieked with delight as the other children raced behind them. The sight made Christina wistful.

Instances of Agnes behaving like a child became rarer every day.

Sarah reached for Christina's hand. 'Are you all right?'

'I was thinking about Will.'

Sarah squeezed her fingers. 'I sense all the missing children. I keep expecting to see them.' Sarah had nursed Tom and Ann's two youngest children until they died within a week of each other in March.

'Are you sure you want to come back to London with us?' Christina asked.

'Ann insists that she is recovered enough to look after Christiana. I belong beside you and George now,' Sarah replied. 'There is more to the world than Alnwick. You've given me the chance to see it.'

'London and Edinburgh are hardly the world. I've promised to go back to Paris again next year. Would you come with me if I can work out a plan?'

'I'd like nothing more.' Sarah's eyes shone with excitement. 'Will you stay with the same family?'

'They have invited me back. Princess Maria, who is Olga's younger sister, wants a portrait like Olga's and I met several other Russian families who were keen.'

'Is there room to take the children?'

'They live in an enormous mansion, but I'd look for an apartment nearby. I think the Princesses would be happy to host us all, but we would be constantly worried about the children making too much noise or breaking something.'

'Noise is guaranteed with four spirited children,' Sarah agreed.

Christina pulled a face. 'I'm certain James won't let me take John. It was enough trouble trying to get him out of London to come here.'

'I'll probably send Andrew back to Alnwick,' Sarah replied. 'Tom has offered him an apprenticeship. Andrew is enthusiastic about the idea, and Tom and I already discussed that he should spend a few weeks in the workshop before he decides.'

The following March, Christina and Sarah travelled to Paris with Agnes, William and Mary. John was angry with his father for keeping him at home, but was consoled with the knowledge that Andrew didn't go either. Their first week in the French capital was rainy, but now they'd been blessed with a series of sunny days. Christina had given herself a few hours off painting to accompany Sarah and the children to the Tuileries gardens. This was definitely the best time of year to visit. Christina's last visit to Paris had been during the summer, when Paris smelled even worse than London.

She and Sarah had taken delivery of new dresses the day before, and the seamstress had made up parasols in the same fabric. Christina cared little about her own appearance, but her artist's eye knew the pair of them, she in palest blue and Sarah in crocus lilac, made a pleasing picture. The girls wore white and William's blue and white outfit had a nautical feel. They looked charming and crisply clean, although history predicted William and Mary were unlikely to remain that way for long.

Christina and Sarah sat on a bench, watching the children play. Agnes entertained her younger siblings by setting Mary's top into a spin and teaching William how to send his hoop off down the path. Sarah sighed and twirled her parasol above her head. 'I will try to remember this day always. To promenade with you in lovely Paris is a moment I was born for.'

Christina smiled at her careful French pronunciation. 'How did the lesson go this morning?' she asked.

'*Très bien,*' Sarah replied, smiling back.

A young lady came to the apartment every day to teach

Agnes French. Then, she stayed on to do beginner lessons for William. As Christina had anticipated, Sarah was more enthusiastic about them than her son.

'How is the painting progressing?' Sarah asked.

'Well, so far. Maria Ivanovna is a beautiful subject, and an accomplished organist. Painting her engaged in her favourite activity lends spirit to the pose.'

'Fair hair and very dark eyebrows are such a striking combination. I wish I had it,' Sarah replied.

'I wouldn't voice that too loudly. Every other woman is longing to have your blonde hair.'

Loud crying shattered the moment. Mary had grabbed William's hoop when he had just managed a successful launch, so he'd pushed her onto the gravel. Agnes's rebuke made him cry, too. Sarah scooped Mary off the ground and Christina took William's hand. 'Mary didn't spoil your game on purpose and gentlemen do not knock over young ladies, William. Shall we walk to Place de la Concorde to view the obelisk again?'

William nodded and ceased crying. The story behind the ancient Egyptian column, newly erected in Paris, had captured his imagination. They made their way along the river to let William gaze up at the obelisk, then headed for home. Christina had them detour past the Baryatinskay villa to allow her to pack away her painting materials for the day. She found a letter addressed to Sarah propped against her easel. Christina's hand shook as she carried it to the court-yard, where Sarah was waiting with the children. The hand-writing was Tom's and unexpected correspondence must surely mean bad news. Sarah's face turned white. She handed the opened letter back to Christina.

Alnwick, April 12th 1837

Dearest Sarah,

I write with the most terrible news. Today, we buried baby Anne beside Charles and Agnes. To lose three children in one year is too much for anyone to bear. Ann found her dead in her cradle, when the child had seemed perfectly healthy the day before. She screamed for what seemed like an hour and hasn't spoken a word since. Christiana and I are locked together in the misery of Ann's silence, only broken by the sound of her cough.

I'll ask you to inform Christina of her niece's death, but please make clear that there is no need for either of you to come now. I know how much you have looked forward to this Paris visit and Christina needs you there.

Andrew continues to show an aptitude for carpentry and I believe he will excel in this trade if he chooses to join me. Thank you for trusting me with his welfare. It provides some comfort to know I have someone to pass my skills onto.

With very best wishes

Tom

Tears coursed down Sarah's face.

'We will pack and go home directly. I can finish Maria's portrait in England,' Christina said.

Sarah shook her head. 'It will annoy Tom if we defy his wishes. I can already see this portrait is going to be one of your best, so the details are important. I will go to Ann as soon as we get home.'

When they all returned to England in May, Sarah went to Alnwick. A few weeks later, the King died and young Princess Victoria became Queen.

James and Christina travelled north as soon as they

received Sarah's letter informing them of Ann's death on 24th August. Sarah had warned them to expect Ann's demise because she had stopped eating. Christina could remember this urge to give up, from her own experience of losing Will so soon after Tiana. She was grateful now that Sarah had helped her find the will to live, but poor Ann had already been ill. She had only brought her own death forward.

The whole family huddled miserably around the graveside in St Michael's churchyard. Tom had raised a large stone to commemorate Charles and Agnes. The stonemason had added Ann's name below the line he had inscribed for her baby only four months before. A whole family wiped out in sixteen months. Tom stood holding four-year-old Christiana in his arms. The child's sobs were the only sound and Christina wondered how poor Tom's legs didn't give way. When the mourners started to peel away from the graveside, Sarah went to his side. 'Pass her to me, Tom. We'll meet you back at the house.' Tom gave her a grateful look. Sarah would remain in Alnwick. It was obvious that she was needed here.

Tom led the procession out of the graveyard. Christina and James fell in towards the back. She became aware of a tall presence at her side. It was John, the brother who was closest to James in age, but the only one Christina didn't really know. He and James were not on speaking terms.

'Are you not stopping to pay respects to your merry widow, James?' He pointed to a grave on their left. 'Or maybe your wife doesn't know she wasn't first choice?'

'For God's sake, John. Today of all days, can we not stand together?' James growled at him. He took Christina's arm to pull her away, but not before she read the name on the gravestone beside her.

Lady Henrietta Askew, widow of Lord Anthony Edward Askew. 12th June 1791 to 14th January 1821.

Christina's chest contracted as the significance of the date sank in. Ahead, Sarah turned around, and Christina caught the look of concern on her face. James had come searching for her in London in April 1821, and they had married a year later. She had always been suspicious about his explanation of why he failed to come back to Kinghorn when he promised, and the delay in tracking her down. Now she had the answer she had never wanted. She withdrew her arm from his.

Chapter Twenty-Five

December 2017, Moscow

I locked myself in the toilet and sobbed into my hands, trying to stifle any noise. Other women came and went. Their happy chatter was a cruel contrast to my state of mind. I strained to hear if they were talking about me. The committee table was right at the front and the most public place to have a marital meltdown. My tears turned to self-pity. I'd arrived on such a high. It hadn't been easy to break into this community, and tonight I'd felt I belonged. Now, I'd been humiliated. How could he have done this to me?

'Anna, are you in there?' Lisa's voice filtered in. 'Please come out. The bathroom is empty. They're all listening to Kerry's speech.'

I unbolted the door. Catching sight of my ruined face in the mirror, I turned my back and leaned against the sink.

'Did you know?' I asked.

Lisa shook her head. 'No. Not until tonight. I'm really sorry, Anna.'

I sighed. 'I wondered if you'd worked it out and been afraid to tell me. The first time I saw them together was the same day I met you. They went into a restaurant as you were getting in the car.'

Lisa looked appalled. 'I didn't see them. Have they been having an affair all this time?'

I shrugged. 'I don't know. Maybe? Perhaps that's why Nick always had an excuse not to meet you.'

Lisa shook her head. 'I don't think Nick knew there was a connection. Dmitry just introduced himself as Oksana's ex-husband. Nick looked really shocked.'

I barked out a bitter laugh. 'God. Is he still here? Does he think he might stay for the dessert? How bloody dare he!'

Lisa shook her head. 'No. He asked me to see if you were all right. Then he left.'

'Of course I'm not fucking all right.'

Lisa put her arm around my shoulder. 'Do you want to come home with us? I can ask Kerry to finish up the auction.'

I turned to the mirror and smoothed down my dress. I licked my thumbs and wiped mascara from under each eye in turn. 'No. I don't want to let you down. What needs doing?'

'Definitely nothing by you. At least stay with us tonight.'

'Isn't Vadim there?'

'Oh, shit. Yes. I'd forgotten.'

I sighed, a weight settled on my shoulders. I couldn't run away. At least not yet. 'I think I'll stay here for a bit. I'll give him time to go to bed before I go home. I'll sleep in the spare room and decide what to do in the morning.'

Lisa took my hand and led me back to the table.

'Is there anything I can do?' Pavel asked. His big, dark eyes looked like he was the one who'd been wounded.

I managed a smile. 'Could you get me a whisky?'

A few minutes later, he returned with a round of drinks. Then he and Dmitry excused themselves. 'Sorry, Lisichka, but tonight I need just one cigarette. I'll be back soon,' Dmitry said.

I took a sip of my drink. I never drink whisky, but the smell of Scotland and the burning in my throat felt harsh yet comforting. Appropriate. 'What are the chances of Dmitry's ex working with Nick? Isn't that a weird coincidence?'

Lisa sipped her whisky with more practised skill than I'd managed. 'Yes, but it's not entirely coincidence. Enerfranc brings lots of expats to Moscow, including me. I joined them in France as a trilingual marketing trainee and they posted me here. Oksana was already working as the Engineering Manager's translator. I first met Dmitry at a company family day. Just before she dumped him for a French guy with better prospects. So, it's not pure coincidence and I'm the connection. I just wish I'd worked it out before.' She took another swig of her drink. This time, she grimaced.

Glamourous couples on the dancefloor, dressed up to the nines, clung to each other in a slow dance. They looked so comfortable together. Had I ever felt that sure of Nick?

'It's nobody's fault. Maybe not even Oksana and Nick's.' I drained my glass. 'The dream of a baby bound us together. The whole thing started to falter when I didn't conceive.'

Lisa raised her eyebrows. 'I think you're letting Nick off the hook too easily. Are you going to give him a second chance?'

I shrugged. 'I don't know. Right now, I can't see it. Maybe I'll go to St Petersburg a few days early. Give myself time.'

Pavel and Dmitry returned. Pavel was carrying the coats we'd checked in.

'Are you sure you can manage without me?'

Lisa hugged me. 'Promise to come round to see us tomorrow. Think about what we can do to help.'

I lay awake all night, but must have fallen asleep after dawn. When I woke, I was astonished to find that my mobile said it was after ten. I pulled on my dressing gown and went into the kitchen. Nick was wearing his jacket, obviously about to go out.

'Where are you going?'

He literally jumped. 'I've been up for hours. I thought you wouldn't want to see me. I decided I should make myself scarce until you calmed down.'

I gritted my teeth. 'I am calm. You can't just run away from this.'

His shoulders slumped. He sat down and dropped his winter boots on the floor.

'Are you going to her dacha?' Now I wasn't calm.

He shrugged. 'Just getting out of the way.'

'You lied to me, Nick.'

'I didn't. There was no physical relationship when you accused me.'

I sat down opposite Nick at the kitchen table and put my head into my hands. 'So this was the first time you had sex, and you got caught? Poor bloody you. Are you telling me there was nothing before? No clinches? No kisses?' I glared at him. I was blazing mad. Nick sat in silence, gazing down at the table.

'Get the hell out of here. I'm going to St Petersburg this afternoon. I'll call you when I've decided what I'm going to do.'

I packed a bag, tears running down my face. Warm gear, my notes, and my laptop. I looked around my bedroom. All these possessions. Was I coming back? Was there anything else I needed? My gaze settled on Christina's desk. I'd never manage both that and a bag on the train. I wrapped it in my dressing gown to protect the corners and put the box in an Ikea bag. I'd ask Lisa to keep it safe for me.

· · ·

Lisa opened the door and immediately enveloped me in a hug.

I left my bags in the hall and followed her into the kitchen. Dmitry was standing at the stove. One twin was flipping small pancakes, and her sister sat on the countertop. Both of them were covered in flour.

'That one needs longer,' the girl on the counter said. I didn't understand her sister's grumpy reply in Russian, but I could guess.

'You will get your turn in a minute, Eva. Let's see how easy you find it,' Dmitry said. He looked over. His sympathetic smile almost set me off. 'Will you have some pancakes, Anna? We've made enough batter to feed an army.'

'I'd love some. Thank you.'

'Coffee?' Lisa asked. 'Let's take it through to the living room.'

'I'm hoping to leave a bag here, if that's okay. I'm going to see if I can get a St Petersburg train this afternoon and it's too bulky to manage.'

'Sure, of course. What is it?'

'Maybe my most precious possession. Christina Robertson's writing desk. I inherited it from my grandmother.'

'A desk?'

'A portable desk. Let me show you.' I retrieved the writing slope from its impromptu wrappings and set it on the living room coffee table.

'Wow, what a beautiful thing.'

'It unfolds to turn into a travelling desk. Isn't it wonderful that I've got something she actually owned?' I unlocked the box and transformed it into the writing slope. 'It's amazing that it still has its ink pot. I plan to get myself an old-fashioned pen so I can use it properly.'

'It's gorgeous.' Lisa knelt to examine it closely. 'Are you sure you need to rush off today? At least stay overnight?'

'You have a house full.'

Lisa shrugged. 'A noisy house is probably good for you today and you can have Vadim's room. He's at ice hockey practice this morning. He'll come back for lunch, then go home to his mum.'

'Are they on speaking terms now?'

'Dmitry smoothed it over. We told him he could stay, but his mum's place is more convenient for school.'

Dmitry and Misha appeared in the doorway. The little boy walked very carefully, holding a small plate in front of him.

'Michael wanted to give you one of his pancakes. He is very proud of his cooking skills,' Dmitry said.

Misha was still dressed in his spiderman pyjamas and his little feet were bare. He looked up at me with huge, serious eyes and offered the plate, bearing one small and misshapen pancake.

'Thank you so much. It looks delicious,' I managed to say.

He grinned and ran to his father, who picked him up and headed back to the kitchen.

'Well done, Misha!' Lisa shouted after him.

The tears started, and I put down the plate. 'I'll have to call the fertility clinic to tell them I'm not coming tomorrow.'

'Oh, Anna. I'm so sorry.' Lisa moved to sit beside me and held me until I stopped crying.

I took a deep breath and reached for my handbag. 'Can I use your internet? I'll send the clinic an email. Easier than talking to them. Also, I need to see if I can bring my accommodation in St Petersburg forward.'

Lisa took a card out of a box on the coffee table. 'The Wi-Fi code and password are on here. But please stay, at least tonight.'

'I know you're being kind, and I realise I'm running away, but if I can get it sorted, I'll go today. I want to fling myself into the Christina research again. It will make me feel better.'

'Have you changed your rail ticket yet?' Lisa asked.

I shook my head.

'Then let me change it for you. I don't think the website is very easy to navigate in English.'

I rummaged in my bag again, pulling things out, looking for the rail ticket printout.

'I'm going to get a coffee top up. Can I get you one?'

I nodded. I found the ticket but also found the little box that Nick had given me. When Lisa returned, I was still holding the box in my hand.

'What's that?' Lisa asked.

'Nick's Christmas present to me. I saw him come out of the shop with Oksana on the day he bought it.'

She set our coffees down. 'Would you like me to put it in the bin?'

I shook my head. 'That would be sacrilege. It's hand-made.' I handed it over.

Lisa frowned as she stared at the picture on the tiny box. 'Mother of god, it's Oksana!' She clapped her hand over her mouth and looked at me with wide eyes.

I started to laugh. In seconds, we were both in helpless hysterics.

Chapter Twenty-Six

May 1839, London

Today marked a high point in Christina's career. She'd had eight portraits accepted by the Royal Academy, and they'd hung three large paintings in their most prestigious rooms. Her skill had been lauded in the high society London papers, and she had a long list of commission requests. Their financial situation was finally stable. Yet walking around the exhibition, she'd rarely felt more dejected. The revelation about Henrietta Askew had undermined her trust in James and he refused to talk about it, insisting it was a figment of his brother John's jealous imagination.

In contrast, James looked like the cat who'd got the cream. He was engaged in earnest conversation with Sir David Wilkie and William Allan, whose paintings were hung on either side of hers. These Scotsmen had risen to the top of the artistic world. Wilkie was now Queen Victoria's official portraitist and Allan had been appointed President to the Royal Scottish Academy. For her part, Christina hadn't the energy for conversation, and no one noticed her slip away. She walked alone, back to her painting of Lady Mary Milnes

Gaskell. She'd posed Mary at her easel with her palette in hand, wearing that particular look of concentrated contentment she used to feel herself but could no longer summon. Christina feared that the empty ache in her betrayed heart would surely soon be evident to others when they viewed her paintings. Might the letter she'd received this week provide her escape route? She certainly couldn't keep going in this frame of mind.

A voice broke her reverie. 'Congratulations, Mrs Robertson, you have captured the creative moment. Has the lady any talent?'

William Allan, standing beside her, was a distinctive man with a mane of grey hair and large side whiskers and, at that moment, sporting an unusually genial smile.

'Thank you. And yes, she has some skills.'

'I came to look for you. I thought I might find you here.'

Christina gave him a questioning look.

'Well, truthfully, I was escaping Wilkie, too. He seeks reassurance that his famous commission for the Queen was not a poisoned chalice. But the truth is, no human could capture Her Majesty's likeness along with the thirty statesmen she insisted should be included in the depiction of her First Council. I'm most thankful she didn't ask me to paint it.'

Christina waited. He'd surely not come to find her to talk about that.

'Also, I'm hoping to lend my influence to help a friend in St Petersburg,' Allan continued.

'A friend?'

'You know I travelled extensively in Russia?'

'Of course. I thought your painting of the prisoners on their way to Siberia was very fine. You must have seen so many fascinating things.'

'I did, and I came to love both Russia and her people. I

was lucky enough to become acquainted with the present Tsar when he was a young man, and it is he who has asked me to speak to you.'

Christina feared that her mouth might have fallen open. She gritted her teeth to reassure herself.

'It seems that your portrait of a Princess Baryatinskaya has captivated the Tsarina. Tsar Nicholas has written to me, asking if I might help persuade you to come to St Petersburg to paint his daughters.'

Christina was momentarily lost for words. A commission from the Emperor of Russia! 'I knew Princess Maria's portrait had been exhibited in St Petersburg, but I never dreamt of such a reaction.'

'You are the talk of the court, Mrs Robertson. Tsar Nicholas is devoted to his wife, and if she sets her heart on something, he will move heaven and earth to fulfil her wish.'

'I'm astonished. I've had an invitation but it didn't make clear it was at the Tsarina's request.'

'It is a tremendous compliment and a significant opportunity. The Tsar has three daughters and I'm certain if you gain their patronage, every family in St Petersburg will clamour for your services.'

'I will give it very serious thought.' Christina's head was spinning. Such a commission could take months to fulfil and it would surely take weeks to reach such a faraway destination. She could hardly tell a man like William Allan that she might consider turning down the chance of a lifetime, because she had children to look after.

'I realise the journey is a big undertaking, but I must confess the very thought of St Petersburg fires me with the urge to return there myself. In my estimation, it is one of the most beautiful cities in the world.'

'How would one get there?'

'Boat is the quickest way to travel, if you are a confident

sailor. There is also a well-travelled route overland from Paris.'

'What about the language? I've heard you are fluent in Russian. I would surely face enormous communication difficulties.'

'The Tsar speaks English, but I'm not sure about his wife. Do you speak French?'

'I've been taking lessons, although I'm far from fluent.'

William Allan shrugged. 'I wouldn't worry about it. French will get you by in court and there is a large British community in St Petersburg who even have their own church services and shops.'

'How intriguing. I'll certainly consider it.'

'Good. The Tsar has said he will oversee all the arrangements to get you there, but I am happy to be the go-between. I am delighted for you, Mrs Robertson. One of my countrywomen becoming the toast of St Petersburg is a joyful prospect.'

'Thank you for that offer and for your kind interest. I'd obviously have to discuss the matter with my husband.'

'Of course. Please let me know if I can do anything further to reassure you. I'd be happy to talk to James. A commission from the Tsar is quite something.'

'Please allow me to raise it with him first.'

'At your service, Mrs Robertson.'

The conversation with James did not go the way Christina had expected. Apparently, the words 'Tsar' and 'William Allan advises' had transformed James's attitude to her travelling overseas. The only fraught point was the plans for the children, she didn't want to leave them behind.

'Eliza's health isn't robust enough to manage the younger children on her own now,' she argued.

James scowled. 'Both boys must stay here. William has only just commenced his lessons with Mr Ambleton. There is no need to disrupt things. He is an independent little chap, and he will be offended if you treat him like a baby. Eliza, John and I will be able to keep an eye on him in your absence.'

Christina wanted to argue, but sensed James wouldn't yield. A royal commission was a career changing opportunity, but thought of leaving her sons behind was agonising. Might Sarah be able to come? She hadn't seen her in nearly a year, but the adventure would be less daunting if Sarah could help with Mary while she worked.

Sarah's reply arrived within the week.

Alnwick, May 21st 1839
Dearest Christina

Let me think. Would I prefer to stay in dull little Alnwick, listening to my mother repeating the same inconsequential gossip three times every week? Or shall I travel to Russia and meet a court full of princesses? Shall I see a city reputed to be as beautiful as Paris? Most of all, shall I share this exciting adventure with you?'I am doing my best to pretend that I am loath to leave everyone here, but in my imagination my feet are doing a jig! I had already begun to make plans to return to London. I've found a suitable local girl called Margaret and Tom has agreed I can start training her up.

Andrew is now a fully-fledged working man. He loves carpentry and shows every sign of mastering the skill. I shall miss my boy, but I'm not sure how much he will miss me. They work long hours and even when he is at home, he is usually found lurking near Tom and Adam, whittling a piece of wood, or pestering them for advice on some tricky joint.

I estimate that I will be confident to leave Christiana in Margaret's care by the end of June.

Yours, with my head dreaming of distant lands.
Sarah xxx

Christina expected Sarah to arrive today. It gave them three weeks to assemble their luggage and make all the necessary plans. Christina, Sarah, Agnes and Mary would travel to Paris at the end of August, to join the Yusupovs on their journey back to St Petersburg. Christina had met Boris Yusupov and his young wife Zinaida on her last trip to Paris. They had been frequent visitors to gatherings in Vladimir Davydov's home. She was glad not to travel with strangers, since they would be trapped together for many weeks.

Christina had only managed a few brushstrokes all morning. Every time she heard a carriage stop in Harley Street, she was drawn to the window. In the end, she was intent on blending paint and missed her friend's arrival. She heard Mary's feet run across the parquet floor in the room below, then the bell rang. 'Sarah!' Mary shrieked. Obviously, Christina wasn't the only one who had been watching the window. She descended to the sitting room, to find Mary balanced on Sarah's hip with her face buried in her neck and Agnes clasped into a hug with Sarah's other arm. Sarah smiled at Christina over the top of Mary's head. There were tears in her eyes. 'I've missed you so much.'

'I can hardly find the words to express it. Welcome back,' Christina replied, tears running down her own cheeks.

The following two weeks were a blur of shopping and dress fittings. At sixteen, Agnes needed an entire trunk of dresses, as did Christina and Sarah. William Allan had warned her to expect a very active social calendar and a need for many formal gowns. Such expenditure all at once made Christina nervous. They were not currently short of money and Allan had advised her to charge the Tsar a sum per portrait that was much higher than any previous commission, but frugality was a habit. Christina was hardly interested in clothes, but seeing excitement on both Agnes and Sarah's faces made her very happy.

There was only a week left before their departure date when she and Sarah finally had a quiet evening on their own. Sarah was staying at George's house, but tonight she'd come home with Christina. James was dining at his club, so they'd planned a quiet supper, just the two of them.

Christina looked up from her copy of *Kenilworth* when Sarah came back from kissing the children goodnight. She was rereading her favourite of Scott's novels. Sarah took one of William's socks out of the darning basket and pulled a stool in beside Christina, leaning back against her chair. Christina put her hand on Sarah's shoulder. 'Leave that. The light's not good enough and you'll strain your eyes.'

Sarah tipped her head back to smile up at her. 'I might say the same about your reading. Where have you got to?'

'Where Amy Robsart meets the Earl of Leicester. I was thinking I'd like to attempt a depiction of the scene. Would you pose for me if I can find some spare time in St Petersburg?'

'Of course, but I hope you don't wish me Amy's tragic end. I have no desire to die for any man.'

Christina looked into her friend's smiling face. She had to ask: 'Sarah. Will you tell me about Henrietta Askew?'

Sarah's smile disappeared, and she looked away. 'Don't you think I would have told you already if I thought it would do you any good? Anyway, I never met her and repeating hearsay is a bad idea.'

'Who was she?'

'A widow, a monied lady. Jane told me Adam and John did some work at her mansion.'

'And James?'

'I heard so,' Sarah replied, her tone flat.

'I saw the dates, Sarah. She died during the months that James was missing from my life. Were they lovers?'

'Who can possibly know that? It was said he spent time at the house. If you need to know more, you should ask him, but I'd advise against raking up the past.'

'It's in my heart, so not only in the past.'

Sarah's eyes were full of sympathy.

'I was so in love with James,' Christina continued. 'It was like a fairy tale, that this handsome boy should have chosen me and I felt so certain of his love. When I was abandoned, I told myself that Robbie must have written some lies to James to scare him away, because I simply couldn't believe that James would be disloyal.'

'Perhaps he did? It certainly sounds like Robbie was intent on hurting you.'

Christina shook her head. 'It dawned on me recently that Robbie never mastered writing. I surely knew that? I wonder if I invented an explanation to save myself from facing the truth.'

'How did James explain his absence when he came to you in London?'

'I was overjoyed when James reappeared. He was full of apologies and he seemed so genuinely delighted to find me. He said he'd been working on a contract away from home and didn't get my letters. When he went looking for me in King-horn, no-one would tell him where I'd gone. I fear now that the contract he was working on was for marriage, and it was only Lady Henrietta's death that prevented it.'

Sarah looked down at the sock in her hand. She stabbed her needle into the pincushion. 'Will you confront him?'

'It's eating me up inside. I think I must.'

'I would advise forgetting it, but if you cannot, then you deserve the truth,' Sarah replied.

The next morning, Christina was woken early by James entering her bedroom. She knew what was on his mind by the look on his face.

'Please, Christina. You will be gone for months. A man cannot live this way.'

Resentment erupted. She sat up in bed. 'Do you think for one moment I find it easy? That I don't miss your touch too? But what about the consequences? Would you have me make this journey pregnant?'

'I'd be careful,' he whined.

'William and Mary both arose from your so-called carefulness. I cannot risk another pregnancy, and I simply could not bear another bereavement. I loved all our children, and the lost ones are a weight in my heart every day.'

He looked at her with those big blue eyes, beseeching, deluded.

'Get dressed,' she said. 'I understand you try not to think of the deaths, but I cannot avoid it. Today is the anniversary of Will's passing. I'm going to lay flowers at the gravestone. Please come with me.'

They walked towards Marylebone through the quiet streets, passing maids on their way to open up the grand houses and butchers delivering to back doors. The roads were almost empty of carriages, it being too early for the gentry to be up and about. Christina carried a posy of anemones she'd bought from a flower girl. In the walled graveyard, the little rose bush beside the gravestone was covered in tiny white buds. She knelt and pinched off the dead blooms to encourage more growth.

'You planted a rose?' James asked.

'Sarah and I put it in last year. She took a cutting to Will's grave, and she tells me it has taken. She did the same thing by bringing snowdrops here from Alnwick.'

'Sarah is a loyal friend.' James allowed his head to sink towards his chest. 'I'm sorry for not coming more often. Three babies is a lot to bear.'

'Four,' she replied.

'What?' James's head snapped up. He looked confused.

Christina gritted her teeth. 'Tell me about Henrietta Askew,' she demanded. She had to deal with that subject first.

James groaned. 'Damn John Robertson. Did Sarah say something?'

'She wouldn't report gossip and said it was better left in the past.'

'Please, let's do that.' He gave her a pleading look. 'It was a long time ago.'

'I have to know. Would you have married her if she had lived?'

James didn't reply immediately. Eventually, he sighed and said: 'I don't know. Henrietta knew I hated the toil of carpentry and house painting. She promised to fund my career as an artist. Promised a life outside Alnwick.'

'So I was your second choice?' Christina's words caught in her throat.

James gave her an anguished look. 'You were always my first choice. I was young. It was a few months of madness, youthful stupidity.'

'You left my pleading letters unanswered. How did you forgive yourself?'

James had the look of a chastised child. 'We found the right path in the end. No harm was done.'

'You are wrong,' Christina replied. 'Come with me.' She led him the few steps to the first Christiana's grave. She took out her handkerchief and knelt to scrub the lichen off the small stone, making the wording clearer. When she got to her feet, she saw the horror on his face.

'You were pregnant? Why didn't you tell me?'

'I believed you wouldn't have wanted to know. Robbie Thomson was watching us in the barn that day. After you left, he came in and raped me. I didn't know for sure that Christiana was ours until I delivered her.'

'That scoundrel defiled you?' James snapped back, his tone outraged.

The disgust in his eyes made her furious. 'While you were paying suit to a rich widow, I endured the shameful consequences of Robbie's violence. Aunt Agnes threw me out when I refused to reveal the father. I was heartbroken by your abandonment and then almost died giving birth to our daughter. She was born too early, just like her sister. When she died, I thought I'd never recover. Perhaps I never did.'

'It wasn't my fault. How could I have known?' Tears were running down his face, but she judged that he was feeling sorry for himself.

'You've been protected from this for twenty years. I carried the pain alone to spare your feelings. I now see that was a mistake. When I'm in Russia, we must both think about our future together. We have to be in this marriage on an equal footing and with no more secrets between us.'

Chapter Twenty-Seven

December 2017, Moscow

L isa insisted on dropping me off at the station. 'Let me know what your plans are. We arrive on the eleventh, so I'll see you then if not before.'

'I haven't really got a plan, but I'll keep you posted. I'm not sure how long my research is going to take.'

'When will Pavel be back in St Petersburg?'

'His plan was to leave this morning, so I presume he's there already.'

I slept through most of the train journey. When I walked out into the station concourse in St Petersburg, Pavel was waiting for me. He took my bag. 'I hope you don't mind that Lisa told me when your train was arriving. I thought I'd see you safely to your hotel.'

'Thank you, that's really kind. It's not far, on the edge of Mikhailovsky Garden.'

We got into Pavel's car and he pulled into the traffic. 'How are you feeling?'

I shrugged. 'A bit numb, still in shock, I think. I hope it's not a nuisance having me here early?'

'Not at all. It suits me. Work is quiet for the next couple of weeks.'

'I've been so looking forward to seeing Christina's paintings and really getting into her story in Russia. It will keep me from moping.'

'I found hard work a good cure for heartache when Liling left.'

'Did she go back to China?'

'Eventually. A couple of months after we split up.'

Pavel stopped outside the hotel. 'Do you want to have a working supper with me? We could look at your list of paintings again and decide which ones I should request from storage.'

'Sure.'

'I'll meet you in the lobby at seven-thirty. I know somewhere within walking distance.'

I checked in, and thankfully, I was on the other side of the building from our previous room. It maybe wasn't the most sensible choice to return somewhere that made me think of Nick. If I decided to stay beyond this week, I'd look around for somewhere else. I sent Nick a text to let him know where I was. Not that I owed him any explanation of my whereabouts, but I didn't want to give him an excuse to call. I certainly didn't want to talk to him today.

I logged into the Hermitage website and pulled out my file of paintings. I wanted to seem professional and prepared before I discussed them with Pavel. There were several things to consider. The book needed paintings which showcased Christina's talent, and also best illustrated her story. Crucially, I hoped to discover more about Christina's life here in Russia. The success of the book would depend on both the pictures and an interesting story. Were there any smaller sized paintings in the Hermitage that might be loaned for the Scottish Portrait Gallery exhibition?

When Pavel arrived I was glad I'd got my hat and gloves, because his headgear suggested we were in for a cold walk. His brown leather hat was fur-lined, including the comical-looking ear flaps. He pulled the hat off and gave me a sheepish look.

'Are you laughing at my hat?'

'No, and please put it back on. When my ears start to freeze, I expect I'll be asking for directions to the shop to buy one.' I tugged my own woollen hat down over my ears.

'I thought we'd go to a dumpling place on the Fontanka River, but it's about a twenty-minute walk. If that's okay?'

'Sounds great.'

The walk along the river was picturesque, the beautiful buildings casting illuminations on the water and icicle-like Christmas lights strung across the river added to the effect. I stopped to gaze at a particularly beautiful yellow and white mansion behind a wrought-iron fence on the opposite bank.

'That's Sheremetev Palace.'

'I recognise that name. I'm sure I've seen a Christina painting of an Anna Sheremeteva.'

'Could be,' he replied. 'It's the right era.'

In the restaurant, Pavel chose us a selection of delicious dumplings. Once we'd eaten, we ordered two more beers, and I spread out my Hermitage images. 'So far, I've only seen the five big paintings of Nicholas I's family.'

'As I said before, most of her paintings are in storage.' Pavel pointed to the images he'd asterisked in the Moscow café. 'But those are in the British collection on the second floor.'

'Nick and I must have missed them when we walked through the British collection. I'll book a ticket to go back tomorrow.'

'To be honest, room 301 is tricky to find. It's no wonder you missed it. I'm working in the museum tomorrow. Send me a text when you're heading there, and I'll meet you.'

I didn't sleep well. I was angry with Nick. Raging at wasting my childbearing years on a cheating bastard. Mocking voices filled my head. 'Poor Anna must be heartbroken. Imagine, when she's only been married a year.' Was it definitely over? Nick had been my whole life. But was I really surprised? I'd known there was a problem and chose to ignore the warning signs.

Next day, I needed a walk to clear my head before my Hermitage visit. I entered the Mikhailovsky Garden via the floral wrought-iron gates. The sign confirmed that the park was here in the 1840s. Some of the large trees would have been saplings when Christina had walked these very paths. The thought made me smile. Emerging from the edge of the wooded area, I took a bridge across the Moika River into a formal garden called the Field of Mars. Apart from the modern dress of the pedestrians, I could easily have been in the nineteenth century. In these surroundings, with a cold blue sky above and a whole day to immerse myself in Christina's world, I was momentarily content. Of course, it only took a second to locate the rejection and loss inside. I should have had my first ovulation stimulation injection this month. What if this had all happened when I was already pregnant with Nick's baby? My gut response to that 'what if' wasn't straightforward. My longing to be a mother was deep-rooted. But now I had to reconsider whether I even wanted to be connected to Nick forever.

I turned in the direction of the Hermitage, took a deep breath, and deliberately put him out of my mind. I didn't have to account for my plans to anyone. A tiny spark of happiness flickered. My life might be in meltdown, but I was free to make my own choices.

Striding up the red-carpeted Jordan staircase to the first floor, I didn't stop to gawk at the grand surroundings. I was focused on going back to Christina's Romanov portraits again. The intricately inlaid wooden parquet was almost certainly the same floor as Christina had walked on. There had been a terrible fire in the Palace in 1837, just before Christina's arrival. Nicholas I had to have the whole place redecorated and many of her portraits were commissioned to replace artwork lost in the fire.

I stopped first at the portrait of Alexandra, the youngest daughter, dressed in pink. I was determined to focus on all the detail. Christina had painted in the date 1840. There was a book open on the balustrade behind this teenager, perhaps indicating her favourite pastime? She held a blue flower in her hand. A cornflower? Her mother on the opposite wall held a white rose. I supposed the flowers held some meaning that viewers of the day would have understood. I'd read some criticism of the Empress's portrait, complaining that it flattered her features, making her look younger than her then forty-two years. Was this the equivalent of nineteenth century airbrushing? The family must surely have liked the portrait, because Christina went on to paint so many more. The painting on the other side of the Tsar was Maria Alexandrovna, who would go on to be the next Tsarina, when Alexander II took over the throne from his father. It surely wasn't coincidence that Christina had portrayed her in a white silk dress, very similar to the Empress's gown. At least one of these royal portraits had to feature in the book. I liked the portrait of Maria, the eldest daughter, the best. She wore a beautiful burgundy velvet dress, and stood with sheet music in her hands beside her piano. Musical instruments were a recurring theme in Christina's work.

I texted Pavel to tell him I was on my way to room 301. I fought my way through a crowd of visitors packed into a corridor of military portraits, took several wrong turns and eventually I arrived at a narrow gallery. Pavel was standing at the end, beside the painting of two children with a parrot.

'I found it! This place is a maze.'

'It is.'

I looked at the painting. 'Who are the children?'

'Most experts consider this one of her best, but sadly, we don't know the names of the children.'

I checked the Hermitage virtual guide to get the description of this portrait and passed my phone to Pavel. 'Read that last sentence.'

They followed the example of the Russian imperial family in showering the Scottish artist with commissions, forgiving her the lack of variety in composition and the sentimentality which made all her sitters look sweet and virtuous.

'It's that same condescending and patronising tone I've come across before. This gallery is full of portraits of military men standing like emotionless statues. Yet, those male artists don't face any censure. Would the parents be happy if she'd painted the children having an argument?'

'You have a point. This will have been written by a curator, but I promise it wasn't me.'

I turned to a small painting which depicted the Empress's

two younger daughters. 'Oh, this is perfect. The same sisters but on a tiny scale. This painting says so much about Christina's style. All the particular quirks of her work. A miniature, featuring a piano and the youngest Princess is viewed from behind. Do you think the Hermitage would lend this to the Scottish Portrait Gallery?'

'Hmm.' Pavel looked dubious. 'I'm not sure I can get you this painting. Esme Stevenson has already asked about us loaning these William Allans.' He gestured to a pair of paintings on the adjacent wall. 'I can't see the directors agreeing to allow three empty spots in the same room.'

'Ah,' I said. 'That's disappointing.' I peered at the Allan painting. A dark, backlit scene, featuring two men on horseback. 'This painting of the Bashkirs is so much smaller than I imagined.' The width was about half a metre and the height was less. 'The Lady Rolle in ermine painting which was displayed beside this in the Royal Academy is two and half metres high.'

Pavel shrugged. 'Like I said, maybe Allan painted more than one version?'

I turned back to the small portrait of the Princesses. 'You get no idea of scale with internet images. I really love all the precise details. This wouldn't be hung high on a wall but at eye level, or perhaps be placed on a desk.'

'I'm sorry. I do agree this is a lovely painting.'

I sighed.

'Don't worry, we'll find you something suitable. Let me borrow your list. I'll talk to the director of the Staraya Derevnya Restoration and Storage Centre. He might have advice on what he's got that would work for the Scottish exhibition.'

'So they're not stored on site?'

'Wait till you see the size of this place. We store more items there than we can ever display in the museum. I'll ask

257

the Director if I can show you around. There are exhibits there that will give you a sense of Christina's world, carriages and sledges and even some clothes. I think you'll find it fascinating.'

'That sounds great. Is it far away?'

'Not too far and we can get there by metro. I've got meetings tomorrow, then everything is closed on January first. I'll try to get us an appointment for Thursday.'

'Of course. I'd lost track of the date.'

'What are your plans for tomorrow?'

'I want to make sure I've covered every lead I can find about Christina's life. I might go to a café because the internet connection in the hotel keeps dropping.'

'You'd be welcome to work at my place, if you like? I'm going to be out all day.'

'That's really kind of you. Are you sure?'

'Of course. You need peace and quiet to work. My apartment's not far from here. I'll text you the address and directions. Can you be there by eight in the morning?'

'Definitely.'

Back at my hotel, I ate the sandwich I'd picked up on the way home. I quickly gave up channel surfing on the TV in my room. They either had no satellite connection, or it wasn't working. Why didn't I pack a book? I reached for my phone to call Mum. The text I sent yesterday told her I was going St Petersburg early, but not why. Reluctance to tell her was stacked against the sudden need to hear her voice. But what was I going to say? Had I left Nick for good? Had he left me? I hadn't even spoken to him since I quit Moscow. I reluctantly changed tack and rang Nick's number. His phone went straight into voicemail. Somewhere in a nearby room, a baby began to cry.

Chapter Twenty-Eight

September 1839, Paris, France

Christina gave their carriage driver the address of the Yusupovs' home. Princess Zinaida had told her their villa was close to the Bois de Boulogne.

'Wake up, Mary. We're in Paris,' Christina said.

Her daughter rubbed her eyes and looked out the carriage window. 'Does the Princess live in a castle?' she asked.

A few minutes later, they swept onto a circular drive. The house ahead of them was the most enormous mansion.

'A castle!' Mary said triumphantly.

Christina and Sarah exchanged wide-eyed looks. They were to stay with the Yusupovs overnight, before setting off for St Petersburg in the morning. This would most certainly be the biggest house any of them had ever slept in. A liveried footman stood beneath the pillared portico. Their carriage stopped, and he stepped forward to open the door. Agnes reached for her hand. She gave her daughter a reassuring smile.

Christina told the footman her name, and he replied that the Princess was expecting them. As they crossed the white marble floor of an echoing hallway, the sound of beautiful violin music got louder. The footman opened a door, and they entered a huge drawing room. Princess Zinaida Yusupova got up from her seat, and the young man who had been playing took his bow away from his instrument.

'Madame Robertson, welcome to our home. This is Nikolai, my son.'

'I'm delighted to meet you again, Your Highness. You might remember my companion, Sarah, and these are my daughters, Agnes and Mary. We are so very grateful that you are allowing us to join you on this journey.'

'The Tsarina is so pleased that you've been persuaded to come. She has asked me to do everything possible to make your journey tolerable.'

Christina saw that both her daughters were entranced. The Princess was extraordinarily beautiful. Dark brown hair fell to her shoulders in shiny waves and her lace-edged pink silk dress hugged her form in liquid-like folds.

There was a knock on the door and a tall young woman with jet black hair entered. 'I'm sure you must all be exhausted after your sea crossing,' Princess Zinaida said. 'Yelena will show you to your rooms. We shall dine at eight. I'd be delighted if you'd like to join us, but I can have some food sent up, if you prefer.'

Christina glanced at Mary, whose pale face and glassy eyes gave away both her excitement and tiredness. 'As you say, our journey was long and I think it best if we get Mary ready for bed soon.'

'Of course. Yelena will make sure you have everything you need. Fortunately, she speaks some English.'

Yelena led them up two staircases to a suite of rooms. 'Look, Mama,' Mary exclaimed. 'I have a tiny bed all of my own.'

True enough, one of the two bedrooms had a full-sized curtained bed and another almost identical but half-sized.

'You are a very lucky girl,' Christina replied. She had worried that she'd find it hard to get Mary to go to bed, but her daughter was already on her stomach on the mattress, kicking her little legs, trying to haul herself up. 'Let me unbutton your boots, Mary.'

Mary squirmed onto her back and stuck out her feet. 'Don't you want some supper before bed?' Christina said, whilst sliding Mary's feet out of her smart new kid boots.

'I send your trunks up,' Yelena volunteered.

Sarah unpinned her bonnet. 'I'll come down with you. We've packed a couple of small ones with our things for tonight. Also, perhaps you could show me the kitchen so I can meet the other staff?'

They had discussed their travelling arrangements before they set off. Christina had been against Sarah setting herself apart as if she were a servant.

'The title of companion is fine if it pleases you, but I'd prefer not to spend the whole time pretending to be a lady,' Sarah had argued.

Something in the tilt of Yelena's head seemed to imply she was pleased with the clarification. Christina's first impression of Yelena was that she seemed rather standoffish, so it was a surprise to see her smile warmly at Sarah as they left the room.

The next morning, they woke early. When Christina pulled back the heavy drapes, she discovered a line of carriages outside. 'Goodness, we are going to be like an army on manoeuvre.'

'Yelena told me we are to have a carriage to ourselves,' Sarah answered. Christina caught the frustrated look on Agnes's face. Her elder daughter had been disappointed not to dine with their travelling companions. 'I'm told this journey might take six weeks, Agnes. You will have plenty of opportunity to get acquainted,' Christina told her.

Agnes shrugged. 'This is such a grand house, Mama. I should have liked to see it.'

Christina had to work hard to hide her sadness during the long hours in the coach. She ached to be so far away from her sons, and her last conversations with James were painful. It was a relief to be rid of her secret, but James's lack of understanding was hurtful. She'd told Sarah he wouldn't cope with the knowledge of the rape. Nevertheless, she'd hoped to be wrong. His self-centred reaction increased the gap between them.

The Yusupovs kept to their own rooms when the party stayed overnight at small coaching inns. However, in Lille, they were invited to their private sitting room in the hotel.

'Nikolai has been practising a new piece, and it's good for him to have an audience, if you wouldn't mind?' Princess Zinaida said.

'We would love that,' Christina replied in French. The boy's playing was beautiful. Being given permission to gaze at him, Christina observed how much he looked like his mother and was mesmerized by his skilful handling of the violin. She itched to capture his image. He was a slight child and looked younger than his twelve years, but his intent expression and flying fingers transformed him from a boy into a gifted musician. They'd spent a lot of time in Yelena's company, and she'd told them that Zinaida was the Prince's second wife, and that Nikolai was their only child. The age gap between the couple was not as large as between Louisa Rolle and her husband, but Christina noticed a similar tenderness. Perhaps older husbands were more appreciative of their luck.

'Do you know the Tsarina well?' Christina asked the Princess.

'Extremely well,' she replied. 'I was her lady-in-waiting before I married.' She explained how the royal couple had met in Berlin when they were very young and that their marriage was a love match. After a few minutes, Mary began to fidget. She swung her legs, which dangled several inches off the ground, and Christina had to place her hand on Mary's knee to stop her. Princess Zinaida whispered something to her husband.

'My wife regrets she cannot speak much English,' Boris Yusupov said. 'She has asked me to translate for her.'

'Please excuse my daughter's rudeness,' Christina replied. 'We wouldn't want to put you to such trouble.'

Princess Zinaida smiled reassuringly at Mary and spoke to Prince Boris in rapid Russian.

'My wife insists it is no hardship and I agree. My translation of her court stories will offer an opportunity for her to improve her English and give your children a break from constant French.'

This settled them into a routine of a violin recital followed by Princess Zinaida's court stories, which they replicated in Brussels, Berlin, and then on into Poland. Christina got permission to bring her sketch pad to their conversations. The Yusupovs had asked Christina to do family portraits when she had finished the Tsarina's commissions. She couldn't paint on the journey, but creating a portfolio of sketches helped her form a vision of the portraits in her head. She would paint Nikolai with his violin. As in her painting of Princess Maria Ivanovna, she'd observed that the boy's features came alive when he was performing.

. . .

The hotels and architecture of Brussels and Berlin bore some similarities and they even came across some of the same guests. However, once they started further heading north, the surroundings and languages made their distance from home very evident. Christina hoped the nightly routine was a steadying factor for her daughters in this disorientating journey. Princess Zinaida was a talented raconteur, and she always inserted a few anecdotes about the royal family's naughty spaniel to entertain Mary. The Princess's stories of the Tsar and his wife portrayed them as a loving couple, devoted to their seven children. However, their court duties required them to entertain, and her descriptions of lavish balls had them all enthralled, including Mary.

On the nights where Agnes volunteered to put Mary to bed, Christina encouraged Princess Zinaida to relax into French and the stories took a different turn. Her husband would leave to attend to his correspondence and the Princess related stories about previous Romanovs, which were definitely not suitable for Mary, or even Agnes's ears. She learnt how Peter the Great had loved a peasant girl, who became his mistress. He went onto marry her and as Empress she led his court, and later his country. Christina and Sarah were particularly fascinated by the scandalous stories of the two female Empresses Elizaveta and Catherine.

'So do you think?' Sarah asked in English. 'Were the stories of our virgin Queen Elizabeth a parcel of lies?'

'Who knows?' Christina replied. 'Somehow I cannot imagine the English lords allowing her to flaunt her sexual needs openly.'

The topic caused Christina to think about her own sorry situation. She was firm in her resolution to have no more children, but she missed physical intimacy. Five years of self-imposed celibacy had been difficult to bear. James imagined it didn't matter to her, which made the pain even worse. Sarah had been a widow for fourteen years. How did she manage?

'Were the Empresses not afraid of bearing illegitimate children?' Christina asked in French.

Princess Zinaida shrugged. 'There are rumours that they both had daughters. Perhaps it would have been more difficult to keep sons a secret?'

A consequence of the Princess's stories was that everyone's French improved. Even Mary had begun to pepper her conversation with French words. Sarah's language skills improved the most. As the journey progressed, Sarah and Yelena had begun excusing themselves once Yelena's duties were over, and they spent more and more of their evenings together.

When they reached the town of Danzig on the Baltic coast, Princess Zinaida announced they would stop for three nights to catch up with laundry. Christina had an urge to stretch her legs, and asked Agnes to keep Mary with her. She worried about Mary's safety amongst the crowds, and so close to deep water in this busy port.

Sarah accompanied Christina on her walk.

'Are you angry with me, Christina? I fear I've been neglecting my companion role,' she said, as soon as they were away from the hotel.

'I miss you in the evenings,' Christina replied truthfully, 'but I'm glad to see you happy.' This was only partially true, but Christina was ashamed to admit how much she was jealous.

'I'd happily spend every hour by your side and the same is true for the girls,' Sarah replied. 'But, after being cooped up in the coach all day, I find it a chore to sit silently in the Yusupovs' company. I must tell you that Yelena has a different nature entirely from the severe and silent character she acquires in her mistress's company.'

'Why do you feel you must be silent with the Yusupovs?' Christina asked.

'I lack your diplomacy and in such company it's not my place to speak. In any case, I'm gathering my own information to aid our success in St Petersburg. Yelena confirms that the royal couple are quietly devoted, but the court is full of intrigue. You have the ear of a member of court and I have access to their servants' tongues. We are a formidable team.'

Sarah took her arm as they walked along the long harbour front, lined with tall-masted ships. 'These high, narrow buildings remind me of Leith.'

'A sort of elongated version,' Christina replied.

Sarah wrinkled her nose. 'It certainly smells similar.'

'To be walking in the fresh air is a joy, fishy or not.'

They strolled into the centre of the city until the musical chiming of the town hall clock reminded Christina of the time. 'We need to get back. Mary's ill-temper this morning is due to going to bed too late last night. If I can persuade her to have a nap, I'll paint this afternoon. Come and entertain me with some of Yelena's stories. You are quite right, I need to approach the court with my eyes open.'

A week later, they reached the coast again in the ancient town of Riga. Yelena advised Sarah that they lacked some essential items for the Russian winter. She took them to a furrier, tucked down a narrow street in the lee of the cathedral. There she helped them all choose fur hats and muffs. Agnes and Mary were thrilled with their purchases, but it was Sarah who looked most impressive. Yelena had picked out a very dark fur hat and placed it on Sarah's head, running her fingers inside its brim to settle on Sarah's blonde ringlets.

From Riga they set off overland again, finally reaching St Petersburg at the end of October. There was an early snowstorm on the penultimate day and its severity reminded Christina of the long, cold, and dark winter ahead. Her forty-third birthday would happen here, and she would miss William's ninth birthday in January. John was thirteen but mature for his years, whilst William still seemed like a baby to her. She sighed and pushed the thought away. Christina trusted Eliza implicitly and whatever James's faults were as a husband, he was an unusually attentive father. Now she was here, she must maximise her time to justify the journey. There was no hope that James would start earning again and the future of her family depended on her success. A man's focus was needed to overcome the misgivings of her motherly heart. Like an Empress, but without the lovers.

Chapter Twenty-Nine

December 2017, St Petersburg, Russia

I t turned out, I'd gone past Pavel's building on my walk along Millionnaya Street, when I was heading to the Hermitage. I entered a cobbled courtyard overlooked by tall old buildings on three sides. Pavel had said I'd find his door number opposite the entrance. The stairway up to the third floor reminded me of Lisa's building. This one was even older, but whereas Lisa's stairwell was gleaming and well lit, this was dark and dingy. Pavel opened the door, and I stepped into a massive apartment.

'Welcome to the 1970s,' Pavel said. 'Perhaps I should have warned you.'

'This is incredible. Do you really live here alone?'

'It's a bit ridiculous, isn't it. I should sell it and buy a modern flat somewhere else.' He shrugged. 'But I like it here.'

The floor was woodblock, and a large chandelier hung from the middle of a corniced ceiling. Other than that, it was as he said, straight out of the 1970s.

'Liling had big ideas to change everything, but my grandmother wasn't keen and I kept stalling. It's a wonder she didn't leave me sooner.'

The apartment certainly felt dated. The furniture was large and constructed of shiny varnished dark wood. I could see a kitchen through an open door. Wood-edged cupboards with red panels. Surely at least thirty years old.

Pavel shifted from one foot to the other. 'I have done some updating. My bedroom, bathroom and study are up on the mezzanine, and decorated for the twenty-first century, I promise.'

I followed his gesture to some stairs in the next room. 'Why are you apologising?' I said with a laugh. 'It's incredible.'

'Incredible, like a Soviet film set, incredible?' He gave me a lopsided smile. 'This is how it was when Dad and I moved in... Come and see the best feature.'

Pavel led me over to the French doors, which opened out onto a narrow stone balcony. The embankment road ran below and ahead was the most incredible view of the Neva River. There was a church on the opposite bank. Its very thin steeple shone brightly, as if made of gold.

'That's the Peter and Paul Cathedral. St Petersburg's oldest landmark. The spire is covered in gilded copper.'

'Oh, Pavel, what a view. This apartment is absolutely amazing.'

'You get it. I should have known you would.' He smiled. 'The wireless network and password are on the table. Just sign in and make sure it works for you.'

I opened my laptop. 'It works perfectly. Thank you.'

'I've left tea and coffee on the kitchen counter. Here's a spare key in case you want to go out and stretch your legs. I should be back late afternoon.' Pavel put on his jacket and shouldered his backpack. 'See you later.'

When Pavel left, I spent a long time watching the river traffic. Apparently, the Neva can freeze over in winter. That would be something to see. This building was only a few hundred yards from the Hermitage. Pavel must have the shortest commute ever, and one of the best views. Forcing myself to sit down and make use of this quiet time, I spent the rest of the morning working on a chapter plan for the book. At lunchtime, I took myself off for a walk to the multi-storey bookshop in the Singer Building. When I reached the junction, I crossed Nevsky Prospekt to be able to see the art nouveau architecture properly. Double-height curved windows, topped by four more elegant, grey granite floors. Female bronzes, weathered to green, lined the top floor below the glass and bronze cupula, with the globe on top. Commissioned in the early 1900s by the American Singer Sewing Machine Company, it wouldn't have been here in Christina's day. Somehow, however, it fitted in with the spirit of St Petersburg. My guidebook said it had been *Dom Knigi* – House of Books – since the 1930s. Inside, it was packed with shoppers, surely a good sign for the cultural health of a city. They had a large English language section where I picked up a book on art history and Turgenev's *Rudin*, which I hoped might get me into the mood of Christina's era. I treated myself to a pastry and coffee in their café before heading back to work.

I'd set the afternoon aside for ancestry research. There were so few confirmed facts about Christina's personal life. I wanted to make sure all the biographical details were as accurate as possible. I downloaded copies of the birth certificates of all Christina's children. Next, I turned to the sad task of looking for death or burial records. I anticipated this might be more difficult. I'd never managed to find burial records for Christina's parents. There were birth records for seven children. Agnes, John, William and Mary had survived into adulthood, but three babies had died as infants: Christiana, James William, and Christina. Three bereavements in four years. My eyes pricked at the thought and the tragic repetition of Christina's own name.

I found a Marylebone burial registration for Christiana, her second child, who was born in the June and died September 1824. How could Christina have coped with nursing a baby then burying her, after just one brief summer? Then I caught sight of a burial entry below Christiana's. An almost identical record. Another infant girl named Christiana Robertson was buried in the same parish in April 1820. I let my hands fall in my lap. Then I realised the significance of the date. Two whole years before Christina married James. More digging convinced me the child was Christina's. Had she borne this tragedy alone? The idea brought me back to thinking about my disastrous personal life, and tears trickled down my cheeks.

The door flew open and Pavel stood there, loaded down with bags of shopping. 'I quit work early. I thought I'd cook you some Russian food.' Catching sight of my face, his smile disappeared. 'What's wrong?'

The kindness in his voice set me off. I started to cry properly. Pavel left the shopping in the middle of the floor. He sat down and put his arm around my shoulder. 'Whatever is the matter?'

'I'm sad for Christina,' I replied, sniffing into my tissue. 'Look what I found.' I brought the records up onto my screen. 'Four of her children died as infants. I knew about three of them, but I found this record of another little girl with the same name, who died before Christina got married.'

'Could it not be a coincidence?'

'Maybe, but look.' I changed the parameters of the search. 'In ten whole years, the only babies called Christiana or Christina Robertson born in London were hers. In fact, the only other in the whole of England is this Christiana, born in Alnwick in 1832. She was the daughter of Tom, James's brother, surely named after her little cousins who didn't survive.' I added another box to the family tree in my notebook.

Christina Robertson Family Tree

John Saunders / Sanders
Grandfather
Born 1726

Jean Bruce
Grandmother
Born 1734

George Saunders / Sanders
Uncle
Born 1774

Margaret Saunders
Mother
Born 1777

John Robertson
Father
Born ?

Christian / Christina Robertson
born 1796

James Robertson
born ?
married 1822

12 elder brothers
& sister

Christiana Robertson
born 1822
died 1880

Agnes Robertson
born 1823
died ?

Christiana Robertson
born 1824
died 1824

James William Robertson
born 1825
died 1826

John Robertson
born 1826
died ?

Christina Robertson
born 1828
died 1828

William Robertson
born 1831
died ?

Mary Robertson
born 1833
died ?

Pavel nodded gravely. 'I see. That is sad, and I think you are probably right.' He gave me a searching look. 'Is that the only reason you're crying?'

I shook my head. I felt I could trust this kind man. 'To be honest, I'm feeling sorry for myself, too.'

'You've been through a lot.'

'Nick and I were about to start fertility treatment. I so wanted a baby.' I took in a long, shuddering breath, trying not to cry again.

'I'm sorry. Have you spoken to him this week?'

'No. I called him yesterday, then twice again this morning. He doesn't answer and doesn't return my calls.'

'That's rude of him.'

'I'm not sure that I can forgive him.'

'You're not sure? Would you go back?'

'That's something I've barely admitted to myself. I imagined he would beg me to come back. Tell me it was a one-off mistake. That it would turn out that my hopes for a baby weren't over. Isn't that absolutely pathetic?'

'Of course not.'

'I'm still working through this. Christina's story makes me realise how lucky I am. I'm mourning my lack of a baby, when she had to bury four.'

Pavel smiled sympathetically. 'Will you stay for dinner? I hate the idea of you spending the evening alone, and I do think we should mark the passing of the year and getting a restaurant table tonight might be difficult. I promise I'm a passable cook.'

'I'd like that. Thank you.'

'I'll make my grandmother's Solyanka casserole. She used to say it was comfort food.'

'Sounds lovely. Grandmothers are wise.'

Pavel produced a bottle of wine and I went over to stare

out the window. 'I can see why you don't have your desk in here. I'd never get any work done.'

Supper was a delicious meaty mixture of sweet, salty, and sour. Very different from an English stew.

'I've got us an appointment to go to the storage centre the day after tomorrow, and the director suggested you might be interested in a family called the Yusupovs. Princess Zinaida Yusupova is the girl in the pink dress you saw in Moscow. We have portraits of her, as well as her young son Nikolai, and mother-in-law Princess Tatyana. It might be worthwhile doing some internet research about them before we go?'

'That does sound interesting. I think I'll move hotel this week. Find myself somewhere with high-speed internet and a proper desk too.'

Pavel looked down and straightened the fork and knife on his empty plate. 'Would you consider moving in here? There's plenty of space. It seems madness for you to pay for a hotel when you can work here.'

My brain raced. My immediate reaction was to say yes, but was it madness to move into the home of a virtual stranger?

'You could try working here for a couple more days before you commit to leaving the hotel. I'm in the office most of the time, apart from tomorrow.'

'That's really kind. Are you sure I wouldn't be in the way?'

'Not at all. Although you might want to check out the décor in my grandmother's bedroom before you decide.'

'You've forgotten my declared affinity with grandmothers.' I smiled. 'Did your mother's family come from St Petersburg too?'

'No, from Boulogne. I never knew my French maternal grandparents. Mama met my father when he was working in Paris. She didn't get on with her family. From what I understood, she more or less ran away from home as a teenager. I wish I'd asked her more about them, though. Fourteen-year-old boys aren't famous for talking to their parents, so I missed my chance.'

'Have you considered searching for them?'

'I should really, especially since I was born in France. Half French and I don't feel it at all.' Pavel shrugged. 'It seems disloyal to go looking. Since she didn't like them, I don't suppose I would either.'

'I only started looking into our family genealogy recently and found out stuff that my mother didn't know.' I told Pavel about my grandmother and her father.

'Was your mother okay about you discovering the truth?'

'Yes. I think her attitude was a bit like yours. She hadn't probed out of respect for her mother's wish to leave it in the past.'

'Perhaps I should look into the French side. Here I am saying I have no family, when I probably have dozens of French cousins. I wonder if Mama might have got back in touch, if she'd lived. I know spending her last few months in a French-speaking country was important to her.'

'I only thought to look into our past because I want to try to tie our family back to Christina.'

'Have you managed it?'

'Not yet. I can't find any trace of Christina's daughters. I've found several mentions of them having come with her to St Petersburg, but then the trail goes cold.'

'Remind me her daughters' names?'

'Agnes, born in 1823, then Mary, her youngest child, was born ten years later.'

'I'll have a look in our archives.' Pavel checked his watch. 'It's nearly midnight. Get your coat. We'll toast 2018 on the balcony.'

As midnight arrived, the air was filled with the noise of bells ringing all around the city. There was also a faint sound of beautiful music. A single high voice, then a chanting choir. The combination sent a shiver down my spine.

'That sounds familiar. What is it?'

'*Shchedryk*. In English, the Carol of the Bells. Russia's most famous carol.' Pavel raised his glass. 'To 2018.'

I raised mine in reply. 'And to the Babushka Appreciation Society.'

Pavel walked me back to the hotel. It had been a lovely evening, but I was fully aware I'd run away from my troubles but not escaped. Alone in my bedroom, I wondered what 2018 would bring. In the space of a week, I'd managed to separate from my husband, and my dream of having a baby had evaporated. How was I going to support myself? My book advance wouldn't last long. What on earth was I doing with my life? A wave of hopelessness swept over me. I steeled myself to call Nick. It went to voicemail again.

'Hi it's me. Just calling to touch base. Em... okay. Call me back.'

I couldn't bring myself to wish him Happy New Year. I cried myself to sleep.

Chapter Thirty

1840, St Petersburg

Christina worked so hard through the long winter that it flew past. Sarah and Agnes took over looking after Mary and she had to concede it might have been difficult to entertain the boys indoors. She was determined to produce her best work and working on such huge portraits was challenging. She had been astonished to be given sole use of a room in the Palace as her studio, but soon realised that working inside the Winter Palace was the only practical solution. The Tsar wanted five huge portraits of himself, the Tsarina, and their three daughters. They'd had an extra-large easel specially made, and Christina requested a set of ladders to work on the upper sections of the portraits. The paintings were destined to be hung together in the domed rotunda situated at the formal entrance to the royal quarters. Emperor Nicholas specified that each portrait must be in the same life-sized scale and formal style.

Christina had painted the youngest daughter Alexandra first, and her parents were delighted. Fifteen-year-old Adini, as they all called her, was a very sweet girl, adored by her

parents and the whole court. The portraits of the Tsarina and
Olga, her second daughter, were completed next, along with a
portrait of the Tsar. Maria, the Tsar's eldest daughter, had
married the Duke of Leuchtenberg the previous summer and
was already suffering from morning sickness by the time
Christina arrived in court. Her little girl had been born at the
beginning of April and in May Maria sent word that she was
now recovered enough to sit for her portrait.

Christina rushed along the long corridor, and down the
grand marble staircase of the Winter Palace. She hoped she
might catch Grand Duchess Maria before she set out on her
daily morning walk with her sisters. It took nearly ten
minutes to get from her studio on the eastern side of the
second floor, to their quarters in the opposite basement.

She caught sight of her reflection in a mirror at the
bottom of the stairs just before she entered the dark corridor
leading to the sisters' rooms. She rubbed the smudge of blue
paint off her cheek with the back of her hand before hurrying
on. Flustered from the rush, she took a deep breath, with her
hand on her chest, then knocked gently on the door. Inside,
she found Grand Duchess Maria and her sister Olga, both
already dressed in their outdoor clothes.

'Good morning, Your Imperial Highnesses,' Christina
said, as she curtseyed.

'Good morning, Christina. You are lucky to catch us. We
might have already left if my sister were not so slow.' Grand
Duchess Olga shouted the last words loud enough to summon
Grand Duchess Alexandra from her bedroom with her hat
and gloves in her hand.

'I am here, Ollie. There is no need to shout,' Adini said.

'Good morning, Christina,' Maria added with a wide
smile. 'Papa said yes to our scheme,' she added. 'I told him my
legs are particularly bad this spring, and I needed the piano to

lean on. Then Mama reminded him how delighted they are with the portrait of Ollie and Adini that you've done for the Cottage, and he agreed I might have my way.'

'Great news, well done,' Christina replied.

'It's not fair,' Princess Alexandra said. 'Papa insisted on me being painted with an outdoor background. It looks as if I've been sent out into the corridor for being naughty.'

'Petulance spoils your appearance, dear sister,' Maria teased. 'You and Ollie already have another painting before I even get my first and everyone agrees you have the prettiest shoulders in all Russia.'

The Tsar and Tsarina spent a great deal of time at the small English-style house they called the Cottage. Nicholas had built this hideaway on an out-of-the-way corner of the Peterhof estate, as a present for his wife. This large house was by no means a cottage. However, compared to the grand palaces Peter the Great had built nearby, it was very modest. This is where the royal family tried to live a simpler life. Empress Alexandra had asked Christina to paint something for its walls. Being given more artistic freedom, Christina had posed Olga sat at her writing desk while Adini played the piano behind her. The view of Adini's back in this small painting featured a deep lace trim across her shoulders.

'Meet me in the music room at ten tomorrow morning, Christina,' Maria said. 'I have a burgundy gown in mind for the portrait. I'll bring it to get your opinion.'

'Excellent. I shall find you there,' she replied.

Later, Sarah and Agnes visited Christina in her studio.

'What time did you leave this morning? I didn't hear the door,' Sarah asked her.

'Just after six, maybe? I wanted to be here at first light.'

'You do realise that the sun rises at two in the morning by

the end of June? You cannot work every daylight hour in St Petersburg.'

'I know, but I'm overdue with the Yusupov commissions.'

'Do you still think we will get home this year?'

'Honestly, I doubt it. The Empress's eldest son has become engaged to a German Princess, and I've promised to paint her when she arrives in St Petersburg. Then, as well as the Yusupov portraits, I've been asked to paint both Vladimir Davydov and his mother. Since all our Russian commissions stem from his patronage, I feel I owe it to him.'

'Then you certainly won't finish before the weather turns cold again.'

'I'm afraid we'll be here until next spring. I'm sorry to keep you away from Andrew for so long. It's really not what I had planned. There are three other families who have promised to match the Tsar's fee if I will paint their ladies. A year's work here should fund us for a decade. I simply cannot turn it down.'

'I understand, but I know you miss your boys, too. Could we not go to England and then return?'

'We could, but it's such an arduous journey, it makes more sense to stay.'

Christina caught sight of Agnes's happy expression. 'At least your soldier will be pleased, Agnes.'

Her daughter's blush confirmed Christina's suspicions. Agnes had just turned eighteen and had adored all the social activity in St Petersburg. She had met a young officer the previous month. He'd now gone on army manoeuvres but had promised to see her again on his return. Christina longed to go home and see her sons, but she realised Agnes would have been heartbroken to leave now. She'd met James when she was only seventeen, so she couldn't argue that Agnes was too young to be in love.

'I heard from Alnwick today,' Sarah said. 'Young Margaret

Threw is to be promoted from housekeeper. She and Tom will marry in October. It is the best possible news, especially since Jane says Christiana has grown fond of her.'

'That's marvellous. I'm sorry you'll miss the wedding.'

'It's fine. Ma wrote that they plan to keep the celebrations very simple.'

Agnes unpacked the contents of her basket. 'We brought you some lunch, Mama. I know quite well that you'll not eat if I don't bring it.'

Christina smiled at her daughter. 'Time just disappears when I'm painting. What are you doing today?'

'I'm going to meet Mary when she finishes school, because Sarah has promised to visit the Empress. Will you return in time for supper?'

'I promise I'll try,' Christina agreed.

Christina kissed her daughter goodbye and turned to Sarah.

'I'll come with you to the Empress's quarters. I should let her know that I'll begin Maria's portrait tomorrow,' she said to Sarah. 'What have you brought for her?'

'It's just my usual tisane. The Empress says it calms her nerves,' Sarah replied.

'I think it's your company that calms her. Who would have thought that little Sarah Lewis from Alnwick would be health advisor to the Empress of all Russia?'

'I sometimes think that she has too many advisors. I concentrate on treating her symptoms.'

Christina linked arms with Sarah as they set off towards the royal quarters, which were on the top floor above their children's suites. They had to pass sentries at several sets of double doors, but in each instance, they were waved through. Only when they entered the Empress's Malachite Drawing Room with its bright green stone pillars, did the last guard ask to see inside Sarah's packet of dried herbs and flowers.

She also opened the jar of lavender cream. One sniff was enough to satisfy him that it was the usual pre-approved items.

Inside the Silver Drawing Room, the Empress was being attended by the beautiful dark-haired Princess Maria Ivanovna Baryatinskaya. Painting Maria had changed Christina's life. Her summons to St Petersburg came after the Tsarina had admired the portrait of Princess Maria in a St Petersburg Academy Exhibition. Christina and Sarah first curtsied to Empress Alexandra, then Sarah walked over to the samovar to prepare tisane for the Empress. 'Good morning, Your Imperial Majesty,' Christina said. 'I'm pleased to inform you I shall begin Grand Duchess Maria's portrait tomorrow. We meet in the music room at ten.'

'I'm delighted. The Tsar wants to have all the paintings hung in the Rotunda for the midsummer celebrations. Has Maria selected a dress?'

'I believe she will bring a gown for my artistic opinion.'

'Then I shall come along to give my maternal view.'

Sarah set the steaming cup of scented tea at the Empress's elbow and drew up a small stool. Empress Alexandra took a sip of the hot drink, then with a deep sigh, she put her hands on the table. 'Maria, come and watch how Sarah massages in her magical cream. This was the first winter since I came to St Petersburg that my hands were pain free, and I fear Sarah won't be here to administer it for much longer.'

'Poor Sarah will have to endure another winter away from her son. I have too many court commissions to leave St Petersburg this year,' Christina said.

'I cannot imagine spending a long time away from my children, so you must forgive my selfishness in confessing that I'm glad,' the Empress replied. Sarah handed the Empress's rings to Princess Maria and began to rub cream into her left hand. The Tsaritsa closed her eyes and Christina thought she was dozing, until she said: 'You may continue to use your studio here to undertake your other commissions, as well as Tsarevich Alexander's fiancée. The Tsar mentioned he'd like to include her portrait in the Rotunda Gallery.'

'I look forward to meeting her,' Christina replied.

Once Sarah finished, they walked back to her studio.

'Agnes has packed enough piroshki to feed a battalion. Will you stay and share my lunch?'

'Of course,' Sarah replied, accepting one of the pastry parcels. She nibbled it as she walked around the room, admiring all the royal portraits. She stopped in front of the Tsar's image, then turned towards Christina with one eyebrow raised.

'Do not say a word. The pose is wooden, and everything except his face had to be done from memory. The Royal ladies were generous with their time, but the Tsar hated to stand still. When I mentioned I needed to paint his uniform accurately, he simply sent me his coat.'

'You did your best,' Sarah replied. Coming over to kiss her cheek. 'Perhaps they will decide to make the Rotunda Gallery ladies only?'

'I should say that there is a chance of that. I can't imagine this austere military painting sitting well amongst a bevy of silk and velvet frocks.'

Christina painted through another winter. Her popularity grew but she made plans to go home. She worried about her boys and feared if she waited any longer, her girls would find it difficult to adjust to London life. Christina had one last important commission to fulfil for the Yusupovs.

She left the palace and climbed into the ornately painted troika Princess Zinaida had sent for her. The driver took off the horses' protective blankets, releasing a cloud of steam from their backs, then he shook the reins, sending them off at a trot. Two white horses flanked a larger bay, whose elegant head was framed by a painted wooden arch. This beautiful piece of craftsmanship held the shafts on either side of the central horse, keeping the troika stable. Christina pulled her scarf up over her mouth, plunged her hands back into her fur muff and sank against the padded seat with a sigh. In the summer she'd made the ten-minute journey to the Yusupov Palace by boat, but a sleigh was by far the nicest way to get around St Petersburg. The near silence of the snow covered streets was disturbed only by the soothing swish of sleigh runners, and the jingling bells on the horses' harnesses.

It amazed her how she'd become used to living in such bizarre circumstances. She'd just walked through the corridors of the Winter Palace with barely a glance at the opulence, and was heading from an Empress's home to paint yet another Princess. Christina glanced at the frozen Neva River, empty of ships now, for the ice would crush their hulls to matchsticks. The spring thaw would come in a few more weeks, and she would join a vessel travelling south from here to England. She longed to see John and William, but the thought of James as her constant companion rather than Sarah made her heart sink. She hoped to hide this dread from Agnes and Mary.

The troika swept over the Red Bridge and along the Moika River embankment. The yellow painted walls of Princess Yusupova's palace looked particularly striking set against the snowy streets and frozen river. Like a butter sculpture on a porcelain plate.

A footman led her up the white marble staircase, which was almost as grand as the one in the Winter Palace. 'The Princess will receive you in her private sitting room,' the footman told her. He managed to imply in his tone that it was a great honour and that she didn't deserve it. In the court full of princesses, grand duchesses and countesses, Christina's low-born status stood out. She knew that her access to royalty and apparent privilege annoyed some people.

The footman opened the door and announced: 'Madame Robertson.' His stress on her simple title emphasised again her unsuitability for a private audience.

'Christina, how lovely to see you.' The footman's wince was almost imperceptible. 'I'm so excited that you're beginning Princess Tatyana's portrait today. Now our wall of portraits will be complete,' Princess Zinaida said.

Christina smiled, then curtseyed to the elderly Princess Tatyana, who was dressed in shimmering black velvet, with a swathe of tasselled ivory silk tied in a turban around her thinning hair.

'Is my outfit suitable, do you think?' she asked.

'Your choice of fabrics is perfect, Your Highness.' Christina was looking forward to painting this lady in her seventies. It created a different challenge, compared to the peachy young skin of most of her sitters. Just then, one of her 'peaches' entered the room. Prince Nikolai had shot up since she'd sketched him on their coach journey, and was already taller than his mother.

'I thought perhaps Nikolai might play while you paint?'

'Perfect idea. This will help Princess Tatyana be relaxed.'

Princess Zinaida helped her mother-in-law out of her chair and bent with Christina to arrange the fur-lined robe. The footman brought over the easel, and Christina got to work immediately. She didn't expect this lady would be comfortable to stand for too long. Nikolai began to play and his grandmother's features immediately relaxed. Christina's pencil flew to capture such a perfect instant.

A maid came in with a tea service on a tray. The gilt-edged porcelain was Limoges and Princess Zinaida usually trusted only Yelena to handle it. 'Is Yelena unwell?' Christina asked.

'Yelena decided to leave my service,' Princess Zinaida replied.

Zinaida was normally inscrutable, so Christina was surprised by the cloud of annoyance that passed over her face.

Christina instructed the troika driver to take her home. The Tsar had given them a generously sized flat on Nevsky Prospekt, close to the Moika River. She opened the front door and went straight to the kitchen, expecting to find Sarah there. Instead, she found Agnes stirring a pot of fragrant stew.

Christina took off her hat and coat and kissed her daughter on the cheek. 'That smells amazing.'

'It's the paprika you smell. I'm persisting with my efforts in Russian cooking.' Agnes held out the spoon for Christina to taste.

'So delicious,' Christina said. 'I wonder if we can get paprika at home?'

'I'll buy some to take back,' Agnes said.

'Is Sarah in?' Christina asked. It was unusual for Sarah not to greet her when she came home.

'She has a headache, so I told her to rest. She wouldn't, of course. I think she's in the sitting room with Mary.'

Christina found Mary kneeling beside the low table.

Her daughter looked up and smiled 'Hello, Mama, I'm drawing a *snegurochka*.'

Christina loved the way Mary peppered her English with Russian and French. 'And what exactly is a *snegurochka*, poppet?'

'A girl made of snow,' Mary replied. 'They told us the fairy tale at school.'

A movement in the drapes caught Christina's eye. Sarah

was standing in the shadows, staring out the window. Even in the dim light and facing away from her, Sarah radiated tension. A shiver of apprehension ran down Christina's back.

'Is something the matter?'

'No, just watching the sledges.'

Christina walked to her friend's side and took her arm.

Sarah gave her a strained smile. 'How was your visit to Moika Palace?'

'Successful. The elder Princess Yusupova is almost as striking as her daughter-in-law. I got some good sketches.' She paused, waiting for Sarah to ask if she'd seen Yelena. When she did not, Christina assumed that this was the source of her low mood.

'Did you know Yelena had left the Yusupovs?'

'Yes. A few weeks ago. The Dutch family she used to work with returned to St Petersburg. They begged her to come back,' Sarah replied.

'I got the impression Princess Zinaida wasn't pleased.'

'The Princess owns thousands of serfs on her country estate, but Yelena is her own woman.'

Christina frowned at Sarah's bitter tone. 'It seems an odd choice to leave a royal household to work for a diplomat's family.'

'She felt loyalty to her first mistress. I can understand that,' Sarah replied.

Was that what kept Sarah by her side for so long? Just a debt of loyalty? Christina's heart clenched. 'Is she happier now?'

'I imagine so. I haven't seen her since she moved houses.'

At that, Sarah walked away. She snatched up Mary's cloak, which had been abandoned on a chair, then left the room. Mary looked up, her little face crumpled in confusion.

Christina saw her own thoughts mirrored in her daughter's face. Had she upset Sarah? Her friend had been very quiet recently. Sarah often used to visit Yelena in Moika Palace. She'd surely miss her companionship. If Sarah's previous happiness depended only on Yelena, their last months in St Petersburg would be miserable. Christina's jealousy of their closeness felt mean-spirited and shameful.

Chapter Thirty-One

January 2018, St Petersburg

Nick didn't return my call. In the morning, I called Mum.

'Hello, darling. Happy New Year.'

'Happy New Year, Mum.'

'So you're in St Petersburg. What a romantic place to spend Hogmanay.'

'You're right and the sound of the bells at midnight was amazing, if not actually romantic for me.'

'What's wrong? I can hear there's something. Did you two fall out?'

'Nick isn't here. We've split up.' I began to cry.

'Oh Anna. Whatever happened? You sounded so happy last week. Excited for the ball and looking forward to starting your treatment.'

'I cancelled my gynae appointment. Nick is having an affair with his translator.'

'Anna! Are you sure?'

I explained all about Oksana's connection to Lisa and about Vadim catching them.

'I'm so sorry.' Mum hesitated. 'Is there no chance of reconciliation?'

'Things have been unravelling since I got back from Scotland. He wasn't very enthusiastic about starting fertility treatment. Maybe he'd already started seeing his future with Oksana.'

'Is that what Nick said?'

'Not specifically. Right now, he isn't even taking my calls.'

'Oh, Anna. What are you going to do now?'

'My research here will take at least another week. To be honest, I'm glad of the distance to take some time to think.'

I described all my Christina news and how Pavel was helping me.

'Well, I'm glad you've got at least one friend there. You are right to be angry with Nick, but I do think you should persevere in trying to talk to him.'

'I guess. But I can't make him take my calls.' I took a deep breath and tried to sound more cheery. 'Anyway, what have you been up to? Did you have company for the bells?' Mum had moved back to Edinburgh in the middle of December.

'Yes. I watched the midnight fireworks from Inverleith Park with Mandy and Jack. Then we had a wee dram at Mandy's afterwards. I was in bed by one. I hope you weren't on your own.'

'I had dinner with Pavel, then we listened to the St Petersburg bells from his balcony. There were fireworks here too. He has this amazing flat, right beside the Hermitage Museum.'

I could hear her brain whirring. 'It's okay, Mum. He's just a friend. I'll call you again in a few days.'

'Call me before if you need to talk.'

'Thanks, and don't worry.'

'Ooh, I nearly forgot. Do you have Christina's writing slope with you?'

'It was too heavy to carry but Lisa is bringing it here in a few days.'

'I meant to tell you to be sure to check the secret compartment. Apparently, if you pull up the little wall beside the inkwell, it should release a hidden panel.'

'That's exciting. I'll let you know if I find anything.'

'I love you so much, Anna. I'm so, so sorry, but there's a room here for you if you need it.'

Pavel answered the door with a bulb of garlic in his hand.

'Expecting vampires?'

'Ha. No. Although St Petersburg on the first of January might be a suitably dramatic entrance. I'm putting together a chicken curry for tonight. Will you join me? Then I thought you might enjoy a drive round town. The roads will be quiet today. Is there anything you want to see?'

'The Yusupovs' Palace, maybe? I plan to go after we've seen the paintings. Get a sense of where they lived.'

'Good idea. It'll be closed today, but we can drive past.'

'Also, Christina is buried in St Petersburg. Do you think we might look for her grave?'

'Sure. Do you know where it is?'

I got out my laptop. 'The Volkovskoe Lutheran Cemetery.'

'We can easily go there,' Pavel said, placing a mug of tea beside me. 'Finding the grave might be tricky, though. It's a huge graveyard.'

'It's so awful that she died here in poverty.'

Pavel grimaced. 'I believe the Tsar became less enthusiastic about her paintings, and didn't always pay her bills.'

'I hope this article is wrong about her being alone.'

'I thought her daughters were here with her. I'll see if I can find anything in the archives.'

. . .

The Moika Palace, the Yusupovs' home, turned out to be an enormous yellow-painted mansion, built directly beside the river and fronted by two-storey-high, white columns.

'Wow!'

'Impressive, isn't it? You should definitely visit. The official tours might be in Russian, but I'm sure they have an app in English. It's also infamous for being where Rasputin was murdered.'

Pavel hadn't been joking about the size of the cemetery. I've always enjoyed walking through graveyards and this one was particularly atmospheric. Large trees created dappled light on the sea of gravestones. Some plots were enclosed with low fences and planted with flowers. Elsewhere were enormous gravestones and family mausoleums. I practised my Russian alphabet by reading the grave names aloud.

'I often wish my father had a grave. Somewhere I could go and visit. After he was cremated, we scattered his ashes in his beloved Yorkshire Dales.'

'My mother has a small memorial in a Brussels graveyard, but I haven't seen it in ten years. Maybe I'll pop over when I'm in Paris.'

'When are you going?'

'We're talking to the Louis Vuitton Foundation about them putting on an exhibition of our Morozov Collection in 2021. We had a similar collaboration in 2016, and it's a massive amount of work. I'm going to Paris to finalise the plan.'

'That sounds exciting. Perhaps I'll try to get over for the exhibition.'

'I'd like that. I'll do you a personal curator's tour if you come.' We walked in silence for several minutes.

'So have you decided to leave Russia?' he said.

'I don't know.'

'Where is your home in the UK?'

'I own a tiny flat in London, but it's rented out. I'd probably go to my mum in Edinburgh.'

'I visited Edinburgh a couple of years ago. I took a Jean-Étienne Liotard painting to an exhibition in the Scottish National Gallery. It's a beautiful city. I'd love to visit again.'

'Well, if I'm there, you must visit me. Mind you, I couldn't put you up if I'm at Mum's. Her entire house would fit in your ground floor.'

We walked the leafy paths for over an hour. Pavel asked another visitor if she knew of any foreign graves and we were directed to a section with many German names. There, an old man told Pavel that some foreign graves were lost when part of the cemetery was destroyed in the 1920s.

'Sorry, Anna. I think we're out of luck.'

'It's fine. I knew it was a long shot. I wonder if anyone would even have erected a gravestone.'

'I can't imagine that the Empress would have left her grave unmarked.' Pavel shrugged. 'She brought her here and commissioned dozens of portraits. Many more than we can trace. Christina might have fallen foul of the politics over Crimea, but I hope their friendship endured.'

'They might have bonded over their experience of childbirth. Seven of Alexandra's children survived to adulthood, but like Christina, she had one almost every year.'

'It's said that the Tsar took a mistress when Alexandra became too ill to share his bed.'

'I wonder how she felt about that. Here am I having a fit about Nick's one indiscretion.'

Pavel wisely said nothing.

. . .

I called Nick again early the next morning. He didn't pick up. 'That's enough,' I said out loud, when I ended the call. I'd promised Mum to try, but I couldn't make him talk to me.

I texted Pavel:

If the offer still stands I'm going to check out of the hotel this morning.

Great, he replied.

Half an hour later Pavel opened his front door. He carried my bag through to his grandmother's bedroom.

The wooden furniture could have been taken from a 1970s G Plan catalogue. The bed's headboard was padded in turquoise velour. The cream candlewick bedspread was topped by three cushions in the same velour fabric. A crocheted doily sat on the kidney-shaped dressing table, below a small smoky-effect glass vase filled with silk flowers. It was as if the old lady had just left.

'Turquoise was my grandmother's favourite colour. I wonder if she was slightly colour blind.'

'Are you sure you're okay about me sleeping in here?'

His expression became anxious. 'Yes. Of course.' He looked around the room. 'God. Is it all a bit too *Psycho?*' He snatched up the vase and reached for a cushion.

I smiled and took the cushion from him. 'Leave it. The room is fine.'

Pavel must have guessed my thoughts when I glanced at the wardrobe. He pulled open a door. 'I got rid of all her clothes. I promise I'm sentimental, but not deranged.'

I laughed. 'I'm really grateful to you for putting me up and so looking forward to doing my research with that view of the river. Where better to imagine Christina's life?'

'I'll leave you to unpack. We should head to the metro in

about ten minutes.' He held up the vase. 'But I'll get rid of this. It's ugly.'

The ground floor of the storage centre housed a collection of large items, including ornately gilded and painted sledges. 'I can just imagine Christina travelling in one of these. It must be so pretty here in the snow.'

'You might see some yet. We usually have snow in January.'

The director arrived, and Pavel introduced me. The explanation that I was writing a book about Christina Robertson got me a welcoming smile. I felt a colossal fraud being treated as if I were a proper art historian. I'd just have to not screw it up now. The director led us to a room where he'd put four portraits up on easels.

The difference in sizes was striking. The painting of the older woman, Princess Tatyana, was as large as the royal portraits in the Hermitage Romanov Gallery. Her grandson's portrait was around a metre high, a charming painting of him holding a violin. Then the two of his mother were about half the size again. I recognised one of these paintings as a smaller version of the large portrait I'd seen in the Pushkin. The second portrait was an absolutely stunning head and shoulders. Zinaida's mass of loose dark curls was threaded through with pearls. Christina had captured every nuance of her off-the-shoulder dress. Royal blue velvet edged in pink silk and translucent lace. 'Oh, I adore this one. Isn't she beautiful?' I turned to Pavel, and he nodded. It occurred to me I was being too gushing. I'd better tone it down for the benefit of the director. 'I'm curious about the very different sizes. Surely they wouldn't hang well together?'

'You are right,' the director replied. 'I would expect there were originally other large paintings on the same scale as Princess Tatyana.'

'I'm sure I've seen a bigger version of that Princess Zinaida one in the Pushkin Museum in Moscow.'

'Have you viewed the paintings in the Moika Palace? It's open to the public and they have their own art,' he added.

'I've booked to go tomorrow.'

'If you are interested, we have dresses belonging to both Yusupova ladies on our fourth-floor costume display.'

'I'll take a look before we leave. Dr Sidorov, this head and shoulders painting would be perfect for the Scottish Portrait Gallery exhibition.'

The director's smile implied he agreed with my choice. I caught the sparkle in Pavel's eyes at my pretence of formality. When the director walked ahead of us, Pavel gave me a huge wink.

'How did I do?' I whispered.

'Great,' he replied.

Reaching for his hand was a spontaneous reaction. 'Thank you so much. I'll recommend Zinaida as perfect for Edinburgh and I can do a whole section in the book around all their family paintings.'

Pavel's huge grin reflected back my own excitement. He squeezed my fingers.

When the director turned around, I snatched my hand away. He gave Pavel a knowing look.

'Nice to meet you, Miss Grieve,' he said. 'Good luck with your project.'

'Thank you,' I said, hoping my embarrassment wasn't visible, and not daring to look at Pavel. So much for my professional pretence.

Chapter Thirty-Two

May 1841, St Petersburg

Christina was working on a small painting at home. The Empress had commissioned a miniature of Maria, her eldest daughter, with her husband and little girl. It was a domestic scene full of tenderness, just the kind of picture she loved to paint. Christina had completed the last of the family's large formal portraits, with the portrayal of young Princess Marie of Hesse, just before she married the Tsar's eldest son and became Grand Duchess Maria Alexandrovna.

Agnes came in. 'You have letters. One from Papa.'

'That's a pleasant surprise,' Christina answered, attempting to keep sarcasm from her voice. James was a very infrequent correspondent. The second letter was from Eliza, who found writing an arduous task, so Christina was grateful for the housekeeper's efforts to keep her up-to-date with life in Harley Street.

'There's a letter for Sarah, too. I'll take it to her,' Agnes added.

Christina took up her letter knife to break James's red wax seal.

. . .

14th May 1841

Dear Christina

Eliza informs me that she has written to you regarding my new lodgings in Beaumont Street. I must apologise for not informing you first. My bedroom in Harley Street has suffered some water damage due to a window leak. The damp atmosphere is intolerable. I have moved out until they are able to make the necessary repairs.

John and William have been splitting their time between Beaumont and Harley Street. I like to look in on their lessons and it is inconvenient to have to keep rushing backwards and forwards, so I have insisted they move here.Both boys are fine and Mr Ambleton reports they continue to be attentive to their lessons. Since you expressed the hope that they shouldn't spend all their days indoors, I am pleased to inform you they recently began riding lessons in the Hyde Park stables. William has also taken up fencing. I know you are against a military career, but riding and swordsmanship are excellent skills for any gentleman.

I'm delighted to hear that Agnes's artistic talent continues to flourish, and I can think of nothing nicer than being able to arrange a salon for you both on your return. However, I quite understand your wish to stay on to fulfil all your commissions. Such an opportunity is too precious to pass over.

It's hard to imagine that little Agnes has turned eighteen. Shall I begin looking for a suitable young man in London? Your extra commissions will supply her with the chance of a dowry, so I might as well start thinking. I thought a saddle would be a suitable gift for John's fifteenth. He has had a growing spurt and is ready for an adult saddle of his own.

Give my love to Agnes and little Mary,
Yours, James

Christina frowned at the letter. Everything about it was troubling. Agnes had written to her father and mentioned that she had become close to one of the Tsar's officers. Christina was annoyed that James hadn't even mentioned Agnes's feelings, and she feared he would be swayed by thoughts of his own long-term advantage. As to his news about the boys, horse riding was certainly a useful skill, but the stable in Hyde Park was one of the most expensive in London. And why fencing? James had never been in the slightest bit interested in fighting. Why would he want it for his sons?

She reread the paragraph about leasing lodgings. Whatever was he up to? Renting another property for want of a bedroom made no sense when both hers and the girls' bedrooms were empty. She picked up the second letter in Eliza's tiny handwriting and took it to the window to get better light.

13th May 1841

Dear Christina

I am writing to confess that I have annoyed Mr Robertson.

We disagreed about certain events being a source of local gossip and a bad example to the boys. I am mortified that my words have led to him taking William and John out of the house. It was the last outcome I intended and I pray you will return soon to rectify the situation.

I hope you and the girls are well. I miss you so much and look forward to you coming home.

Yours
Eliza

. . .

Eliza's letter confirmed her suspicion that James's reason for moving was nothing to do with a damp bedroom and there was obviously some scandal that he hadn't mentioned. Was he gambling again? Or something worse? Eliza would not have spoken out unless sorely tested. It was most certainly time to go home.

Christina looked up to find Sarah in the doorway, in tears. She jumped up to put her arms around her friend. 'Whatever is the matter?'

'It's a letter from Jane. Ma had a fall. They fear for her life.'

Christina's already troubled heart felt like it would break from the shaking of Sarah's sobs on her shoulder. Although she had seemed to have come to terms with Yelena's absence over the weeks, it was the first time they'd embraced in months. Eventually, Sarah was consoled enough to stop crying.

'I fear I've delayed our departure too long,' Christina said. 'Let's go to the English Embankment this afternoon to book a passage. We need to get you home to Alnwick as soon as possible.'

Two weeks later, Agnes came to Christina's room, dressed for the ball. She wore a white, lace-trimmed dress inspired by the gown Queen Victoria had worn for her wedding the year before. Seeing her tentative expression, Christina reached out for her hand.

'Am I overdressed, Mama?' Agnes asked. 'I don't want people to think I'm putting on airs.'

Christina smiled at her daughter. 'You look beautiful, and it is impossible to overdress for a ball in the Winter Palace.

You have an invitation and should walk in with your head held high.' The Romanovs had a habit of sending out the prized ball invitations on the actual day, so Christina was grateful that the Empress had given them some warning that Agnes, Sarah, and she would all be invited.

'Is Lieutenant Ponkin in town?'

'Yes,' Agnes replied. 'He has asked me to keep the first dance for him.'

Agnes dipped her head to try to hide her blush. Christina was torn about what to hope for from this evening. There was a long tradition of young men asking for their lady's hand in marriage during a court ball. If Agnes's beau was going to ask her to marry, it would have to be soon. Their ship to London would leave at the end of next week. Agnes loved this boy and Christina wanted her to be happy. But was young love a good enough reason to marry? Look at how her feelings for James had faded. Klaas was a career soldier and his father had been in the Russian Imperial Army before him. His role tied him to the Tsar and Russia. Would Agnes decide not to come home? Also, while these were relatively peaceful times, a soldier's life was dangerous. Agnes's nervous face was full of hope, but Christina's stomach churned with anxiety.

Later that evening they queued in a long line of carriages waiting to drop off their passengers at the Palace. Christina stared out the window, trying to memorise each precious detail. Her life treading these much loved streets and royal corridors was coming to an end.

Sarah was sitting opposite. Despite the worry about her mother, Christina knew she was excited to go home to see Andrew. Now sixteen he might be unrecognisable from the boy she left behind. They had found a ship bound for Newcastle, which would get her home quicker, but it meant

Sarah would sail the very next day. Christina was distraught at the thought of her leaving, and she had no idea when she would see her friend again. Sarah met her gaze; her smile made Christina's heart tighten. She looked so beautiful in her eau de Nil gown and much younger than her thirty-five years. Sarah would surely have many dance partners on her last night in St Petersburg.

'What did the Empress say yesterday?' Christina asked.

'She shed a few tears and so did I, but she wished me well on my journey.'

'Are you fully packed?'

'Yes. I have already sent my trunk to the ship. I only have to put away the things I've used today. Not that I'll need this gown in Alnwick.'

Christina smiled. 'Perhaps not, but I'm sure there will be suitable occasions in London.'

'I doubt if I'm needed in London anymore. Tabitha is doing a good job for George.'

'I hope you'll arrive and find your mother recovered, and if so, I will certainly need you. Were you thinking of staying on in Alnwick?' Christina felt panicked at the thought. Might she lose both Agnes and Sarah?

'Goodness, no. I've long outgrown Alnwick. If Ma is better, I might offer to help set up George's new house. The move will create a lot of extra work.'

'I'm glad Uncle George has found a quieter street for his retirement, but I'm going to miss not having you both just around the corner.'

Their carriage reached the entrance. The lady alighting ahead of them looked back to check that her maid was attending to her long train. There was no mistaking Yelena's dark hair and haughty profile as she gathered up the end of the train and followed her mistress into the Palace.

'Is that Yelena's Dutch mistress?'

Sarah nodded. Her face was extra pale, and two red spots had appeared on her cheekbones. They joined the crowd, waiting to ascend the stairs. Yelena was several flights ahead of them, still carrying the silk train. Christina whispered in Sarah's ear. 'Try to catch up with her. You must take your chance to say goodbye.'

She watched Sarah weave her way in Yelena's direction.

The ballroom was full. Triple-height candelabras filled the room with the smell of wax, and the candlelight twinkled reflections on the many bejewelled ladies. The noblemen in Nicholas's court wore a myriad of multicoloured uniforms. It was said that he found the uniforms so useful in establishing the ranks in the crowd, that he'd instigated a similar system for the ladies. Their formal attire included intricate gold embroidery on their white dresses and long velvet cloaks. These were so heavy that the ladies talked about 'putting on their armour'. The Empress's attendants, in their green and red velvet cloaks, began to filter into the room, signifying her imminent arrival. Christina had painted so many of the guests present that she and Agnes were inundated with ladies coming over to wish them a safe journey.

A hush in the room marked the royal couple's entry. Empress Alexandra was resplendent in her shimmering gown and crimson velvet robe. She wore a diadem on her head, as did her daughters. The Grand Duchesses had similar outfits, but each in their own chosen colour of velvet. Surely no court in Europe could outdo the Romanovs for splendid spectacle. Chords from the orchestra signalled the dancing was about to begin. The Tsar took his wife's hand, and they danced side by side in a graceful polonaise. Warm glances between them in that first solo circuit made Christina envious of their closeness. They had been married for over twenty years and were clearly still in love. When the floor opened to everyone, Lieutenant Klaas was one of the first to claim his partner. The sight of Agnes gliding around the ballroom looking so happy brought tears to Christina's eyes. She was pleased for her daughter, but tonight, standing watching all those couples, she felt particularly alone.

'I see you are sad to leave us.'

Christina turned to find Princess Maria Ivanovna beside her. 'It's time I went home but you are right, Your Highness. I've been happy here.'

'The Empress sent me to detain you. She wishes to speak to you this evening.'

Christina bowed her head. 'I am at her service.'

The orchestra struck up the notes of a lively mazurka. Klaas and Agnes were one of the most enthusiastic couples. He sped Agnes across the floor and Christina and Princess Maria both smiled at the sight.

'It seems little Agnes is quite grown up,' the Princess commented.

The young soldiers stamped out the rhythm and whirled their partners around. Klaas and Agnes's smiles got wider as the dance progressed, and at the final flourish of the music, Klaas grasped Agnes around the waist and held her above him. They were too far away to hear his words, but Christina clearly saw him mouth, 'Marry me.' When he set Agnes down, her daughter was weeping tears of joy. Christina resolved to ensure no one stood in the way of her daughter's happiness.

Agnes led Klaas over towards them. 'I'm glad you are here, Your Highness. Your portrait brought me to St Petersburg and I've found my destiny here.' She took both Christina's hands and bowed her head. 'Klaas has asked me to marry him, Mama. Please give us your blessing.'

'You have my blessing in all you do, Agnes. But do you mean you will not come home?'

Agnes smiled at her partner. 'Klaas is keen to earn his promotion to provide for me better, and he understands I miss Papa and the boys. He will write asking Papa's permission for our marriage. If all goes to plan, I will return to marry him next year.'

'Congratulations, my dear.' They all turned round to find the Empress standing beside them. 'I hope you will all return for the wedding. In fact I came to persuade your mother to stay.'

Christina and Agnes sank into full curtsies. When she rose, Christina replied. 'I'm honoured by your request, Your Imperial Highness. However, I've been away nearly two years and I really must go home.'

'Could you delay for a few more months? The Tsar will submit your royal portraits to the Imperial Academy of Arts Exhibition in the summer. You must keep it to yourself, but he will also recommend that you be admitted as an Honorary Member.'

Princess Maria Ivanovna gasped. 'Oh, congratulations, Madame Robertson.'

A surge of pride almost made Christina waver in her resolve. She didn't know of any other artist who had been granted membership to the Scottish, English and Russian Royal Academies. This exceeded her highest ambitions. Then she remembered the urgent tone of Eliza's letter. 'I can barely express my gratitude to you and the Tsar for your enduring support. However, I know you understand my maternal feelings, too. My boys have reached a critical age and I've neglected them. However, I promise I will return if it is at all possible, and if I am invited again.'

'I truly hope so,' the Empress replied.

'I shall visit you before I leave, Your Imperial Highness.

The portrait of the Duchess of Leuchtenberg's family is almost complete. I believe you will be pleased with it.'

The Tsarina smiled, then she and Princess Maria moved back towards her ladies-in-waiting.

Agnes hugged Christina. 'What a marvellous evening for us both.'

'I am delighted to be welcomed into such a talented family,' Klaas said. 'Allow me to fetch you both some champagne.'

Agnes looked around, her brow furrowed. 'We should be celebrating with Sarah. I want to tell her my news. Where is she?'

'I was thinking exactly the same thing,' Christina replied, scanning the room. Yelena's mistress was nearby talking to the Dutch Ambassador's wife, but Yelena wasn't with her. Most likely she'd been sent home once her mistress and her train were safely delivered into the ballroom. Might Sarah have gone with her? Would she have left without saying goodbye? Christina pushed her injured feelings aside. It was petty to begrudge them a few last hours together.

Klaas returned and handed them glasses of champagne.

Christina raised a toast. 'To Agnes and Klaas and their long, happy life together.'

Christina saw a new bloom in her daughter's face. She must try to remember this look, so she could capture the image on canvas.

The music started again, this time the tune was a waltz. Klaas emptied his glass in one and grabbed Agnes's hand. 'I wish this night to last forever, and to keep you dancing in my arms.' He pulled her towards the floor.

Agnes laughed and handed Christina her glass. In an instant, they were swallowed by the crowd in this most glamourous of ballrooms. Christina was struck by a thought. The memories of tonight would fade unless she did something to prevent it.

She put down the glasses, slipped out of the ballroom, and sped down the corridors towards her studio. She must capture the moment in her sketchbook. Such a complicated composition was perhaps beyond her skills, but she owed it to Agnes to at least make an attempt.

Christina halted outside her room. The door was slightly ajar, and she'd heard a noise. She slid through the gap, then stopped dead. One candle flickered in a single chamberstick on the corner of the marble fireplace, but the moon lit up the scene. Yelena was perched on the edge of Christina's desk with her head flung back. Her eyes were closed and her legs wrapped around the shoulders of the person kneeling in front of her. She groaned in ecstasy, and Christina gasped. Yelena opened her eyes. She looked straight at Christina and placed her hand on Sarah's head, pulling her closer. Her eyelids flickered, and she moaned.

Christina turned and fled.

Chapter Thirty-Three

January 2018, St Petersburg

The Yusupovs' Palace was a place of extraordinary contrasts. Extreme luxury and opulence, then a small room in the basement with macabre wax figures of Rasputin and his assassin. Most importantly for my work, they had a couple more of Christina's portraits on the walls. The rest of the day was spent diving into research on the Yusupovs. I discovered they had a large house in Paris. Had Christina met them there first?

Pavel must have spent much of his day thinking about my research too, because when he came home, he was full of news.

'You're right about Christina bringing her daughters to St Petersburg. I found Agnes mentioned several times in Grand Duchess Olga's papers. Also, we store two little watercolours by a Mary Robertson. The style is very English and previous curators have accredited them to Christina's daughter.'

'Mary? That's interesting. Then both her daughters painted. A Miss Robertson exhibited at the Royal Academy in 1843, but that must have been Agnes. Mary was only ten at the time.'

'So, far from abandoning her daughters, she tutored at least one of them to professional standard,' Pavel said with a smile. 'You need to look for concrete proof. Historians often get things wrong and once it's in writing, it gets quoted as fact.'

'It looks like her sons stayed with her husband. James and their two boys are listed as living in a house in Beaumont Street on the census from June 1841. There's no record of Christina and the girls. It seems they arrived home later that year.'

I opened up my spreadsheet listing all Christina's Royal Academy paintings and pointed to 1843.

'Agnes and Christina exhibited together, which must have been extraordinarily unusual. It's the same year Christina showed a portrait of Tsar Nicholas together with Tsarina Alexandra.'

'I wonder what happened to that painting?' Pavel said.

'I've only been able to track down a tiny proportion of the art she displayed at the Royal Academy. Eighty-five per cent of her portraits are missing.'

'Also, you can assume that she painted many, many more portraits than she displayed there,' Pavel added.

'It makes me cross that she has been forgotten.'

Pavel squeezed my shoulder. 'She will be remembered better when your book comes out. Do you want some tea?'

I nodded and followed him into the kitchen. 'So what did Princess Olga say about Agnes? I found an article online that said she married a Dutch army officer called Ponkin.'

'Dutch? That sounds more like a Russian name. There's a famous conductor called Ponkin. I found out something else about Agnes.' A big grin spread over Pavel's face. 'I think you'll be pleased.' He handed me my mug of tea, and we went back to the living room.

'I might have found your missing link. Princess Olga

mentions Agnes as a widow. It seems this Ponkin was a soldier who was killed in the Crimean War, but Olga also describes herself as delighted that Agnes is to remarry a Scottish widower. One of Empress Alexandra's doctors, a man called Donald Phillips.'

'Really? I wonder if he brought her back to Scotland.'

I moved back to my laptop and typed the names into my favourite Scottish ancestry site. I found no marriage certificate, but they might have married in Russia. An hour later Pavel brought me a glass of wine. I smiled up at him. 'Thanks.'

'I've ordered in some pizza. I figured you might be here for a while,' he said.

I shifted my search to looking for a daughter. Pavel had said Princess Olga's papers had tied Agnes's second marriage to 1857. She would have been thirty-four. After another hour, I began to despair. I didn't even know if Agnes had come to Scotland and my lack of the language prevented me searching Russian sites. The name Phillips would be no help if Agnes had a daughter fathered by the soldier, but there were no Ponkins on the Scottish site. Finally, I found a little boy. A David William Phillips born to an Agnes and David Phillips in Newington, Edinburgh, in 1859. Could he be my Agnes's son?

The pizza delivery driver turned up at the door. Pavel joined me at the table and I pushed my laptop aside. 'Sorry, I've been terrible company tonight.'

'No problem. I'm busy doing some research of my own. It's a secret, but I'm dying to tell someone,' he said.

I crossed my heart. 'A solemn Babushka Appreciation Society oath. I can keep a secret.'

'Have you ever been to Amsterdam?'

'Yes. Twice. It's a fabulous place.'

'I have a friend called Paul, who works there for the

Hermitage's sister museum. A head-hunter approached him for candidate recommendations for a Senior Curator job at the Rijksmuseum. He called me to ask how I would feel about him suggesting my name.'

'So you might move to Amsterdam?'

'I don't know. It depends on the salary. It's a more expensive place to live than St Petersburg. Anyway, I've agreed to update my CV. If they like my experience, I'll go and meet them when I'm in Paris.'

'Wow. That's big news. Wouldn't you miss living here?' I waved my arm towards his view.

'Yes, but there are no promotion prospects for me in the Hermitage. The senior curator is a world expert, and I can't see her retiring anytime soon. I guess there's no harm in talking to them.'

I went back to my search and struck gold with the 1861 census. Two-year-old David Phillips lived in Edinburgh, with his mother and father Agnes and David. He had an elder sister, three-year-old Sarah.

The next leaps were achieved within half an hour. A Sarah Robertson Phillips married a David Linton in Edinburgh in 1880. Her daughter Mary Robertson Linton was born in 1884. Here was the concrete connection to my grandmother Edith. Sarah Robertson Phillips, who was presumably born in St Petersburg, since the birth was not on Scottish records must surely be Christina's granddaughter and my great-great-great grandmother. 'I've found the direct line of descent!'

Christina Robertson Female Descent

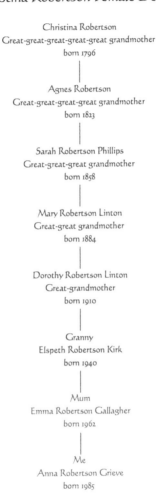

Christina Robertson
Great-great-great-great-great grandmother
born 1796

|

Agnes Robertson
Great-great-great-great grandmother
born 1823

|

Sarah Robertson Phillips
Great-great-great grandmother
born 1858

|

Mary Robertson Linton
Great-great grandmother
born 1884

|

Dorothy Robertson Linton
Great-grandmother
born 1910

|

Granny
Elspeth Robertson Kirk
born 1940

|

Mum
Emma Robertson Gallagher
born 1962

|

Me
Anna Robertson Grieve
born 1985

Revisiting Christina's St Petersburg was uplifting. During the day, I experienced moments of real elation. Visualising this book and how I could bring Christina back into the limelight. Later, when my mood sank, I laughed at my conceit. I wasn't a proper author. The gallery would cancel Christina's exhibition inclusion and the book would bomb. At night, I couldn't sleep. Nick's abandonment set me adrift. I'd believed he loved me, yet in an instant he'd gone. The mood swings were exhausting.

Being in St Petersburg was like being suspended in time. Living alongside Pavel was comfortable, but it was a short-term hiding place and I had to be an imposition. I'd expected contrition from Nick. The ongoing silence suggested the opposite.

It would take weeks to explore all the Romanov summer residences. I chose to go inside the two most associated with Nicholas I, which were also the most contrasting. I travelled out of town to Peterhof and Tsarskoe Selo.

The Cottage Palace was a weird place. A large house, but tiny for a Romanov family. Victorian gothic mixed with something slightly off. I wondered if Menelaws, the Scottish architect, was proud of it. The interior definitely had a 'cottage' feel, lots of floral prints and wallpaper. Pavel had said that many of Christina's smaller paintings formerly hung here. This month, it was decorated for Christmas, perhaps based on historical images. Did the Empress bring influence from Germany, as Albert did to Victorian England?

A few days later, I followed a Russian guide around the huge Catherine Palace. It was very reminiscent of the Winter Palace, with intricate floors, fancy ceilings, chandeliers, and an overload of gilding. I came across a haunting Christina portrait of Alexandra, the youngest daughter they called Adini. I was pleased to see a Robertson portrait still here but sad to remember her story. She died of tuberculosis when she was only nineteen. Her premature baby died too.

Next morning, I opened my laptop with a clear plan. I mustn't squander more time down St Petersburg rabbit holes. I assembled my chosen images and finally began to tell Christina's story.

My phone beeped. A text from Nick.

This is so very difficult for me. I know I've behaved badly but you have to believe me that I'm suffering too. I'm sorry but I don't feel ready to talk about what I'm going through and it's not something you can help with. I'm assuming you will stay on in St Petersburg to spend the weekend with Lisa? I'm not going to come. I need more time to think.

The selfish bastard. Who said he was still welcome?

I sent Lisa a message.

You will not believe the text I just had from Nick! Call me when you are free.

My phone rang immediately. 'What has he done now?'

I read the text to her.

'Oh, honey. I wish I was there to give you a hug,' Lisa said.

'I'm so angry with him, I can't face coming back. Do you think you could bring me a few more of my things? I hate to ask you when you already have that desk to carry.'

'Of course. The artwork is being couriered to St Petersburg, so we don't have much luggage.'

'Are you bringing the children?'

'No. Are you kidding me? I'm about to do Christmas for the second time in two weeks. I've earned my week off. Dmitry's mum is moving in here for Russian Christmas and staying on while we're away. She'll manage my little monkeys with Mila's help.'

'Lisa...' I hesitated to ask. 'Is Nick still seeing Oksana?'

I heard her breathe in. 'I'm not sure.'

'He is isn't he?'

'I think so.'

'That's it then. It really is over. God. Do you think she's been in our flat? Will he actually ask her to pack my bloody bags?' I was reduced to ugly sobbing.

'I'll do it. Send me a list. I'll clear out the lot if you like.' Lisa sounded furious.

'Would you? Just one case. I packed in such a state that I'm short of clothes and I left some precious things behind.'

'Just tell him I'm coming. I'll take Dmitry with me.'

In the evening, I asked Pavel if he could put up with me for a bit longer.

'You're welcome to stay as long as you like.'

'Nick is being such a dick. I might not go back to Moscow at all.'

'That guy needs his head examined.' He went upstairs and returned with his laptop. 'I've got some work to do. Quiet company might encourage me to concentrate.'

'What are you working on?'

'A press release about the Louis Vuitton exhibition. They're going to run an article in the *Moscow Times*.'

'Do you think they might be interested in an article about Christina?'

'Great idea!'

'I'm putting together a pitch for various journo contacts. I'll need publicity for the launch and really need to drum up some extra income from all this work. Would the idea of Russia honouring a British artist who has been forgotten in her native land be a good angle?'

'Definitely. I'll send you the *Moscow Times* editor's email address and you can mention that I'll endorse it. I've done several articles for them in the past.'

Pavel worked in silence for a few minutes. 'Did you do any freelancing after you quit your London job?'

'Nick said my visa didn't allow working, and being a journalist would make it difficult to get permission.'

Pavel raised his eyebrows. 'There are ways around it.'

I set about writing a pitch. Christina had coped with both tragedy and family separation and continued to produce great work. I had to use her mindset.

We worked in companionable silence for an hour until Pavel sat back and rolled his shoulders. 'I think we've earned wine.'

He brought me a glass of his favourite Russian red.

'Do you have plans for Christmas?' I asked. 'Please don't feel you have to change them because I'm here.'

'Not really, although I usually go to Mass on Christmas Eve. I'm not very religious, but I always went with my grandmother. Would you like to come?'

'I'd love that. And what would you like for dinner? It's my turn to cook.'

'Can you do a proper English Christmas dinner with gravy?'

'I don't think the two of us would get through a turkey, but I'll roast a chicken.'

The next evening, we ate our Christmas dinner, then got ready to go to Mass.

'You'll need to cover your hair in church. I've kept a couple of my grandmother's scarves.' Pavel came back with three scarves. 'I lied about getting rid of all her clothes. Do you think I'm a sentimental idiot?' he asked with a wry smile.

'Of course not.' I chose a white scarf with intricate lace embroidery. 'Will this be too fancy?'

'No. You'll fit right in. Wear your winter boots. It will be cold and we'll need to be comfortable to stand for about an hour and a half.'

I tried on the scarf in the mirror. It had a delicate scalloped edge and a network of embroidered daisies. 'Thank you for lending me this. I'm honoured.' He smiled at me in the reflection. 'What was her name?'

'Marina.'

'Such a lovely name.'

I was surprised to discover Pavel's grandmother took her Christmas Mass in Kazan Cathedral.

'It's a working church,' Pavel explained, as we strode past the floodlit square in front of the Hermitage. We crossed Nevsky Prospect beside the Moika River.

'Christina's apartment was on this corner,' I said. 'It's a shame the original building has been torn down.'

Behind the massive curved colonnade fronting Kazan Cathedral, the church had a huge green dome, modelled on St Peter's Basilica in Rome.

'Have a look around,' Pavel suggested. 'I'll save our places here.'

I did a circuit inside the church, giving myself a crick in my neck from staring up at the painted dome. When a cleric wearing an elaborately embroidered gold robe came in, I squeezed back through the crowd to Pavel. The priest started to chant, then two massive gold doors opened to reveal a priest with a blue hat in front of an altar table.

'That's the Archbishop,' Pavel whispered.

The man began his own sonorous chant, which was echoed by a singing reply from the choir, filling the cathedral, and swelling up into the dome itself. I understood hardly a word, but it was a sensational experience. After an hour, I shifted from one foot to the other.

Pavel smiled and offered his elbow. 'Are you tired? Lean on me.'

I wasn't tired, but the comfort and warmth of another human being was wonderful after the pain and loneliness of this week. I didn't believe in God, but the surroundings required a prayer of thanks for the friendship of this kind and gentle man.

Chapter Thirty-Four

July 1841, London

Their ship sailed into port at first light. The carriage was able to speed through London at that early hour and it brought Christina, Agnes and Mary to Harley Street before seven in the morning. The front door was bolted, so Christina had to ring the bell. A maid she didn't recognise opened the door and looked at them in confusion.

Eliza's voice came from the stairs behind her. 'Who is it at such an hour, Maisie?'

When Eliza saw them, she burst into tears. 'You're home! I'm so glad to see you.' She crouched to welcome Mary into her arms. 'My baby, I've missed you and you've grown so much!' She hugged Christina and then Agnes. 'Agnes, look at you! Already a lady.'

'I'm sorry not to send word ahead. I was able to get an earlier passage than I expected,' Christina said.

Agnes extricated herself from Eliza's embrace and squeezed past her. 'I want to tell Papa my news,' she said, heading up the stairs.

Eliza's eyes widened in panic.

'Is he here?' Christina whispered.

Eliza shook her head.

'The boys?'

'No. I'm sorry,' Eliza replied.

'Wait, Agnes,' Christina called. 'Eliza says Papa has gone out of town on business.'

She and Eliza caught up with Agnes standing in James's bedroom. The bedclothes were undisturbed.

Christina could smell lavender. She associated it with baby Christina's death and James knew she never had it in the house. She walked to the window, which showed no sign of damage. The smell was stronger here. When she touched the drape, something fell off the window ledge and rolled to her feet. A bottle of lavender water.

Mary burst into the room.

'Mama, the boys are missing!' She turned and took in James's bed, then burst into tears, burying her face on Christina's skirts. 'Mama, everything has gone wrong.'

'Papa didn't know we would be back today. He has obviously taken the boys off on some adventure. They'll be back soon.'

Christina looked towards her elder daughter. 'Isn't that right, Agnes?'

Realisation dawned on Agnes's worried face. 'Don't be a goose, Mary. You're just tired and hungry. Shall we go and make some porridge?'

'Excellent plan, Agnes. Then, Mary, I believe you were up too early and a nap in your own bed is just the thing to mend your spirits.'

Mary stopped snivelling and took Agnes's outstretched hand.

'I'll just check on our luggage,' Christina said.

On the stairs, Christina slipped the bottle into Eliza's pocket. 'What number?' she whispered.

'Oh Mistress, I don't think—'

'What number?' she repeated.

Eliza looked down at her feet. 'Forty-nine B,' she replied.

The driver had deposited their luggage in the hall. Christina instructed Henry, her long-serving footman, to take the two heavy chests up to her studio. 'Lock the door and give the key to Eliza.'

'Of course, madam,' he replied. 'Shall I pay the driver and let him go?'

'No. I have an errand to run.'

'Forty-nine B Beaumont Street,' she told the driver.

She stepped out of the chaise, just three streets away. Christina gave the man his fare. He smiled at the generous tip.

Christina pulled the brass bell and stood back from the wooden door of what appeared to be a large apartment building. A curtain to the left of the entrance twitched, and she saw John's face at the window. Seconds later the front door flew open, and William threw himself into her arms. He was almost her height already, and John, who stood behind him was a full foot taller. They were both in their nightshirts.

'My boys,' she said, with tears running down her cheeks. 'Will you invite me in, John, or persist in standing on the step in your nightclothes?'

'Mama, I don't think...' John said.

'Would you prefer to have this conversation in the common stairwell, John?'

She followed her sons into the flat. 'Get dressed quickly. Your sisters are waiting to see you at home. Poor Mary cried to find you missing.'

A door opened, and a woman with a cloud of curly red hair stepped out, wearing only a silk robe. The scent of lavender filled the air.

James shouted, 'For God's sake, boys, who is banging

doors?' He appeared in the doorway behind the woman. 'Christina, you're back.'

'Clearly.'

James crossed his arms over his chest, naked beneath his unbuttoned nightshirt.

'Mary is distraught to find you missing. I'll take the boys back with me now.' Christina gritted her teeth and fought the urge to cry. She was a fool not to have anticipated this disaster. She'd feared it, but hoped she was wrong.

The woman, her face ashen, disappeared back into what must be a bedroom. James was dumbstruck. His ridiculous bare legs stuck out from under his nightshirt. She was married to an imbecile. She turned to leave.

'Christina, wait,' James said.

'How dare you,' she replied.

Christina summoned a smile when her sons came out of the bedroom. They were dressed, although it was clear that William had tucked his nightshirt into his trousers.

'Do I need to bring anything else, Mama?' John asked, glancing nervously at his father.

'No need right now. Papa will organise that later.' She glared at James, and he nodded. 'Boys, I would like you to say you were overnight with a friend. It's a white lie, for Mary's sake. Papa and I have some talking to do.'

The boys left and she turned to face James. 'I'm exhausted from my journey and I need to think. Please drop off the boys' trunks today and come and see me at eleven tomorrow.' James nodded, his expression grim. 'Come alone,' she added.

Christina lay awake all night. She couldn't fool herself that she'd thought James had been celibate all this time, but she had never imagined he would expose his behaviour to the boys. There had been men in St Petersburg who'd thought a woman travelling alone might be open to their advances, but she had given them no quarter. She worked so hard to fund this family, and presumably that included James's mistress. A pretty woman of no more than thirty. Christina allowed herself some hours of angry tears. The colour of the girl's hair gave her particular offence. Her own had been a few shades darker in her teens, but its fiery hues had faded with every difficult year that followed. As dawn approached, her grief solidified into angry determination. She must pursue the best interests of her children.

At first light, Christina went to her studio to begin turning her sketches of Agnes's engagement night into a painting. The rhythm of it helped settle her nerves.

Agnes came in with cups of chocolate and bread still warm from the oven. She kissed Christina on the cheek. 'You look tired, Mama, and I see that my role in reminding you to eat remains necessary.'

'Thank you, my darling. You look tired too.'

Agnes placed the tray on the table and sat down. She spoke with her head bowed. 'I made John tell me about her. He fumbled his explanation of his whereabouts and William already blurted out a name. John is truthful by nature and he has been carrying a heavy burden. Papa told the boys that you and he had come to an arrangement, but John doubted it. He worries he should have told you.' She looked up. 'I am so very sorry. I shall never talk to Papa again.'

Christina touched Agnes's fingers. 'I am as upset as you are, but never is too strong a word. We had no such arrangement, but sadly, taking a mistress is not so very uncommon.'

'I knew from St Petersburg that it was ordinary. It's just I hadn't thought of my papa as such a low and ordinary man.'

'He will come at eleven.'

'I cannot face him.'

'Perhaps you and John could take William and Mary to Hyde Park. Your father and I must discuss practical matters. As for your part, Klaas gave you a letter to deliver. I believe you are brave and strong enough to deliver it in person, as you promised.'

Agnes gave a deep sigh and nodded. 'Not today, but I will pray on it. I'll go and find John.' She stood up.

'Tell John that he and I will talk later and that he has done nothing wrong. I shouldn't have asked him to lie. There will be no more of that in this house.'

Agnes lifted the tray with empty cups and made to leave.

'What is her name?'

Agnes replied, without looking at her. 'Lucy Fisher.'

It was ten after eleven, and Christina began to wonder if James would come. Then she heard his footsteps on the stair and he burst into the room, his expression thunderous.

'I hope you didn't expect me to knock. I'm unused to being given an appointment to enter my own house.'

So that was how it was going to go. 'I assure you that I have had to get used to many new notions in the last twenty-four hours,' Christina replied.

He sat on the chair opposite. Neither of them spoke. James stretched out his legs in front of him and gave a deep sigh. 'I'm sorry,' he said.

'Are you? Sorry for what? For breaking your marriage vows? For breaking my heart? For causing our sons distress and misplaced guilt? For making Agnes declare she never wants to see you again?'

James screwed up his face. 'I admit the first, but I intended none of those other things. And are you really heartbroken? You ceased marital relations long before you went to Russia, Christina. What did you expect? No man can live that way.'

'What do you know of my heart? But you do know why I want no more pregnancies. Do you imagine celibacy was easy for me?'

He shrugged. 'Women's desires are different.'

The vision of Sarah and Yelena flashed into Christina's head. 'You have no idea what you are talking about.'

'Many men are openly promiscuous within their marriage. I am discreet. Lucy is the only one.'

'Miss Lucy. What a pretty and innocent name. Like her face, but not her nature.'

'It's Mrs Fisher. She's not a bad person. Her life has been difficult. Her husband blamed her for not giving him children and he abandoned her.'

'The poor woman obviously has terrible taste in men.'

James flung the gloves inside his hat. 'Did you only ask me here to taunt me? I have to tell you that I am prepared to come back but I cannot promise to give up Lucy.'

'Your loyalty to your mistress is touching, and you can reassure her that I certainly don't want you back.'

James appeared stunned. He looked around their large drawing room, as if realising his comfortable life might be about to change.

'In law, this is my house,' he said quietly.

'And how do you propose to fund it? I wager that paying for two houses has dented our bank balance. I might decide to get back on that ship before it leaves and take all the Russian silver with me.'

'You wouldn't leave the boys again.'

'Perhaps they would choose to come with me. The girls loved St Petersburg and the English schools are excellent.'

James glared at her. She took a deep breath. 'I had not intended to lose my temper with you. We cannot repair what you have broken, but we must do what is best for the children. I'm going to insist they all live here and not in an adulterous house.'

'Lucy lives with her mother.'

'I saw the evidence to the contrary.'

'She sometimes stays overnight. I cannot be seen to visit her in her home.'

'I can't decide if you caring about her reputation makes this better or worse.' She took a deep breath. 'I need to spend some time with the boys and we must decide what we tell Mary. In the meantime, please conduct your extramarital affairs out of our sight.'

James got up to leave. He turned back at the door. 'Please, Christina. Ask Agnes to forgive me.' For the first time, his face showed genuine remorse.

'That is in your own hands,' Christina replied. 'She has a letter for you. A young man in St Petersburg has asked for her hand. Klaas is from a good family and is an officer in the Russian army. She has decided to marry him.'

James looked horrified. 'A Russian? She wants to live in Russia?'

'I told you we all liked St Petersburg and Klaas is half Russian, his mother is Dutch. Agnes adored you, James, yet I heard her crying in the night. If you seek forgiveness, then approving her choice might help. Assuming I can persuade her to talk to you.'

James replaced his top hat. 'Tell her to send for me when she is ready.'

After he left, Christina went into her studio and locked the door. She examined all the floorboards until she found a loose one. She took the shovel and then the poker from the hearth and levered it free. Each chest was filled to the top with leather bags containing silver roubles. She lined the gap in the floorboards with a scarf, then dropped in as many bags as the space would take. Hearing the children's voices downstairs, she left the room, locking the door behind her.

After supper, Agnes gave her an envelope.

'I found this letter for you on the hall table. Is everything all right?'

Christina's heart skipped to recognise Sarah's handwriting. 'It will never be all right, but a letter from Sarah is a welcome distraction.' She tore open the envelope.

'What is the news from Alnwick?' Agnes asked.

She scanned through the letter. 'Sarah reports that her mother is alive and out of immediate danger. However, she is confined to bed with a badly broken ankle. She plans to stay in Alnwick for the foreseeable future.'

'That's good news and bad. Sarah's support would have made this horror more bearable.'

'Yes, but we have each other,' Christina replied.

Sarah should have been the least of her worries, but she found it weighed heaviest on her heart. She'd waited in vain for Sarah to return after the ball. In the morning, she'd found her bedroom empty and a note on her bed.

I've gone early to the ship and didn't want to disturb you. Have a safe journey. I'll come to London when I can.

Once she'd processed the shock and disquiet of witnessing the scene with Yelena, Christina realised she was in an impossible situation. She didn't know if Yelena had told Sarah they were seen. She wanted to tell Sarah it shouldn't damage their friendship, but couldn't possibly put those words to paper. In any case, Sarah obviously loved beautiful Yelena. Clumsy words might make things worse and drive Sarah away for ever. Her heart had been already aching long before she'd come home to London. The only thing to do now was concentrate on her children.

'I need to show you something.' Christina led Agnes into her studio and locked the door behind them. She picked up one of the leather pouches from a chest and poured the silver coins on her bed. 'I made a promise there would be no secrets, but...' she swept her hand over the bed and the chests on the floor. 'I believe this represents more money than earned by any artist in the whole of England. Everyone underestimates my worth, including your father. It's dangerous to keep it here, so I must soon ask Papa to take it to the bank. I fear that such a large sum will tempt him to be extravagant, so I'm keeping some back.'

Christina bent down and peeled back the scarf hiding the bags of coins in the floor space. 'A quarter of this will go back to St Petersburg with you and the rest is for the others.'

Agnes sat on the bed and stared at the floor. 'Thank you, Mama. I've been thinking I should try to make some money from my own art. Do you think I'm good enough?'

'Yes. Not Academy standard yet, but you have the potential.'

'Then I will work as hard as you did to hone my skills.'

Christina hugged her daughter and slotted the floorboard back.

'Goodnight, Mama. I'll come back before breakfast to start work on my portfolio.'

'Goodnight, Agnes. When you are ready to speak to your papa, I'm hopeful he will support your marriage. Tell him you want to achieve Royal Academy entry. It will please him and he can help you meet the right people in London. Now, I'm going to see if John is still awake. I must know what ambitions he has for his future.'

After Agnes left, Christina took a bag of silver roubles from the chest. She penned a note to George.

We are home and I hope you will visit us soon. I long to see you and have a request. News of my father's death doesn't touch my heart, but I want to send some money to my half-sister. I have a bag of roubles to be exchanged for sovereigns. I am hoping you might ask your Leith friend Angus to deliver it anonymously into Isobel's hands.

Best wishes, Christina

She left the sealed letter on the hall table, with a note asking Henry to have it hand delivered.

Chapter Thirty-Five

January 2018, St Petersburg

I was engrossed in my newly purchased art history book. It was fascinating to learn some artistic context for Christina's world.

Pavel came in with a mug of tea and pushed over the cover to read the title.

'I wanted to have a broader view of the art scene in Christina's day.'

'Did you buy it?'

'Yes.'

'You needn't have. There's a copy on my bookshelves. Come and see.'

I followed Pavel up to the mezzanine. His study area was lined with bookshelves. Hundreds of art books.

'Wow! It's like a library.'

'Let's see.' He ran his finger along a shelf, pulled out and handed me two large books. 'These are both nineteenth century, but feel free to browse and help yourself. Most are in English.'

I flicked through the first beautifully illustrated volume. 'Thank you. All these books must have cost you a fortune.'

'They were acquired over a long time. Many of them when I was studying.'

'History of Art?'

'To the point of obsession. I did a masters in Budapest then came back to St Petersburg to do my PhD.'

'Then it's Dr Sidorov?'

He shrugged. 'I only use the title for work purposes.'

Pavel carried the books downstairs for me.

'I had a place to study History of Art and English Literature at Edinburgh Uni,' I said. 'I sometimes think turning it down was a mistake.'

'Why did you?'

'I was seventeen and in love with a boy. He was going to Brighton, so I decided to go straight into studying journalism there.'

'But the boyfriend didn't work out?'

'Not forever, but we were together for ten years.'

The doorbell rang. Lisa stood on the threshold weighed down by my suitcase as well as the bag containing my desk. She cast her eyes around the large room. The table was strewn with my papers.

She grinned. 'Look at the two of you, holed up in here.'

I laughed. 'Please tell me you didn't struggle upstairs with those on your own.'

'No. Dmitry walked me up to the door, but he's gone back to the Uber to check in at the hotel and dump our stuff. He'll be back soon.' She pulled a bottle of champagne out of her large handbag. 'Can I put this in your freezer, Pavel? It's warmed up on the journey.'

'What are we celebrating?' he asked.

Lisa gave him an exasperated glare. 'We are celebrating Christmas and surrounding Anna with so much love she might suffocate.' She walked over and pulled me into a hug. 'Also, a child-free week in my favourite city calls for champagne. My children are lovely, but they're exhausting too.'

She placed Christina's desk on the table. 'One precious object, safely delivered.'

My hands were immediately drawn to stroke the box. 'I don't know how to thank you. It's such an awkward thing to carry.'

'The look on your face is thanks enough.'

I opened the writing slope and ran my fingers along the rear compartment. I removed the crystal inkwell, took the lid off the pen compartment, then pulled the edges of all the sections towards me, looking for a catch.

'What are you doing?' Lisa asked.

'Mum says these sometimes have a secret compartment. It's released by pulling the inkwell wall.' I put my finger and thumb over the section divider. The small piece of wood came straight out and the whole panel below sprang forwards.

Lisa's cheer brought Pavel from the kitchen. 'What's going on?'

The exposed compartment had two drawers. One contained an engraved metal pen.

'It's beautiful,' Pavel said, 'and perhaps old enough to be Christina's. Can I see it?'

I passed him the pen.

'It comes apart,' Pavel said.

'For the ink?'

'No, it's a nib pen, they just dipped it an inkwell. Maybe for spare nibs?'

Pavel pulled the two parts of the barrel apart, revealing paper curled inside. The surge of adrenalin caused a tiny tremor in my outstretched fingers. The note looked square but one corner sprang out of a fold, transforming it into four star points decorated with flowers. It unfolded into one sheet of paper, several lines of handwriting were in the middle. 'It's like origami,' I said.

'That's a traditional Victorian love note,' Pavel added.

'What does it say?' Lisa sounded as excited as I felt.

'The writing is tiny and hard to decipher, and it's very faded.' I took it to the window.

Pavel and Lisa came to look over my shoulders.

'There's a trick for faded documents, using yellow acetate. Perhaps I've got some upstairs,' Pavel said.

'The first line is a date. June 1847. That's the year she came to St Petersburg the second time.'

'St Petersburg! That's in the third line,' Lisa added.

Pavel arrived back. 'No acetate, but a yellow plastic file might help.' The yellow contrast revealed the left hand of the note, but not the right.

June 1847

Dearest Christina,

I have only ever loved you. Then some undecipherable words.

We belong together in St Petersburg. More illegible words. Then only one letter instead of a signature. 'Is it an L, or maybe an I?'

'Surely it must be her husband,' Lisa said.

'Maybe? It doesn't look like a J, and if James came here, he certainly didn't stay. I kind of hope it's not him.'

'Blimey, has Nick put you off all husbands for life?'

'No, but it would blow my theory that she travelled abroad to avoid being pregnant.'

'Menopause? How old was she in 1847?'

'Could be. She was fifty-one,' I answered.

'I'll take it into our archive department,' Pavel said. 'They have equipment to enhance old documents. Doesn't this give you what you hoped for? You hated to think she was alone in St Petersburg.'

'You're right. And whoever wrote this is expressing undying love.'

The doorbell rang. Pavel let Dmitry in.

'Good timing. We've just found another reason to celebrate,' Lisa said. She swooped in on the old-fashioned coupé glasses behind the glass doors of Pavel's grandmother's cupboard. 'Ooh, these are adorable.'

Pavel brought in the bottle.

'This is proper stuff, too. As much as I love all things Russian,' Lisa paused to kiss Dmitry on the cheek, 'champagnskaya is not the same.' Dmitry smiled indulgently at her.

Lisa opened the bottle and filled the glasses. Dmitry handed mine and grinned. 'I think your Nick is little bit terrified of me.'

I spurted out my sip of champagne. 'What did you do?'

'Nothing,' he said, with a mischievous look.

'He told Nick he had behaved like an absolute shit to you, and that if Vadim brought home, even a whiff of complaint, he would send in his particular friends,' Lisa said.

'Who are his particular friends?' I asked.

'Ach. Dmitry's friends are all painters, but he looks like he might know gangsters. That's enough.'

We all laughed. Lisa sat beside me on the couch and gave me another hug. 'How are you doing?'

I shrugged. 'All right, I guess.'

'You should be pleased to know that Nick looks like shit.'

I screwed up my face. 'I don't know what to feel about him. No doubt he is in a state, but after being together for all these years, you'd think he would want to talk to me about it.'

Lisa grimaced. 'He gave me a letter for you. But open this first.' She pulled the familiar colourful gift bag out of her handbag.

I frowned. 'I don't think I want it back.'

'I know the woman who runs that shop. Open it.'

I unwrapped the box from its tissue. It was the lacquer box I'd picked up first in the shop. The blue-eyed woman standing in a sleigh, holding a whip in her hand and was looking resolutely over the heads of her white horses.

'That's you. Getting the hell out of your past and owning your future,' Lisa said.

I laughed. 'Thank you. It's perfect.'

'Let's go out,' Dmitry suggested. 'What about the pub next door to our hotel? I'll go ahead and grab us a table.'

Dmitry left, and Lisa handed me an envelope.

'I told Nick he should call you if he'd something to say, but hey...'

'I'll just get my hat,' Pavel said, tactfully leaving the room.

I stared at the letter, hesitating to open it.

'You could keep it for later?' she said.

I opened the envelope. 'No. I need your moral support.'

Dear Anna

I know I should come to St Petersburg and confess face to face, but I'm too ashamed to even do this by phone.

My sperm sample results revealed that I'm infertile. I feared this ever since you brought that leaflet from Scotland as I had mumps when I was a teenager.

I got the result on the day of your charity ball and I fell to pieces. All those years of longing to be a father were pointless. Oksana was there to comfort me. We've become close. I believe she now knows me better than anyone. In that moment when I felt a failure as a man, she convinced me it doesn't matter to her. I'm ashamed to have hurt you with my behaviour. I also feel terrible that I watched you go through all those months of disappointment when the problem was with me all along.

If I were a better man, I would have shared my fears before the test. Perhaps you would have stayed with me to plan a different future together. The truth is, I cannot see any future for us. We hoped and dreamed of a baby together for too long. I can't imagine living beside you, when surely a tiny part of you would always blame me. Every time I caught you looking at a pregnant woman or a new-born, it would kill me inside. I don't know whether my relationship with Oksana will work out long term, but for now she makes me feel wanted.

I will arrange to be out of the apartment if you want to get in. Or I can organise to have your stuff shipped back if you prefer. I wish you all the luck in the world and I hope you find a father for your baby.

Nick xx

I was stunned into silence and passed the letter to Lisa.

'This is all about him. He hasn't thought about your feelings at all. He hadn't even the balls to tell you himself.'

I shook my head. My heart ached. 'It's not just the end of my marriage. I've squandered my last child-bearing years on someone who surely never really loved me at all.' I caught my breath, stifling a sob.

Lisa grabbed my hands. 'Don't you dare cry for that bastard. You've had a lucky escape.'

I shook my head.

'Don't you realise?' Lisa said. 'You would never have conceived with him. He hasn't even given you the loving offer of other options. A sperm donor, for example, but now you don't need his permission.'

'I suppose... My brother is having a baby through surrogacy. An egg donation from his husband's sister. But Euan is part of a family. Could I manage on my own?'

'Why not? Did you imagine Nick was going to be much help?'

I smiled. 'No. Not really. But I'd need a donor.'

'Your brother managed it and he overcame the need for a womb. You just need a cooperative friend.'

'Blimey, it's a big ask. How exactly would you phrase that?

Hi, random bloke, would you like to father my baby and be tied to me forever?'

'You could ask me,' Pavel said. He stood in the doorway wearing his leather hat and a nervous expression. 'If a Russian bloke isn't too random?'

I smiled at him in disbelief. 'Would you really do that for me?'

Lisa whooped and jumped off the couch to kiss him. 'Do you have any whisky, Pavel?'

He shook his head.

'Then let's go and find Dmitry. A Scottish-Russian pact of such magnitude has got to be toasted with whisky.'

'Thank you,' I said, going on tiptoe to hug him. 'We need to talk about this seriously. It would be a huge gamble, but I have a feeling our grandmothers would approve.' I kissed him. He grinned and hugged me again.

Pavel and I paused our late night walk back from the pub beside the enormous Christmas tree in front of the Hermitage in Palace Square. Draped in blue and gold lights with a single star on top, it was breathtakingly beautiful. I slipped my hand out of my mitt and reached for his.

'I'm a bit of a mess. It's not the right time to plan a baby.'

'It's a gift from me if you want it. No strings attached.'

He wrapped his fingers around mine and put both our hands in his pocket. 'Let's go home, it's freezing.'

Chapter Thirty-Six

March 1846, London

Uncle George's burial took place in All Souls Cemetery in north-west London. A bitter March wind whipped Christina's hair loose and against her face. Her heavy grief was tempered by being pleased to have spent lots of time with George these last five years. George liked to sit in her studio whilst she painted, and he visited her more often in James's absence. He loved to hear about the Rothschilds and the Clintons, but her stories of the Romanov court fascinated him most of all. He used to call her 'my niece who paints princesses'.

'I owe everything to you,' she'd told him for the umpteenth time.

Three years previously, when Agnes had eight paintings accepted by the Academy Exhibition, he'd insisted on attending. They'd travelled together to the new Royal Academy premises in Trafalgar Square. He'd needed John's arm to walk beside Agnes to view her exhibits, but for a while, the excitement gave him a new lease of life. Christina was so glad he'd lived to see it. Thoughts of Agnes far away in St Petersburg made her eyes smart again. She turned away not to upset Mary.

Since George had no descendants and all his siblings were dead, Christina was chief mourner. At seventy-two, George had outlived most of his contemporaries. Arthritis had prevented him painting for many years. Nevertheless, there were many representatives from the artistic community. David Roberts nodded to Christina from his place with the group of artists on the other side of George's grave. James stood amongst them. They mostly managed to be civil to each other these days, but she was glad he kept his distance and hadn't brought Lucy.

'Papa is alone. I might stand with him?' William said.

'Of course,' Christina agreed.

Now fifteen, William had been young enough to adapt to his parents living apart. John, on the other hand, had never entirely forgiven James. Now he stood tall and proud on the other side of Mary. Christina looked around for George's friend Angus. On arrival, she'd approached him discreetly to offer her condolences. Despite George's age and frailty, he'd had no recent crisis, but passed away quietly in his sleep. A good way to go, but they had all been unprepared. When they lowered the coffin into the grave, Angus was unable to contain his grief. Catching sight of him walking away alone was heartbreaking to see.

When Angus reached the cemetery gates, Christina saw a veiled lady dressed in black enter. Even without a glimpse of blonde hair, Christina knew Sarah immediately and the joy of recognition struck straight to her heart. She had feared that the letter to Alnwick might not reach her in time. Sarah stopped beside Angus and embraced him, before hurrying towards the graveside. Her particular empathy with George and Angus's situation made a lot of sense now. Christina wondered if George had known about Sarah?

The minister said a final prayer, then Christina threw her handful of earth on the coffin, followed by John. Sarah looked up towards Angus's lonely figure, as if to say, this is for you when she threw her own.

Christina took Sarah's arm to walk back towards the carriage. 'How is your mother?'

Sarah sighed. 'More or less bedridden. I believe she could have learned to walk again once her ankle injury healed, but she refused to use a stick and now she lacks the strength.'

'I'm so sorry for her and for you. I never saw you settling back in Alnwick.'

'It was certainly not my plan, but I find myself trapped. Adam's Ben is as lively as his five brothers. Ma complains their house is too noisy for her, and that's one of the few things we agree on. She cannot return to live there.'

'I'm sorry. How do Tom and Margaret get on?'

Sarah's face lit up. 'I think I would go mad without their company. Margaret had another little boy in January. He's a darling, but I have to admit her William is my favourite. Three is such a lovely age, and he reminds me so much of your boys. Your William looks so grown up now,' Sarah added, looking towards where he walked ahead with James.

'I believe he might overtake James in height,' Christina agreed.

'Is he close to his father?'

Christina nodded. 'The pain of growing up without my father made me determined to encourage their relationship.'

Mary interrupted. 'What happened to your father, Mama?'

'He died,' Christina answered. She caught Sarah's eyes above Mary's head. She'd told the elder two the story of her early life before Agnes returned to St Petersburg, but couldn't yet face a grilling from curious and talkative Mary. At fourteen, Christina judged her too young to give truthful answers to her inevitable questions.

'What did he die of?' Mary persisted.

'Would you mind if I don't talk about this today of all days, Mary?'

Sarah gave her a sympathetic smile.

'Will you stay with us tonight?' Christina asked.

'If that is all right? Tom's Christiana is staying overnight with Ma, but I promised to return tomorrow.'

'Of course. I'm looking forward to showing you Bentinck Street.

After supper, they settled in the drawing room. Mary plonked herself down on the couch beside Christina, who resisted the urge to sigh. Agnes had been her constant companion on return from Russia. When she left to marry, Mary assumed she could take over. Christina had indulged Mary, and there was little chance of a private conversation with Sarah.

'What news of Agnes?' Sarah asked.

'She is very well.'

'You must have been sad to miss the wedding.'

'Of course, but Klaas couldn't get the leave to come here. Agnes stayed in London much longer than she initially intended.'

'George wrote to me about Agnes's Academy exhibits. He was so proud.'

'I doubted anyone could have been prouder than me, but he was so very pleased for her.'

'Might you visit her in St Petersburg?'

'I didn't dare be away when George was so frail. I might consider it now.'

'I want to go back,' Mary piped up. 'It's not fair that I was too young to attend court balls.'

Christina laid her hand on Mary's arm, hoping to dissuade her precocious daughter from talking.

Mary didn't take the hint. 'Did you hear that your friend Yelena left St Petersburg?'

Sarah's eyes widened. 'No,' she replied. 'Yelena speaks English, but doesn't write it. We lost touch.'

Mary moved out of Christina's reach. 'Agnes told us there was such a scandal with her mistress.'

'Mary!'

Mary ignored Christina's warning. She had a wicked glint in her eye. 'Apparently, her husband accused her of having a perverse affair.' Mary took obvious delight in giving the word 'perverse' emphasis. 'He sent her back to her family in Rotterdam. She took Yelena with her. Can you imagine the fuss! Poor Yelena, losing her place in St Petersburg over her mistress's bad behaviour!'

'Mary, I'm ashamed of you for repeating such gossip. If Agnes meant you to read her letters, she would address them to you.'

Mary tossed her head. 'Agnes's life is exciting and mine is so dull. I'm not a child anymore, Mama.'

Christina stole a glance at Sarah. She had managed a neutral expression, but the tell-tale red spots on her cheeks gave away her emotions. Christina felt guilty. She should have told Sarah about Yelena herself, but hadn't known what to say. She wasn't sure if Agnes knew any details of the Dutch woman's disgrace, but was in no doubt about what Sarah would assume.

Nevertheless, Sarah forced a smile. 'I wouldn't concern yourself about Yelena, Mary. She wouldn't have wanted to be left behind.'

Surely the tremor in Sarah's voice was caused by recalling the love she had lost? Christina hoped she might return to St

Petersburg. Now she feared Sarah would never want to go back.

George had been like a father to Christina and his loss left her so low that she was glad of the excuse to withdraw from society. The following year she forced herself to mix more and when she met David Roberts at the theatre, she invited him to visit their new home the next day.

'This is really beautiful, Christina,' Roberts said, gazing around the walls of her Bentinck Street drawing room.

'Thank you. I'm happy here. The studio and drawing rooms are better in this house, and the gas lamps are a revelation.'

'You must be very proud of Agnes's Royal Academy success.'

'Very proud, but I miss her every day.'

'I heard you'll visit her in St Petersburg?'

'Mary and I will go after William joins his regiment this summer. It wasn't what I wanted, but he is determined. It seems likely he will travel to India. How can I argue with his ambition to see the world?'

'Travel will be good for him.'

'Will you take some tea?'

'I'd love some, but not before I view this painting. I'm thoroughly intrigued.'

'My studio is upstairs. The painting is so far from my usual style that I'm nervous. I want your truthful opinion.' They mounted the narrow staircase. The canvas was hung opposite the windows, covered by a sheet.

'An enormous painting. How exciting!' David Roberts said.

Christina gripped the edges of the sheet. 'You must tell

me if it's too sentimental to show in public.' She tugged the cover away. She'd depicted Walter Scott's heroine Amy swooning in the arms of her earl.

'Christina, not a portrait but a scene, and it's stupendous! It's the lovely Sarah in fancy dress, but who is her beau?'

Roberts' admiring expression did seem genuine, but looking at it again, her courage wavered. 'I was right. It is too much. No one will accept it.'

'Utter nonsense. It's clearly one of your best works. The rendition of the details, the light on her dress, all masterfully done. Surely it's a painting that tells some story?'

'It's my imagining of a scene from Scott's *Kenilworth*. Sarah was my model for the sketches in St Petersburg. I originally planned it as a thank you gift for the Tsarina. She and the Tsar are huge fans of Scott's work. I discovered the story of tragic Amy Robsart was her very favourite.'

'This must have taken you months and it's beautiful. You have to exhibit it.'

Christina flushed. 'It's been a private project, a challenge to see if I could achieve something on a grand scale. I fear I've made it too big.'

Roberts smiled at her. 'Listen to yourself. You set yourself a challenge and you more than succeeded.'

Christina shrugged. 'I'm glad you think so.'

After tea, Roberts sat back. 'You are a wonder, Christina Robertson. A painting that exceeds the quality of Sir William Allan's Scott illustrations, and the best Dundee cake south of the Tay.'

'You flatter me. The cake was George's favourite and we couldn't get it here, so I took the recipe from an aunt.'

'I pray to witness William Allan's face when he sees this. I'm sure it was your success that persuaded Allan to return to the Tsar's court. He executed his Peter the Great painting in the Winter Palace, but he complains everyone still calls the studio Christina's room.' Roberts flung back his head and laughed.

Christina allowed herself a smile. 'I would never laugh at Sir William. His intervention got me to St Petersburg in the first place.'

Roberts picked up his hat and stood to go. 'You must promise me that the public shall see that painting.'

Christina made no reply.

'Seriously. Why not put it into the British Institution Exhibition? I'm submitting a large painting again this year and it's the right place for something of this scale. The public will love it as much as I do, and you can still take it to your Tsarina if you want to. Sarah must surely agree.'

'Sarah is still in Alnwick. She hasn't seen it completed.' In fact, Sarah hadn't seen it at all, but Christina didn't want to admit that.

'You must invite her to its exhibition. Your friendship with Sarah is like mine with David Hay. Since neither of us chose our life partner wisely, we must depend on our excellent friends.' He tipped his hat. 'I shall approach the British Institute Directors to find out if they still have room. I cannot allow your masterpiece to languish beneath a sheet.'

Once Roberts had left, Christina went back to stare at the painting. It was without a doubt her most personal piece of work. Not just because it featured Sarah's face but because of what it stood for. In many ways, it summed up her own life. The endless struggle between ambition and love, just like the characters in Scott's story. Christina wasn't falsely modest and believed she'd achieved her aim to paint from imagination and on an epic scale. Whether critics and the public would accept it from her was another question. Childrearing years were behind her and her artistic success was beyond her wildest dreams. That struggle was over. This painting had been her indulgence and also her consolation.

How could she tell him that this was all she had left of Sarah and that she was reluctant to live without it?

The loss of her friendship with Sarah made artistic ambitions seem insignificant in comparison.

Chapter Thirty-Seven

May 2019, Edinburgh

I ran my fingers along the gleaming black slate mantelpiece. Mum and I had squealed with joy when we discovered the fireplace boarded up on one of the shop walls. The landlord gave me permission to restore it and now it formed the central feature for my lovingly created room sets. The cooperation with an Edinburgh interior designer was a very lucrative side hustle to the antiques shop. I sourced elements to their client brief. Certain reproduction items usually formed the core. This time a vast overmantel mirror and authentic-looking wall lights. The art varied according to client taste. For this person, a pair of antique oil on canvas landscapes. The designer had practically purred when she came to take photographs today, then she called to say her client wanted everything within an hour of leaving the shop. Even although the commission was shared with the designer, it covered the shop rent for the whole month. Today had been a great day. Lisa waited for me in the front section of the shop. She turned in a circle, admiring the walls hung with old paintings. 'You have made such a good job of this place.'

I leaned into the windows to pull down the security shutters. Lisa walked ahead of me onto Dundas Street and I set the alarm.

'Most of the antiques are still sourced by Mum. But she is coaching me and I love our joint trips to old house clearances. It's amazing what people have hidden away.'

'And are you enjoying your course?'

'I absolutely love it. Studying art history part-time allows me to combine it with working here. My head is bursting with everything I'm learning.'

Lisa hooked her arm through mine and we headed up the hill towards Edinburgh town centre.

'So no chance of a test tube baby?' She stuck out her bottom lip. 'It's such an excellent story, I so wanted it to come true.'

I laughed. 'I briefly considered it, but with a chance to start my life again it would have been a mistake. Instead I've invested in me. Mum says I have a knack of choosing paintings that will sell. I even correctly identified a couple of portraits by sought after artists which went onto sell for serious money.'

'Any Christina Robertsons?'

'Not yet, but I keep hoping.'

'Dmitry and I are going to try to come over for the exhibition.'

'That would be great! My brother's coming too. I'm desperate to meet baby Edie.'

'Dmitry's excited to visit Edinburgh, and I think we'll bring the kids.'

'Brilliant! What's going on in their lives?'

Lisa shared all her news while we walked along George Street. As we approached Contini's Italian restaurant, Mandy appeared around the corner. 'I invited Mandy to join us. I want you to meet her.'

'How lovely and it's your birthday, honey. Great to make a party of it. I'm just so glad my conference fell this weekend,' Lisa replied.

I introduced Lisa to Mandy, then we followed a waitress to a booth. Lisa stared up at the elaborately corniced ceiling of this former bank. 'What an amazing place,' she murmured.

'I've got the perfect birthday present for you,' Mandy said and took a shiny new book from her handbag.

'Oh my god, the proofs are in!'

'I have a whole box for you at home. I'll drop it round tomorrow.'

The weight of the book in my hands. The lovely cover with Christina's painting of Princess Zinaida. It was a dream come true. Emotion almost stole my voice, but I managed to whisper, 'Thank you.' I flicked through the pages, pausing over the gorgeous colour illustrations, then passed it to Lisa.

'Congratulations, Anna. I love this,' Lisa said.

'I'll give you a proof to take home, you can have that one if you like.'

'Thank you, I'd love to read it, but you have to sign it for me.' She flicked back to the beginning. Opening at the dedication page, which simply said:

For my granny, Edith Robertson Gallacher.
Also for Pavel and in honour of our Babushka Appreciation Society.

Lisa looked at me wide-eyed. 'Does that mean you guys are together?'

I smiled. 'We kept it kind of quiet. I wanted to give us room to be sure. But there have been lots of weekend visits. Me to lovely Amsterdam and Pavel coming here.'

Mandy looked over my shoulder and smiled. 'Here he comes.'

I jumped up to hug him. 'You managed to get away!' His surprise arrival made this birthday gathering perfect.

'Happy birthday, my love,' he whispered in my ear. He kissed both Lisa and Mandy on their cheeks, then sat down. 'The book!' he said, sounding as excited as me.

'You've got the prime spot,' Lisa told him, passing over the proof.

Pavel grinned. 'It's sad to report that this gorgeous author is exploiting my contacts for academic endorsements,' he said, in mock seriousness.

'I think that might be her publisher,' Mandy added. 'We are thrilled with how many people have agreed to take an author review copy.'

'I think you will approve of Anna's birthday present too, Mandy.' Pavel handed me a large envelope.

It contained a brochure. 'Lithuania.' I smiled but was puzzled. I knew nothing about Lithuania.

'Next month maybe? I didn't book anything yet. I know you need to check with your mum, but the Baltic coast is lovely in June. Also the coastal city of Klaipeda used to be called Memel. That's where William Allan was shipwrecked and lived until he travelled onto Russia. Might give you inspiration for the new book.'

'Sounds amazing.' I kissed him. 'I'll ask Mum but I would think I can get away. My uni year will be over.'

We ordered our meals and the wine waiter brought prosecco.

Mandy raised a toast. 'You are about to become a published author, Anna. The happiest of birthdays to you.'

'To Pavel and Anna,' Lisa added.

I raised my glass too. 'And to Christina Robertson and also my lovely granny, who gave me the clues to unlock my path to happiness.'

Chapter Thirty-Eight

June 1847, London

O n the opening day of the British Institution
Exhibition, Sarah arrived just in time to accompany her to the Pall Mall viewing. Christina was
nervous and not chiefly about the painting's reception. She
was resolved to talk to Sarah about the incident with Yelena.
Surely, enough years had passed for Sarah to come to terms
with the loss of her lover. It was pure cowardice on her part,
not to have raised the awkward subject. Leafy St James's
Square was full of birdsong and the weather was perfect for
walking. She squeezed Sarah's arm against her own ribcage.
'It's so lovely to have you here.'

Sarah's smile helped her nerves to settle.

'But I'm surprised to see you still in black. I gave it up
earlier this year. You know George would not have expected
you to persist.'

Sarah dipped her head, hiding her face under her bonnet
rim. 'It's not for George. Ma died six weeks ago.'

'What?' Christina stopped walking. 'I am so sorry. Why
did no one tell me?'

'I made Tom promise not to. You didn't really know Ma. You would have rushed to come up, and I didn't want you to feel obliged.'

Christina flung up her hands in exasperation. 'Obliged? You are my best friend in the world. What have we come to if we cannot lean on each other? How did we let that happen?'

'You are right and I'm sorry,' Sarah said. She glanced up with fearful eyes. 'When Yelena told me you'd seen us, I was so mortified. My behaviour was unforgivable.'

Sarah strode on again, and Christina ran a few steps to catch up. She grabbed Sarah's hand as they negotiated a path through the carriages on Pall Mall. She pulled her to a halt in the British Institution doorway. 'It is I who is to blame. I didn't know how to talk about it, and couldn't find words to comfort you when I knew you were heartbroken. I'm not a worthy friend.'

Sarah looked puzzled. 'Yelena could never break my heart.'

A male voice shouted her name. 'Christina! Wait for me.' Roberts joined them in the doorway and offered them his elbows. 'Let's go in together. I've been looking forward to this for weeks.'

The doorman gave them a catalogue and waved them through.

'We are in the same room, but your painting is first,' Christina said. Glad for the chance to gather her wits after Sarah's words.

They stood in front of David Roberts' large painting of a market scene.

'Where is this place?' Sarah asked.

'Coutances in Normandy. My Dieppe market scenes sold well, so I'm hopeful I'll get bids. But tell me, Mrs Lewis, what did you think of yourself as a Scott heroine?'

'Please call me Sarah. And I've yet to see the finished work.'

'Oh hurrah. I wanted to witness this moment. Come along, ladies.'

Christina's painting was easy to spot, since it took up most of one wall. A group of ladies in front of it were being noisy in their praise.

'Oh, Christina. It's so beautiful,' Sarah said.

'Do you think people will recognise you?' Roberts whispered to Sarah.

'I shouldn't think so. Swooning in the arms of a handsome nobleman is not my customary pose.'

Christina laughed out loud.

'This calls for a celebration,' Roberts declared. 'I've brought you a gift to take to St Petersburg. I left it at the Athenaeum for safe-keeping. Walk with me there, then we'll take a carriage to Browns.'

'A gift? You are too kind and I'm intrigued. Can we celebrate at Bentinck Street? I'm expecting James to bring Mary back within the hour.'

'You're going back to St Petersburg?' Sarah asked.

Christina met Sarah's eyes. She thought her heart might break in two in response to her sad expression.

'You won't travel this time, Sarah?' Roberts asked.

'Until recently it would have been impossible...' Sarah's voice trailed off.

'Would you want to come with us?' Christina whispered, still holding her gaze and her breath.

'I can think of nothing I would like more,' Sarah replied.

'Another reason for celebration! Wait right here.'

David Roberts' ebullient reaction mirrored the joy surging through Christina's body. She took both of Sarah's hands. 'It would make me beyond happy to have you back by my side.'

'It is what I long for too.'

They hugged right there in the middle of the London street.

Roberts appeared carrying a painting-shaped parcel tied up with brown paper and string. He opened his jacket to reveal a bottle of champagne held against his side. 'It's not a day for tea,' he declared.

Roberts opened the champagne in Christina's drawing room. She undid the string to unwrap what turned out to be David's painting of Kelso Abbey.

'Thank you. A memory of Scotland to hang in our St Petersburg apartment. I can think of no better gift.'

Just then, Mary burst in.

'Where have you been, young lady? Have you no interest in your mother's art?' Roberts said in mock admonishment.

'Mary has inherited my artistic talent but also her father's love of society. Given the option of going with James and William to Ascot, she had no difficulty deciding,' Christina replied.

Mary's hair was coming down and her high colour suggested she'd had a successful outing. 'We had the best day, Mama. Papa's horse won and we had champagne!'

'Then you must have another,' Roberts said.

'I'm not sure...' Christina thought Mary might be excited enough.

Her daughter pulled a face. 'I only had one glass with Papa. Are we celebrating your exhibition?

'That and the news that Sarah will come with us to St Petersburg.'

'Really? That is the best news!' Mary embraced Sarah and accepted the half glass that Roberts poured for her.

David Roberts stayed on for another hour. Mary dominated the conversation with stories of her Ascot adventures. Sarah caught her eye across the room and smiled.

Christina got ready for bed. She decided to write a thank you note to send to David Roberts in the morning. On opening her writing slope, she found an illustrated and folded note addressed simply 'Christina'. She recognised Sarah's hand. It unfolded to first reveal a star decorated with flowers. Inside was a message.

June 1847
Dearest Christina,
I have only ever loved you. No one else ever came close.
We belong together in St Petersburg. Your friendship and having you beside me is all I need.
S
xxx

Christina knocked softly on Sarah's door. Her friend was in her nightgown with her hairbrush in her hand and her long blonde hair tumbled over her shoulders. Christina sat on the end of her bed and clasped Sarah's hands.

'I don't think I can give you everything you need,' she said, looking deeply into Sarah's eyes.

'I love you as you are. Just your companionship will be enough.' Sarah lifted Christina's fingers. 'The touch of your hand, the warmth of your hug.'

'I've managed to turn my back on my physical needs, but you are too young.'

Sarah sighed. 'Yelena taught me things and gave me experiences I never imagined for my life. Her love was only for her Dutch mistress but she was jealous of you. Yelena was delighted to hurt you and I could never forgive her. It was the thought of losing you that broke my heart.'

Sarah stood and they embraced. Christina's heart brimming with happiness.

Just then, Mary's voice came from the corridor. 'Mama, where are you?'

'Your excellent chaperone,' Sarah said and raised her eyebrows.

Christina laughed. 'I believe keeping that girl under control in the Russian court will be a challenge for us both.'

Author Note

The Paintress is a work of fiction.

The inspiration for the book came from my own incredulity on discovering five huge paintings of the Romanov royal family in the St Petersburg Hermitage Museum by a Scottish painter I'd never heard of. Anna's story is fiction including her family tree, but her research mirrors my own.

Little is known about Christina Robertson, so I used author's licence to create a private life for her. However, where there were facts: a profusion of birth/baptism registrations and a full catalogue of her Royal Academy exhibitions, I built my story around them.

Her self-portrait in the V&A shows a small and ordinary looking woman. The successive births and deaths she had to endure were commonplace in the nineteenth century. However, her artistic successes and her achievements in St Petersburg tell us she was extraordinary.

Sarah is entirely my invention. Every woman needs at least one good friend.

Afterword

If you enjoyed this book I would be hugely grateful if you could write a review. Thank you!

Scan to reach The Paintress Goodreads page. Reviews mean SO much! Thank you.

You might also enjoy my 2023 historical adventure/romance. Find The Girl Who Fled the Picture here:

amzn.to/3rh9U73

Acknowledgments

The support of my family has been absolutely crucial. Thank you for your patience and love, Mark, Louise, Calum and Helen.

Writing is tough. If you are thinking of taking it up, I would encourage you to join a writing group. You need writer friends who will tell you the truth but also have your back when things go wrong. My current writing group of Alison Belsham, Hannah Thresher and Kristin Pedroja are like my family and I love them.

In the course of my research, I was lucky enough to meet curator, Elizavetta Renné from the State Hermitage Museum in St Petersburg. Lisa's support and cooperation has been invaluable.

Historical fiction author Sara Sheridan mentioned Christina Robertson in both *The Fair Botanists* and *The Secrets of Blythswood Square*. Her encouragement to complete this project was heartening and I'm thrilled that she loves the novel.

Thank you to The Romantic Novelist Association, particularly the RNA Facebook Indie Chapter.

Finally, thanks to Debi Alper and Helen Baggott for their expert editing and Rachel Lawston for her beautiful cover.

About the Author

Jane Anderson is an Edinburgh based writer of historical fiction. Born in Fife, Jane originally studied English Literature at Edinburgh University. She spent most of her working life living in countries as far-flung as Vietnam, Azerbaijan and most recently, Egypt. She has travelled extensively, including to St Petersburg. Retelling history from the point of view of women is where the fun begins.

This novel was inspired by viewing Christina Robertson's paintings of the Russian royal family in St Petersburg's State Hermitage Museum. Jane published *The Girl Who Fled the Picture* in 2023. You can read more about this author's writing life on Jane's website:

https://jane-anderson.co.uk/